Empire and War

By Michael G. Bergen

The Rutherford Chronicles
A tumultuous family journey through the 20th Century

Part 2

"This is a war to end all wars."

— Woodrow Wilson, 1917. President Woodrow Wilson made the saying famous, invented by the British futurist writer and social commentator H. G. Wells. Wilson predicted WWI would be the last war in his article "The War That Will End War," published in The Daily News on Aug. 14, 1914.

"Only the dead have seen the end of war."

— George Santayana, 1922. The Spanish-American philosopher said this statement to counter President Woodrow Wilson's words in his book Soliloquies in England and Later Soliloquies.

"I wish those people who talk about going on with this war, whatever it costs, could see the soldiers suffering from mustard gas poisoning. Great mustard-coloured blisters, blind eyes, all sticky and stuck together, always fighting for breath, with voices a mere whisper, saying that their throats are closing and they know they will choke."

— Nurse Vera Brittain, 1933. Brittain was an English Voluntary Aid Detachment nurse, writer, feminist and pacifist, and the quote can be found in her 1933 memoir, Testament of Youth.

"Never think that war, no matter how necessary, nor how justified, is not a crime."

— Ernest Hemingway, 1946. Hemingway was 18 years old when he volunteered as an ambulance driver for WWI. He suffered physically and mentally from the horrors of war. As a novelist, he used his writing to show the criminality of the war.

For my late grandfather, who kept his good humour to the end!

And for all who lost ancestors in that horrible war.

Contents

Prologue

At the start of part 1 of this series, I asked the following questions:

Why does warfare captivate each generation's youth, motivating them toward joining conflict? Is it the proud military uniform acting as an attraction to the opposite sex? Is it because military service offers global travel and adventure? Or is it the pride of protecting one's country?

In this quest for my family history called The Rutherford Chronicles, I learned just how frightening, painful, and undesirable war can be. The Center for International and Security Studies in Maryland has documented all the wars and conflicts of the twentieth century that resulted in 231 million deaths. So, why do we keep falling into its dangerous trap? Why allow warmongering politicians to send each generation's youths into battle? What accounts for our enduring captivation with war heroes, and why does each generation seem to ignore the previous generation's blunders?

Those are the questions I seek answers to in The Rutherford Chronicles. This second book of the series continues my family journey.

Part 2 of this series is again about Joe Rutherford, a veteran of the Boer War, who enlists and faces the horrors of World War I. Captured early in the conflict, he endures four years in German POW camps, clinging to hope and friendship amidst brutal conditions. His story is one of resilience, survival, and the enduring power of human connection.

The emotional heart of the story is Joe's unwavering determination to return home to his family. This deep love and longing drive his resilience and give him the strength to endure years of captivity. His connection to his wife and children, even from afar, felt deeply moving and palpable.

A central underlying theme is the brutality and futility of war. From the senseless violence of the trenches to the inhumane conditions of the POW camps, the story reveals the devastating impact of war on individuals and communities. The detailed descriptions of battles, the casual mention of staggering casualty numbers, and the suffering on both sides create a powerful anti-war message.

Another key theme is the power of human connection and resilience. The friendships formed in the trenches and the camaraderie among the POWs offer a glimmer of hope amid the darkness. Acts of kindness, shared laughter, and unwavering support deeply touched me and helped Joe and his friends survive. These moments of connection, amidst such bleak circumstances, really underscored the strength of the human spirit.

Other underlying themes are the brutality and futility of war and the power of human connection and resilience. It touches on fear and anxiety, boredom and frustration, sadness and grief, hope and resilience, joy and relief.

The next book, No. 3 of this series, Empire and Tyranny, is about how Joe recovers from this horrific episode. It joins him again as he grows and cares for his family through the chaotic years leading up to and including the next crisis, World War II.

§

WESTERN FRONT 1914–18

Farthest German advance September 1914

German offensive in summer of 1918

Front line beginning of 1915

Allied offensive in fall of 1918

Armistice line 1918

© Encyclopædia Britannica, Inc.

1914—Movement and Stalemate

1.   From Ennetières, France to Hamelin, Germany

Despite not knowing German, Joe and Mike understood the "hände hoch" order. They had learned to "hande in die lug" when capturing Dutch-Afrikaans-speaking fighters in the 2nd Anglo-Boer War in South Africa, and the German command sounded similar to them. Besides, their captors' attitudes and hostile gestures reinforced their understanding. Realizing they had no option but to surrender, they discarded their weapons. They raised their hands while turning to face their enemy at close quarters. It was the terrible moment they had never reckoned on experiencing—eye-to-eye with the enemy.

The Allies defended Ennetières-en-Weppes by Lille in France during the Battle of Lille-Armentières. But it fell to the Germans on 20 October 1914. That struggle cost the 2nd Battalion of the Durham Light Infantry (2/DLI) four dead non-commissioned officers (NCOs) and men, 46 wounded and 177 missing. [1][2] The British Army assumed the unaccounted-for Durhams were dead, missing in action or taken captive, Joe Rutherford and Mike O'Brien among the latter. The enemy killed Major Blake, too, and injured Lieutenants Beart,

---

[1] Non-Commissioned Officers – Sergeants and Corporals
[2] S.G.P Ward, *Faithful, The Story of the Durham Light Infantry*, Naval and Military Press, 1962

Gilbertson and Norton, who they left dying in enemy hands.[3]

For Joe and Mike, 20 October 1914 ended their war on the Western Front. It was just one month and one day from the first rudimentary British trenches in the Aisne region two months after the war started. Joe Rutherford was a slight, 5-foot, 7-inch, good-looking man with dark hair and a moustache. Mike O'Brien was a strong and scrappy 5-foot 7-inch man with dark, curly hair. They were both Jarrow-born Geordie, working men of Irish descent[4]. The marras were now part of a group of captive British soldiers in the care of Imperial Germany[5].

The captured soldiers' destination was a German Imperial Army POW camp somewhere in Germany; which one and what that holds in store for them, or whether they would survive it, was anybody's guess at this stage. But, despite having fought through horrific battles with their enemy, they were still unharmed. They had survived an ordeal by fire on the Western Front but were now POWs!

"I'm ready to die," whispered Mike. "This is the worst thing that could have happened to us, Joe! But I'm ready to die for my king and country."

---

[3] Ibid
[4] Geordie is a nickname for a person from the Tyneside area of North East England, and their dialect.
[5] A marra is a workmate or friend in the Geordie dialect spoken in North East England

"Aye, that's true, Mike," murmured Joe while gathering his thoughts. "I have never even thought of this happening to us, but I'm not prepared to die. I can't die because I have a wife and bairns at home. And nor should you be my old friend, for your wife's sake. We will survive this war the way we did the last. I told Mary that, should I die, she was free to remarry. But this upset her; she cried, so we didn't discuss it further. We also discussed the possibility of injury. And she said she would nurse me back to full health as soon as I was home. But we never discussed the possibility of capture by the enemy. Our training didn't cover it, and it never occurred to me, although, based on our experience in the South African War, it should have."

"Aye, Ruth and I had more or less the same talk," said Mike. "She became upset, too. So, I guess that's a topic you should best leave unsaid with women."

"Nee, Mike," said Joe. "It's right to talk about it. You're tied together now, so you need to share such thoughts. It's how you speak of it that's important."

"Aye, Joe, but I'm sure you're better at it than I am."

This brief sequence summarized it for most British POWs. The last thing an early Great War soldier expected at the Front was capture. They entered the war understanding that their lives and limbs were at risk, which they accepted. After the first battles they had lived through in this war, they expected the possibility of injury or death, and they came to terms with it. But being captured and imprisoned by the enemy was beyond their imagination or comprehension. Being taken prisoner was, to them, the ultimate failure. When detained, the only thing that went through their minds was that they had disappointed everybody. They felt they had betrayed their fellow soldiers and regiment, their country and king, their community at home and their loved ones.[6] It was the most humiliating thing that could have happened to any soldier during this war.

Their German guard rebuked them again, poking them with his rifle with a loud and stern warning, "Nicht sprechen!" ("No talking!") A German officer nearby translated this command into English for the assembled British prisoners. "No talking. Take off your equipment and leave it here," he said, pointing to a pile of discarded rifles and other military equipment. "Keep quiet and do what the guards tell you." The men followed orders but could hold on to personal items such as letters, pay books or photos of their sweethearts and children. An interrogating German officer later examined these.

There was loud shouting and the occasional gunshot as the Germans herded together more surviving Tommies into a tight group on the edge of the village. They were now under German control. They could not see much at first, but soon

---

[6] Richard van Emden, Prisoners of the Kaiser (The Last POWs of the Great War), Pen & Sword, 2012

enough, their companions appeared out of the acrid smoke-filled gloom, most of whom had glum looks on their faces. A few of these recent arrivals were resisting the guards. The Germans brought the few more challenging ones to heel through brutal blows to their bodies with rifle butts. They shot those who gave the enemy any reason to execute them, even if not permitted by the war conventions. Those Tommies, too, soon realized that any further resistance was futile. The marras recognized a sizeable group of Sherwood Foresters coming in their direction. The prisoners' numbers had swollen to a group of 100 or more. Then there were East and West Yorkshiremen, Moroccans and French soldiers too, many of whom Joe had fought alongside in his first battle. They appeared out of the mist and smoke, shuffling forward as a group. No one dared utter a word. They awaited their fate in stony silence while their captors barked incomprehensible blasts of commands and degrading insults in English or French occasionally.

Joe gave Mike a sideward glance and grimace, but he avoided provoking tension with the guards by talking. Their immediate future was very much on their minds. To the best of Joe's knowledge, they had received no information during training on the rules of war for prisoners. They couldn't know that Chapter II of the Geneva Convention, signed in October 1907 at The Hague, focussed on prisoners of war.

"Prisoners of war are in the hostile government's power, but not of the individuals or corps who capture them. They must humanely treat all POWs. All prisoners' belongings, except arms, horses and military papers, remain the POW's property[7]."

However, a Durham officer POW knew of this convention. He shared his knowledge with as many lower-ranking men as he could before being separated from them and officers going to separate camps.

"Remember, men; you are soldiers, not animals," he said. "You mustn't argue, since you might provoke them. Just remember your rights and discuss any grievances you have at the right time with a German officer."

Now and then, they got another harsh nudge in their back or neck from a German rifle to move them on quicker, which they daren't protest.

Mike couldn't hold back, muttering, "Bloody Huns!"

"Careful, Mike," Joe reminded him, but it was too late.

"Was? Was hast Du gesacht? (What? What did you say?)" asked the guard, yelling. Mike looked surprised and shrugged his shoulders. But the guard wasn't happy with that gesture. He was sure he had heard "Hun" and knew it was an insult.

---

[7] Convention (IV) respecting the Laws and Customs of War on Land and its annex: Regulations concerning the Laws and Customs of War on Land. The Hague, 18 October 1907.

Empire and War

Before the war, British propaganda claimed that the Germans descended from the warlike Asian Huns, whom Attila's reign made notorious. Kaiser Wilhelm II started this myth with his statement during the Boxer Rebellion in China. He ordered his army to act brutally towards the Boxer rebels.

"We will show no mercy, and we will take no prisoners. Just as a thousand years ago, the Huns under Attila won a reputation of might that live on in legends, so may the name of Germany in China. It will be such that no Chinese will even again dare so much as to look askance at a German."

British propaganda later used the term "Hun" from this speech during the Great War as a derogatory label for the Germans. The spiked Pickelhaube helmet, or pickaxe bonnet, worn by German forces mimicking the headgear of the Huns in battle, reinforced the analogy. As a result, the terrified Tommy prisoners feared their captors might live up to their reputations. Their supreme commander was the same Kaiser, Wilhelm II.

The guard grabbed Mike and spun him around to meet his rifle straight on. "Was has Du gesacht?" he yelled. Then, a German officer close by spoke to the guard. "Lass das sein, Korporal. Wit mussen weiter. Keine scheiße."

No one translated that for the British soldiers, but whatever the officer said defused a dangerous situation. Sanity returned, and the column resumed its progress. The Germans herded the prisoners to a mustering point on the road out of Ennetières towards the new German lines. After a march of two hours, they arrived at a wire enclosure. It resembled a rough cage where the Germans had already assembled at least 200 to 300 or more British, French, and Moroccan prisoners. There, they waited in groups as their captors rounded up more and more.

"Shite," cursed Mike in a whisper. "Are we animals or soldiers?"

"To these guards, we are just animals," said Joe. "They could shoot us like deer or whatever."

This holding pen the Germans called a Dulag, short for the German Durchgangslager (transit camp). Before being sent to a POW camp, a captured prisoner of war had to pass through these Dulags. They were impromptu stops where the Germans gathered them, interrogated and noted their details before dispatching them to their onward destinations in Germany.

The Great War was the first war in which both sides of the conflict agreed to track POWs via the International Red Cross in neutral Switzerland. That organization was only 51 years old in 1914. The Red Cross required the captors to detail the following information: the name and surname of the prisoner; their ID number, rank, and unit; the place and date of capture—Lille (Ennetières), 20 October 1914; any injuries; the destination POW camp once known; and their last pre-war residence address. So, the German interrogator jotted down the details and reported the capture of Joe, Mike, and the others to the Red Cross.

"This place is disgusting," said Mike in a whisper. "There's nowhere to sit that isn't wet or plain mud."

"Aye, and it's bloody freezing," said Joe. "But we must survive this, Mike."

The men were already so weak and demotivated. Hundreds of disheartened men descended onto the wet ground to rest or sleep through the few days their captors held them there. They received little for hunger or comfort, and running water was unavailable; they only found a few buckets of drinking water scattered about, with a tin cup attached to them on a string. Their captors provided long trenches dug next to the fences as open-air latrines but didn't provide paper wipes. More humiliation! But what else could they do but resign themselves to their fate?

In these compounds, medics first gave the wounded men first aid. Medics sent those with serious injuries requiring further treatment to a nearby German field hospital. Many of the men had injuries, and what food they received was scant nourishment. The most vulnerable among them were dying. Every morning, guards investigated the enclosure to see if anyone had expired during the night. They would pick up any corpses and take them to a shallow trench outside the wire cage. There, they discarded the bodies and covered them with lime and soil.

"My God, look how many of us prisoners there are," said Mike. "We're dropping like flies. Is that any way to treat our dead companions?"

"Aye, poor buggers. Wounded, I reckon. Or sick with a fever. They couldn't make it under these bloody awful conditions," said Joe. "No, I'm sure that it's not allowed to treat the dead the way they are treating them. I hate these Huns too, Mike."

But even during this dreadful time, Joe and Mike renewed old friendships. They made fresh acquaintances among the Sherwood Foresters and Yorkshiremen with whom they had fought at the Aisne. They traded memories of their torrid battles and bonded at once, brothers in arms, the battlefields creating lifetime friendships among fellow combatants.

"That's one good thing about the military," said Mike. "I like and respect these chaps already; we have been through so much together."

"Aye, Mike," said Joe. "They are a magnificent bunch of laddies. There we were, side by side, fired upon by the Boche in the Aisne trenches or while running through the bog and turnip fields of French Flanders. We have suffered a lot together, cheek by jowl. What a gathering of wayward heroes we are here."

"Aye. Now we are prisoners, one and all, suffering at the hands of these Huns," murmured Mike, this time with more caution. "What more will we live through together now?"

Among the old acquaintances rekindled was Walter (Walt) Lane of C-Company, a close friend and fellow "Durham," even though he was born in Leeds. Walt was a tall, handsome man with brown wavy hair but no moustache.

"Howay, Come on, Walt! They got you too, old friend," said Mike while hugging him.

"Aye," said Walt. "I got careless, and they caught me at Ennetières."

"Aye, us too," said Joe. "Looks like our war in the trenches is over. But what will become us now is up to God and the Boche."

"Aye," said Walt. "God and the Boche, for sure."

"Well, it's good of you to join us."

"My God, look at this," said Walt.

"There are men from so many units here, only a few of whom I recognize—it's a mixed bag of British fighting men. But look at how filthy this cage is. Do they expect us to sit or lie in that?"

"Well, at least we aren't the only losers," said Mike. "More of them keep coming. I hope we do the same to the Boche on the other side of the Front!"

"Aye, Mike, but I'm sure we are treating them better than they are treating us," said Joe. "Not that it will change much. There are so many of them."

The march to the Dulag had not been without incident. The occasional stray, friendly bullet or shell from the British side of the front lines had wounded or killed Allied soldiers and Germans. They had to circumnavigate the shot holes in the road, too. A fresh set of guards escorted them, including German lancers on horseback. And then a few nasty incidents unfolded in front of them.

A few cantankerous Tommies defied the guards in one incident, and a scuffle ensued.

"Get back in line, you," shouted a German guard.

"Up yours, you bloody Hun," said one soldier. "I answer only to British officers, not scum like you."

Then another such protest broke out a short distance away, and then another.

"You can't treat us like cattle," shouted another Tommy.

"Yeah," called another as the protests grew. "We're men, not animals."

The guards called in the lancers, who charged into the ranks on horseback. Under the direction of the German guards, they speared the protesting Tommies like wild pigs with their lances. To them, the objections voiced by the British prisoners were equivalent to resistance or trying to escape, and it gave them an excuse to rid themselves of ill-tempered men. It also ensured the rest toed the line.

"Shite, Mike; did you see that?" murmured Joe to his marra. "They just did the same as the British officers' sport of Pig-Sticking in India, with the same disgusting result. Do you remember that?"

"Aye, Joe," said Mike. "These are cruel bastards. We had better behave ourselves and stay out of trouble for now. Otherwise, we'll end up on the end of one of those lances."

A German soldier noticed them talking to each other and shouted, "Wovon sprechen Sie, (What are you talking about?)" while lowering his rifle in their direction. In this instant, so soon after their capture and the lancer incident, they froze in terror.

"I don't know what he's saying," whispered Joe. "He looks like he could shoot us without a problem."

"Aye, Joe. Or bring in one of those lancers back to stick us," said Mike, reaching his hands even higher and nodding to the guard, "let's be careful."

Joe and Mike weren't sure what he was saying, but they understood his intent. So, they both held their hands higher in the air and called, "Nix, nix, nix." They had learned that this word meant "nothing" and hoped it would placate their antagonist. That satisfied the guard for the time being. They found their reaction with "Nix, nix, nix" humorous, laughing with his buddies, and humiliating the Tommies even further.

After what seemed an eternity, the Germans mustered them on the road under the watchful eyes of their guards. A much more significant number of Prussian Uhlans lancers on their horses joined the others. Uhlans were Polish-Lithuanian light cavalry armed with lances, sabres and pistols and a celebrated unit of the Imperial Army. Under their watch, a long march to an unknown destination began. They now numbered over a thousand POWs. Instead of being proud armed fighting men, they were a rag-tag shuffling crowd of lost souls, separated from their rightful place on the other side of the Western Front.

They moved away from France and meandered through the Belgian countryside under German control, far from the front lines. When officers weren't present, the guards could be provocative and violent as they coaxed the lagging soldiers to keep up with the march. The Uhlans used their lances from their horses to jab and jostle the prisoners to keep pace[8].

After two and a half hours of lumbering along narrow lanes through Belgian farmlands, they arrived at a railway siding where a cattle train awaited. The German wards instructed them to entrain 40 to 50 men per wagon. Once loaded, German soldiers went through the cars with buckets of water and a few loaves of black bread, their nourishment

---

[8] Richard van Emden, *Prisoners of the Kaiser (The Last POWs of the Great War)*, Pen & Sword, 2012

for the journey to Germany. The Germans then shut and locked the doors of the wagons and waited for a locomotive to arrive. After four long hours of waiting in such cramped quarters, the engine reversed into the station and hooked up the cars.

However, even before that, the men noticed there were no toilets!

"How the hell are we going to have a shite in these overcrowded wagons?" asked Mike scornfully. "Do they expect us to shit on the wagon floor like cattle?"

"Aye, Mike," said Joe. "It looks as if we can expect anything in this war."

"Maybe they'll stop occasionally and let us off for relief," said Walt, who had attached himself to Joe and Mike by then.

The duration of their journey depended not only on the distance to their destination, but on other delaying factors. The train diverted to sidings from time to time to make way for passing supply trains from the other direction. They were on their way to the Western Front.

They stopped at intervals along the way, and the guards ordered the prisoners out of the train to relieve themselves. On these occasions, they sometimes received more water and bread. The journey was slow going, confined and unpleasant. But, away from the mud and Uhlan lancers, their spirits lifted somewhat.

Then, in the dead of night, they rolled through a city.

"Where are we?" asked a soldier.

"It must be Brussels," called another.

"Howay, another city on our list of experiences, Joe," said Mike, nudging his marra.

"Aye, and another capital city of Europe," said Joe. "Where to next stop?"

"Berlin?" suggested Walt with a chuckle.

The next day, the train crawled through a pastoral and forested landscape on the edge of the Ardennes in eastern Belgium. It arrived that evening at Aix-la-Chapelle, or Aachen, on the German border. The train crawled through the station where hundreds of German men, women and children had gathered for the sport of chastising enemy POWs passing through from the front. The din was horrific as they screamed invective and threw objects such as stale bread and rotting food at the passing cars. It relieved the men that the train hadn't stopped. They feared for their lives with this angry mob, and a few hungry soldiers even ventured to eat the best bread and food they could find.

This hostility was but a passing phase. At the start of the war in August, the German citizens were friendly and hospitable. They even showed sympathy for the soldiers by handing them gifts of food and drink when they stopped at the border stations. However, the German Army's high command was most unhappy with this practice. So, they issued new orders and placards hung at train stations, instructing the locals to admonish their enemies. They spread rumours among German citizens of the horrors the British soldiers had perpetrated against their German counterparts on the Front. At train stations, they hung mannequins dressed in Allied uniforms by the neck, visible to prisoners passing by in trains.

"These people hate us," said Mike. "Don't they know we didn't start this shite war?"

"To them, we are the enemy," said Joe. "Didn't you see those posters in the station? And those scarecrows in our uniforms? The Kaiser is telling the German people we are the monsters."

"It's amazing how simple folk can be so hate-filled," said Walt. "Are they like that with their own people?"

"I don't know about you, Laddies," said Joe. "I'm getting stiff and uncomfortable standing in these cars for hours. If this goes on much longer, how are we going to sleep? Standing up?"

"I'm sure we wouldn't treat our prisoners like this," said Mike. "These Huns are barbarians!"

But, for another two days, they trundled across Germany, passing through the impressive city of Cologne with its towering cathedral towers. They crossed the famous Hohenzollern Bridge over the River Rhine, used by the German army trains travelling to and from the Western Front. Then, they turned north and went through industrial towns such as Leverkusen, Wuppertal, Gütersloh, and Bielefeld.

Empire and War

Between these busy industrial cities, they saw peaceful rolling forests, farmland and tiny villages, some surrounding ancient castles on hilltops. The wooden slats of the cattle cars impaired their views of the panoramas, but what they saw differed from England and France, and it intrigued them.

"What a beautiful country," said Mike. "Is this to be our new home?"

"Aye, Mike. It is beautiful and so different," said Joe. "Who knows how long we'll be here?"

"Aye, and who knows how our jailers will treat us," said Walt? "What will life be like as prisoners? If it's anything like this train trip, we're in trouble. Shit, I need to stretch out and rest for a while!"

"No such luck, Walt," said Joe. "I guess we'll get that at our destination."

Their life was fraught with questions, but these working-class men from North East England continued their exploration of the world. And despite their apprehensions and discomfort, they felt excitement, too. They explored Africa and India within the British Empire. Within the past few weeks, they became acquainted with the French, Belgian, and German countryside, cities, and villages. Without appreciating the nuances of the distinct cultures they were experiencing, they could see and take in the differences. They were learning about early twentieth-century Europe, a diverse industrial powerhouse similar to the one they already knew back home.

The prisoners completed the slow and excruciating 330-mile journey from Ennetières, France, to Hamelin, Germany, in three days.

"Well, we'll soon find out where we're going, Laddies," said Joe. "It looks like we might be there. Look at our welcoming committee. You know, we are lucky to be alive. And I, for one, will try to make the best of whatever we are about to experience."

"Well, Laddies," said Mike. "I wouldn't trust the Huns because they are the ones who put us in this mess."

§

2.   *Internment at the Hamelin POW Camp from October 1914 to 17 June 1916*

Arrival at Hamelin, Germany

After a few days and nights of cramped travel, the prisoners arrived at their destination—Hamelin (Hameln), a town in the northeast of Germany. The train stopped before entering the station and then diverted onto a deserted parallel track next to a country lane. Then the guards opened the creaky wooden doors of the train carriages once more, and the men poured out onto the road. There were dozens of armed German soldiers waiting to greet them. The guards mustered the prisoners and marched them to the camp close by.

Empire and War

The Imperial German Army had allocated the German 10th Army Corps quarters at Hamelin as a Prisoner of War camp. It was in a shallow valley with quiet pastures and wooded hills behind it. It was a mile from the town made famous by the Pied Piper, whose legend was that he had rid the city of its rats and children.

"This doesn't look so bad," said Joe. "We seem to be in the countryside."

"Aye," said Mike. "Forest and pastureland. Very peaceful, but as prisoners."

"Just like our County Durham countryside," said another. "I almost feel at home."

"We're not inside the camp yet," said Joe. "So, maybe we should see what they have waiting for us there."

But they were in for a shock. At the start of the war, the Germans boasted of a quick and historic victory with fewer casualties. So, the vast number of prisoners of war they were receiving from the two fronts surprised them. They had made no preparations for holding so many prisoners. At first, the Germans converted the existing army Kaserne (barracks) into POW camps, and most were inadequate given the vast onslaught of prisoners. In October-November 1914, when Joe's group arrived at Hamelin Camp, they were lodging prisoners in shallow trenches covered with canvas awnings. Filth and vermin were everywhere. They gave each prisoner one blanket and bedding filled with wood shavings. Washing facilities had one tap for 7,000 men! [9]

"I thought we had left the bloody trenches behind," said Mike as they entered the camp.

"Everything will be better," said a German guard close by who could converse in English and had overheard Mike's comment. "You will soon build houses where you can live."

"Houses?" queried Mike in surprise.

"Well, you know, houses made of wood. I think you call them barracks, Ja? Small, but very warm and comfortable," said the guard.

"That's good to know. What's your name?" asked Joe.

"Klaus," he said. "I will be your guard while you are here."

"Well, my name is Joe. And this here is Mike, and that is Walt over there. We are friends from the same regiment and city in North East England—Jarrow, on the Tyne River. How do you know English?"

"Pleased to meet you," said Klaus. "I lived in London for many years before the war and enjoyed living and working there. But now, I am back home in Germany and guarding you British POWs. Now, go to registration, where they will tell you where to go and what you can and cannot do here."

---

[9] Heather Jones, *Violence against Prisoners of War in the First World War*, 2011

The marras noted he differed from the other German guards they had encountered up to then, and they felt a sudden relief. He didn't display the same stern looks as the other German guards they had met. So, despite the misery and antagonism they had experienced in these first few weeks of their war, things here were improving. They could have been dead!

"This place serves as the parent encampment for many satellite work camps," said Klaus.

"We call it a Stalag, shortened from Stammlager or base encampment, and our word for an officer camp is Oflag, shortened from Offizierslager."

"So, we have learned new German words," said Joe. "Dulag, Stalag and Oflag. How useful!"

"Aye, brilliant," said Mike. "Does every German word end with lag?"

"Only those that have to do with lagers," said Klaus. "A lager is a camp."

"Lager is also a beer," said Mike.

"Oh, Ja," said Klaus with a laugh. "I know English lager, which differs from our beer, but I liked it."

The truckloads of wood and other materials would take a few weeks to arrive so the prisoners could start building. In the meantime, the POWs adjusted as best they could to the camp's appalling temporary freezing wet living conditions. At least during the day, they sent the POWs to work on local road projects or farms.

§

Autumn Work at a Nearby Farm

"They say they will send us to work on a nearby farm," announced Joe. "Don't ask me what work they will assign us."

Being city boys, Joe and Mike had never worked on a farm before, so they didn't know what to expect. Before dawn the following day, the farmworkers arrived at the camp with massive draught horse-drawn wagons to collect their POW workers. They parcelled out the POWs in groups of up to 20, accompanied by one or two armed guards to ensure security and to act as interpreters. They then set out in the pre-dawn darkness to the allotted farms, where they were to spend a day in the grain fields.

"I'm looking forward to this," said Mike, peering into the night. "Although I don't know what we will be doing."

"Shovelling pig shite?" asked another prisoner in their group.

"Nee. Plowing work at this time of year, I should think," said a soldier-prisoner beside him.

"Have you worked on a farm before, my friend?" asked Mike. "I haven't, and I know Joe hasn't either."

"Aye, for many years," said the fellow POW, who introduced himself as Mac. "I left a farm in County Durham for this army, and now it looks like I'll work for the Germans on one."

"We were shipbuilders in Jarrow," said Joe. "So, this will be a fresh experience for us."

"Don't worry, Laddies," said Mac. "I'll look out for ye."

"Thank ye, my marra," said Joe.

Dawn had pushed off the darkness of night as the wagon made its way over a forested hill into a valley of farmland surrounding a hamlet. As they arrived at their allotted farm, dawn had broken. A pleasant older woman met them with an enormous pot of tea and hard biscuits at a table outside a rambling barn.

"Herzlich Willkommen," she said with a smile. "Tee und Kekse?"

One of the camp guards translated the welcome of the farmer's wife, who helped fill their mugs with the piping hot refreshment.

"Well, we're off to a pleasant start," said Mike, smiling at the woman and nodding his head to show his gratitude.

"Aye, farmers and their wives welcome strangers most of the time," said Mac. "So, that's a pleasant sign."

Within a few minutes, Farmer Schmidt and his permanent workers arrived with another four enormous draught horses. The farmer signalled to follow him, and they went out into stubble fields from the last harvest. There, they hooked up the horses to waiting plows. They then split the group into four teams, each led by the farmer and his workers. They divided them by field and gestured to the POWs to watch and learn.

"Wait a minute," called Mike to his companions. "Are they teaching us how to handle these monster horses?"

"It sure looks that way, Mike," said Joe, surprised too.

"Don't worry, Laddies," called Mac. "I'll wager these horses know better than their handlers what they should do. You will just have to learn the commands."

"In German," asked Walt?

"Aye," said Mac. "Do you think these fine German horses speak English?" Which raised a chorus of nervous chuckles among the men.

Joe's farmworker made the sound "brrrr," and the horse lurched forward. The plow lurched and dug into the soil. Off they went in a straight line towards an invisible goal at the end of the field. When they reached it, the farmworker said, "Rechts." Sure enough, the horse turned right and aimed for another goal at the right angle from the first. And so it went, field by field. *Simple,* thought Joe. When Joe had completed the area's perimeter, the worker made the sound "brrrr" again, and the horse stopped. He then called upon another POW to take the reins. One by one, the POWs learned the essential skills for controlling the giant horses.

Once they were ready, the farmer called his farmworkers and left the horses with the POWs to continue plowing the fields. On the way back to camp, they exchanged experiences with one another using a lot of animation and strange command sounds. One by one, the POWS declared their most harrowing moments. But it amazed them and filled them with pride. They had mastered the art of plowing in one day.

"You were right, Mac," said Mike. "Those giant horses know what to do. And the commands are easy enough. And now, I'm a farmworker," he announced with pride.

Back at camp, they wasted no time retiring to their mats in the trench for a brief night's sleep. However, Klaus awakened them to another day of working in the fields in no time. This farm work lasted three weeks while they waited for the building materials. In those three weeks, they completed the plowing for the farmer. The farmer's wife arranged a sumptuous meat and potatoes meal on the last day of plowing the fields. And the farmer found a cask of good German dark beer to wash it down. It was a joyous celebration of work that was well done and much appreciated.

"That gives us new job skills when we return to civvy life," boasted Joe.

"Aye, most useful," said Mike. "I could work on a farm when I return if Ruth doesn't mind moving into the country."

"Those German farm girls were most appealing," said Walt. "Their daughters, I believe."

§

We Build the Barracks

Then, one day, a long convoy of trucks loaded high with timber arrived. With lots of shouting and excitement, the guards ordered the POWs to unload the supplies. Once the offloading was complete, the guards mustered them on the parade square, and they brought the prisoners to attention as the Camp Kommandant mounted a portable podium. He was a man of medium height in a handsome Prussian uniform, complete with an array of medals and a sword. He also wore a polished black leather Pickelhaube helmet with an ornamental metal spike on top. He also had an imperial moustache and monocle.

"Good morning," called the Kommandant in perfect English. "I have news for you. As you know, we have received lots of timber, and that is for your new barracks. And the other news I have for you is that you will build them. The sooner you have them ready, the sooner you will move into them and make them warm and comfortable."

He looked around the parade square to measure the reaction to his pleasant news. He knew the announcement was to please them. The inadequacies of the temporary accommodation chilled the men to the bone and afflicted them with various minor illnesses.

"So," he said, "we want volunteers to report at once to the camp headquarters for the following jobs: architects or architect assistants, carpenters and experienced construction supervisors. We have the standard plans for the barracks and marked the plots where you must build them. We will assign the rest of you to construction teams. You can start at once. If you need any tools, the guards will help you find them. We only have so many tools, so a few of you may have to wait a while or share with other teams. Get to work."

The Kommandant then did an exemplary about-face and departed while the parade sergeant dismissed the assembly. Camp HQ registered prisoners with the required specialist skills. Afterwards, the guards grouped the rest into teams of 95 to 100 men by nationality. They allocated them to the predefined plots for the construction work.

The weather was clement, so work began at once, most getting into it enthusiastically, POWs and German guards alike. The guards excused injured prisoners from labouring, but the remaining POWs threw themselves into the various tasks with verve despite their reduced motivation. In no time, the camp was a hive of work and the rat-tat-tat of scores of hammers erecting one barracks after another. For the war-weary POWs, it was a much-welcomed distraction from their pain and anxieties. Although they were well into the

Northern Germany autumn chill, they enjoyed this construction work and didn't notice the cold. It was meaningful work aimed at improving their living conditions. It was much better than sitting in a flooded trench on the front with bullets and shells screaming past them in every direction. It was also comforting to know they could soon move out of their temporary accommodation's rotten, vermin-ridden ditches into new, clean, warmer housing. And it motivated them. They knew the quicker they built and outfitted the barracks, the sooner they were to live in comfortable conditions.

"Come on, Laddies," called Mike. "Let's get moving and show the others what these Geordies can do."

"I'm with you the whole way, Mike," said Joe.

"Me too," called Walt and most others in their group.

The prisoners set up an informal contest amongst work gangs to see who could make the huts quickest and to the best quality standards. And then they set about their tasks with enthusiasm. Construction went fast, and once completed, Hamelin Camp comprised 100 wooden barracks of the same form and size, radiating from a central point, each capable of accommodating 100 men. The work teams had each crafted the many three-tier bunks required for the barracks, and the camp provisioned cloth bags and dry straw for mattresses. From its days as an army Kaserne, it had a theatre, a canteen where the prisoners could shop and a YMCA hall for gym exercises and other activities. They had made enough accommodations to house the current population of prisoners and guards and moved into it before the onset of winter. The camp authorities provided a stove and chimney for the middle of each barrack and rationed cut wood.

"So, we are ready," declared Mike to the guard. "This is where we will live."

"Ja. Here and in the work camps," said Klaus, "depending on what they assign you to do occasionally. You will be wherever you need to be."

"Do you mean we will be workers?" asked Joe. "What are the work camps?"

"Yes, workers; that's it," said Klaus. "Work camps are temporary camps with work projects."

This was news to the group, most of whom expressed approval since they thought it better than sitting daily in their barrack at a loss, Joe among them. Others didn't trust the German intentions.

"What work will we be doing?" asked Mike.

But Klaus only said, "You will see, Ja."

Klaus then explained the camp had a post office in the canteen, from which they could send and receive mail and parcels. They distributed and collected the post from this central camp to and from the satellite work camps when necessary. Upon arrival, guards gave each prisoner a pre-printed "First Capture" postcard and ordered them to fill it out immediately. By checking the right words, the prisoner informed his family he was 'Sound,' 'Wounded,' or 'Ill'. Klaus explained that "once your family has received the card, they will know where to respond to and where to send care packages."

This card was spectacular news for the prisoners so far from home. At last, their families would know they were still alive and where and how they lived. It was an exciting moment when they had re-established communication with home. Their families learned at last that Joe and the others were not only active but in good health. For the prisoners, it provided a lift of their spirits.

"This place isn't so shabby," said Walt. "I mean, we can survive here, can't we?"

"That's for sure," said Mike and Joe in unison.

"It's much better than we thought," said Joe. "Although it's not home, it's better than being shot at and freezing at the Front."

"Aye, for sure," said the others.

"A home away from home," said Mike with a sneer.

The POWs settled into their unfamiliar environment, the routine of hard work, and two meals of thin soup and black bread daily. It wasn't enough for a working man. So, before long, hunger became a feature of most prisoners' lives. In time, they could look forward to deliveries of food parcels, which soon arrived to add to their scant camp food. These packages were from the Joint War Organization of the Red

Cross and the Order of St John. They contained "luxury" items such as butter, biscuits, chocolate, condensed milk, dried fruits and vegetables. The Red Cross provided scarves, jumpers, cardigans, shirts, pyjamas, blankets, gloves, and socks. They meant these items for their physical comfort against the elements of winter. Tens of thousands of women across the Empire contributed their time, labour and money to make this extraordinary service possible. Many prisoners received care packages from home, too. They contained more chocolate, tobacco, home baking, hard candy, liquor, toiletries such as shaving articles, knitted socks and scarves, smaller items of homemade clothing, photos, books and magazines. The camp guards and elected POWs inspected the packages and distributed them to their intended recipients. As a general custom, they shared such packages amongst fellow prisoners, whether from the Red Cross or home. These gifts kept them alive and buoyed their morale.

"Look, Laddies," called Mike. "I've built a brick stove outside to cook our food in these empty milk tins."

"Howay, Mike," said Walt. "What a grand idea. Now, all we need is the food to cook on it."

"Aye," said Mike. "Like those rabbits running around the camp. And if we get more farm work, maybe we can ask for a few potatoes? Mac says he knows plants we can collect outside the camp and use as greens."

Many of these soldiers had joined the war effort, unemployed and plagued by hunger in the belief the British Army provided for them. As prisoners, they still suffered hunger—not a fair trade! But they lived in the hope they had more chance of surviving the camps than in the trenches of the Western Front. And they became creative about finding more food in their restricted environment.

§

Daily Life at Hamelin

The daily routine of the POWs began with reveille at 5 A.M. from the parade square.

"Another shite day in this camp, Laddies," groaned Mike as he rolled from his middle bunk and stretched.

"Aye. It's another beautiful day in Germany," said Walt, still in his top bunk. "In our new bungalows."

"Our holiday from the trenches," chuckled Joe, stumbling toward the ablutions.

"Aye. What do you think the camp has in store for our amusement today?" asked Mike.

The men had half an hour to wash, dress, have tea and bread and muster for a roll call. They then worked either within the main encampment, in the town of Hamelin, or at other working camps nearby. After work and on Sundays, they played various outdoor sports when the weather permitted, football being a favourite, except they lacked equipment. Teams shared balls and whistles from Sunday to Sunday, an unsatisfactory arrangement. In the evenings, they played various card games or other leisure activities or just talked among themselves and told stories to stay amused. Sometimes, the prisoners organize concerts or other forms of entertainment. But for most, fatigue and hunger were the dominant features of life in a POW in the camps early in the war.

After completing the most urgent construction tasks, the commanding officer directed workgroups for separate projects outside the Stalag. They ordered the best builders to stay behind to continue building barracks for more expected POW arrivals or other required construction or general camp maintenance jobs. The men then settled into their alternative life, whatever that entailed. Most were so relieved! It wasn't home, but it sure as hell wasn't the horrific and life-threatening conditions of the trenches of the Western Front! While they settled into the camp, they soon worked on various projects in and around Hamelin. It wasn't home for sure, but it was the best they could hope for.

"This isn't the life I had in mind," said Mike. "I must make the best of it. We didn't have the sense or courage to stay out of this war, so we have no other choice."

"Aye, Mike," said Joe. "We should have known better after South Africa. But it sucked us into this war, like everybody else. What else can we do?"

"It must be harder for you, Laddies," said Walt, "having wives and children."

"Aye, that it is, Walt," said Joe. "That it is."

But soon enough, the men settled into a routine at Hamelin Camp. They spent their days working for their German masters. In the evenings and nights and on Sundays, the authorities left them to their own devices, albeit checked on at regular times by the guards. They often huddled around the woodstove to keep warm while talking or recounting stories of their experiences in the war or their pre-war lives. Before they had books, it was their only entertainment, so this pastime was essential to them; few could read. And even if they did, many repeats of their stories.

While Joe and his marras began their incarceration as POWs in Germany at the end of October 1914, the Great War raged on both Fronts. Prisoners tried to stay informed of its progress as best they could. They got this not from the Germans, who only announced their victories and British defeats, but from recent arrivals from the Front. In this way, they learned soon after their arrival that Lord Frederick Roberts, 1st Earl Roberts of Kandahar in Afghanistan and Pretoria, died at eighty-two on 14 November 1914. He was one of the most successful British military commanders of his time, a distinguished, decorated and honoured Field Marshal of the British Army. He led the British Army in India and the campaign to defeat the Boers in South Africa. "Little Bob" had gone to France to encourage the Indian Army Corps with whom Roberts had such an affinity. But he caught a chill upon landing there and died three days later of pneumonia at St. Omer.

"Little Bob is dead; can you believe it?" said Joe one day.

"He was a fine old general," recalled Mike. "I remember you mentioning him before we enlisted for the South African War."

"Aye. Little Bob left South Africa before we arrived there," said Joe. "His gigantic shadow was still there until the war ended."

After a while, the routine became monotonous. There was only so much to discuss when confined to a POW camp.

§

We Start a Football League

With boredom creeping in at Hamelin Camp, the authorities became concerned with the possibility of unrest. They realized the prisoners needed diversions in their free time. So, the Kommandant ordered a large consignment of footballs and whistles. Their arrival and distribution raised the spirits of the POWs at once. Joe and his growing band of fellow POW mates organized a football league with Joe as manager. His team had men from the Durhams, Sherwood Foresters, 1st Dorsets, Cheshires, South Wales Borderers, Royal Irish, Gordon Highlanders, 4th Dragoon Guards and sailors from the Royal Navy. They were a mixed group with two shared passions: football and survival. With such a mixed party of soldiers and sailors, they didn't know what to call themselves. Then someone came up with the name "POWers." "It's a stupid name," they thought, but it stuck.

"It reminds me of our navy days off West Africa," said a sailor called Wyatte from HMS *Astrea*. "We became avid rowers on the rivers. And it was the most enjoyable exercise."

The Germans had taken the sailors in Joe's group captive on the west coast of Africa. Their ships were the second-class cruiser HMS *Astraea*, the gunboat HMS *Dwarf* and the Condor class sloop HMS *Rinaldo*. They had been fighting the Germans in Togoland, Cameroon and South West Africa along the continent's west coast since the war began. Before arriving in West Africa, HMS *Astraea* had been in Zanzibar and German East Africa on the east coast of Africa. These East African countries were German colonies invaded by the French and British soon after the outbreak of the Great War in 1914.

Joe pulled the team together, so they elected him as team manager.

"Right, lads, if we do nothing else in this bloody camp, we should come together as a grand team," Joe began. "We need to practise every chance we can get. They say practice makes perfect. Now, what positions have you played back home?"

With that, the POWers team players bonded together as athletes. Years later, they said their passion for their game and team helped them survive.

At first, the prisoners grouped the teams by country, such as the Tommies, Aussies, Kiwis or New Zealanders, Indians, French, Italians, Belgians and Russians. But as the number of prisoners grew into the tens of thousands, dozens of teams of mixed nationalities emerged. Sunday was football day in all seasons except winter; they had drawn up a roster and schedule, so the contests began. A programme committee representing unique areas of the camp turned into makeshift football fields and organized the program. Despite malnourishment and a gruelling week of working twelve-hour days in the work camps, the POWs always found enough energy to play and cheer their hearts out on Sundays.

Football became their raison d'être, a favoured distraction, exerciser and morale builder. Most POWs considered life in the camp to be bearable as long as they could have their sport. These men and their women at home were the lucky ones. Thousands of soldiers were dying or maimed at the Front. But POWs were out of danger for a while, so football, camp work, and care packages kept the men going.

Besides his passion for football, Joe restarted his old habit of collecting and redistributing any information he could find on the war. It included battles and Allied victories or losses. He soon resumed his role as a raconteur and storyteller within his barrack, keeping his companions appraised of progress in the war or recalling adventures.

§

Looking back to the Race to the Sea

One evening, an inmate asked Joe how he had ended up in this camp. Joe replied with his usual zeal. He started by recounting the stories of his and his marras' experiences so far in this war.

"I'm sure our story won't be new to you," said Joe. "Or much different from your experiences, so I hope it won't bore you."

"Don't worry about that, Joe," said one of the gathered inmates, "We've nothing else to do, and we've heard that you are a storyteller."

"Aye, that he is," said Mike. "He used to tell us what was happening in the South African war before we got there in 1901. He's good at it, you'll see."

"Alright," said Joe, mustering his storytelling skills. "So, I'll start with our 'Race to the Sea' and our capture at Ennetières."

"That is such a fancy name for hell," said somebody.

"Aye, it is," said Joe. "I'll explain why they called it that. After a lengthy journey around Great Britain and through France, the 2/DLI arrived on the Western Front late on 19 September. We came during the First Battle of the Aisne, which had started on 13 September and was still raging. We walked straight into it. But that is another story I'll get to later. You asked how we ended here, so I'll do that first.

"When the Battle of the Aisne was over, we joined the Race to the Sea, as they called it," said Joe.

"I don't know whether you know this, but the British Army introduced the War Diary in this war. I learned of this when I was on reserve and helping to prepare for the 2/DLI mobilization, and I followed the entries from the first day of the war. The 2/DLI War Diary began on 4 August, the day we entered the war, and they have been keeping them up to date ever since. So, I'll give you examples as I tell my story, beginning as we left the Chemin des Dames above the River Aisne on 1 October 1914. I copied most of these as personal records in my diary. What follows in this story is long-winded. But bear with me. That's how it was, and I need to tell it as it was."

His audience nodded their approval since, having been there, they could expect this next part of the story. Handwritten or typed War Diaries recorded a daily account of the activities of every British, Dominion, Indian and Colonial Army unit on active service. The British Army required every unit to carry this out according to the Field Service Regulations dating from 1907. The War Diary recorded the unit's role in battle or on a mission. It was the commander's responsibility of every military unit to keep the War Diary current. For centuries, the Royal Navy and every ship worldwide had kept logs for the same reasons.

A junior officer recorded the day's events each evening and had it signed off by a senior or commanding officer. In addition to the completed official War Diary Army Form, the junior officer might include sketches, messages, maps, and Operational Orders as appendices. They might sometimes nominate the War Diary as an Intelligence Summary. Commanders used this information for intelligence on the enemy and as a historical record for future planning[10].

"As background," said Joe, "The Germans wanted to reach Paris and claim victory over the French. However, the Allies stopped them at the Marne, and we held them at the Aisne. However, there was still a gap between the North Sea and the English Channel that the Germans could get through

---

[10] http://www.greatwar.co.uk/research/military-records/british-army-war-diary.htm

to march to Paris. So, this gap triggered a race between both sides to outflank the other to reach the North Sea first. So, from 17 September, the war had moved into a new phase. A hectic series of flanking movements developed between the French-British and German armies toward the Channel and North Sea ports, a race to the sea. The British then ordered the BEF (British Expeditionary Force) to move with haste from the Aisne to the left of the Allied line closest to the Channel. They thought the BEF might enjoy the advantages of better communication with England there.

"This is how we experienced that race to the sea from the Aisne," said Joe.

§

War Diary: VENDRESSE to Vauxtin, 1 October 1914

Left VENDRESSE at about 10.30 P.M., marched to VAUXTIN and billeted.

"The 2/DLI left the trenches at 22:30 and marched the seven miles to Vauxtin," said Joe. "There, we billeted for the rest of the night. The commander established the Battalion Headquarters in the village priest's house. Although heavy shells were falling nearby, most exhausted soldiers fell asleep and didn't hear the noise until they awoke in the morning."

"In the priest's house?" asked one of Joe's companions.

"Aye, a likeable fellow, too," said Joe. "He took pity on our officers and invited them to stay with him. It was a sizeable house next to the church. Of course, he didn't have enough room for all of us, so we other ranks billeted outside."

"The Diary continued the next day," said Joe.

§

War Diary: Vauxtin to CIRY, 2 October 1914

At 7 P.M., we marched to CIRY and took over a line of defence from 4th Division cyclists who, early in the evening. Had taken over the defences from the West Riding Regt and the K.O.S.B.'s until our arrival.

"Then, at 19:00 hours on 2 October, we marched the ten miles to Ciry and took over the line from the 4th Divisional Cyclist Company. Early in the war, the army added a cyclist company to each British division. For example, the 4th Division included the 4th Divisional Cyclist Company. Recruitment efforts aimed at practised cyclists. The leading roles of the cyclists were in surveillance and communications, such as message distribution. The army equipped them as infantry units to give mobile firepower if required. They carried out trench-holding duties and manual work once the mobile phase of the war had settled into entrenched warfare. They also carried out patrol work and traffic control duties behind the front lines."

"Aye, I remember that," said one of Joe's companions. "I saw a poster to enlist men for the 48th (South Midland) Divisional Cyclist Company. It read, are you fond of cycling? Why not cycle for the King? Bad teeth, no bar!"

The audience laughed at the "Bad teeth, no bar" statement.

"I remember they started in the South African Cape Colony," said Mike. "Do you remember, Joe?"

"Aye, Mike," said Joe. "How could I forget it? But that is another story." He then continued his story of the Race to the Sea.

"So, as I was saying, late on 2 October, the 2/DLI relieved the 4th Divisional Cyclist Company. They were south of the juncture of the River Aisne with the River Vesle near Ciry. The German and British patrols exchanged shots day and night on either river bank. The central position was on the railway line, but they placed pickets well in advance on the Vesle bridges."

"We waved off the 4th Division cyclists there," recalled Mike. "Ever since our episode with bicycles of the Cape Cycle

Corps in the Karroo, we've had a soft spot for those fast-moving soldiers. But that's another story, isn't it, Joe?"

"Aye, Mike," said Joe. "The bicycles of the 4th Division looked better than the ones we had back in South Africa. And they must be most useful for getting away from bombardments."

"We could sure use them instead of this constant bloody marching we're doing, said our good departed marra Jack."

"For three weeks following the trench fighting," said Joe, "both sides suffered frontal attacks and attempted to encircle each other's flank. We were all rushing to gain the upper hand on France's northern coastline and Belgium's southern coast. As the Germans advanced toward the Allied left flank, the Allies aimed for the German right side. Such constant movements were typical during this campaign."

"Interesting, Joe," said one of his companions. "I've heard of the Race to the Sea but never knew what it meant."

"Aye, well, there you have it. But while this was happening, my third child was born on 4 October 1914," said Joe. "I learned this later in a letter from Mary. As my wife and I had agreed, she named her Mary, but they soon called her Molly to distinguish her from her mother."

This wasn't an isolated example. Many soldiers found themselves cut off from rapid news from home while they were incommunicado.

But once they re-established communications with their loved ones in the POW camp, they received such home news faster.

"That is the hardest thing of being here," said a listener. "Not only are we cut off from the families we left behind. For those of us whose wives have had children since leaving home, we won't know them until we get back if we ever do!"

"Aye, but our wives can now use public photographers to have pictures of our families made," said Joe. "I've asked my Mary to do that for me."

"Aye, that's an excellent point," was the reply.

§

War Diary: Ciry to St. REMI then LARGNY, 7 October 1914

We were relieved at CIRY by the LANC. FUS. at 2 A.M. and rejoined the brigade by march route at St. REMI. Remained there until 6 P.M. when we marched to LARGNY

"Our turn to move north came at 2 A.M. on the 7th of October," said Joe.

"It took us several days to reach our destination by various means. We started with a long march southwest beside the canal from the Aisne to the Marne, to Saint-Remi by Reims."

"The Lancashire Fusiliers relieved us at 2 A.M., so we only got away at 4 A.M. to march thirteen and a half miles to St Remi with 18 Brigade. We arrived at St Remi at 9 A.M., went into billets, and had breakfast. Then we spent the day there resting until 6 P.M. Then the brigade tromped over twenty miles to Largny-sur-Automne."

§

War Diary: Largny to St. SAUVEUR (OISE), 8 October 1914

Marched at 2 P.M. to St. SAUVEUR (OISE)

"On 8 October, the column didn't start until 2 P.M., when we marched the fifteen miles to St Sauveur on the River Oise," said Joe.

§

War Diary: Entrained at Le Meux, the 9th of October 1914

We marched at 5 P.M. and entrained at LE MEUX at 9:20 P.M.

"At 5 P.M. on the 9th, the Brigade marched the four and a half miles to Le Meux, where we boarded a French Railways train of cattle cars. The train carried us one hundred and forty miles through the night and the next day. It travelled via Etaples, Amiens, Abbeville, and Desbres to Arques, which was twenty-five miles from Calais and Dunkerque on the English Channel."

"I'm not complaining," said Mike. "Have you noticed we've been spending a lot of time marching and on trains over here?"

"It's better than what we went through back in the trenches," said Joe.

"Oh, aye, I agree," said Mike. "Just saying. But did you notice how they downgraded us on those transports? We started in third-class cars with the British Railways. Then they downgraded us to forty men or eight horse carriages on the French Railways. And now cattle cars! What's next?"

"Donkey carts," said Joe, to loud laughter from experience. "Or French trucks, maybe?"

"Aye, do you remember how Jack asked where we were heading," recalled Mike. "I said to the beaches, maybe in a Rolls Royce?"

"You joke, Mike," said Joe to his Rolls Royce comment. "The major mentioned that Rolls-Royce was building an armoured car for this war. We may see them soon enough."

"Aye, but only for the generals, I reckon," said Mike, the audience shaking their heads in agreement.

§

War Diary: Detrained at ARQUES, the 10th of October 1914

Disembarked at ARQUES and went into billets.

"On 10 October, the brigade detrained at Arques, Pas-de-Calais, still in France. There, Major Crosthwaite noted he spent the night in a brewery. We then marched to a farm two miles away, where we rested throughout the Sunday. We were now in a flat, low-lying country, with dykes and slow rivers lined with willows and thorn hedges. The ground was so saturated that trenches weren't possible, so we built breastworks [11] instead."

---

[11] A breastwork is a temporary fortification, often an earthwork thrown up above ground to breast height to provide protection to soldiers firing over it from a standing position.

§

War Diary: Arques to WARDRECQUES, the 11th of October 1914

We marched to WARDRECQUES, arriving about 9 A.M., bivouacked throughout the day, and went into billets at night.

"The next morning, we marched the three miles to Wardrecques, arriving at 9 A.M.," said Joe.

"There, we spent the rest of the day in fields, resting and waiting for another unit to leave their billets. Then, at night, we moved into the vacated premises."

§

War Diary: Wardrecques to HAZEBROUCK, the 12th of October 1914

Went in French trucks to HAZEBROUCK, arrived there at 3 P.M., and went into billets.

"The next morning, a convoy of French army motor trucks arrived at Wardrecques. So, we climbed into the French trucks, and they then transported us to Hazebrouck, arriving at 3 PM.

The whole brigade formed in Market Square, and then we marched to an old factory where we sheltered for the night.

"We had arrived in the region where the British III Corps was concentrating, covered by the 2nd Cavalry Division. Rumours circulated we were going to attack the Germans on the Belgian border."

General William Pulteney, a distinguished veteran of the Anglo-Egyptian War of 1882 and the Boer War of 1899, ordered III Corps to continue progressing on 13 October towards Bailleul. The plan was for a general advance, so the III Corps advanced with both its divisions in line. Three columns of the Sixth Division, including the 2/DLI on the right, moved towards Vieux-Berquin and Merris, east of Hazebrouck. Fourth Division moved in two columns towards Flêtre, north-east of Hazebrouck. The Cavalry Corps advanced to the northeast of the Mont des Cats, a small 490-foot hill near the town of Godewaersvelde on the Belgian border.

§

War Diary: Hazebrouck to VIEUX-BERQUIN, 13 October 1914

Marched to VIEUX-BERQUIN at 2 P.M., advanced to the attack of Ferme Labis and Les Trois Fermes. The attack was successful. Casualties.

"I told my marras the generals were readying us for an attack," said Joe. "I'd heard that we were to attack farms where the Boche troops were dug in. Then, the order came to fix bayonets."

"Shite. We will be very close to the enemy," called Mike. "I'm ready."

"We were in French Flanders," said Joe. "For those of you who've been there, you know it."

French Flanders is on the border with Belgian Flanders, where they still speak a Flemish dialect of Dutch. They have divided French Flanders into Maritime Flanders or French Westhoek on the North Sea. Dunkirk is a vital port there, and the French dialect Picard-speaking Walloon Flanders is where Lille is the principal city. The Lys River divided the two French Flanders regions.

During this war, the Western Front cut through the length of France until it crossed over from French Flanders into Belgian Flanders close to Ypres and Passchendaele. It blocked the German Right Flank from entering France on its intended path towards Paris. It became a region of several of the fiercest battles of the Great War.

"We were in French-speaking Walloon Flanders," said Joe.

"We then moved to Vieux-Berquin, 10 miles from Armentières and the Belgian border and fourteen and a half miles from the Belgian town of Ypres. The Dutch call it Leper.

At Vieux-Berquin, we joined the action at 2 P.M. when we arrived at the left of French General Antoine de Mitry's cavalry corps. We were opposite the enemy entrenched behind the Méteren Becque. The Méteren Becque waterway is a straight, ten-mile-long canal, twelve feet wide at the top and ten feet deep. It had been dug into the flat fields near Méteren to drain them into the River Lys.

"The cavalry corps refused an infantry appeal for help since they were engaged in battle. This forced the III Corps to launch a frontal assault on the German lines. The 2/DLI stretched out with the other regiments. We then received the order to attach bayonets and attack Ferme Labis and Les Trois Fermes.

"Right, me marras, here we go again," called Mike.

Mike, in the Hamelin audience, grimaced as the story gained momentum.

"We crossed a bog, sinking up to our waist in frigid water and mud, then reached a plowed field. Look after yourselves," I said to my marras. "They say we must cross this muddy field under fire while returning fire without protection!"

"Shite," said our marra, Jack. "Bloody madness!"

"Then the attack began," said Joe. "Hundreds of troops were shouting while running through the mud while firing through their comrades at the enemy. The Germans climbed out of their trenches and ran towards us, too. It was madness, as Jack said! Bullets whizzed past us in every direction the whole time, while shells exploded randomly across the entire field. British guns were lobbing projectiles from behind our lines into the German defences on the other side of the Méteren Becque. The noise of battle was horrific, and smoke covered the entire battlefield, so it was difficult to see ahead of our bayonets! And men were dropping too often around us."

"Stick with me, Lads," I yelled to my marras.

"Right next to you, Joe," called Mike.

"Right behind you, Joe," yelled Fred.

"I'm with you too," called Jack back from just ahead of me.

"So, on and on we ran," said Joe. "Weaving around our fallen wounded and dead fellows in the mud. But then I noticed Jack stumble and fall face-first into the mire."

"Jack's hit," I shouted. "I'll check him out. Keep going."

"I dropped to the mud and crawled back to check on my marra," said Joe. "Sadly, Jack had taken a bullet through his forehead."

"He's dead, a bullet to the forehead," I called forward to the others. "Jack's gone!"

"Keep going, my marra," said Mike, looking back. "Keep going as fast as you can. Catch up with me. They will collect and bury Jack after the battle."

"So, we ran through the hail of bullets and shrapnel from exploding shells. More men dropped to the mud when hit," said Joe.

"Soon enough, we came upon the enemy and engaged in one-on-one combat. We were thrusting our bayonets into very young Germans as we went and dodged the German blades as best we could.

"Then, it had ended," said Joe. "We were the last men standing. Not one German soldier had survived the charge. And they were all so young!

"Still, we couldn't rest. The Major ordered Mike, Fred and me to run forward to prevent the Germans from destroying a bridge over the canal. We arrived too late since the Germans had completed their preparations and, after setting the bridge on fire, they had retreated. The enemy had set fire to a chapel in the village of Sailly sur Lys, too, while they were at it. So, the major moved us to another outpost position, where we captured one German soldier and found another dead at the side of the road. The captured German spoke English and told us that the dead man's name was Krupp, and he had a wife and two children living in London."

"What an insane war," complained Fred. "I suppose he lived in London too when this all began, then signed up with the Fatherland. Crazy!"

"Aye, and bloody dangerous, Laddies," I said. "It's a miracle we didn't end up like Jack."

"After what seemed an eternity, the battle was over by the end of the day," said Joe. "It cost III Corps 708 casualties. The Germans wounded one officer, 2/Lieutenant Smith, and 60 NCOs and men, many of whom died from their wounds later in hospital. The Germans killed two 2/DLI officers, Lieutenant Parke and 2/Lieutenant Storey, a sergeant from Shildon, County Durham, who had received his commission just ten days before. They killed only 11 2/DLI NCOs and men, Jack among them, despite charging through the hail of bullets and exploding shells out in the open. Medics quickly bandaged Mike's left thigh muscle after a bullet went through it. Fred and I came through unscathed.

"I inquired about Jack and learned that they planned the burial of those killed the next day. The British had decided not to send bodies to their homes in Britain, burying them in makeshift cemeteries behind the Front close to where they fell. They had a service and burial the following afternoon at

Vieux-Berquin. And I got permission for us to attend. 'Will you join me?' I asked my marras."

"For sure," said Mike and Fred in unison.

From the earliest battles in the first weeks of the fighting on the Western Front, the number of military deaths was in the tens of thousands. The scale of casualties in the Great War was unparalleled. Thousands of soldiers were being buried on the battlefields in individual or communal graves by their comrades. Their comrades often buried them where they fell in action or dug into the sides of the trenches. But they buried the majority in a burial ground on or near the battlefield. They buried those who died of their wounds in a hospital behind the fighting lines in a cemetery nearby. Often, it would be in or near a town, village cemetery or a purpose-created annexed burial plot. They put up simple wooden crosses or markers to mark the graves and noted brief details of the deceased individuals. They registered the official burials, marking their locations for present-day visitors.

"Mike's wound was sore but not severe, so he rejoined us that afternoon. We were still mourning the loss of Jack, our beloved friend of so many years, and attended his burial early that morning at Vieux-Berquin. There was only a small gathering for Jack and a half-dozen other Durhams at the make-do cemetery close to the battlefield. The battalion chaplain led a quick service and an army prayer for the dead soldiers.

"There was no hymn, no taps and no further words," said Joe with tears mounting. "It was all so rushed. We said Amen, then paused for a few moments of reflection. Then, we returned to our units to face another battle. I'll miss him."

"Aye, our old marra," remembered Mike. "He was a fine laddie."

"We then reminisced over the times we had enjoyed together as we returned to our company position. Our close-knit little group of marras was mourning. We had endured childhood struggles and travails together in the colliery. We worked together at the Hawthorn Leslie shipyards, then survived more than a year of the South African War. We lost Billy in the Boer War and now Jack after such a brief time in this war.

"Damn wars," I sputtered. "Why do we have to have them?" Mike approached me after the burial and grasped me in a manly hug.

"To make the rich richer," said Mike, sticking to his old grudge. "But we didn't start this one either. The Boche did that and dragged us into it."

"I think this one will continue for a long time," I said. "I can't see how we'll be home by Christmas. And look how many of our fellow soldiers and sailors are dead or maimed so far!"

Empire and War

"When they ordered us to fix bayonets, I felt a strange sensation go through me," said Mike. "It was a mixture of fear and excitement, believe it or not."

"We did the practice charges and thrusts in training, but killing a junior Boche soldier was terrible. But I had to do it. It was him or me. I'll never forget pushing my blade into that young man and the horrible look on his face as he cried out. Terrible! Will we ever get used to it?"

"I felt the same way, Mike," I said. "And I don't think I'll ever get used to it."

"Did you laddies notice how they charged fearlessly through the bullets and exploding shells?" asked Mike. "But as soon as they saw the flash of our blades, it terrified them. I suppose that's why the army ordered it."

"Aye, I noticed that, too," I said. "And did you see our plane bring down that Boche plane?"

"Aye," said Mike. "That was belta!"

"It's a new war, Laddies," said Joe, speaking to his Hamelin audience. "We saw nothing like it in South Africa."

"Aye," said a listener who had experienced the same charge. "Frightening! Before, we just had to worry about who was in front of or behind us. We must look out for what happens above us, too!"

"I still haven't gotten to where they took us captive," said Joe. "I can see you are all ready for your bunks. So, I'll continue this story another day."

His companions agreed all around and shuffled off to their bunks for the night.

§

Mary Hears from Joe

One day in the second half of November, Mary got her first communication from Joe - a postcard. It was a strange pre-printed postcard with incomprehensible German print on it. But she recognized Joe's handwriting in their address.

Above it, in English, she read, "To be forwarded immediately to England."

On the flip side, at the top, it read "Fill up this card immediately!" in print, followed by "I am a prisoner of war in Germany."

The prisoner's details are as follows: "Name, Christian name, Rank and Regiment," filled in by Joe in his handwriting. Mary then noticed the most crucial information in line with the printed items "Sound," "Wounded," and "Ill." Joe's handwritten "Yes" beside "Sound" filled her with relief and joy. Then, at the bottom of the card, they printed the return address of the Hamelin Camp.

Half wailing and half laughing, Mary broke into hysterical tears of relief. She hadn't known whether Joe was alive or dead. She last received a letter from Joe at the Western Front on 18 October. It had been so unlike Joe not to write; he had done it almost daily. Soon after Joe's last letter, the Army sent her a telegram that said only that her husband was "Missing in Action."

"What does missing in action mean?" she had asked her sisters. "I want to know whether Joe is still alive. How can he be missing?" The telegram hadn't provided her with any comfort. She found it worse than declaring Joe killed in action. "Where is he? Is he injured? When will I know for sure what has happened to him?" A wail often heard across Great Britain and the British Empire was the lament of the loved ones of the soldiers and sailors of the realm "missing in action."

But with his simple pre-printed postcard, Mary knew Joe was alive and sound! She turned to the children and said, "Your Da is safe. Alive and well! He is fine. But Ma doesn't know when he's coming home." She then grabbed them and rushed to tell her siblings.

"Joe is alive and well," she declared to her family.

"How on earth do you know?" asked one of her sisters.

"Look. I got a postcard from Joe," said Mary. "He is in a German prisoner of war camp in Germany. And it said he was sound. My God, I am so relieved."

"So, when is he coming home?" asked her sister.

"Oh, they didn't mention that," said Mary. "Maybe he'll tell me in a letter? Or, maybe he doesn't know."

"I've heard Ruth Anderson O'Brien got the same postcard from Mike," said another sister.

"Thank God for that, too," said Mary. "Mike is Joe's longest and best marra. And Joe is still very fond of Ruth. I must look her up again. Have you heard anything about Jack and Fred?"

"Nee… nothing," said her sister. "Not a word."

§

Looking back at Joe's Capture at Ennetières

The same companions gathered another evening to hear the rest of Joe's story about how he and Mike had ended up in the Hamelin POW camp.

"Good to see you are still interested in our story," said Joe. "It can't be so different from yours. This story is the last chapter of how Mike, I, and many of you got into this bloody camp."

§

War Diary: Advanced to LE VERRIER, 14th October 1914

Advanced to LE VERRIER and battalion billeted on the RAU DU LEET.

"The attack on Ferme Labis and Les Trois Fermes being over, the Germans moved back towards Lille under steady pressure from the British infantry," said Joe.

"We pushed the enemy line back along the River Lys towards the village of Menin in Belgium. By 14 October, we Durhams had advanced to Le Doulieu. We then cautiously turned southeast to cross the Lys by a broken bridge at Sailly, the one we had tried to protect.

"During the first two weeks of October, the leading British force had advanced eastwards. The 2nd Corps first moved towards La Bassée. The 3rd Corps moved towards Armentières. The 1st Corps followed them north of Ypres at the end of the third week. They turned on the famous St Omer-Aire-La Bassée defence line. Then, after the success at Méteren Becque on 13 October, the 3rd Corps drove back the enemy through Bailleul and Armentières towards Lille and was awaiting further orders."

§

War Diary: Marched to SAILLY, 15 October 1914

War Diary: Marched to Bois Grenier, 17 October 1914

Marched to BOIS GRENIER, two companies took up a line between TOUQUET and LE QUESNE and returned to outposts at BOIS GRENIER in the dark. Casualty 1 O.R. killed.

"On the evening of the 15th," said Joe, "the Germans took up an outpost south of Sailly. We remained near Bois Grenier until the night of the 17th, engaging in minor encounters with the enemy. Mike and I didn't take part in those."

§

War Diary: Attack on Ennetières, 18th October 1914

Ordered to make a demonstration to test enemy strength at LA VALLEE, at 3.45 P.M., attacked ENNETIÈRES; the attack was successful. Casualties.

"When the high command ordered Major-General Pulteney to advance through the River Lys valley, he complained that this could have exposed his right flank to danger," said Joe.

"It forced him to drive the Germans off the Perenchies Ridge first. To do this, he ordered the 6th Division to test the strength of the enemy forces between La Vallée and Perenchies and to push them back if they could.

"So, at 3:45 P.M., they ordered us Durhams to advance at La Vallée and attack the village of Ennetières. The advance guards walked on the grass verges to deaden their noise, passing groups of French cavalries. One of these groups was a detachment of cuirassiers[12]—I struggle to say that—their cuirasses, body armour and helmets by then rusty. One called out to our company, Hullo, Tommie, I was at Oxford."

"La Vallée was at the edge of a rise on which the Lille fortresses stood. We began our demonstration[13] under heavy shrapnel fire, and they sent us southeastward towards Fort d'Englos. Our company advanced through a bog in extended order for a hundred yards when a hail of bullets came from the right, left and front. Shrapnel from exploding shells once more rained on us. Beyond the bog, we were into farm fields filled with turnip plants."

"Drop!" was the order at that point. "So, my marras and I fell flat and attempted to conceal ourselves behind the turnip greens while shrapnel from exploding shells rained down. We then rose and rushed forward through the turnip field with no cover.

---

[12] French cavalry regiments that still wore a covered cuirass, a piece of armour which covers the torso. and plumed helmet on active service

[13] According to the Department of Defense Dictionary of Military and Associated Terms, in military terminology, a demonstration is an attack or show of force on a front where a decision is not sought, made with the aim of deceiving the enemy. A related diversionary manoeuvre, the feint, involves actual contact with the enemy, unlike a demonstration.

"Drop," I shouted again. The bullets were so thick now that we could only lay our faces sideways on the mud and lie flat.

"Are you injured, Fred?" I called.

"Aye, sore but no open wound."

"We advanced again with caution, reinforced by the men before us, then dropped and remained there for two hours while the bullets were thick. Then, just before dusk, Fred risked a look over the turnip tops and got a piece of shrapnel in the shoulder. Letting out a scream of pain as he rose his body just above the turnip leaves. A rifle bullet struck Fred in the stomach. He collapsed into the mud between the vegetables, writhing in his death throes. Once again, assisted by Mike, I returned to help our marra but to no avail; Fred was dead. The Germans had reduced our small group of Jarrow shipyard marras to two."

"We had no choice but to leave Fred where he was as we moved on," said Mike.

"Despite intense rifle fire, the 2/DLI got as far as Ennetières before dusk," said Joe.

"By 5 P.M., we had taken Ennetières, and at 8 P.M., the action over, we searched with caution for shelter. The streets were empty, or so it seemed. Mike and I came upon a house on the principal street where we entered and encountered an appalling sight. Having searched the entire house and found no one, we entered the cellar, where we found a horror scene. In the dim light from the cellar door, we could see the outlines of many bodies. The floor was littered with arms, legs, and heads. It was nothing more than a heap of bloodied dead villagers. We concluded the Germans had herded and executed them in the cellar. In one corner, an older man and woman lay shattered by a grenade. We moved to help the old man, who was still alive and moving, but he died soon after we got to him.

"It shook us to the core. So, we left that house and moved through the village. There were no bodies of German soldiers anywhere—their army had removed them. However, we came upon a small group of six French Dragoons we had seen patrolling the previous night. To our horror, Mike and I saw that someone had removed their eyes, ears and noses.

"What the hell is this?" cried Mike. "These Boche are barbarians!"

"Then, a little further along, we found a Frenchman standing erect but dead in the corner of a brick wall. They had removed his eyes, nose and ears too."

"What are we dealing with here?" I murmured to Mike. "Savages? Let's get the hell out of here."

"Such terrible scenes were frequent at the start of the war while villagers clung to their homes and meagre belongings while the war raged and closed around us. Mike, Fred, and I did our best against the enemy during that battle. And we saw terrifying battle conditions. Our marra Fred was dead. Another marra dead! Neither Mike nor I had worrying injuries, but coming so hard after the last fight, we felt bruised and shaken."

"We are getting into more and more of these tussles, Joe," said Mike with a sigh after the battle

"Aye, that we are, Mike," I said. "And we are losing more and more of our marras. How long do you think we have to live in this war?"

"Well, Fred is joining his Mary in Heaven," said Mike. "And that will please him. He was a good old soldier! And Jack is right next to them. How long we have is anybody's guess, but I reckon we won't be living a long life, Joe."

"In this successful battle for the Allies, which thrust a small salient into the line," [14] said Joe. "The enemy killed Lieutenant Conant and Captain Northey and four soldiers. The Boche also wounded 74 NCOs and men, and 29 were missing, presumed dead or captured. After nightfall, the battalion, relieved by the 2nd Foresters, moved back to a reserve position at Fetus, a mile northwest of Ennetières. [15] C-Company remained forward in a local reserve with the Sherwood Foresters at La Vallée, next to Ennetières.

---

[14] A **salient** is a battlefield feature that projects into enemy territory. The salient is surrounded by the enemy on three sides, making the troops occupying the salient vulnerable. The enemy's line facing a salient is referred to as **are-entrant** (an angle pointing inwards). A deep salient is vulnerable to being "pinched out" across the base, forming a **pocket** in which the defenders of the salient become isolated.

[15] S.G.P Ward, *Faithful, The Story of the Durham Light Infantry*, 1962

"Our troops pushed German cavalry and Jägers [16] back towards Lille until 19 October. But German infantry reinforcements of the 6th Army [17] had arrived during October, boosting their strength."

§

War Diary: In reserve at FETIS, 19th October 1914

In reserve at FETUS, one mile south of ENNETIÈRES, Major Blake's Company (C) left in reserve to Sherwood Foresters at LA VALLÉE.

"So, German attacks against the British 6th Division began from 7:00 A.M.," said Joe.

"After a one-hour bombardment of heavy guns and howitzers, the German assault was part of an offensive on either side of Ypres to encircle the British forces. The leading Germans attacked the right flank of the British line towards

---

[16] Jäger is a German military term adopted in 1631 by the landgrave of Hesse when he first formed an elite infantry unit out of his professional hunters (Jäger) and rangers (Forstleute, or forestry people) in the Hessian Army. By the early twentieth century, Jäger units were part of the Imperial German, Austro-Hungarian, Swedish, Dutch and Norwegian armies. They corresponded to the rifles, light infantry, chasseurs à pied or bersaglieri units of the British, French, Italian and other armies. While such units still enjoyed considerable prestige and high esprit de corps, their training, equipment and tactical roles had for the most part become aligned with those of the line infantry of their respective armies.

[17] At the outbreak of the Great War, command of the 6th army was given to Rupprecht, Crown Prince of Bavaria (Kronprinz Rupprecht von Bayern). The 6th Army initially comprised units of the Bavarian Army with additional Prussian units. During the execution of Plan XVII, the 6th Army was stationed in the Central sector, covering Lorraine. In August 1914, in the Battle of Lorraine, the 6th Army managed to hold against the French offensive. After the Western Front turned to a stalemate and the opposing forces formed lines of trenches, the 6th Army was based in Northern France.

Ennetières, where it merged with La Vallée. Their infantry advanced in rushes of men in skirmish lines supported by machine-gun fire."

The First Battle of Ypres and the Battle of the Yser River were the last battles fought between the Allied Powers and Germany in the Race to the Sea. By early October, the German troops had taken Antwerp farther northeast, and the Allied forces held Nieuport on the North Sea near Ypres, Belgium. Under the command of Field Marshal Sir John French, the BEF reinforced the French-Belgian troops at Ypres. Another battle started on 19 October 1914, with the Flanders Offensive run by German Chief of General Staff Erich von Falkenhayn. He ordered the German 4th Army, under Prince Rupprecht of Bavaria and General Albrecht of Wurttemberg, to attack the Allied troops. They planned to take the city of Ypres and concurrently engage the Belgian forces at the Yser.

"The British fought off the first German attack with small arms fire," said Joe. "So, the Germans made another attack on Ennetières at 1 P.M. But they failed. In a drizzle of rain, the Germans attacked again at 3 P.M. but were driven back by the British. The German artillery bombarded the Brigade positions from the northeast until dark. At night, the Germans sent three battalions of their 52nd Infantry Brigade to rush our British ranks.

"This German attack broke through, and two companies of their Reserve Infantry Regiment 125 entered Ennetières from the west. Four units of German Reserve Infantry Regiment 122 and a battalion of Reserve Infantry Regiment 125 broke in from the south. They surrounded and captured several British platoons. Another attack from the east led to the British infantry east of the village retiring to the west side of the town. Then, German troops advancing there from La Vallée, which had fallen after 6 P.M., surprised and captured them. The entrapped troops fought on until 5:15 the next morning. However, the German infantry didn't take advantage of the success. British soldiers on the northern flank withdrew to a line one mile west of Prémesques, leaving behind our C-Company as a reserve to the 2/Sherwood Foresters."

§

War Diary: Fall of Ennetières, Tuesday 20th October 1914

In brigade reserve, at about 8.30 A.M., 3 companies were ordered to go to LA VALLEE. Soon afterwards, two companies, B and D Capt. Wood and Capt. Birt was sent to support the East Yorkshire Regt at PARADIS. At 1 P.M., C.O.

ordered the remaining company, Captain Taylor's (A), to PARADIS. There was a gap in the firing line between the East Yorkshires and Stafford Regiments, which Capt. filled up. Wood's company and one platoon of A-Company under 2nd Lieut. Beard, about 3.30 P.M., Capt. Birt's company (D) was ordered to support the West Yorkshire Regiment on the right of the East Yorkshire Regiment. At about 4.30 P.M., the C.O. ordered to take all the men not engaged back to LA VALLEE, comprising only three A-Company platoons. On the way to LA VALLEE, we met the O.C. Sherwood Foresters. They stated that a large force had turned his right flank and that LA VALLEE was in the hands of the enemy after two unsuccessful attempts to enter it. The three platoons of A-Company withdrew to FETUS to prevent any further advance of the enemy on that flank. As far as was found out, Major Blake took some of his Company (7 platoons) into a factory and did good work from the upper storey. They brought overhead fire to the enemy attacking the Sherwood Foresters. A heavy shell fell into the building, wrecking it and smashing some machinery. Major Blake was killed. It is not known how many of the men were killed or wounded. The remaining platoons of C-Company under Lieut Norton were sent to the right flank to protect the right flank of the Sherwood Foresters during their retirement. Lieut Norton was wounded and taken prisoner. It is supposed that many of his men not killed suffered the same fate as only 23 NCOs and men of C-Company returned.

Casualties: Officer killed - Maj. Blake. Wounded & missing - Lieut Norton. Wounded - 2nd Lieutenants Beart and Gilbertson. 4 OR killed, 44 injured, and 177 missing.

The pressure exerted by the BEF III Corps, whose line projected in a salient from Prémesques to Ennetières, appeared to the Germans to threaten Lille. They had held Lille since 11 October and at once ordered a counterstrike, which fell on the 18th Brigade's small salient on 20 October. Being in reserve, the 2/DLI companies reinforced the other battalions as they came under attack. Of the Durhams, Major Blake's C-Company went to the Foresters at Ennetières and La Vallée; Captain Birt's D-Company went first to the East Yorkshire at Paradis and then to the West Yorkshires on their right; Capt. Wood's B-Company moved to the East Yorkshires. Capt. They ordered Taylor's A-Company to follow soon after. [18]

"Mike and I soon found ourselves separated from D-Company, so we joined a platoon of C-Company under Lieutenant Norton until we could find our way back.

"We heard the Germans were using three-quarters of the 44,000-man Royal Württemberg XIII Army Corps in the storming of Ennetières. [19] So, they swamped our 2nd Foresters, who formed the garrison. The German attacks came upon them soon after 1 P.M. from the east, the southeast, and the southwest. But only after dark did a German assault from the west burst into the village. Even though a few soldiers held out in the house in La Vallée until

---

[18] S.G.P Ward, *Faithful, The Story of the Durham Light Infantry*, Naval and Military Press, 1962

[19] The XIII (Royal Württemberg) Corps was commanded by General der Infanterie Max von Fabeck, within the 5th Army commanded by Generalmajor Wilhelm, Crown Prince of Germany: 26th Infantry Division & 27th Infantry Division. The XIII was, effectively, also the army of the Kingdom of Württemberg, which had been integrated in 1871 into the Prussian Army command structure, as had the armies of most German states. The corps was originally established as the Württemberg Corps Command (Korpskommando) in 1817. It became the XIII Army Corps when it was integrated into the Prussian numbering system on December 18, 1871, shortly after the Franco-Prussian War.

the early hours of the 21st, the enemy destroyed most of the battalion.[20]

"Major Blake took two platoons of C-Company into a sugar factory. From there, they fired on the attackers from the upper storey. A massive German shell fell into the building, smashing the machinery and killing and crushing the men inside, including the Major. The other two platoons, under Lieutenant Norton, took part in bitter fighting after dark in the village's south.

"Mike and I had always provided cover for each other, working as a compact fighting unit. We stood crouched with our backs against the wall of an abandoned house in Ennetières while looking over a low barrier in front. There was a fierce firefight. And it was so dark we couldn't recognize anything in the gloom except for the many flashes of rifle fire. Lieutenant Norton and the others weren't far from us, but we could hear the Germans approaching from every direction. Lieutenant Norton's company had retreated into the village. But it was only a temporary escape. It was now looking bleak for us all. And Mike and I were alone and surrounded by Germans!

"Look out there, Mike," I whispered while looking into the darkness. "They aren't ours, that's for sure!"

---

[20] *Ibid*

"Aye, it looks like we're trapped here," whispered Mike. "Finished."

"Aye, I reckon you are right," I said. "The Germans have surrounded us. What happens now? I can't imagine, Mike. Could this be our end?"

"We can't run," said Mike, "or they'll shoot us for sure."

"Aye, let's stay put. I hope the Germans miss us," I said.

"I don't think there's much chance of that, my marra," said Mike. "As far as I can see, we're finished!"

"Not yet, Mike," I said, "but if we raise our rifles, we will be."

Somebody cried out in the distance, "They shot Lieutenant Norton!" Shots were still ringing out in that direction. We saw the distinct shapes of the many German soldiers approaching mere yards away. Their gleaming bayonetted rifles held from their hips at forty-five-degree angles, and their menacing pointed helmets identified them as German. I couldn't stop trembling. And I heard Mike's rapid breathing and gasping from time to time. Then, we listened to the tramping of boots on cobblestones. "Where were they going?"

"They are approaching us," whispered Mike.

And then we heard "Hände hoch!", "Hands up," from one of the approaching Germans. "Drop your weapons! No weapons! Hände hoch!"

§

"So, that was that, Laddies," said Joe with a smile. "That's how we got here. So now, after a tense transfer from there to here, you have us among you."

That brought applause and comments of "well told," "that's how it happened," and "Thank God we survived that ordeal, all of us!"

"Aye, well, I'm not sure how we survived it either," said Joe.

"Now I have more war stories to tell you another day when you are ready. It's about how we got into this war and how we survived the Battle of the Aisne in the first trenches of the Great War. I'll continue them when we find some time."

"Grand, looking forward to it, Joe," said a companion. "A few of us were right there with you."

§

3. *Christmas 1914*

Before they knew it, Christmas Day 1914 was upon the Allied soldiers in the POW camps and the trenches of the Eastern and Western Fronts. The Kaiser hadn't met his promise to his armies of bringing the soldiers home for Christmas.

"No Christmas cheer this year, Laddies," said Joe as they arose that morning. Despite it being a Friday, the authorities declared a long weekend of free time. "No Christmas dinner with our families, no presents and no Christmas service in our church at home. Just knocking around together in this barrack so far from home on a miserable day. It's a sad state of affairs in which we find ourselves."

"Aye, Joe," said Mike. "It's a bloody dismal Christmas this year."

"Dismal, dark and cold," said Walt. "What the hell will we do for the next three days?"

"Wait, Laddies," piped up another. "I have just received a Christmas package from home, and I'm willing to share."

"Me too," called another, and another, and another.

"Me too," said Joe.

Before long, a chorus of voices offered their contributions to a Christmas dinner that dismal holy day. And then, on the day, the unthinkable happened. Guard Klaus appeared with two other guards carrying a load of "Christmas gifts" from the establishment.

"Hello, gentlemen," said Klaus. "It pleases me to announce that the Kommandant wants you to enjoy this important religious day in Germany. We call it 'Weihnachten', and it's the most important day for us. Here are a large roast ham, potatoes and a case of German beer from the Kommandant."

The men stood as if stunned for several seconds while the surprise registered. Then Joe broke the silence. "Klaus, you and the Kommandant are guardian angels," he said. "Merry Christmas."

"'Und', I have more news," said Klaus. "The Kommandant told me that there's a truce happening on the Western Front. Isn't that amazing? Maybe the Kaiser was right? Maybe the war is over today!"

"Listen, Laddies," called Joe. "Klaus says there's a truce on the Front. A truce!"

"Howay, Laddies," called Mike. "Is the war ending?

"We hope so," called Klaus. "Maybe we can be brothers again?"

Christmas 1914 became a surprise merry event in Hamelin POW camp. It seemed a miracle and created a joyful atmosphere in an otherwise dismal environment. The Kaiser had promised an end by Christmas; this must be it. There were cheering and impromptu drumming noises throughout the camp. On Christmas Day, 1914, the POWs at Hamelin and elsewhere rejoiced in the truce and sat down to a hearty Christmas dinner. Joe and his companions enjoyed a sumptuous German roast ham and potatoes, washed down by a strong German Bock Beer. They topped it off with English Christmas pudding and cake from their shared home packages. It was a joyous day.

Empire and War

The men soon learned the facts about the Christmas Truce. On 7 December 1914, Pope Benedict XV suggested a temporary pause of the war to celebrate the holy day of Christmas. The combatant countries refused an official ceasefire, but on Christmas Day, 1914, the belief the war could end ran the entire length of the Western Front like lightning. Many soldiers in places along the Western Front declared an unofficial truce. There were widespread unofficial ceasefires, and one hundred thousand British and German troops took part in the unofficial cessations of hostility along the Western Front. [21] The Germans mounted candles and Christmas trees in their trenches. They sang German Christmas carols, to which the British responded by singing English carols. The soldiers shouted Christmas greetings to each other. A few crossed no-man's-land and exchanged small gifts, such as food, tobacco and alcohol, and personal souvenirs like buttons, badges and hats. The artillery and rifle fire fell silent, and they even held joint Christmas church services in places. A few soldiers used this short-lived ceasefire for a more sombre task: retrieving the bodies of fellow soldiers who had fallen within no-man's-land. In many sectors, the truce lasted through Christmas night; in others, it continued until New Year's Day. [22]

---

[21] Thomas Vinciguerra, "The Truce of Christmas, 1914," *The New York Times*, 25 December 2005.

[22] David Brown, "Remembering a Victory For Human Kindness – WWI's Puzzling, Poignant Christmas Truce," *The Washington Post*, 25 December 2004.

A separate Christmas truce occurred on the Eastern front, where the Austro-Hungarian commanders made the first move. The Russians reciprocated, and the soldiers met in no-man's-land [23].

Alas, they never repeated the 1914 Christmas Truce. Threats of disciplinary action quashed any future attempts at holiday ceasefires on the Fronts. However, the Christmas Truce of 1914 proved that a thread of humanity and Christmas spirit still existed at that early stage of the Great War.

§

---

[23] Max Hastings. William Collins, *Catastrophe 1914: Europe Goes To War*, 2013. – 'On Christmas Day in Galicia, Austrian troops were ordered not to fire unless provoked, and the Russians displayed the same restraint. Some of the besiegers of Przemyśl deposited three Christmas trees in no man's land with a polite accompanying note addressed to the enemy: 'We wish you, the heroes of Przemyśl, a Merry Christmas and hope that we can come to a peaceful agreement as soon as possible.' In no man's land, soldiers met and exchanged Austrian tobacco and schnapps for Russian bread and meat. When the Tsar's soldiers held their own seasonal festivities a few days later, Habsburg troops reciprocated."

1915—The year of searching for a breakthrough

The Women of Britain Go to Work

As Joe, Mike, Walt and their fellow prisoners settled into their new winter routine in Hamelin, so did their women at home. Mary and Ruth had prepared their own Christmas packages of home treats and sent them to their husbands.

By then, the Home Front was undergoing significant changes. They enlisted women to help with the war effort. Mary and her sisters volunteered to work wherever and whenever needed, with or without pay. Her mother and other older female family members cared for their children. Joe sent home most of his 1s 1d per day soldier's pay to his wife and family. He could do this since he neither smoked nor drank and needed much cash. But the POWs still didn't know whether they would continue receiving their pay.

"My biggest worry is not for myself," said Joe to Mike. "If we don't get our pay, we can still eat and survive, thanks to the Red Cross. Even as prisoners, they care for us, thanks to the Kaiser. But what happens to our families? Who will help them?"

"Aye, Joe," said Mike. "I have the same concern about Ruth."

Empire and War

"The government must help them out," said Walt. "This war is not the fault of our women."

"You know, it's tough enough we have to go to war to protect our country, but it's tougher on our wives and families," said Joe.

"I sure hope our country is helping them."

From the beginning of the Great War, losing the principal wage earner created severe hardship for many families. The call-up of reservists and Lord Kitchener's recruitment drive diverted hundreds of thousands of men to the Western Front. At first, unemployment increased from the war since specific markets like luxury goods collapsed. The effect on the wartime economy increased the stress for the women on the Home Front. The government soon realized they could not get men to volunteer for service if they could not care for their homes and families.

So, the British established thousands of charities for basic comforts, including clothing, books and food—for British and Empire troops. They set up charities for medical services and support for disabled service members and organizations to relieve distress at home. In 1914, the local churches asked for donations and volunteers to prepare care packages for the British POWs. The women of Tyneside threw themselves into this task with zeal. With the sudden influx of wounded men from the Western Front, the local hospitals appealed for volunteers to help with their overwhelmed kitchens and cleaning staff. Again, the women of Jarrow stepped up to do whatever they needed to do with enthusiasm and humour.

Early in 1915, Mary met Ruth one Sunday in town. They had become close friends, bonded through the closeness of their husbands. "Y'areet hinny," [24] greeted Mary. "Have you heard from your gadgie?" [25]

"Aye, that I have," said Ruth. "He's canny [26], same as your gadgie, I expect?"

"Aye, Joe is canny too," said Mary. "I've just heard from him again. He's written to me and telling me as much as he's allowed. I don't think he can say much about their life there. But he drops hints, and he sounds alright. And I guess it's better than them getting killed at the Front. That's all we hear of these days."

"Aye, you're too right," said Ruth. "So many men are dying or returning with the most terrible injuries. A cousin of mine has returned blind, shot through the eye and head. He's finished."

Mary showed Ruth her latest postcard. "This time, it has a photo of the camp on the front," said Mary. "Just look at the entrance to the camp. And all those solid-looking wooden cabins behind it. Joe says the prisoners built them. And look

---

[24] Geordie for honey, a term of endearment, wife, female companion or life partner.
[25] Gadgie is a Scottish or Northern English term for a man or boy, boyfriend or loved one; but also for a person considered to be of little importance or worth.
[26] Geordie for good, nice, or pleasant

beyond the camp. See the rolling farm fields with forests on the top of the hills. It looks pleasant enough."

Joe had vowed to never give Mary any sad or upsetting news from the camp. He instead tried to stay on the light side and emphasized that he was well and, if not happy, at least living in satisfying circumstances. In that way, he also got around the German censors. Mary turned the card over and read the back to Ruth.

"Dearest Mary,

"Enjoying my holiday in northern Germany. Housing is warm and comfortable since we built it ourselves. Food is not as good as yours, but our guard tells us that German black bread with thin soup is good for us. Loved your parcel and shared your fruitcake with my friends at Christmas. They loved it.

"Can't wait to see you and the children again.

"Tell Johnnie and Violet that their Da is grand and that they and baby Molly are behaving well.

"Loving you, my dearest Mary, Joe."

"What a lovely card, Mary," said Ruth. "Joe has a knack for writing, doesn't he?"

"Aye, that he does," said Mary, smiling and heaving an enormous sigh. Her husband was alive and safe and still had his sense of humour.

"They have the luck of the Irish, those two," Ruth giggled.

"Aye, that they do," said Mary. "Joe has lost so many of his marras in two wars. Billy died in South Africa, and now Jack and Fred dying on the Western Front. So many men are dying in this war."

"How are you doing, Mary," asked Ruth. "Are you coping?"

"Aye, I'm fine," said Mary. "Joe is sending home most of his pay, so we're not suffering. We don't know how long that will last, so I might need to find paying work."

"I know what you mean," said Ruth. "I'm lucky I still have a job at the mansion. And we have no bairns the way you do."

"Aye, but one on the way, hinny," said Mary. "You'll need every penny for the two of you."

Before the war, few women worked, apart from primarily single female servants of the grand houses, teachers, nurses, seamstresses, sales clerks, and workers of the cloth mills. On Tyneside, it was the "white mice" of Malings Potteries or the infamous tough ropery lassies.

However, as the Great War progressed, more and more men left Britain and its industry for the Western Front. The yards, factories, and municipal services were under severe strain to meet the increased demands of the war effort. The same was true in agriculture. Men had left the estates and farms en masse, leaving an acute shortage of workers and a worry about the continued food production. Most of the grand houses of Britain lost their young gardeners, leading to their rapid decline.

At first, Belgian refugees filled the gaps, but soon, that wasn't enough. So, the women of Britain started filling that void and taking up the strain. It was unprecedented, and those who initially expressed skepticism about women taking over men's work were in for an awakening.

Mary was with her friends on a Sunday after the church service. There was a noticeable shortage of younger men and a preponderance of women and older men in the church.

"Well, my hinnies," said Mary. "We have to pitch in and take over the work of the men here at home!"

"Howay, Lassie," was the collective response.

"Maybe things will turn out right at last if we do," called another, to shrieks of glee from the other ladies in the church hall.

"What do ye have in mind, Lass?" asked another.

"I'm strong," said Mary. "I'll do whatever they want me to do. Where can I find a job?"

"I've heard the factories and yards are battling to get their orders out because of a lack of workers. I know a few hinnies that have gotten jobs," said another.

With that, Mary and her female friends sought paid employment at various factories and services. They did not pay the women as much as the men, but they provided income for the household. The women of Britain rolled up their sleeves and went to work for their men abroad, their communities and their nation at war. They'd work for the duration of the war in the places left vacant by the hundreds of thousands of men who had gone off to war, many not returning. It was a revolutionary phenomenon that changed British society forever.

Most of the women Mary knew had started work in munitions factories elsewhere, involving long commutes in company-provided transport. But Mary wanted to stay closer to home, so she approached someone senior she knew at Hawthorn Leslie. Joe had worked there for many years, both before the Boer War and between the wars. Hawthorn Leslie had never used women, but as Joe's wife, they took her on, starting with menial tasks in the yard. In 1915, Hawthorn Leslie was very busy. Hawthorn Leslie built two C-Class light cruisers, which were laid down before the war. They launched HMS Carysfort in November 1914 but were still outfitting the ship on schedule for a June 1915 completion. The yard was working on HMS Champion for a May 1915 launch and a conclusion in December 1915. Twenty Destroyers were under construction, floated, fitted, or planned at Hawthorn Leslie during the war. Also, the yards had Royal Fleet Auxiliary vessels and merchant ships under construction during this time. There was lots of work and too few men to carry it out.

But the job was challenging, particularly in winter. Most tasks were monotonous; the conditions were often severe, and the workdays were long. Since it was so cold, they nicknamed one section of the yard 'Siberia,' and the company only allowed workers two toilet breaks a day for up to three minutes. Workers perched toilets above one long trench; they provided neither toilet paper nor doors, though men and women used separate facilities and brought newspapers from home. [27]

The working wives of Hawthorn Leslie veterans soon understood the harsh conditions under which their husbands had worked before the war. It made them even more determined to succeed in their new endeavours no matter the circumstances. They were far more cheerful than the men, singing and calling to each other across the yards. The women settled into alternative lives and enjoyed their newfound independence and the rewards of paydays. They saw far less of their families except on Sundays, just as it had been for their men. Older members of their families looked after the children. Everyone pitched in and soon adapted to an alternative way of life in wartime Britain.

When the women met after church a few weeks later, they all worked in paying jobs.

"Howay, Mary," called one. "How's the job at Hawthorne Leslie?"

---

[27] Jo Bath, Great War Britain: Tyneside, Remembering 1914-18, 2015

"Grand," said Mary. "Well, lots to do and building callouses on my hands."

"Champion, Lassie," said the other. "Me too. I found a job with the tram company. I'm working now as a conductor, but they said they might teach me how to drive a tram since they need drivers."

"I'm at Palmers," piped up another. "They have a full order book for warships, cargo and passenger ships. I'm working there as an inside painter."

"Well, I'm still at the mansion," said Ruth. "The boss is still making lots of money, so they are keeping all their staff. They've put me in charge of the chambermaids and increased my pay slightly. And since they lost a few manservants, they are replacing male roles with women, would you believe?"

"That's what's happening everywhere, Ruth," said Mary. "Just look among our small circle of friends at how many of us have taken over male roles, myself included."

It soon became apparent women were every bit as capable of performing most tasks apart from the most physically challenging. They filled the gaps in the factories, mines, transport, and commerce. They fulfilled the burgeoning requirements of hundreds of new companies that had sprung up to manufacture weapons, munitions, and other items required for the war effort. Women filled the missing help on the farms, taking up hoes and spades and learning to drive the horse teams and steam traction engines. They became tram conductors and drivers and took over the delivery of goods as carters and lorry drivers. It soon became clear that few women couldn't or wouldn't do it.

"It's an unfamiliar world we're living in, my hinnies," said Mary. "A strange world."

§

The Bets are On for the Gallipoli Campaign

By January 1915, the football fields were under snow; their first season had ended well before Christmas. The prisoners then looked for other ways to amuse themselves when not working. Those who could read enjoyed books sent by the Red Cross and letters from home. They spent hours seeking information and conversing about recent developments in the war. They also knew the Great War was also in Africa, the Eastern Mediterranean and the Middle East. Word trickled through to Hamelin even though few POWs arrived from those far-off theatres of war. Many of the recent arrivals knew of it.

Joe rekindled his old habit of collecting all the facts entering the camp that he could get and made notes on the few scraps of paper he could find. He became the primary source of information on the war for all who knew him. And this gave rise to an additional source of entertainment— gambling. This was not new to the soldiers; gambling was an everyday activity back home. But the war provided ample events to bet on.

"Who'll win the next battle?" asked Walt Lane. "Us or the Boche?"

"Anybody's guess," said Mike. "I've heard the boys are making bets using the camp money. Maybe we should get involved in that, not that it's worth much?"

"It's not about how much we win," said Walt. "It's the game and the winning that counts."

"Well, they first have to hear when the battle has started before they place any bets. But what if it's over by the time we hear about it?" asked Joe. "Or if it lasts a long time?"

That baffled everyone, but Walt, who they could see was a practised gambler, said, "That doesn't matter. In quick games, players make quick decisions and win or lose the bet. We must wait for the outcome no matter how long it takes for the lengthy ones. And for the ones that have ended, it's too late to place bets. Simple."

Joe then kept a log of the events and actions as they transpired, a private War Log of sorts. He kept track of the wins and losses, too. He had become a central source in the British section for what was happening in the war.

"What the shite is this new trouble brewing in the East, the Dardanelles or whatever? What and where the hell is that?" said Mike one day.

"Another bloody British disaster," said Walt. "They have told me that Winston Churchill may have had something to do with it."

Early in 1915, the British took control of the Dardanelles Strait, where they could create a path to Russia. They could then attack Constantinople, the capital of the Ottoman Empire, a Central Powers ally of the German Empire. On 13 January, the British War Council approved plans for a naval operation to force through the Dardanelles. News of this approval reached the men simultaneously as they heard of the French submarine *Saphir* lost after running aground in the strait.

"It's in Turkey," said Joe. "I met a British soldier who had just arrived here the other day. Before he arrived, he heard the news in letters from his brother at that battle. But it's only just starting. The Turks attacked Russian Black Sea ports on 28 October, he said. Then, our navy bombed Turkish forts at the entrance to the Dardanelles on 2 November. Then Britain declared war on Turkey on 6 November. And Mike, I asked where the Dardanelles were, and he told me it's a waterway or strait in Turkey that divides Europe and the Gallipoli Peninsula from Asia. It is sixty miles long and extremely narrow, three and a half miles at its widest point. And deep enough for even the largest ships and submarines to navigate."

"Why do they want to go so far from the Western Front?" asked Mike. "They should finish the job there."

"Because the Ottoman Empire of Turkey is part of the Central Powers with Germany, Austria-Hungary and Bulgaria—our enemies," said Joe.

"So, what I've picked up is that the Allies have wanted to attack them for a long time. That part of Turkey is important to them because of the Dardanelles. Ships heading for the capital of Turkey or on to Russia must go through the strait to get there. Russia is an ally of ours. So, we must support them."

"Sounds like madness," said Mike. "Don't they have enough to do on the Western Front? Crazy!"

"Well, Laddies," said Walt, "Sounds like we're in for another good fight. So, time to open the betting."

"Now that's a bloody marvellous idea," said Mike. "The Allies versus the Central Powers. I'm with you on that."

"I'll go along with that," said Joe.

And no sooner had they let the word out on the betting than scores of POWs were signing up for the contest. The bets were on for the Gallipoli Campaign.

§

The Death of Jimmie Burgess

One day in late February 1915, Joe received the news from Mary that her brother Jimmie had died in the war. Joe announced the death of his brother-in-law to his companions.

"I just heard from Mary that on 5 February her younger brother, James or Jimmie Burgess, died on the Western Front. He was a twenty-five-year-old private with the 2nd Battalion of the East Yorkshire Regiment, The Duke of York's Own."

"So sorry to hear that, Joe," said Mike. "I remember Jimmie well. He was such a nice young man and an excellent Jarrow baker."

"Aye, that's right; he was a baker before he joined the army," said Joe.

"My stories on India and Africa inspired Jimmie, so he enlisted in 1911, right after my wedding with Mary, you might remember. My stories of Africa and India fascinated Jimmie, a sixteen-year-old apprentice baker when I returned from India. He spent hours with me, listening to stories of my adventures abroad. Jimmie joined the 2nd Battalion East Yorkshire Regiment because it was in the Cantonment of Kamptee, near Nagpur, central India. That's where his battalion was in August 1914 when war broke out. They returned to England in December 1914 to join the 28th Division at Hursley Park near Winchester. The Army mobilized them immediately to France from Southampton, three months after us. Last month, they landed at Le Havre with the 83rd Brigade in the 28th Division. The Army concentrated the 28th Division between Bailleul and Hazebrouck, near Ypres and Armentières. Remember that area? They arrived in the trenches on 15 January 1915. But he was dead three weeks later, along with many others from his battalion."

"I'm so sorry, Joe," repeated Mike. "What a bloody tragedy and what a shite war. How many more like Jimmie are dying every bloody day? How many women and families are living through such tragedies? You two were close, weren't you?"

"Aye, Mike," said Joe. "He was my favourite among Mary's brothers. He was two years younger than Mary, and they were close. So, we became close friends in the five years we were together in Jarrow following my return from India. I remember our nights at the pub and the family days together on Sundays."

"Aye, I remember that too," said Mike. "He often joined us at the pub. I was fond of him, too."

"Jimmie followed my example in 1911, enlisting and shipping off to India," said Joe.

"We wrote letters to each other while Jimmie was in India. I just heard from Mary that his battalion had returned from India and joined the fighting on the Western Front. The 1st Battalion East Yorks landed at St Nazaire at the same time as we did. But the 2nd Battalion arrived at Le Havre between

16 and 19 January this year. Then they made their way to Ypres. My God, and what happened there? Jimmie died three weeks after arriving at the Front and qualifying for his medals. What a bloody tragedy! Poor Jimmie."

"Aye, Joe, it's a tragedy for sure," said Mike. "Let's hope it was quick."

At home, the news had shocked the Burgesses and Rutherfords. Jimmie had been with them a few weeks earlier, his first visit since leaving for India. It had been a quick visit since his battalion was hurrying to join the just-formed 28th Division at Hursley Park before leaving for the Western Front.

"He had looked so smart and proud in his uniform," wept Mary. "Jimmie regaled us with stories of his time and adventures in India, just as Joe had done before him. Now he has left us, snuffed out in the prime of his life at 25."

There were no parents to grieve for Jimmie since his father, John Robert Burgess, had died not long after Jimmie had joined the army. His mother, Margaret Veitch Burgess, passed away in 1903, one year after the birth of her last child, Ellen. But there were three brothers, John Robert Jr., William Souter and Harry, and sisters, Mary Caston Rutherford, Sarah Ellen, Margaret and Ellen. They were all now mourning his passing. Their first loss of the Great War came as a shock.

Jimmie's eldest brother, John Robert Jr., had arranged a memorial service a few days following the news. Once the Army returned Jimmie's dress uniform and personal items, we were ready for his funeral. They held the ceremony at St Paul's Church Jarrow, the family place of worship, marriages, christenings and funerals. St Paul's Church and Monastery has a long and distinguished history. The church has been a place of Christian prayer and worship for over 1,300 years. The two families and other close friends gathered at St. Paul's Church on a crisp late winter's day early in March. As the congregation arrived, the organist played the haunting tunes of George Butterworth's 'A Shropshire Lad' before starting the service with the 'Abide with Me' hymn. They placed Jimmie's uniform on a stool at the front of the church as the only evidence of his existence, his corpse buried on the Front. During the ceremony, the vicar gave his eulogy to the congregation.

"We gather here today to remember James Burgess in this peaceful and sacred home of the soul of the Venerable Bede. We offer solace to those grieving for his bravery and tragic passing.

"I christened Jimmie in this historical place of worship twenty-five years ago and watched him grow into a hardworking and good-looking young man. I cherished seeing his handsome and cheerful face looking up at me during our services, and my wife and I enjoyed the many gifts from his baking oven. But instead of a promising future as a baker in Jarrow, Jimmie signed up with the British Army to be a soldier overseas. I suppose it was in his blood, for as you know, the

Burgesses were and still are mariners and world explorers. Jimmie Burgess was an exemplary man, and we shall miss him.

"Oh, I understand that our grand army and navy must protect our nation and Empire from enemies. And I admire and support the brave soldiers and sailors who fulfil that purpose of protecting our great King George. But I have never had to bless so many departing souls as I have in these few short months of this war. I am saddened by it, and I share your grief. No, I am appalled by it! So many sacrifices! So many of our young men have sacrificed their lives in such a brief space of time. And we are not alone. Every parish church of this vast Empire is mourning their losses and consoling families as we are today. Every one! I pray our great generals do their utmost to protect our young men and bring this war to a swift end.

"So, we gather here today to remember Jimmie and to thank his soul and those others who have sacrificed themselves for this nation against an evil foe. This foe has chosen a path of pain and blood to pursue questionable goals. They seek to expand their Empire and grow their wealth no matter the cost! And our sons are part of that cost.

"Our Jimmie was a wonderful man. He was one of our best. You, who I know so well as good, wholesome people, must now learn to live without his presence in the flesh. But no matter where his body is on that gruesome battlefield, his soul rests here with us and the Bede. And it's his soul we cherish and honour today. May God the Father, the Holy Ghost, and God in Jesus bless and look over you."

And with that ending, the congregation responded with a tearful "Amen."

The vicar then led them in the Lord's Prayer and left them to contemplate his words while he strolled to the church entrance. The organist played 'Abide with Me.' There was a prolonged period of silent memories, interrupted only by the sniffles of the women and the occasional throat-clearing of the men. Then, the congregation arose individually, and the family, followed by their friends, filed out of the church. The vicar offered his condolences, goodbyes and other advice to as many who stopped to greet him.

They then returned to John Robert's home for a wake.

"First, the children and I lost Joe, but at least we know he is alive. Now, their Uncle Jimmie has left us forever," cried Mary. "Please, God, send my Joe back in good health!"

John Robert and his wife, Edith Sarah, comforted her. They tucked into a spread of whatever the women could find in those hard times of dwindling fortunes, including Brown Ale for the men.

There were a few men from the 1st Battalion East Yorks in Hamelin, including those who became prisoners along with Joe. He sought them out to find out whether any of them had known lads from the 2nd Battalion and Jimmie in particular. But he had found no one so far.

Joe wrote a letter to Mary on receiving this terrible news. He expressed his profound grief and attempted to reassure her in simple (and to the German censors acceptable) terms.

"Dearest Mary,

"I hope you are well enough, even though this must be hard for you. Losing Jimmie is a tragedy. But let me assure you, you still have me despite being so far apart. And you still have your other brothers. I remember you and the children day and night and talk to you, knowing we will be together soon. Give enormous hugs and kisses to my children, and don't let them forget me.

"Sending all my love to you, Joe."

§

Winter Work in the Forest

When the guards mustered the POWs one frigid morning in February, they told Joe's group to prepare themselves for work in the woods with the foresters.

"Go back to your barrack and dress for hard work in the forest," called Klaus. "Wear the warmest clothes you have. The wagons will be here to collect you in half an hour."

Bundling up in anything they could find to ward off the cold, the men exchanged words on what they could expect on this work assignment.

"Anybody ever worked as a forest worker?" asked Joe

"Aye," piped up one. "I worked for a while in a forest in Durham.

"What will we be doing?" asked Mike.

"The work is sawing, chopping, and hauling logs to the sawmill," he said. "They will have a team of experienced forest workers for the sawing and chopping. So, I reckon we'll be hauling."

"No problem," said Mike. "What do we need to wear?"

"Make sure you wear very thick, warm socks if you have them, and the warmest gloves you have, too," he said. "Oh, and a warm hat."

As luck would have it, the Red Cross had provided the men with winter clothing before Christmas, including warm socks, gloves, sweaters, knitted caps and warm coats. So, the men kitted themselves out for winter work in the forest.

"Right," called Mike. "I'm ready; let's go." And the others echoed his call and strolled to the meeting point.

"Has anybody done this work before?" asked Joe, but he got no response. "Howay, look at those beautiful horses."

Right on time, a sizeable horse-drawn sled arrived with a team of four magnificent chestnut-coloured draught horses with blond manes, tails and leg feathers.

"Those horses look like the ones our breweries back home use," said Joe.

"Aye, they are noble beasts," said Walt.

The guards gestured for the POWs to climb on board; then, they set off in the same direction as the farm they had worked on the previous autumn. It was a brisk, lucid morning as the first light was just appearing to the east; a bracing breeze and blasts of loose snow brushed their faces as they glided through the valley toward the forest. But this time, when they entered the hilltop woods, the sled veered off onto a forestry track. Before long, they had arrived at a large clearing where forestry work had begun. There, the forester and a team of forestry workers awaited them, saws and axes in hand.

"They look like serious working blokes," said Joe.

"Aye, and look at the weapons," said Mike to meek chuckles from his companions.

"Come on, Laddies, we're serious working blokes too," said Walt. "We're up to this."

The forester greeted the POWs with a grunt and distributed them through gestures among his teams at once. The teams then spread out into the woods, setting to their work at once of downing, trimming and cutting the spruce trees into manageable lengths. They provided the British POWs with large clamps to haul the logs to one side as they completed pruning them. Then, they uncoupled the horses and used them to pull the tree lengths back to the sled where the POWs loaded them.

This work continued throughout the day with brief tea breaks with bread in the morning and afternoon and a lunch break with black bread and cheese.

"I'm enjoying this," said Mike to Joe, who was working on a neighbouring team.

"Aye, me too, Mike," said Joe. "It was cold this morning, but I'm not cold anymore."

At lunch, all the teams returned to the central clearing and divided themselves by nationality. Apart from gestures, there was no communication between the German forest workers and the POWs. The prisoners worked hard, and a cautious warmth and mutual respect developed between the masters and their helpers.

"They're not an evil bunch of blokes," said Mike.

"Just like us, somewhat," said Joe.

"Do you mean hardworking and not getting enough to eat?" asked Walt. "I'm sure they're better fed than us."

For several weeks until the first signs of spring appeared, the British POWs worked with the foresters daily. They returned to barracks at night while the forestry workers returned to their families. It was so unfair, but such are the realities of wartime.

§

News Updates on the Gallipoli Campaign

By the end of February 1915, the prisoners at Hamelin Camp started receiving news updates on developments in Turkey. The Allies launched the Gallipoli Campaign on 19 February. This news came not from prisoners arriving from that campaign but from prisoners from the Western Front who had heard of it.

People knew it as the Dardanelles Campaign or the Battle of Gallipoli, while the Turks called it the Battle of Çanakkale. It was a series of military operations in Turkey for the rest of that year. The Allied powers, Britain, France and the Russian Empire, sought to weaken the Ottoman Empire by taking control of the strait that provided a supply route to Russia. But, from the start, it got off on the wrong foot when an Allied attack on Ottoman forts guarding the entrance to the Dardanelles in February 1915 failed.

One evening in April, Joe's companions asked him to explain what was happening in Turkey.

"Aye, that I can do, although I don't have all the facts yet," said Joe.

"We carried out a first serious attack on the Dardanelles on 19 February, using our battleships HMS Cornwallis and HMS Vengeance and the French battleship Suffren."

"What happened?" asked Mike. "I've heard nothing about that."

"From what I've heard, it's complicated," said Joe, referring to his notes. "I've learned that the French Minister of Justice, Aristide Briand (or something like that), wanted to attack the Ottoman Empire in November, but the Allies rejected this. Then, our government tried to bribe the Ottomans to join the Allied side, which also failed.

So, later that month, Winston Churchill, as First Lord of the Admiralty, proposed a naval attack on the Dardanelles. Churchill wanted to use old rundown battleships in the Dardanelles operation, with a minor occupation force provided by the army. Those ships could no longer operate against the more modern German High Seas Fleet, and I suppose Churchill thought they would be helpful in Turkey.

Then, on 2 January, Grand Duke Nicholas of Russia asked Britain for help against the Ottomans as Russia began a major offensive against Austria-Hungary in Russia's Carpathian Mountains. These mountains border the empires of Turkey and Russia on the Eastern Front. This request set the stage for the Gallipoli Campaign.

"Has Churchill opened another Front for Britain?" asked Walt. "Is that what you are saying?"

"Aye, it sure looks like it," said Joe, then continued his narration. "Further news arrived of an attack on 25 February, led by Vice-Admiral John de Robeck aboard HMS Vengeance. And it carried on into March. On 10 March at night, Commodore Roger Keyes and the battleship HMS Canopus continued the bombardments."

"So, if I get this right, there are now three fronts in this war," said Mike. "The Western Front with the British and French. The Eastern Front between Russia and Germany. And now a new Mediterranean Front with the British and French against the Ottomans?"

"Aye, Mike. You've got it. And I've heard something else interesting," said Joe. "Remember Ian Hamilton from the South African War? Kitchener appointed him the British Army Mediterranean Expeditionary Force commander in March."

"Now, we know of those two gentlemen," said Mike.

"You told us about General Ian Hamilton's march from Bloemfontein to Pretoria with Lord Roberts during the Boer War before we arrived. But I remember Kitchener well from South Africa and India. Arrogant bastard!"

"Aye, and when he first became Minister of War, he launched a major recruitment campaign at the start of this war, if you remember," said Joe.

"You might remember too that Winston Churchill was a war correspondent during the South African War. It's a small world, isn't it?"

"Aye, it sure is," said Mike. "A small world full of haughty rogues!"

Later, news arrived that the Turks were laying mines in the Strait.

"Commodore Keyes conducted night-time minesweeping operations," said Joe. "On 18 March, mines sank three of our battleships. They damaged the battlecruiser HMS Inflexible and three of our battleships. Turkey has defeated the last attempt by the British and French fleet to force the Dardanelles."

"It's not looking good for us over there either," said Walt. "We can't even find the mines? We are in the shite everywhere!"

"Aye," said Joe. "Time to adjust the odds?"

"Aye," agreed Walt, deep in thought. "Time to adjust the odds."

On 22 March, at a conference between Hamilton and Vice-Admiral John de Robeck aboard HMS Queen Elizabeth, they set up an amphibious landing on the Gallipoli peninsula. Australian and New Zealand troops (ANZACs) were to play a significant role alongside the British and French.

"Right," said Walt. "So, we must keep our ears open for that action. Gentlemen, the betting is now reopened."

That offered a moment of entertainment and excitement or disappointment for the bored prisoners. The prisoners seriously needed entertainment! Life had become monotonous, especially during their spare time in the barracks. So, in addition to the betting, they sought other forms of entertainment for the dull moments when the weather was too miserable for football.

§

Memories of our Arrival in Saint Nazaire and the Western Front

One cold Sunday during a blizzard and too much snow for football, Joe's fellow prisoners huddled near the wood stove in their barrack to keep warm. A few were sitting, and others were standing and stomping occasionally. As always, the talk revolved around the war. What else?

"It's bloody freezing in here, Laddies," said one of the group. "At least we're safe...I hope. I still have nightmares of our brief time in the trenches. There we were, cold, wet and bloody unsafe."

"Aye, I agree with all that. But it's freezing here because the Germans won't give us more wood," said Mike. "Cheap bastards!"

"Aye, that's for sure," said Joe. "I still have nightmares of the hell of the trenches, too. There were no stoves, just artillery shells, bullets and rain."

"I'll never forget that," said Mike. "We didn't know it could be so bad, even after our time in the Boer War of South Africa."

On the Western Front, as both sides settled into the war's first winter, the weather proved more trying than the enemy. Artillery bombardments destroyed trenches, which were still shallow ditches at that phase of the war. Inclement weather and eliminated pre-war drainage ditches led to widespread flooding. But the soldiers had to stay in the line no matter how cold or wet they were.

A diary entry of 7 January 1915 of Rifleman William Eve of the Queen's Westminster Rifles said it all:

"Poured with rain all day and night. The water rose till knee-deep when we had the order to retire to our trenches. I dropped my blanket and fur coat in the water. I slipped down when getting up on the parapet and got soaked up to my waist. I went sandbag filling and then sewer guarding for two hours. I had no dugout for sleeping. We had to go through about two feet of water in one place. They sniped at us a bit. While getting water, someone shot Roache, and while going to his aid, someone shot Tibbs. He lay in the open all day; that evening, someone brought him in; he was unconscious but still alive. Passed away soon after that."

Rifleman Eve remained in the trenches until January 1915, when the Army invalided him home with trench foot. That was a common medical condition during this war, caused by prolonged exposure of the feet to damp, unsanitary and cold conditions of the trenches[28].

"Tell us your story of our arrival at the Western Front, Joe," suggested Walt. "You do that so well. And we've got nothing else to do."

---

[28] National Army Museum, London.

"You mean about our introduction to the first trenches of the war at the Aisne River?" asked Joe.

"Aye. Tell us. Not that we need reminding," said several of the other Durhams assembled. "We'd like to hear your version, Joe."

"Aye, no problem," said Joe, "Let me start with our arrival in France."

"The 2/DLI arrived in Saint Nazaire from Southampton on the 10th and 11th of September with 27 officers and 1,000 men," said Joe. "Think of that now, 1,000 men! Where are they now? Anyway, we were far from alone when reaching Saint Nazaire. It looked as if half of the British Army was arriving."

"Aye, that it did for sure," said a listener, laughing.

"The first unloading port was Le Havre at the mouth of the Seine River, closer to Paris and the Front. However, the retreat of the BEF forced the British Base Depot to fall back on Saint Nazaire, a small, quiet seaside town in the French province of Brittany, Western France. Saint Nazaire has a substantial harbour on the Atlantic Coast with a lengthy fishing history and shipbuilding on the Loire River estuary. In this war, St. Nazaire became the disembarkation and unloading port after Le Havre for most Allied troops heading to the Western Front.

"When we arrived and caught sight of St Nazaire, we saw a nice little coastal town," said Mike. "It looks a little like Sunderland, at the mouth of the River Wear on the North Sea,

County Durham. That's another great shipbuilding and fishing port near where we come from."

"Aye, it does, Mike," I said. "We only glimpsed it, and we disembarked and marched straight to camp. But it was enough to see the yards from a distance. So, for us men from Tyneside hoping to experience a French shipbuilding town close up, they disappointed us. 'But Major Crosthwaite went into town today, and he reported that there was little interest in it [29].

"Aye, officers can go into town, but they leave us here in this bloody camp," said Jack. "We might have found a pub!"

"Aye, but I guess they think we've seen enough shipbuilding ports for now," I said. "And look at what we have available here. It isn't necessary to go into town. Droves of locals have arrived at the camp, selling everything from wine to tobacco to bread and sausages. They were doing a brisk business and making lots of friends by giving out samples for free. Citizens of the town were giving out gifts of food and wine, too. It was such a spectacle."

"Aye, and that's why they wouldn't let us go in there," said Mike. "What for if they were all here?"

"At 10:30 A.M. the following morning, orders came for the battalion to march to a point where we were to entrain at noon," said Joe, continuing his story.

---

[29] John Sheen, "The Steel of the DLI (The 2nd Battalion of the DLI at war 1914-1918), Pen & Sword Books, 2009.

"We mustered and marched to the railway station in the pouring rain only to find no train waiting. At 4:30 P.M., our allocated train arrived, and we entrained the first half of the battalion for Coulommiers on the other side of Paris.

"They transported us in cars identified by a sign painted on each side as *Hommes Quarante et Chevaux Huit*. Remember that? The Tommies called them The Forty and Eight, a shortened translation of forty men and eight horses. They told us that these cars were France's standard form of troop transport during this war. But one unhappy Durham said the Hommes 40 was only Hommes 34."

The audience nodded and chuckled, remembering the cars well.

"Aye, and you must remember those cars were small, stubby and box-like, only twenty and a half feet long and eight and a half feet wide," said Joe.

"We needed twenty-five cars to transport a thousand men from our battalion. And they needed more for the two or three dozen horses the officers had brought from England. They transported the officers in a more comfortable passenger car."

"It soaked us through and through," called a listener.

"Exactly. So, we stood among the 2/DLI men before climbing into one car together," said Joe.

"Hundreds of men from many regiments milled around in other groups talking, shouting, smoking and laughing while waiting for the command to entrain.

"How the hell are we going to get forty men into that?" asked Mike.

"Aye, well, we're small chaps and good marras!" called another.

"Aye, but just leave me bum alone," joked another, evoking much laughter.

"Well, the rain has stopped, so I may take my chances on the roof," yelled yet another.

The audience chuckled knowingly at these comments, too.

"Now, we had just finished a sea voyage, which had left many feeling sick," said Joe. "So, back on dry land, there was a carefree spirit amongst us. We joked and laughed and cajoled each other until ordered to entrain, after which the commotion subsided. But we jostled and pushed to get ourselves into choice positions at narrow slats at the top of each side for fresh air and a view. They squashed the rest into the middle of the cars.

"Move along and make room for the eight bloody horses," quipped someone, to a loud outburst of laughter and more jests.

"Keep the sergeant away from the horses, lads; he may hurt them somehow." Said another.

"Aye, or try to mount them!" said yet another.

The audience laughed again, enjoying Joe's recollections of their journey across Northern France.

"After an hour, the train was ready to pull out of the loading zone," said Joe.

"My marras and I had found places standing together at the open slat windows for the journey. Sitting or lying was out of the question in such crowded conditions.

"We eventually moved off into the peaceful countryside of Brittany, as they call that region of France. The commotion amongst us continued nonstop as we shouted and joked among ourselves, calling out to more distant marras in cars ahead or behind us. We waved through the slats as we passed civilians and called to them. And as we saw hinnies, we whistled and called to them too."

"Hey, sweetheart, have you ever tried an Englishman?"

"You are so beautiful!"

"We were all in friendly spirits, excited by being on dry land again and about our journey into an unknown adventure. Little did we know then what we know now. But as the hours passed, the noise petered out through fatigue and boredom. All one could hear was the creaking of the cars, the clicking of the wheels and the gentle puffing of the locomotive far ahead of us.

"We travelled over 300 miles for many hours east through Nantes, Angers, Le Mans, past Chartres and the outskirts of Paris at a distance. At first, we travelled through a rolling region with many farms. Cattle were in the fields, and we crossed several rivers with dozens of watermills. We travelled for many hours across a flat plain with many miles of grain fields, which the French call the Breadbasket of France. Sixty miles southwest of Paris, we spotted a majestic cathedral in the distance, soaring into a bright blue sky above that unexciting plain. We learned it was in a city called Chartres. The train continued its journey after a brief stop to take on more coal and water. But instead of entering Paris, we passed it via a detour from a distance. But we could see another great cathedral and an enormous steel tower rising above the surrounding buildings. Now we've seen everything. Newcastle, Capetown, Bombay, Lucknow, Chartres and Paris.

"What an exciting life we're leading," I said.

There were a few nods of agreement and a few groans.

"Aye, Joe, you're right," said Mike. "But seeing those famous Parisian ladies we've heard so much about would impress me more."

"Aye, I've heard about them, too!" said Jack. "But you're married now, Laddie, so behave yourself."

"Aye, but a man can look, can't he?" said Mike.

"That comment reawakened the conversation and banter amongst us in the carriage," said Joe.

"Everyone had a Paris lady joke or something similar and couldn't wait to throw it into the mix. It amused us for most of our remaining trip."

Too soon, they had left the panorama of Paris behind them, travelling another 40 miles east across the Île-de-France [30] towards their destination. After a few more hours of uneventful and creeping travel, they arrived at Coulommiers, a town renowned for its canals, Brie cheese and the Commanderie of the Knights Templar. At the Coulommiers station, they came to the end of their arduous train journey and disembarked. But there was no time for rest or sightseeing.

"Remember we assembled and marched the four and a half miles through a flat and damaged farming landscape to our billets at Saint-Germain-sous-Doue," said Joe to Mike and Jack.

We were heading toward Château Thierry and the Western Front. "French troops had destroyed the bridge over the Grand Morin River at Coulommiers to slow the advancing German Army. So, we had to cross the river on a pontoon bridge. It was our first proof that the war had passed through this region. As we marched, we saw more damage from the war. We weren't close enough to hear the guns of the Western Front, but we were close enough to get an idea of what we

---

[30] The Île-de-France, or Island of France, is a large flat region that surrounds Paris.

might soon experience. There was still general joking and laughter on our march, a cheerful atmosphere, and spirits among the troops were still high."

They passed a pleasant evening in billets when the marras had a few last minutes of peacefulness as they sat outside their tent, recalling their progress so far.

"What a trip that was, Laddies," I said. "We've had a pleasant introduction to France."

"Aye. It was grand," said Mike. "I wonder when our holiday ends?"

"Soon enough," said Jack. "The lieutenant said we are not that far from the Front. The only problem is, we still have to march the rest of the way."

"What of that war damage we see, Laddies?" I asked. "Bloody frightening. They are using wicked guns by the size of those shell holes."

"Aye, and did you notice the bullet holes in the houses?" said Mike. "And the demolished farmhouses. Memories of the Boer War, Laddies?"

"Aye," said Jack. "But somehow, I feel this one might be much worse."

"How are you doing, old man?" asked Mike of Fred.

"Hanging in there," said Fred. "You needn't fret over me. I've done enough marching to keep up with the best of you."

They had removed their boots and putties and soaked their feet in saltwater. But they were soon to embark on a strenuous 75-mile march northeast to the Front through heavy rain over the next few days.

§

War Diary: Château Thierry, 15 September 1914

The Battn marched to CHATEAU THIERRY (25 miles) and entered billets at midnight.

"On 15 September, the 2/DLI rose at Saint-Germain-sous-Doue and began our 25-mile march to Château Thierry on the Marne River," said Joe.

"On that march, we saw the damage of warfare everywhere around us. We first saw abandoned trenches and massive shell holes since the front had moved. We came across ruined and abandoned farm buildings along the route. The Germans held Château-Thierry for a few days in early September 1914 during the first battle of the Marne. Evidence of this battle was everywhere for us to see, a sight that drove home the realities of this war. We met army medical trucks loaded with wounded soldiers from the Front as we marched to replace them. The happiness and carefree spirit of the earlier days dimming somewhat."

I turned to my marras and, with a sweep of my free arm, said, "Looks as if we're close, Laddies. Do you hear the booming of the guns in the distance?"

"Aye," said Mike. "Brace yourselves for a fight!"

"Haddaway, man, we never saw this much damage from battles in South Africa," said Jack, looking concerned. "Did you see the size of those shell holes?"

"You're right, Jack," said Fred. "They have destroyed everything here."

"Aye, Jack," I said. "But have you forgotten the destroyed farms in the Boer War? The British flattened those poor farmers' farms. It looked a bit like this in places."

"Aye, that's true, Joe. But this looks much worse than anything I've ever seen," said Fred. "It looks like the Germans have nasty weapons."

"It was a long march, and we encountered more British motor trucks with red crosses on the doors coming from the Front with wounded Tommies on board," said Joe.

"The signs of destruction were everywhere: the damaged roads, trenches, shell holes and broken telegraph wires. When we marched into Château Thierry after dark, the entire town was in darkness, and we could see few people. The officers noted the Germans had done enormous 'wilful damage' to the buildings. That night, we were unhappy in the rough billets where we rested from midnight, soaking our tired feet in pails of salted water."

"Have you noticed the billets are getting rougher?" asked Mike.

"Aye, but they've told us that the trenches are even worse," I said. "So, we had better get used to it."

"Aye, and I guess we'd better get used to the noise, too," said Jack. "That shelling never stops."

"The lieutenant told me we are only forty miles from our destination," I said. "What we are hearing is the Front."

"Shite," called Mike. "We're in for it, Laddies, that's for sure."

"Aye, and no turning back now," said Fred.

§

War Diary: Tigny, 16 September 1914

Marched to TIGNY (18 miles) and billeted.

"The next day, an early start before daybreak saw us trudging another eighteen miles to the village of Tigny," said Joe.

"It was raining and wet when we started but cleared up after an hour. The large farm housed the entire battalion, and they billeted us there. The officers bought fresh eggs from the farmer. But when they asked for red wine, the Germans had already taken most of the farmer's supply, leaving only two or three bottles. The farmer complained to the British officers, one of whom spoke French, saying he had hidden the only food and wine the Germans hadn't discovered for the family. They even took many of his chickens and a pig."

"Never mind the wine," joked Mike when he heard this. "How can we get a few Broons?"

"When we get back home, Mike," I said, "I don't think the army will bring us our favourite ales out here."

"Bloody Boche, cleaning out that farmer," said Jack. "We never did that on our travels."

"Aye, you're right there, Jack," I said. "They have no manners."

To which he got a few chuckles.

"I heard a rumour circulating that one of our Durham lads collapsed of exhaustion and died on that last march," I said.

"I'm not surprised," said Mike. "We've been marching for days, and if the laddie wasn't fit or even sick, he couldn't make it."

"That night, we caught up on a much-needed sleep," said Joe. "The first proper night's sleep since arriving in France."

§

War Diary: Chacrise, 17 September 1914

Marched to CHACRISE and billeted.

"On 17 September," said Joe, "the battalion marched the five miles to Chacrise and billeted."

§

War Diary: Chacrise to Dhuizel, 18 September 1914

Left CHACRISE at 2:50 P.M. and marched through BRAINE to BOURG, halting at midnight to 4 A.M. 19 Sept. at DHUIZEL.

"The next afternoon, the march continued 14 miles through Braine to Dhuizel, two miles short of Bourg-et-Comin near the front," said Joe.

"We arrived at midnight and entered billets. Then we rested until dusk the next day, but the sounds of constant cannon fire were unsettling. We were now close to the front line, and the racket of shells, machine guns and rifle fire were horrific."

"I'm feeling uneasy in my gut, lads," confessed Mike.

"Aye, Mike," I said. "I think we are in for a pounding once we get there."

"Well, Laddies, as I've said, there's no turning back now," said Fred.

"Aye, this is it, my marras," said Jack. "We are soon to get to know our enemy."

"These sentiments were rippling across the entire battalion," said Joe.

Scenes of destruction and towns with no life and damaged trees stripped of leaves and branches. The constant rumblings of the distant guns and the planes buzzing overhead penetrated that part of their minds that signals fear. The apprehension was rising among these men as they approached the battlefield.

"Fred was right. There was no turning back—that is desertion, punishable by firing squad once caught. Our lives were on the line, and the excitement we had felt on the way there had vanished. We were now to confront our fears and meet the enemy head-on in this hell on earth.

"To make matters worse, rumours circulated through the battalion that the Royal Flying Corps surveyed the Aisne and the Chemin des Dames. One pilot reported that 'they are waiting for you up there, thousands of them.'"[31]

§

---

[31] Norman Ferguson, *The First World War: A Miscellany*, Summersdale, Chichester, UK, 2014.

Empire and War

Memories of our Arrival at the Aisne Trenches

"This is the story of our first battle of the Great War," said Joe. "The First Battle of the Aisne was the Allied follow-up offensive against the right wing of the German First Army. Alexander von Kluck led the First Army, and Karl von Bülow led the Second Army.

After the First Battle of the Marne in early September 1914—the Miracle on the Marne, where the French halted the German army's blitzkrieg—they retreated.

There was a nervous shuffling among Joe's audience. They had all been there and were replaying those hours and days with Joe's help, bringing back many uncomfortable memories. But no one asked Joe to stop his story.

"Well, we were entering the Battle of the Aisne," said Joe. "One of the earliest battles of the war. We've since learned the Aisne region is no stranger to military action. As a hilltop route above the River Aisne, the Chemin des Dames ridge has seen many battles through the centuries since ancient times. This ancient road is one of the best routes to Paris from Eastern France. It was important to the military, too. They've told me the Romans fought there. And French Emperor Napoleon's junior soldiers beat an army of Russians and Prussians there too."

"The Romans? The Prussians? Emperor Napoleon?" said another in the audience. "Then us, the British!"

"Aye," said Joe. "Us and the French against the Germans. As some background on this battle, following their defeat at the Marne, the Germans withdrew 50 miles north to the River Aisne. The BEF arrived at the southern banks of the Aisne on 12 September after marching 160 miles in three weeks. It had been an arduous and demoralizing trek for the British, who were suffering from exhaustion and hunger when they reached the Aisne banks."

On the night of 13 September, the BEF crossed the Aisne using pontoons or half-demolished bridges in a dense fog. The Germans had selected an escarpment at Chivres-Val as their best defensive position. Then, the French Fifth Army crossed the Aisne at Berry-au-Bac and captured the eastern tip of Chemin des Dames. The British and French faced fighting uphill in full view of the Germans.[32]

Neither side could budge the other, nor since neither retreated, the impasse hardened into a stalemate that locked both parties into the narrow strip of the Western Front. On 14 September, Commander-in-Chief Sir John French ordered the entire BEF to entrench, but few entrenching tools were available. Soldiers scouted nearby farms and villages for pickaxes, spades, and other implements that could do the job. They dug shallow pits in the soil that became the first trenches of the Great War. These were at first meant only to give cover

---

[32] Norman Ferguson, *The First World War: A Miscellany*, Summersdale, Chichester, UK, 2014.

against enemy observation and artillery fire. But these entrenchments were just the start of an unfamiliar form of warfare.

§

War Diary: Troyon, Chemin des Dames, Saturday the 19th Sept. 1914

Left BOURG at dusk and took over the trenches north of TROYON from the 2nd Brigade. The entire battalion occupied the trenches at about 1 A.M.

"By 19 September, we had arrived near the trenches. It was our day of reckoning," said Joe. "Leaving Dhuizel before daybreak, we stomped to Bourg-et-Comin on the Aisne in the early hours. We had a wash and breakfast there and tried to dry out our clothes. Bourg had tremendous damage from the German shells, and they had destroyed the bridge over the Aisne. So, the battalion crossed using a pontoon bridge the engineers had provided to enter the town. But the Command ordered us to move from Bourg to avoid another shelling, so we marched a mile north under cover of a big hill. We went through our first shelling of the war and passed many dead horses as we advanced. For the first time, we saw massive holes in the ground caused by big German percussion shells known as Coal Boxes or Black Marias."

The German Army used the 3-inch field gun and could fire high explosives 11,250 yards. But they possessed more formidable artillery - howitzers that could project heavy shells and create enormous craters. German artillery used the 4-inch Feldhaubitze 98/09 during the Battle of the Aisne. This gun could fire the Feldhaubitzgranate 98, the 35-pound high-explosive shell or the Feldhaubitzschrapnel 98, a 28-pound shrapnel shell.

German artillery also used the German 8.3-inch Lange Mörser M 16/L14.5 (long mortar) with a calibre of 8.3 inches and a range of up to 11,000 yards. They raised its barrel to an acute elevation angle, meaning they could position it behind hills and ridges and fire on the enemy positions on the other side. German engineers designed the howitzer for siege warfare, and it fired various projectiles during the Battle of the Aisne. The shells included high-explosive shrapnel and small, high-velocity shells, known as "whizz-bangs" or "Jack Johnsons" by the British. They emitted black smoke, caused the most devastation, and could blow a crater 20 feet wide and 10 feet deep. Such explosions destroyed villages, levelled trees and vaporized men [33].

---

[33] Paul Kendall, https://thehistorypress.co.uk/articles/the-first-trenches-of-the-first-world-war/

"We British could only deploy old pattern 6-inch howitzers. These were inferior to the German howitzer and were 'flat trajectory' guns, meaning they could not reach the German artillery behind the ridges [34]."

"That same evening at dusk, we moved cautiously up the hill to relieve the weary 2nd Brigade," said Joe.

"The brigade was in shallow improvised trenches on the Chemin des Dames north of Vendresse-et-Troyon. These trenches differed from what we learned in training and offered little shelter. On the 2/DLI's left was the 1st East Yorkshire Regiment, and on their right lay the 1st West Yorkshire Regiment, the last right-hand battalion of the British Army. The 2nd Sherwood Foresters were in reserve behind the front line."

"Beyond us lay a force of Moroccans of the French Armée coloniale, the extreme left of the French 5th Army," said Joe, rechecking his notes. "In front of us awaited the German 7th Army, made up of 44,000 men in five Corps of fourteen divisions. [35] It had rushed from the eastern part of the Front to fill the gap found by General Haig's men on 13 September. They were still fresh compared with Kluck's tired German troops lower on the Aisne. Major Robb's D-Company occupied the 2/DLI's left trenches; next to him was Major

---

[34] Ibid

[35] Formed at the outbreak of Great War, the 7th Army formed the extreme left (southern) wing of the German Armies on the Western Front. During the execution of the French Plan XVII, the 7th Army covered Alsace, successfully repulsing the French attack in the Battle of Lorraine. It then took part in the Race to the Sea.

Blake's C-Company; then Captain Northey's A-Company; and on the right, next to the West Yorkshires, was Major Mander's B-Company. They posted pickets in front of each unit, who, nervous on their first active service, fired on their trenches during the night, causing casualties. But apart from that, the first night was quiet. My marras and I crouched as low as we could in the positions the lieutenant had assigned us, didn't we, Mike?"

"Aye," said Mike with a chuckle. "We were like worms, flat on the ground."

"The night was black except for the flashes of guns and exploding shells, and there was no direct one-on-one combat at first," recalled Joe.

"There's not much bloody protection in these trenches," murmured Mike. "How can we stay safe here?"

"Aye, I don't know where we should hide from the Boche aiming at us over there," I said. "They are so close we could reach out and touch them."

"Is this it?" asked Jack, alive at the time. "Two lines of soldiers facing and shooting at each other in the rain and mud? Is this our new war?"

"Looks like it," I mumbled. "It's a bloody miserable state of affairs."

"Aye. There is no protection against those bloody Boche shells," said Mike. "Well, Laddies, it was nice knowing ye. God knows how long we'll survive out here."

"Let's try to be positive, Mike," I said. "We must survive this and return to Jarrow, just as we survived South Africa. Our women and children are waiting for us, so we have to fight for that. And apart from those bloody shells, it's not too bad."

§

War Diary: Troyon, Chemin des Dames, 20th Sept. 1914

Owing to the battalion on the right giving way, reported to be caused by a white flag incident, our right flank. Was enfiladed[36] by the German machine gun and suffered loss until the battalion in reserve reoccupied the trenches on the right flank. One Company and a half on the left flank left their trenches and advanced and suffered loss until they returned to their trenches.

"But the following day was another story," said Joe.

"The Germans attempted to win back the ridge through heavy counterattacks. From the moment a week before when the Allies forced them from it, they were unsuccessful. On September 20, soon after we arrived at the Front, the German

---

[36] Enfilade is a volley of gunfire directed along a line from end to end.

7th Army attacked the area between the French and British forces. It was a grey, icy morning, the weak light of dawn creeping into the trenches and occasional heavy showers. My marras and I were in Major Robb's D-company. We liked the major. We considered him a professional officer and friendly with his men."

"I agree. Our major was a friendly fellow," said Mike. "Straight from Indian roots; born there, I believe."

"Aye, that he was," I said. "Born in British India as an overseas Englishman. He was an excellent leader, fair, and besides, an affable man."

"I have heard he fought on the Indian North-West Frontier and Burma with the King's Own Yorkshire Light Infantry before joining the 2/DLI," said Jack.

"Well, I know how that must have been, Laddies," said our older marra, Fred. "I was there, but with a Scottish regiment. I've heard, too, that Major Robb distinguished himself over there."

"Before he came here, he taught officers at Durham University," said Joe. "So, he must be smart."

"Then, from the trench, looking out across the scarred terrain to the German entrenchments, we saw movements," said Joe.

"We saw German soft uniform caps and spiked helmets appearing from time to time above their parapets as the German troops prepared for their attack. The morning was misty and dark, and the rain started pouring in sheets. Our fingers had stiffened, and we weren't sure how to fire our weapons should the enemy charge.

"Bloody hell," whispered Mike then. "I don't have a comfortable feeling, Laddies. Sitting in these open shallow trenches with the rain beating on us? It's bloody freezing and dangerous. We have the German Army staring at us from a few yards away, and those movements may mean they will soon attack us."

"Aye, Mike, this doesn't look good for us," I agreed. "But we had bloody well do our best to survive. I reckon the Boche is just as wet and freezing as we are. Keep your heads low, and let's watch what's happening around us. Stay alive!"

"And those Moroccans next to the West Yorkshires? Are they fighting men?" asked Jack.

"I bloody well hope so," said Mike.

"Minutes later," said Joe, "the Germans launched a fierce attack along the Allied line. It began with the horrific storm of an artillery barrage. With the wind and beating rain, it became a storm of fire and water. Shells exploded before and behind the trenches and even overhead, raining shrapnel on us unsuspecting newcomers. The German machine guns and rifles opened fire along the line. Bullets whizzed past us, embedded themselves in the earth mound behind us, or ricocheted off boulders and helmets. It was so loud that we couldn't communicate with each other. The smoke, rain and mist made it impossible to see the enemy. And it continued nonstop for over an hour."

"Keep your heads low, Laddies, and return fire as best you can, yelled a corporal near us."

"How?" cried Mike. "I can't see the bastards!"

"Just fire in their direction," yelled the corporal. "They'll get the message, and we might down a few."

"After the first shocks, which had frozen us in our positions, we rallied our strength and nerve and fought back as hard as we could," said Joe.

"The noise was deafening, the whizzing bullets terrifying, and the sound waves and shrapnel from the exploding shells battered our line nonstop.

"We'll give you as much as you are giving us, you bloody Hun," yelled Mike while unloading his rifle over and over in rapid-fire towards the German line.

The army equipped the British Tommy with the Short Magazine Lee-Enfield rifle, with each magazine carrying ten rounds. They had named it after the American inventor James Lee and the Royal Small Arms Factory at Enfield in north London. The army trained British infantrymen to fire 15 rounds per minute and hit their target at an effective range of 550 yards. German soldiers used the Mauser Gewehr 98 rifle, which had served them since 1898. Its bolt action prevented any rapid fire. [37]

"Mike's fellow Durhams along the line did the same," said Joe. "As I did, too. After a few minutes of preparing their guns, the British artillery also returned shells in rapid fire. And between the blasts from the guns were cries of pain from our fellows. It was terrible."

"The Moroccans on our right came under the massive attack too, panicking and retreating. So, as the Moroccans pulled back, the officer commanding 1/West Yorkshire Regiment moved one of his companies to cover the gap caused by their retreat. The Moroccan officers rallied their men for a while, and they moved forward again. There was total confusion. And not knowing the British moved into their position, the Moroccans opened fire on the 1/West Yorkshire Battalion, which suffered thirty casualties, friendly fire and complete chaos!"

"I told you so," called Jack as loud as he could. "You can't trust those Moroccans to get things right!"

"I think we are in the same bucket here, Jack," I yelled. "No matter where we come from. They are probably recruits with no battle experience like most of us."

"A bloody dangerous bucket," screamed Jack.

---

[37] Paul Kendall, https://thehistorypress.co.uk/articles/the-first-trenches-of-the-first-world-war/

"Despite the heavy losses around us, the four of us survived our first real ordeal by fire," said Joe.

"After more than an hour of bombardment, machine gun and rifle fire, things settled briefly. The constant din died somewhat, but the Germans occasionally kept up heavy artillery and rifle fire to remind us they were still there. And we returned fire in response. This calm period allowed us to catch our breath, pull back our injured and dead companions and call up ammunition reserves.

"Then, at 10 A.M. hours, the Germans relaunched their attack. Their troops came over the top of their parapet and charged the Moroccan line. A robust Moroccan defence supported by the West Yorkshires beside them checked it. Then, at noon, a third offensive started under cover of a heavy rainstorm, and the Moroccans again fell back. And once more, the courageous West Yorkshire men moved eastward to cover the vacated ground, their commanding officer requesting help from the 2nd Cavalry Brigade. But before the reinforcements arrived, the Germans occupied part of the Moroccan position and fired along our line, causing many casualties."

"Watch it, Joe," screamed Mike, pointing towards the fire. "The bastards are firing on us from over there and where the Moroccans were, bloody cowards. They've caught us in a crossfire; it's a bloody disaster!"

"Then the Germans showed a white flag from their trenches and came forward as if to surrender," said Mike. "Remember that, Joe? The surprised West Yorkshires fell back too, sending a few men ahead to handle the surrender."

"Aye, Mike," said Joe.

"You pulled yourself flat behind a bend in the trench as best you could, but we could hear the bullets whizzing past our faces from the German line."

"Bastards," yelled our marra Jack. "They put up the white flag to trick us!"

"Haddaway, man. Did you see that?" shouted Mike. "They ordered the West Yorks to disarm the Germans and to take them as prisoners. But as the West Yorkshires levelled their rifles and approached the enemy, the German first row moved aside and dropped. Behind them were six machine guns that opened fire on the West Yorks. It was a massacre, and I saw the entire thing. Bloody bastards!"

"Now they're firing on us," shouted Jack. "Dammit! They could finish us here!"

"Nee," I yelled, "Let us finish them!"

"At last, B Squadron of the 18/Hussar's cavalry arrived and rallied the West Yorks," said Joe.

"The 9/Lancer's cavalry dug in behind the Moroccans, stabilizing the trench again. News of the cavalry's arrival spread throughout the infantry ranks along the firing line, raising morale at once. A cheer went up among our lads.

Then, the Sherwood Foresters regained the lost trenches with a dashing charge, forcing the Germans back to their positions. And as they ordered the Foresters to counterattack, they gave the Durhams orders to drive the Germans out of their fortified nest on the side of a hill. That we did in a fierce fight."

"Despite that minor victory, the entire brigade had suffered terrible casualties. Our D-Company suffered an ordeal of bullets and shells and, trying to take a stand where the Germans were, the resulting losses were at least twelve to one. They fought with sheer bravado, led by Major Robb. But the cost was high."

"Watch your heads," I reminded my marras. "Keep them low, or you'll get shot."

"Keep them low where?" yelled Mike. "We have nowhere to hide out here!"

"Mike was right," said Joe. "We were out in the open with our position exposed to the enemy. We were easy targets for the Germans. Bullets whizzed by in every direction once more; it was a miracle we didn't get shot, even though the Germans downed many of our companions. Shells were arriving and exploding over and around us again and again. We escaped injury or death from those, too. We pushed forward, full of shock and rage, dodging and diving as we approached the enemy. There were corpses and writhing injured soldiers everywhere, creating even more obstacles for us to avoid. Another brave bid to lead A-Company into action resulted in the Germans shooting one of our officers, Lieutenant Twist. Private Jackie Warwick of the 2/DLI lurched to the rescue with tremendous courage and brought the lieutenant back into the British trenches."

"They've shot Major Robb too," I shouted to the line. "Then Lieutenant Hare shouted out, 'Rescue him!'"

"And again, Warwick jumped into action."

"To hell with this," Warwick said. "I'll risk my lot and get him."

"We followed close behind him. Then Private Joseph Howson, a Darlington man engaged in relief work, fell wounded. So, Warwick got him back as far as us, and we dragged him back to safety in the trench. Warwick saved Private Maughan on a third try, but the hero's crowning feat was to rescue Major Robb. Warwick had to dash over the crest of a hill to within thirty yards of the German trenches.

"Lance Corporal Armin recalled this action to me and my marras from his perspective: [38]

"Warwick ventured out cautiously under our guidance," said Armin.

"We could see both the enemy and his position. He got to the major and dragged him along the ground until Warwick could lift and carry him back. Private Warwick didn't do this brave act without injury, although I don't believe it was too

---

[38] John Sheen, *The Steel of the DLI: The 2nd Battalion of the Durham Light Infantry at war 1914-1918*, Pen & Sword Military, 2009

severe. And as he returned, he received a rousing cheer from his companions. It was a cheer that a real British Hero most deserved [39]."

"Two hours later," said Armin, "We were most surprised to see the form of Colour Sergeant Kent on the skyline, with Private Bootes on his back. The boys laughed at the sight, but as he came nearer, they gave him a rousing cheer and welcomed him into the line again. He had proved himself a proper hero that day, too. We suffered heavy losses; the enemy must have been at least twenty to our one, but the enemy losses must have lost twice as many as ours."

"Private Jackie Warwick was the celebrated Hero of the Day. His officers were so impressed they recommended him for the Victoria Cross. We had many heroes that day."

"Howay, Corporal," I said. "Well done. We also went out there to pull back our dead and injured marras. What else can you do? Leave them there to die?"

"And well done to Private George Harrington, too," said Mike. "What a bunch of heroes we are!"

"Harrington crawled along and got him back," said Joe. "To use his own words: 'Right under the bloody noses of the Germans. It was a hard job to get him in, and in my effort, someone shot me in the back, and I fell.'"

---

[39] John Sheen, *The Steel of the DLI: The 2nd Battalion of the Durham Light Infantry at war 1914-1918*, Pen & Sword Military, 2009

"Ignoring the dangers, my marras and I pulled back several downed comrades, too," said Joe. "You don't question why. In the heat of those moments, we did it without even thinking. The scene was one of total mayhem, but we succeeded in either rescuing our injured marras or recovering bodies under heavy fire."

"What the hell," shouted Mike, resigning himself to his fate. "If we get shot, we get shot!"

"Aye, no point in sitting around protecting ourselves when our marras are dying," I added. "And did you see that chap, Harrington? What a hero he was!"

"Private George Harrington of the Sherwoods, a native of Walsall, Staffordshire, engaged in collecting the wounded too," said Joe.

"He volunteered to run out twice under heavy fire to bring in disabled men."

"Where are these heroes now?" asked a listener.

"Who knows?" said Joe. "Only God knows. He could even be dead. No, he's probably dead!"

"The battle calmed, and the battalion rested overnight. Then, in the early dawn quiet, an officer appealed for a volunteer to find out where the enemy was and see what they were doing. Since he had rescued men under fire the day before, the brave Private Harrington stepped up to the mark again and said he was ready to go. Just before dawn broke, he ventured into no-man's-land and found where the enemy had burrowed. Harrington gathered vital information and returned to the relative safety of the battalion's lines. The information he brought back proved to be of great value to the British gunners.

"Alas, Major Robb didn't make it. He died that night in a field hospital at Troyon. His men mourned him. We all mourned him. He was an officer much loved and honoured by his regiment, a brave leader, and a courteous gentleman[40]."

"So, there you have it, Laddies. The 20th of September 1914 was the 2/DLI's introduction to an unfamiliar form of warfare and our ordeal by fire. The battalion passed the test with flying colours. Mike, Jack, Fred and I survived our first day of hell. It was our veteran, Maras's, first battle of the Great War. Between us, we had lived through a war in distant South Africa. And now we had survived this horrific battle, too. But alas, as I've told you, we lost Jack and Fred later.

"This action had hardened the battalion. But it ended with many casualties. The Germans killed Major Alexander Robb, Major D'Arcy Mander, Captain Harry Hare, Lieutenant Roger Marshall and Lieutenant Charles Stanuell. They injured Lieutenants Wilfred Twist, William Grey-Wilson, John Gales, Colin Mearns, and Charles Baker. Casualties in the ranks were heavy, with 36 men killed and 92 wounded." [41]

---

[40] John Sheen, The Steel of the DLI: The 2nd Battalion of the Durham Light Infantry at war 1914-1918, Pen & Sword Military, 2009

[41] S.G.P Ward, Faithful, The Story of the Durham Light Infantry, 1962

Such casualty numbers were not surprising. Trench warfare was new for both sides of this war. The Germans designed their military training and equipment for a mobile war to achieve victory within six weeks. But trench warfare became the byword for stalemate and futility in conflict, and it mired both sides along the Western Front early in the war. The Germans adapted their weapons to the new circumstances. As noted above, siege howitzers lobbed massive shells into Allied trenches. Skilful use of trench mortars, rifle grenades and hand grenades against British troops enabled the Germans to inflict severe injuries on the Allied forces. The Germans used searchlights, flares, and periscopes effectively in the trenches.

The British equipped a few of their aeroplanes with radio sets and used them to report troop movements. But aviators soon recognized the value of directing or spotting artillery fire. On 24 September, Lieutenants B.T. James and D.S. Lewis, flying over the German lines, detected three well-concealed enemy gun batteries. These were inflicting severe damage on British positions. They radioed back the locations of the guns and then circled while waiting to help place the gunner's exploding shells.

Anti-aircraft fire was half-hearted and inaccurate. The BEF used only percussion-fused shells, often missing their targets. Canadian sources reported, "Not one in several hundred ever hit its aerial target and often fell back to earth in the British lines and burst there [42]."

"The 2/DLI remained in the same trenches for the next five days," concluded Joe, "which passed without further attacks materializing, although the mischievous enemy fire was continuous and troublesome. There were no entries in the War Diary until the end of the month."

§

War Diary: Troyon to Pargnan, 26 Sept. 1914

Relieved in trenches by the 2nd Brigade and marched to PARGNAN, arriving shortly after midnight.

The 2nd Brigade relieved the 18th Brigade, including the 2/DLI, at 10 P.M. on 25 September. They then marched back to Pargnan, several miles from the line but still within range of the German guns.

§

---

42 S.G.P Ward, Faithful, The Story of the Durham Light Infantry, 1962

War Diary: Pargnan to Vendresse, 27 Sept. 1914

Left PARGNAN at 9 A.M., marched to N of Bourg to form a reserve to the 3rd Brigade. At dusk, marched to VENDRESSE to support 3rd Brigade in trenches N of VENDRESSE.

The next day, they moved to a reserve position in a forest north of Vendresse-Beaulne to support the 3rd Brigade, which was withstanding a powerful attack. Then the 1st Brigade relieved the battle-weary 3rd Brigade.

In the evening, the 1st Brigade relieved the 3rd Brigade in the trenches.

By 28 September, the Allies had lost 13,541 men killed, wounded or captured, many of them French. The 2/DLI lost five officers and 36 men killed and 92 injured on their first day in the trenches, their first battle. Of the 1,026 men of the 1st Battalion, Royal West Surrey Regiment, only 34 soldiers survived. [43] And there were many similar shocking statistics along the 400 miles of the Western Front. They didn't know how many German casualties resulted from this battle so early in the Great War.

---

[43] Norman Ferguson, *The First World War: A Miscellany*, Summersdale, Chichester, UK, 2014

Empire and War

Trench warfare began on the Western Front in mid-September 1914 when the Durhams arrived. These first trench excavations were dug quickly and were shallow and crude, leading to significant casualties this early in the war. [44]

§

Back in the Hamelin barrack, the story session came to a close.

"How the hell did we survive that action?" Mike asked. "It was horrific!"

"Luck," said Joe. "Pure bloody luck! And lots of ducking and diving, too."

"My God, what a bloody awful war," said Mike. "We were in a few difficulties in South Africa, but never as bad as this! And we lost so many officers and men in such a brief time. Laddies, that was our first full day in this shite war," said Mike, "how many more such days are we going to have?"

"Well, remember how I said there's a hell of a crowd of Huns out there? So, I reckon it will last a while longer," said

---

[44] As the war continued, the excavations became more sophisticated. They dug the trenches on fighting lines twelve feet deep. They cut them in a zigzagging or stepped pattern. Later, fighting trenches broke the sequence into fire bays connected by access traverses. They called the banked earth on the lip of the entrenchment facing the enemy the parapet. Beneath that was a step for firing a rifle. They called the embanked rear lip of the trench the parados, and it protected the soldier's back from shells falling behind the entrenchment.

They kept a unit's time in the front-line trench brief; from as little as one day to a week or two at a time before being relieved. Over time, on an individual level, they might divide a typical British soldier's year up and rotated: 15% front line, 10% support line, 30% reserve line, 20% rest and 25% other. Other breaks included, for example, time in hospital on sick leave, travelling, leave, training courses, etc.

Joe. "The Germans thought they could take Paris in 45 days and end the war. But the problem is, we stopped them and are now dug in along these bloody trenches, staring at them. And we were well past the 45 days! We asked then if there were any bets on making it home by Christmas.

"That's how it was, and now we are here, well past Christmas, in a POW camp in Germany. But before you fall asleep, I must tell you a funny story I heard from our corporal. There was an Irishman named Pat in our Durham ranks, most likely from our hometown. A large German in a nearby trench harassed Pat during his quiet moments, and Pat had enough. This German had a habit of popping his head up and having a shot at the British soldiers at night.

'I will stand this no longer,' said Pat. 'If I get in a shot at him, we will have peace.'

"They told Pat he was not to open fire until he had his orders," said Joe. "He didn't wait. The next time the German appeared, Pat shot him. Then he proclaimed: And it surprised the German since he had never had a bullet in his head. It may have gone against orders, but it had assured Pat's rest that night."[45]

Then Mike related another brief story that another Durham had just told him. "You know how difficult it has been to get the Germans to show themselves?" he began. "Well, a

---

[45] John Sheen, The Steel of the DLI: The 2nd Battalion of the Durham Light Infantry at war 1914-1918, Pen & Sword Military, 2009

Durham one day yelled 'Waiter!' And a host of German heads popped above their parapets, met by a hail of Geordie bullets!"

After a few rare and hearty laughs in these trying times and asking where he heard such crazy stories, the group went off to their bunks. "Tomorrow is another day of hard labour," someone grumbled.

§

Spring Labour at Hamelin Camp

Spring and more pleasant working conditions arrived in Northern Germany at last. The football season was back in full swing, too, and the POWers were doing well, having won three out of five matches and gaining in strength.

The camp authorities dispatched Joe and his mates to various road maintenance projects in the Hamelin district. In that way, they were getting an excellent overview of the region. Joe thought it was a lovely town with extraordinary buildings, so different from Jarrow or Newcastle. It, too, was on a river, the Weser. But this river was much smaller, cleaner and prettier than the Tyne River, spoiled as it was by industry. The houses of Hamelin were tall, elaborate structures made of daub and wattle with many floors and windows. They painted the walls white and the beams dark brown with elaborate decorations in various colours. He could see that the citizens took great pride in their town and smiled when the British prisoners admired their houses.

Once, he and his team were working on the street in front of the Rattenfängerhaus, the rat catcher's place, a renowned elaborate half-timbered seventeenth-century building. They know it too as the Pied Piper's House. Not that anyone believed the Pied Piper had ever lived there or that the Pied Piper even once existed. But they called it that because of the legend.

The following postcard Mary received was a photo of the Hamelin town centre, with the Rattenfängerhaus front and centre.

"Dearest Mary,

"This shows you the lovely town near our camp. The big house in the middle is where the Pied Piper rat catcher lived before he ran away with the town children long ago. That's what happens when you don't pay the rat catcher, haha.

"I have been working there fixing the cobblestone streets of the town. Last week, I was making the cobbles too.

"I hope you and the children are well and happy even without me. Please give my children an enormous hug and kiss for me.

"Greetings from Old Germany. Sending you my love, Joe."

This card about a rat catcher baffled Mary, but she assumed it was a local story or one of Joe's tall tales. But the most crucial thing was Joe was still alive and communicating. As always, she shared his communications with her siblings and closest friends. She carried a pack of his letters with her everywhere.

§

The First Use of Poison Gas in the War

In early May, Joe had another report to make to his companions one evening.

"The Germans have used a new and terrible weapon at Ypres," said Joe. "They used poison gas on Allied troops on 22 April. They dumped hundreds of tons of chlorine gas at night on the French soldiers first, who couldn't escape the gas as it spread throughout a wood. It blinded them, and many died an agonizing death."

This news shocked his companions, and they didn't know what they should make of it. They had never heard of soldiers using poisonous gas in battle. So, in their silence, Joe continued with his report.

"The Germans launched the Second Battle of Ypres from 22 April to 25 May 1915 for control of that strategic Flemish town in western Belgium," said Joe. "They had fought the First Battle of Ypres the previous autumn. We know all about that. But on 22 April, German forces shocked the Allied soldiers by firing over 150 tons of lethal chlorine gas against two French colonial divisions. Word of this attack caused panic among the other divisions, being the first to use a deadly gas, and it devastated the Allied line. The Germans intended this secret weapon as a breakthrough to change the balance of the stalemate on the Western Front.

"This battle also marked the first time a colonial force, the 1st Canadian Division, defeated a European power in Europe. They fought the Germans and won at the St. Julien and Kitcheners' Wood Battles. They named Kitcheners' Wood after the French name, Bois-de-Cuisinères, or forest of kitchen cookers or stoves, not after Lord Kitchener. French troops housed their field kitchens there, so our troops called it Kitcheners' Wood."

That Canada was automatically at war when Britain was at war was unquestioned, and Canadians from coast to coast pledged support for Britain. Leader of the opposition at the time, Sir Wilfrid Laurier, spoke for most Canadians when he proclaimed,

"We must let Great Britain know and to let the friends and foes of Great Britain know that there is in Canada but one mind and one heart…"

"All Canadians are behind the Mother Country."

Prime Minister Robert Borden, calling for a supreme national effort, offered Canadian help to Great Britain. Great

Britain accepted the offer and immediately ordered the mobilization of an expeditionary force.

With a regular army of only 3,110 men and a fledgling navy, Canada was ill-prepared to enter a world conflict. Prime Minister Borden ordered the Minister of the Militia and Defence, Sam Hughes, to train and recruit an army for overseas service. From Halifax to Vancouver, thousands of young Canadians hastened to recruitment offices. Over 32,000 men gathered at Valcartier Camp near Quebec City within a few weeks. In October 1914, the First Contingent, Canadian Expeditionary Force (CEF), was on its way to England in the largest convoy ever to cross the Atlantic Ocean. Also sailing in this convoy was a contingent from the still separate British self-governing colony of Newfoundland. Canadian authorities politely but firmly rejected a suggestion to incorporate Newfoundland's men into the Canadian Expeditionary Force.

Upon reaching England, the Canadians endured a long, miserable winter of training in the mud and drizzle of Salisbury Plain. In early 1915, authorities deemed them ready for the front line.

The first Canadian troops to arrive in France were Princess Patricia's Canadian Light Infantry, formed entirely from ex-British Army regular soldiers at the outbreak of war. The "Princess Pats" landed in France in December 1914 with the British 27th Division and saw action near St. Eloi and Polygon Wood in the Ypres Salient.

Veteran British troops introduced the 1st Canadian Division to trench warfare in February 1915 after the division arrived in France. Following this brief training, the Division took over a section of the line in the Armentières sector French Flanders. Faced with the realities of d'— __ death, their illusions of military glory o' __appeared [46].

"The 7th Canadian Inf— , battalion lost their Colonel, an officer I kr __mething about," said Joe.

"He was in South Africa and wrote a book about his experiences on Field Marshal Frederick Roberts and General Ian Hamilton's march from Bloemfontein to Pretoria.

They raised the 7th Battalion at Camp Valcartier, Quebec, in September 1914 with an initial strength of 1,223 officers and men. Its first Commanding Officer was Lieutenant-Colonel William Frederick Richard Hart-McHarg of the Duke of Connaught's Own Rifles (DCOR). Lt. Colonel McHarg was a veteran of the Boer War and a Vancouver attorney. Five BC militia units raised the drafts that comprised the 7th. The 6th DCOR contributed 353 volunteers; the rest came from other Regiments around the province.

"I heard from another Canadian who arrived later that a bombardment began at nine A.M., soon after an airship had

---

[46] https://www.canada.ca/en/news/archive/2014/08/canada-beginning-first-world-war.html

flown over them dropping markers. The 7th Battalion held on by sheer determination, withstanding horrific shell fire, chlorine gas and constant attacks and counterattacks by the enemy. They held until relieved but suffered the loss of 650 casualties wounded, killed or captured. Six officers, including the commanding officer Lt-Col Hart-McHarg, and 176 NCOs and men died. Canadians should remember the events of 24 April 1915 for the sacrifice of the 7th Battalion commander and Boer War veteran from British Columbia. They buried Lieutenant-Colonel Hart-McHarg, who had died at forty-six, in the Poperinghe Old Military Cemetery, Poperinghe, Belgium."

"If the Germans captured those chaps before the bombardment," asked Mike, "how do you know the ending?"

"Ahh, you might well ask," said Joe, chuckling. "I heard it from another Canadian captured after that battle. They've been arriving thick and fast, so I guess they are doing their job in this war. Pity about William Hart-McHarg, though."

"Well, I don't know who he is," said Walt. "I bet on the Canadians and won!"

"Another Canadian present at this battle was Major John McCrae, and by coincidence, he was also a veteran of the Boer War.

They appointed Major McCrae as the medical officer and second-in-command of the First Brigade of the Canadian Field Artillery. He treated the wounded during the Second Battle of Ypres in April-May 1915 from a hastily dug 8-by-8-

foot (2.4m × 2.4m) bunker. This bunker was in the back of the dyke along the Yser Canal about 2 miles north of Ypres.

A six-inch, high-explosive cannon shell burst during the battle on May 2nd, killing McCrae's friend and former militia member, Lt. Alexis Helmer. He was 22, and his burial inspired McCrae's famous poem *In Flanders Fields*, written on 3 May 1915.

Possibly because of that tragedy in his life, Command ordered McCrae away from the trenches on 1 June 1915. He was to set up the No. 3 Canadian General Hospital at Dannes-Camiers near Boulogne-sur-Mer, southwest of Calais on the English Channel. The hospital operated in Durbar tents for eight months. However, after suffering from storms, floods, and frost, the army moved it into the old Jesuit College in Boulogne-sur-Mer in February 1916. Brigade-Sergeant C.L.C. Allinson, who served with John McCrae, wrote, 'McCrae told me what he thought of being transferred to the medicals and pulled away from his beloved guns. His last words to me were: "Allinson, all the goddamn doctors in the world will not win this bloody war: what we need is more and more fighting men."

In a letter written to his mother, McCrae described the battle as a 'nightmare,'

"For seventeen days and seventeen nights, none of us have had our clothes off, nor our boots even, except occasionally. In all that time while I was awake, gunfire and rifle fire never ceased for sixty seconds. And behind it all was the constant background of the sights of the dead, the wounded, the maimed, and a terrible anxiety lest the line gives way [47]."

The Allied forces comprised two French and six British divisions, including the Canadians fighting seven German divisions. The French lost 21,973 men, and the British lost 59,275. German losses amounted to 35,000 men.

But the most infamous legacy of this battle was the first use of gas in combat.

§

The Gallipoli Landings

"Howay, Laddies," said Joe one day at the end of April. "We are landing on the beaches of Gallipoli. General Ian Hamilton is in charge."

"So, we're moving from the sea to the land," said Mike. "Where did you hear that, Joe?"

"Aye, that we have. Now, the fight begins. The moment of truth," said Joe. "I heard of the landings from a recent arrival this morning."

"The betting is open," said Walt. "Who will win this battle?"

---

[47] In Flanders Fields, Veterans Affairs Canada

"Well, we haven't been doing so well there on the water," said Joe. "So it's anybody's guess how we'll do on land."

While the 2nd Battle of Ypres ended on 25 April, British Empire and French forces made amphibious landings on the Gallipoli peninsula. The British 29th Division and elements of the Royal Naval Division, accompanied by French troops, landed at Cape Helles. Australian and New Zealand Army Corps (ANZAC) landed at Anzac Cove, as they called it, on the European side. And French forces made a diversionary landing at Kum Kale on the Asian shore.

"On 26 April, the Australian submarine HMAS AE2 became the first Allied vessel to pass through the Dardanelles into the Sea of Marmara," said Joe.

"On 27 April, the British submarine E14 passed through the Dardanelles to start a three-week tour. The Turks mounted a counterattack on the same day but couldn't drive the Anzacs into the sea. On 28 April, at the First Battle of Krithia, British and French forces suffered 4,000 casualties for little gain. But the British reinforced the Anzac landing with four battalions from the Royal Naval Division."

And so, the news from the Dardanelles continued, sometimes good, sometimes not so good. The betting POWs of Hamelin followed the events as best they could, their mood swings depending on the news, as recorded by Joe.

"On 1 May, the French submarine Joule struck a mine and sank in the strait," reported Joe. "On 6 May, the Second Battle of Krithia started at Cape Helles, the British 42nd (East Lancashire) Division landing as reinforcements. This battle ended on 8 May, but one-third of the Allied soldiers became casualties. With the failure of the second battle, Hamilton asked the British Secretary of State for War, Lord Kitchener, for another four divisions."

"On the 12th of May, the Ottoman torpedo boat Muavenet-i Milliye sank HMS Goliath at Cape Helles," said Joe.

"On the same day, the Australian 1st Light Horse Brigade arrived at Anzac Bay as reinforcements, and on the 13th, New Zealand Mounted Rifles Brigade arrived as reinforcements."

"Five days later, Turkish forces mounted a massive attack using 42,000 men, but the Allies repulsed them, suffering 10,000 casualties," said Joe.

"More reinforcements arrived at Anzac Bay—the Australian 2nd and 3rd Light Horse Brigade."

The negative news continued to arrive in Hamelin.

"The German U-boat U-21 sank HMS Triumph on 25 May," said Joe. "The same U-boat sank HMS Majestic two days later. On 4 June, British and French forces mounted a limited attack in the Third Battle of Krithia but couldn't reach their objectives. Even by the end of July, the Allies were not making any progress but were suffering huge losses of men. It was looking bleak in the Dardanelles for the Allies."

§

Then Joe heard of an unrelated tragedy that pierced deep into his heart.

"Mike, I've just heard that a German U-boat sank RMS Lusitania on 7 May in Ireland," said Joe, "killing 1,200 passengers and crew."

"My God," said Mike. "Wasn't she a sister ship of the Mauretania?"

"Aye," said Joe. "Do you remember how we watched the launch of Mauretania in 1906? But the Scots built Lusitania on Clydeside."

"Bloody Germans," said Mike. "Killing 1,200 civilians. Bastards."

Sinking the Lusitania caused worldwide anger. In Britain, across the British Empire and in the United States, they met it with fury. [48] But the Germans justified the act since they claimed the ship "carried contraband of war," and the Americans classified it as an "auxiliary cruiser." The sinking caused a powerful reaction and protests in the US since 128 of the 139 American citizens on board drowned. The incident

---

[48] Jones, Howard, Crucible of Power: A History of U.S. Foreign Relations Since 1897. Rowman & Littlefield, 2001.

shifted public opinion in the neutral United States against Germany. It influenced their deliberations leading up to the US declaring war two years later.

§

Throughout April and May, Joe's group continued working on various projects for the municipality of Hameln. But as summer arrived, Guard Klaus announced the delightful news they had wanted to hear for a long time. They would work again on Herr Schmidt's farm for the next few months.

§

Summer Work at the Farm

It was a bright, warm morning in June when the farm wagon and its team of horses drew up to collect the British POWs to help at the farm. Its arrival exhilarated the men since they had enjoyed Schmidts' hospitality before and looked forward to working in the fields.

Once again, Frau Schmidt and her gorgeous daughters met them with tea and biscuits. But this time, the men could say 'Guten Tag Frau Schmidt' and 'Danke schön, Fräulein' when the daughters handed them each their breakfast. It was like returning home.

The farmer and permanent staff led them into the fields and showed them what needed doing, primarily weeding and pest control. The farmer had sowed the crops in the spring, and the young plants' needed care. In other fields, the rapeseed plants the farmer had planted in the autumn had finished blossoming, and the seeds were ripening.

As before, the two daughters, in their billowing skirts and snow-white blouses, headscarves and wooden clogs, arrived at noon with tea and bread spread with thick lard. Once again, the men could say "Danke schön, Fräulein" with enormous smiles and giggles as their reward. The lunch break lasted the usual 30 minutes, during which the men ate and caught a brief nap before being called back to work. At dusk, another piece of bread and a drink arrived before the wagon transported them back to the camp.

"It's grand to be back there," said Joe as they returned to camp that night.

"Aye, of the work the Boche force us to do, I enjoy this best," said Mike. "I don't mind working for those people, even if they don't pay us. They treat us well, and they treat us with respect."

"Aye, and they need us. And seeing those Fräuleins again does my soul wonders," said Walt.

Then, in mid-July, farmer Herr Schmidt appeared with two helpers laden with more tools. Joe and Mike studied the long forks and scythes with curiosity. They were to help with the grain harvest.

"Those look like wicked weapons," said Mike.

"Aye, they're not weapons but farm tools for harvesting grains. I noticed wheat, oats and barley in the fields," said the farm-knowledgeable Durham Mac. "I bet we'll be harvesting them today."

The farmer led the POWs into the fields surrounding the farm buildings and showed them how to use the scythes. Farmer Schmidt then gave each a blade and gestured to try it.

"Shite. This isn't as easy as it looks!" said Mike to the farmer's amusement.

"Don't worry, Mike," said Mac. "I'll help you laddies get used to them. You'll be experts by the end of the day."

And he made good on his word. He showed Joe, Mike and Walt the best techniques for keeping the scythe blades sharp. He showed them how to master the smooth sweep of the scythe to achieve the broadest strokes through the wheat with one swing. Then he showed them the best position of the whetstone holder of their belt to optimize the swift movements from belt to blade. He also taught the ideal technique and the number of times they should stroke the edge to keep it sharp. They soon caught on and enjoyed the novelty of working as farmers' helpers.

"This isn't too bad," said Joe.

"I'm getting the knack," said Mike.

"Aye, me too," said Joe.

"Aye, here too," said Walt. "My muscles are complaining a little."

As always, the two sisters arrived in the fields at noon with tea and bread spread with thick lard. After the lunch break, the work continued until dusk, when another piece of bread and a drink arrived, and the wagon came to transport them back to the camp.

"I knew it," said Walt on the way back. "I've rediscovered muscles I had forgotten, and they are aching!"

"Aye," said Joe and Mike. "We know what you mean."

They also learned how to stack the hay as "ritter," or knights, as the Germans called them. These standing knights of hay collected and transported to the farm buildings to separate the grains. They had learned grain harvesting from beginning to end. On the last day of the harvest, the farmer's wife arranged another fantastic meal of meat and farm-fresh vegetables. And the farmer brought a cask of good German dark beer to accompany the meal. It was another joyous celebration of work well done for the Schmidts and much appreciated.

In most respects, except for the lack of family, summer was a pleasant time for the POWs. Yes, they were prisoners. And yes, the food they received in the camp was inadequate. But the farm's summer and early autumn working days made up for those sacrifices.

§

The First Use of Flamethrowers in the War

One day in August, Joe reported on another significant engagement called the Battle of Hooge to his companions.

"I've just heard the Germans have introduced an unknown weapon at a place in Belgium called Hooge, two and a half miles east of Ypres," said Joe.

"What is that now," asked Mike? "Isn't gas enough?"

"They shoot ignited liquid gas with a weapon they call a flamethrower," said Joe. "They are now burning our soldiers out of the trenches!"

"Bastards."

"Aye, and the new arrival I was talking to said the weapon throws a huge flame many yards. Frightening!"

On 30 July 1915, the Germans put their new weapon, the 'flammenwerfer' or flamethrower, to devastating use against the Allies at the Battle of Hooge in Flanders, Belgium. This battle represented the first principal deployment of the flamethrower, one of the most feared weapons introduced during the Great War. Eleven days before, British infantry had captured the German-occupied village of Hooge near Ypres by detonating a massive mine. Then, using the flamethrowers to frightening effect, along with machine guns, trench mortars and hand grenades, the Germans reclaimed their positions on 30 July. They easily penetrated the front lines and pushed the

British forces back to their second trench. They lost a few men to actual burns. But a British officer reported later that the horror weapons had a significant demoralizing effect.

"The Germans have taken Hooge back from us," said Walt, "I lost another bloody bet!"

"Aye," said Joe. "They did it using flamethrowers! Can you imagine what it must have been like there?"

"What's this bloody world coming to?" asked Mike. "Now they're burning soldiers to death! How rotten is that? How low can these bloody Boche go? Fire is the one thing that terrifies me."

This fight, known as the Battle of Bellewaarde, took place on a half-mile square battlefield and involved several British battalions. In 12 hours, they killed over 1,000 men and wounded 3,000.

"Well, if they use poison gas and now flamethrowers, what can we expect next?" asked Joe. "We are losing bets everywhere, Laddies!"

"Meaning that the Allies are losing everywhere," said Walt.

§

Before too long, the word was out in camp that a massive British offensive was underway at Loos in French Flanders. This battle was the British contribution to the Third

Battle of Artois, an Anglo-French attack known to the Germans as the Herbstschlacht (Autumn Battle). Since it was a British offensive, bets in Hamelin favoured the British for this one.

§

News of a Major British offensive

Compared with the small-scale British efforts of spring 1915, the Battle of Loos, from 25 September to 14 October, was a major offensive against the Germans. They referred to it at the time as 'The Big Push,'

Six British divisions took part on the flat open ground that the British Generals loathed for an excellent reason. Stocks of ammunition and heavy artillery were inadequate. It was the most prominent British attack of 1915, the first time the British used poison gas and the first mass engagement of Kitchener's New Army units. The French and British tried to break through the German defences in Artois and Champagne to restore a war of movement. However, despite improved methods, more ammunition, and better equipment, the German armies contained the Franco-British attacks, except for limited losses of territory.

British casualties at Loos were twice as high as German losses, and they considered it a failure. They had criticized Field Marshal Sir John French before the battle.

However, because of this British failure, John French lost his remaining support in the Army, Government, and the King. As a result, Douglas Haig replaced John French as Commander of the British Expeditionary Force (BEF) in December 1915.

Nobel laureate, novelist, and poet of the British Empire Rudyard Kipling was one of many British and Irish parents who lost a son to this war. [49]

"Bloody hell," said Walt. "We've lost another one, and I've lost another bet!"

"You're not alone there, Walt," said Joe. "Everyone's lost in this battle."

Maybe it was because so many had lost their bets on Loos and appeared to be failing at Gallipoli. Or because of the deep disappointment caused by the British defeats instead of expected victories. However, the British POWs entered a period of deep depression. In many discussions, the blame fell on Sir John French's shoulders.

"Arrogant bastard," said Mike, "I always knew he'd fail us one day. They say women are more important to him than his duty!"

"Aye, a real buck and women's man," said Walt. "They say he had an enormous scandal in India when he had an affair with a fellow officer's wife. They nearly court-martialled him!"

---

[49] Ronan McGreevy, Rudyard Kipling's first World War tragedy, The Irish Times, 5 May 2015

"Aye, and word has it he has been arguing with the French General Lanrezac, and the other French Generals don't appreciate him either," said Joe.

"I don't think one should argue with fellow soldiers in the heat of war," said Joe.

"None of our politicians, the King or Lord Kitchener, approved of him. I guess that's his end. Hopefully, Haig will do a better job?" said Mike.

"It's a pity, though, because he was a genuine hero in South Africa! I remember and even saw him in the Cape twice," said Joe.

"How far the great Generals can fall," said Mike. "Remember General Buller?"

"Aye, I sure do," said Joe. "He fell from grace after the catastrophes in Natal."

"If you are a General, you must never lose a campaign!" said Mike.

"They say we lost at Loos because the Germans were on the slag heaps and colliery towers overlooking a flat plain where our troops were."

"Why didn't the generals see that?" piped up another.

"Bloody stupid," said Mike. "These generals don't care how many soldiers they lose. We mean nothing to them!"

§

More Work at the Schmidt Farm

Throughout the summer, Joe and his companions assisted the Schmidts. They had become indispensable to the success of that farming family. The men and their employers had grown much closer. When they arrived from the camp early in the morning, Herr and Frau Schmidt and their daughters and permanent staff greeted them enthusiastically and warmly. The men had learned more German words, particularly Walt, since he had chatted at length with the Schmidt daughters at every opportunity. They were teaching each other their respective languages and making progress.

They continued their journeys to the farm when autumn arrived to help turn the fields. But after a few weeks, they had finished the work, and their time at the farm ended. And just as they had done at the end of last year's work, the farmer's wife arranged a sumptuous lunch of meat and vegetables. And once again, the farmer rolled out a cask of dark beer for the meal. It had become a traditional celebration of work well done and much appreciated.

After an emotional departure on returning to camp that night, the men were silent and deep in thought. They missed the Schmidts during the winter. Walt missed seeing Traudle, the sister with whom he had grown fond. They missed the pleasant and healthy days in the fields as they helped the Schmidts through the crop cycle. And they assumed their next assignment would be the hard winter work in the forest. But more than that, they fought deep and confused feelings. They were at war with Germany. But they had grown fond of a kind and generous German family. They battled to understand what was going on in the world.

"Shite," said Mike. "I will miss those people and their farm. It's a crazy world and a crazy war!"

"Aye, that's for sure, Mike. They're kind people, just like us," said Joe.

"I think I could live here without a problem," said Walt nostalgically. "My German is getting better, too."

Joe and Mike just smiled back at him.

§

First Anniversary as POWs - 20th of October 2015

On Tuesday evening of 20 October 2015, Joe and his fellow POWs from Ennetières commiserated over the first anniversary of their imprisonment in Germany.

"One year, Laddies," announced Joe that morning. "We've been prisoners for one bloody long year!"

"One year working for the Hun," said Mike. "What have we got for it? Nix!"

"Not much," said Walt. "Apart from a football team, our German friends on the farm, aches and pains and weight loss."

"Our loved one's even less!" said Joe. "My Mary has had to go out to work. Same as most of our women. What is happening to this world?"

"It will never be the same," said Mike, lowering his head.

"It will never be better," said Walt.

"A sad state of affairs," said Joe. "We do not know how long we will be in this hellhole! But, at least we are alive."

Life in the camp had deteriorated because of the massive influx of prisoners from the Western Front. There were now tens of thousands of British, French and Russian POWs at Hamelin. The camp food had changed little. However, the Red Cross and home packages of food and essential articles of clothing still arrived, maintaining an acceptable level of comfort. The hygiene and physical health standards were unsatisfactory, but they survived despite minor ailments. And for those who were able, the daily sorties to work outside the camp meant they spent little time there. So, despite their complaints, the Hamelin POWs weren't suffering as much as their comrades in the trenches. They maintained their spirits on their off days through sports and entertainment, such as self-developed plays, concerts and a growing English library. But, after their first year at Hamelin

Camp, Joe and his marras were very aware of the effects of captivity.

"I don't mind the work," said Joe. "When we can't play football, there's nothing else to do here. And I miss my family so much."

"Aye, and the Broons," said Mike. "Our times with our marras at the pub."

"We've been losing too many battles and bets," said Walt. "We can't even beat the Turks. How are we going to beat the Germans?"

"Warfare has changed so much in that year," said Joe. "Nor has 1915 been a successful year for either side, as far as I can see. The war is still stalemating on the same lines and trenches as last year."

"Aye, and the Germans introduced poison gas warfare and flamethrowers, hoping they would achieve a breakthrough," said Mike.

"I can't imagine what it would be like in such a war anymore."

"This war has seen the start of air warfare," said Walt. "A soldier has to look around him on the ground and watch what's above him, too."

The land and sea forces used planes for scouting and surveillance only at the start of the war. However, fighter aircraft armed with machine guns appeared in 1915. On 1 April 1915, the French pilot Roland Garros became the first to shoot down an enemy aeroplane. After that, both sides equipped their planes with guns and dropped bombs on enemy lines. They introduced tactical bombing of targets such as enemy airbases that year.

"Both sides started air raids this year," said Joe.

"You might remember British planes from Dunkirk bombing German cities like Cologne, Düsseldorf and Friedrichshafen in the autumn of 1914, including the sheds of the German Zeppelins."

"I remember," said Walt. "The Germans carried out air raids on English towns in December 1914, followed by Zeppelin raids from January this year. They bombed London on the night of 3 May to 1 June this year."

"It isn't going so well for Germany and the Kaiser, either," said Joe. "Their original plan to encircle Paris failed since we stopped their rapid advance. This halt caused the stalemate on the Western Front. The gas attacks didn't give them the breakthrough they needed, and the Allies sought revenge with poisonous gas against them, too. The German armies also faced significant Allied offensives in 1915. I've also heard the war is not going so well for the Germans in Africa, either. As our football sailors told us, French, British and Belgian colonial troops invaded Togoland and Cameroon in western Africa. And in Southern Africa, they had lost German Southwest Africa."

"Aye. The Kaiser hasn't had it all his way," said Mike. "Still, he has made our lives a living hell, here, in the trenches and at home!"

§

The End of the Gallipoli Campaign

On 15 October, the army relieved the commander of the Mediterranean Expeditionary Force, General Sir Ian Hamilton, of his duties. By 15 November, Field Marshal Herbert Kitchener, the Secretary of State for War, was in Gallipoli. After his visit, he recommended they evacuate the Anzac and Suvla troops. So, on 7 December, the British Cabinet ordered the removal of the British soldiers. The press declared the Gallipoli Campaign a colossal failure, adding that it was Churchill's fault.

"Aye," said Joe. "Those at the top of that disaster, Churchill, Kitchener, Hamilton and Stopford, are being dropped a notch or two."

"So they should, haughty bastards," said Mike. "They got us into that mess!"

Churchill's responsibility in Gallipoli ceased once they deployed the army under Hamilton. Incompetence and hesitancy plagued the invasion by military commanders. Still, Churchill became the scapegoat, and he took heavy criticism for his involvement. The disaster at Gallipoli severely hurt his reputation and standing in British politics. Field Marshal Lord Kitchener took a hard knock as the Secretary of State for War. The Army fired Sir Ian Hamilton, and this defeat finished his military career. They also dismissed Lieutenant-General Sir Frederick Stopford since he had led the failed amphibian attack on Suvla Bay. They had recognized and decorated them for their service during the 2nd Anglo-Boer War and many earlier Victorian campaigns. However, after the disaster of Gallipoli, people discarded and vilified them.

"Our politicians and generals can do whatever they want without regard for the cost of men," said Mike, disgusted. "Always the same old bloody story! How many men died out there?"

No one could answer Mike, but the estimated cost of Gallipoli in soldiers was later determined to be over 160,000 British and 27,000 French casualties in battle. Another 165,000 were sick or dead from disease. 57,000 thousand men died on both sides of the fight. The war at Gallipoli killed one-fifth of the 50,000 Australians, and 15,000 New Zealanders sent there and wounded another fifth.

New Zealand and Australia remember the Gallipoli Campaign as a significant disastrous event despite them being a small minority of the Allied forces. The campaign was a "baptism of fire" for both nations, linked to their emergence as independent states. They commemorate the landings on 25 April every year in both those countries as "Anzac Day."

The Ottoman Empire had between 240,000 and 315,000 dead, wounded or sick.

§

4. *Christmas 1915*

Christmas 1915 was a non-event for the POWs in the Hamelin Camp, as on the Western Front. A few units arranged ceasefires on the Western Front, but the truces were far fewer than in 1914. The high commands of both sides had passed down orders prohibiting truces. The POWs huddled in their barracks, attempting to warm themselves by the wood stove.

"Do you think the Kommandant will surprise us with a Christmas meal this year?" asked Walt.

"I doubt it," said Joe. "I've noticed a change of attitude by the Germans; they are angrier, shouting more. They seem to be unhappy with the war, too. Have you noticed?"

"Aye," said Mike. "I've noticed."

"Me too," said another, and another, and another.

British High Command replaced Field Marshal French with General Douglas Haig because of the disaster at Loos. The catastrophe at Gallipoli forced Liberal Prime Minister Herbert Asquith to swallow a bitter pill by forming a coalition government with the Conservatives. The latter insisted on the removal of Winston Churchill from his cabinet duties. They then appointed Churchill to the sinecure office of Chancellor of the Duchy of Lancaster. It required little or no work and gave him limited status and financial help. Churchill lamented, "I am the victim of political intrigue—finished."

"I've heard that Winston Churchill has rejoined the army as a lieutenant colonel in the Royal Scots Fusiliers on the Western Front," said Joe.

"It's about time he did something useful," said Mike. "Is Kitchener still in his lofty position? And why the hell can't he end this bloody war?"

§

1916—The year of attrition

A New Phase

The year 1916 began with the Gallipoli Campaign. That campaign ended with an official Allied defeat and Ottoman victory on 9 January, ten months, three weeks, and two days after it started.

The Western Front stretched 400-plus miles from the Swiss border through France and Belgium to the North Sea. On both sides of this Front, military strategists planned monumental battles to break the deadlock.

For the British POWs at Hamelin, the war was dragging on too long. The novelty of working in a foreign land had worn off. Isolation from their families and loved ones for such a long time had turned from fear to frustration to anger.

"It's enough, now," scowled Mike one evening before going to his cot. "We've got to leave this place and go home."

"Are you mad, Mike?" said Joe. "How do you propose we do that?"

"By breaking out," said Mike.

"How?" asked Walt.

"I don't know yet," said Mike. "It's time we started making a plan. We must work out how to get out of here and go home."

"I'm all for planning," said Joe. "I'll start hearing around camp whether anyone has broken out before now."

"Let's all search for a map of the area to see where we are and to plan a route to safety," said Mike.

"I'm with you," said Walt.

§

But the war raged on all Fronts.

On 21 February, the Germans made the first move at Verdun on the eastern border with Germany.

That is a boundary created by the Franco-German War of 1870 when France lost the provinces of Alsace and most of Lorraine. The attack on Verdun resulted from a plan by the German Chief of General Staff, Erich von Falkenhayn. He wanted to "bleed France white" by launching a massive German attack on a narrow stretch of land with a historic sentiment for the French—Verdun. The area around Verdun contained twenty principal forts and forty smaller ones that had protected the eastern border of France from German invasion, modernized in the twentieth century. Falkenhayn believed the French couldn't allow these forts to fall since the national humiliation would have been too much to bear. By fighting to the last man, Falkenhayn believed the French would lose so many men that the battle would change the war's course.

So, he sent 140,000 German troops to attack on 21 February 1916. The Germans had complete air supremacy, too, with 168 planes—the largest concentration of planes in history. The French only had 30,000 troops available to oppose the Germans. On the day the battle started, 1,200 German artillery guns fired 2,500,000 shells along a six-mile line of the French front. They needed thirteen hundred ammunition trains to supply these guns.

"At least they didn't involve us in this fight," said Mike. "This war continues with us elsewhere."

"It will only end when we have beaten the Boche," said Walt. "They keep sending in their millions to fight us on every front."

"First Marne, followed by Aisne, Ypres, Gallipoli, Loos... not to mention the Eastern Front, and now Verdun," said Joe.

"We have seen one battle after another and no end in sight. But at least the British aren't involved in that fight."

The French put General Philippe Pétain in charge of the defence of Verdun. There was only one road from Bar-le-Du accessing the city, and this road was only twenty feet wide, and modern vehicles battled to pass one another. Pétain moved 25,000 tons of supplies and 90,000 soldiers into Verdun using 6,000 vehicles. The French gave the road the name Voie Sacrée (Sacred Way). But despite enormous military strengthening, the French lost 133,000 men at the hands of the invading Germans. The Germans suffered massive casualties, too; by the end of April, they had lost 120,000 men.

As the battle moved through the spring of 1916, Pétain asked his commander-in-chief, Marshal Joffre, for more and more men, but Joffre refused. The Marshal wanted the men for an attack on the Somme they were planning. He replaced Pétain with General Nivelle—a soldier who believed that the most successful strategy was to be on the offensive at all times. Nivelle introduced air warfare at Verdun. By summer, he had achieved a modicum of air supremacy over the Germans. But the horrors of the land battle at Verdun continued.

French reconnaissance pilot Roland Garros revolutionized air fighting when he mounted a Hotchkiss machine gun with a mechanical interrupter mechanism on the cowling of his Morane-Saulnier L.

However, the system at the time had issues. So Garros added deflector wedges to the rear of the propeller blades to protect the wooden propeller from being shot to pieces whenever he opened fire on German aeroplanes. With this setup, Garros became the world's first fighter pilot.

Dutch aviation pioneer Anthony Fokker developed a gun synchronizer by the start of July 1915, thus changing how pilots fought the war in the air. From then on, German and Allied fighter pilots fought each other in the sky. The war produced such renowned aces as Britain's Albert Ball, James

McCudden and Edward 'Mick' Mannock, and Canada's 'Billy' Bishop. Others included South Africa's Andrew Beauchamp-Proctor, France's Georges Guynemer and Germany's Max Immelmann, Oswald Boelcke and the renowned Red Baron Manfred von Richthofen. Roland Garros downed four planes during the war, one short of becoming an 'ace' before being hit and killed by German ace Hermann Habich.

§

"The Dutch border is 125 miles from here," announced Walt a few days later. "That's via the most direct route to Oldenzaal."

"Several days' walk while dodging the Germans," said Joe.

"The Germans will patrol that road," said Walt. "So, we must find the smaller roads or pathways to get there unnoticed."

"Well, we know a few German words now, most of all, Walt," said Mike.

"So, with the right clothing, we should be able to blend with the locals, maybe even hitch a ride or two. What do you think?"

"You may be right, Mike," said Joe. "Let's plan our getaway. We must get out of here."

The men agreed, and from then on, they spent their days and nights doing surveillance and planning for their escape from Hamelin Camp.

§

The Sea Battle of Jutland

And while the land battles raged on, another massive action lined up at sea. The Battle of Jutland was the most noteworthy naval battle and the only full-scale clash of battleships during the Great War. Britain's Grand Fleet fought the Imperial German Navy's High Seas Fleet for one day from 31 May to 1 June 1916. It was called The Battle of Jutland, in the North Sea near the west coast of Denmark's Jutland Peninsula. It involved two hundred and fifty ships and 100,000 men.

The British Empire fleet comprised 151 combat ships, including vessels from Canada and Australia, under the command of Sir John Jellicoe. There were 28 British battleships under the control of Rear-Admiral Sir Hugh Evan-Thomas; 9 battlecruisers under the leadership of Sir David Beatty; 8 armoured cruisers; 26 light cruisers; 78 destroyers; one minelayer and one seaplane carrier.

The German Empire fleet comprised 99 combat vessels under the command of Vizeadmiral Scheer. There were 16 battleships, 5 battlecruisers under the orders of

Vizeadmiral Franz Hipper, six pre-dreadnoughts, 11 light cruisers and 61 torpedo boats.

They fought this colossal battle, starting on the afternoon of 31 May, with gunfire between the German and British scouting forces. When the first warships met, British Admiral John Jellicoe positioned his ships before the daylight faded, scoring many direct hits that forced German Admiral Scheer into retreat. Both sides claimed victory, but Britain still controlled the North Sea despite this indecisive battle.

By total darkness at 10 P.M. on 1 June, British losses had reached 6,800 men and 113,300 tons of warships. This loss included three battlecruisers, three armoured cruisers and seven light destroyers. The Germans lost over 3,000 men and 62,300 tons, including one battlecruiser, pre-dreadnought, light cruisers, and torpedo boats.

HMS Queen Mary was the last battlecruiser built by the Royal Navy before the Great War; she lost 1,266 crewmen. The destroyers Laurel, Petard and Tipperary picked up eighteen survivors, and the Germans rescued two. [50] But the worst British tragedy of this battle was the battlecruiser HMS Indefatigable. Of the 1,119 crew on board, only three survived! The German torpedo boat S16 rescued two survivors: Able Seaman Frederick Arthur Gordon Elliott and Leading Signalman Charles Farmer. They picked up a third

---

[50] "HMS Queen Mary – Battle of Jutland [ship's crew] Survivors." Imperial War Museum & D C Thompson. Archived from the original on 7 November 2017.

survivor, Signalman John Bowyer, but *The Times* reported him on 24 June 1916 as a crew member from Nestor [51].

When the British men at Hamelin Camp heard of this battle, the captive sailors of the POWers football team took the most interest. They explained the struggle in terms the soldiers could understand.

"When you soldier go into battle, you're in companies or battalions or divisions or Corps of hundreds or thousands of men marching or running towards the enemy," said Wyatte of HMS Astrea.

"You have your guns lowered and firing and your bayonets set for one-on-one combat."

"Or, you stand behind a parapet in a forward trench firing at your enemy a few yards away, and I'm willing to bet you felt alone."

"Aye, so much is true," said Mike. "We did both. And aye, if we looked enemy soldiers in their eyes, we were one-on-one."

"Well, when you are a sailor, you are part of a team. Not too different from in football, but with a much bigger team," said Jonny. "As in football, every position has a job to do. Each player, from the goalkeeper to the defenders, midfielders to the strikers, will have a set position and a specific role during

[51] "John Bowyer - WW1 memorial and Life Story." Imperial War Museum & D C Thompson.

a 90-minute football game. A match, or battle, has two teams fighting each other; each team has a captain."

"Got it," said Walt.

"In the navy, each ship is a team with engineers, stokers, gunners, helmsmen, cooks, navigators, and a captain," said Wyatte.

"At Jutland, we had 151 teams, and the Germans had 99 teams, and we were fighting each other simultaneously."

"That's many teams," said Mike. "Who makes sure they know what to do?"

"I'm glad you asked that," said Wyatt. "They grouped the 151 ships by ship types and squadrons, each with a super-captain - a commodore. And at the top was a super-super-captain, Vice-Admiral Jellicoe. He and his staff worked out where to position each group of ships for the battle to inflict the greatest damage to the other side—the 99 German ships."

"Aye, got it," said Mike. "I guess it's the same with our generals' moving battalions around a battlefield."

"They equipped each team with weapons," said Wyatte. "So the teams lined up and shot at each other like you do in battle. The smaller ships have 6-inch or 8-inch guns, the ones you know from the front. However, battleships have 13.5-inch or 15-inch guns can shoot much farther and with much more explosives when they hit. When a battleship fires its main 15-inch guns, either 8 or 16, fire at once, depending on the design; imagine that—it's horrific. And when those 15-inch shells hit their mark, the result is a total wipeout."

"Howay, man, that must be something to see," said Joe. "If you can see it with the smoke everywhere, as in our battles."

"At least you sailors don't have to live in stinking, muddy, rat-infested trenches," said Walt.

"Aye, that's true," said Wyatte. "We haven't much space, but at least we live in a warm, dry, clean space. Until your ship sinks, that is. Then it's lights out!"

"Sounds as if we lost out there," said Mike.

"Aye, it first looked like that," said Wyatte.

"Still, the Germans lost two ships they valued, the battlecruiser SMS Lützow and the light cruiser SMS Rostock, and a few others. And they had to admit they were up against a dangerous enemy in us at sea. So, since then, they have backpedalled. They'll think twice before trying that again."

From a strategic perspective, Jutland proved to be as decisive for the British as the Battle of Trafalgar on 21 October 1805. They had driven the German High Sea Fleet home, and it only went back out three more times for minor sweeps during the rest of the war. As with the French after Trafalgar, the Germans turned to commerce raiding. In his after-action report to the Kaiser on 4 July, Scheer renounced future surface encounters with the Grand Fleet. Instead, he demanded the defeat of the British economy by using the U-boats against British trade.

Although the Battle of Jutland disappointed the British public, Churchill noted that Admiral Sir John Jellicoe was "the one man who could have lost the war in an afternoon." Instead, Jutland proved Vice-Admiral Jellicoe's mettle and ended Germany's ambitions on the high seas. [52]

"I've heard that since the Admiral didn't sink more German ships, it disappointed the people at home," said Wyatte.

"The navy says he made no mistakes, and the German High Seas Fleet retreated. Defeat would have been a disaster for Britain. I'm sure we'll remember him as a great British admiral."

But the soldiers at Hamelin concluded they preferred their chances on land to drown in a freezing ocean.

§

Soon after this sea battle, Field Marshal Horatio Herbert Kitchener was to meet his end on 5 June 1916, aged sixty-five. He sailed from Scrabster to Scapa Flow in Scotland on that day aboard HMS Oak. At Scapa Flow, he transferred to the armoured cruiser HMS Hampshire to transport him on a diplomatic mission to Russia to attend negotiations. Just

---

[52] The Reader's Companion to Military History. Edited by Robert Cowley and Geoffrey Parker. Copyright © 1996

before 19:30, en route to the Russian port of Arkhangelsk during a Force 9 gale, Hampshire struck a mine west of the Orkney Islands. It sank in ten minutes. The just-launched German submarine U-75, commanded by Curt Beitzen, had laid the mine. Kitchener drowned with over 600 others. [53]

Not everyone mourned Lord Kitchener's demise. C. P. Scott, the editor of *The Manchester Guardian,* commented. "As for the old man, he could not have done better than to have gone down, as he was a great impediment of late."

Lord Northcliffe agreed: "The British Empire has just had the greatest stroke of luck in its history."

But War Correspondent Charles Repington was kinder. He acknowledged Kitchener's stature and popularity with the public. But he noted too that "his old manner of working alone did not consort with the needs of this huge syndication modern war. He made many mistakes. He was not an agreeable Cabinet man. His methods did not suit democracy [54]."

When news reached Hamelin, it provoked similar positive and negative reactions.

"Serves him right," said Mike. "As you know, I hated that toffy bastard."

---

[53] Byron Farwell, Eminent Victorian Soldiers, Norton, New York,1985
[54] Brian Best, *Reporting from the Front: War Reporters during the Great War*, Pen & Sword Military, 2015

"Aye, but he was a fine soldier and leader, Mike," said Joe. "Who knows, we may have lost the battle in South Africa without him. Look at Buller."

"Aye," said Mike, "He wasn't the gentleman Lord Roberts was."

And with that, the discussion about Lord Kitchener ended.

§

Even before any June news of Jutland or the death of Lord Kitchener reached Hamelin, the Kommandant made a special announcement at a morning roll call. The men were to leave Hamelin, destination Celle, sixty-five miles north. This news brought both exhilaration and anxiety among the prisoners. It meant the euphoria of change for a few and fear of the unknown for others. This dilemma was genuine, too, for Joe's small group of friends and the POWers football team since they had spent twenty months at Hamelin.

"I don't know whether that's agreeable news," said Joe. "After all the hours we've put into our planning."

"Aye, that's for sure," said Walt. "Let's first see where we are going. Who knows? Maybe our efforts will be of use there?"

"I heard from Klaus that it's a place called Celle; Cellelager is the camp's name," said Mike. "Sixty-five miles northeast of here."

The Germans determined the date for transferring Joe and another thirty-nine of his fellow POWs to be 17 June 1916. The men later learnt that the Germans had closed the Hamelin camp, although they never found out why.

Before Joe left Hamelin, he sent a photograph of his friends in the POWers football team home to Mary. A German photographer from Bremen, Georg Ludwig Koch, photographed them in their uniforms, with footballs on the ground in front. On the back of the photograph, the team friends were each noted in handwriting:

"Gurnett 1st Dorsets, Nicholls 4th DG (Dragoon Guards),

"Rogers *Rinaldo* HMS, Smith S Forest ND (Nottinghamshire and Derbyshire Regiment), H. Jones *Astrea* HMS, T Reeves *Rinaldo* HMS, Wyatte *Astrea* HMS, Haines Cheshires,

"H Templin HMS *Astrea*, J Franklin SoWB (South Wales Borderers), S Tallon HMS *Dwarf*,

"Dobson R Irish (Royal Irish), Lane DLI (Durham Light Infantry) and Balcham Gordon H (Gordon Highlanders)."

Joe wasn't in the photo since he had been ill and in bed on the day they took it, and he was the manager, not a player.

It was their last "official" photograph since they didn't move on to Cellelager as a complete team.

§

5. Internment at the Celle POW camp 17 June 1916—3 February 1917

Transfer from Hamelin to Celle

On 17 June, the guards awakened the Hamelin prisoners at dawn. The POWs had tea and bread and then attended the roll call as usual. The camp authorities mustered the POWs into a marching formation. They had their meagre belongings slung over their shoulders in plain cloth bags. Then, they marched through the gates of Hamelin Camp for the first time since they had arrived so many months earlier.

A fleet of open livestock trucks parked along the road awaited them. The guards then oversaw the loading of the prisoners, vehicle by vehicle, and sent them on their way to Celle.

Cellelager (Celle Camp) was another German 10th Army Corps camp a few miles from Celle at Scheuen on the Aller River. Built before the war, the Germans used the forced labour of early Russian prisoners to complete the POW camp by the end of 1914. They positioned it on sandy soil near pine forests in a scenic and peaceful region on the edge of the Lüneburger Heide or Lüneburg Heath.

The Heath is a vast scrubland, geest, and woodland area in the northeastern part of Lower Saxony in northern Germany. They derive the English term geest from the Low German word güst, which means dry and infertile. It is an Old Drift landscape characterized by the sandy deposits left over from the Ice Age. As a result, geest lands have ancient moraines and outwash plains. In the depressions between the raised flats are wet meadows with poor drainage, creating bogs. Towns of the Lüneburg Heath include Celle, Lüneburg, Munster and Soltau. Of these, only Lüneburg didn't have a POW camp.

It was a warm, lucid summer day with fluffy white clouds rolling in from the North Sea against an azure blue sky. As they drove the 66-odd miles northeast, they could see subtle changes in the landscape. Taking a wide berth around the famous Prussian city of Hanover and edging closer to the fringes of the Lüneburg Heath and Celle, they saw many changes. Large and elegant red-bricked farm buildings enhanced by oak beams and thatched roofs graced the landscape on the roads they followed. At first, the scenery was like that of the region of Hamelin. It was rolling terrain with well-cared-for farmland and pastures in the low-lying areas and forests perched on the hills. As they reached the Hanover region, the surroundings were unbroken to the horizon. It took several hours of driving with one or two brief pauses for relief. So, the prisoners had every opportunity to survey their surroundings and assess them in more detail. When they arrived at Celle, they were in a wild, unkempt expanse of grasses and heather, interspersed with birches and conifer trees such as pines and junipers.

"This region looks poor," said Joe. "No fields of grain. No woods for forestry."

"Aye, all we've seen are sheep with a few goats, cows and horses occasionally," said Mike. "Along with those huge farmhouses."

"One guard told me they have salt mines here," said Walt. "Do you suppose that is where we will work?"

"I hope not," said Joe. "I don't want to enter a mine again."

"Nor I," said Mike. "We've done enough of that in Jarrow."

"I wonder what else they could use us for?" asked Joe. "No grain farms; no forests; just sheep and mines."

"Aye, so maybe we'll be back to working in the town," said Mike.

"Or tending sheep," said Walt with a wide grin.

The summer days lasted longer, so the sun had not yet set when they arrived at Scheuen Camp. There were POW camps in Celle for both officers in the Castle (Schloss) and other ranks at Scheuen in wooden huts, one bunk above the other. The camp guards met them there, made a roll call, and allocated them to their wooden barracks. The food was much like at Hamelin, but they found the soup abominable. There was one canteen for the entire camp where inmates could buy cakes, needles, thread, buttons and apples with camp money. A football field and a theatre were available for the prisoners' amusement, but not much else. Again, the guards gave the men postcards to inform their families of their new location.

"At least our women will know where we are," said Joe. "Even if we can't be together."

"Aye, but the war continues," said Mike. "So, who knows when they'll see us again, if ever?"

"Don't despair, Laddies," said Walt. "We will make the best of this and work on our plans to go home."

"That we will," said Joe.

"For sure," said Mike. "I need to get home to see my wife and son."

The following day, their routine continued much the same as at Hamelin. There was the usual wake-up call before dawn. They washed and ate the same poor breakfast of thin soup and black bread. A roll call and assignment to their respective work parties followed, and their working day began.

Work at Celle was much like at Hamelin: road works, local maintenance projects, help for local farms, and salt mining. Six miles east of Scheuen was a salt mine called

Mariaglück near Höfer. It was a new mine opened that year to extract common salt and potash salt at a depth of nine hundred yards. It was not a favourite work assignment, even for the coal miners amongst them, because of the effects of salt. The guards preferred anyone with coal mining experience for that assignment, sending all the unhappy Durham coal miners to the salt mine.

"There are many work camps," said Joe. "One, in particular, should interest us. They call it work camp Celle VI, and it's in the peat moors at Vehnemoor, ninety miles northwest of Celle. There, they use the camp inmates to harvest peat moss. My enquiries have discovered that it's an excellent workplace and only thirty miles from the border of neutral Holland."

"That's for us," said Mike.

On his arrival, Joe wrote home, telling Mary they had transferred him to a new camp. The card had the postal address to which Mary could respond.

"Dearest Mary,

"We have arrived at a new holiday encampment—Celle Camp. More or less the same conditions as Hamelin, but with more salt. I am still active and healthy. Celle Camp, the Red Cross, and you are looking after us, so I expect we will be fine here, too.

"We have a few extra members for our football team. Everyone is keen, as always.

"Give my love and well wishes to my children. Thank you so much for their photos!

"Love you, my dear wife. Joe,"

Not being experienced miners, they assigned Joe and his marras to work for the local roads department, much as they had in Hamelin. The road works allowed them to visit Celle and smaller villages in the region.

"Celle is much the same as Hamelin," said Joe on their first visit. "Look at the houses; very like those we saw in Hamelin.

There was an enormous square in the centre of the town, which accommodated a farmers' market twice a week. The road works department never worked in the marketplace while the market was on. However, one day, a water pipe burst, and the roadworks sent the POWs to fix it. The burst pipe was in the centre of the square and caused much consternation among the farmers selling there. So, the work gang removed the cobbles and dug them down to the gushing pipe. They repaired the leak within two hours and closed the hole, leaving the relieved farmers to continue trading.

"Did you see all that food?" asked Mike.

"Aye, it brought tears to my eyes," said Walt.

"Amazing," said Joe. "There don't seem to be any shortages here."

"Look what they feed us instead," said Mike.

"It's a bloody disgrace," said Joe. "They treat us worse than their animals!"

"Thank God for the Red Cross and our families," said Walt. "We'd starve otherwise."

§

Football and Betting Re-established in Celle

The transferred POWers men reconstituted the team in Cellelager with a few of the Hamelin team members and the rest of the recruits. They soon settled into their Sunday football routine within an existing camp league, which injected renewed enthusiasm into an old pastime.

"I miss the old team," said Mike. "Still, it's grand to have another team together here. A few of these new chaps are excellent players."

"Aye. It's a talented team," said Joe. "We just need to practise and get in as many games as possible."

"It's great to be playing again," said Walt. "It keeps us fit. Well, as fit as we POWs can get, anyway."

Having transferred in June, they had the entire summer to practise and play on Sundays. But their sport didn't interfere with their plans to escape. One evening, the marras met in secret outside their cabin.

"We need to start all over," said Joe.

"Aye, but our situation here is like at Hamelin," said Walt. "We are outside the town, so we need not worry about being seen among many people. But they guard the camp well, so we need to find a way of getting out without them noticing for a few hours. We all need to look out for that, but I'll find a map and look at a likely route to Holland."

"We need to get out on more jobs to check out the neighbourhood," said Mike.

"Let's keep our eyes and ears open," said Joe. "We might get a few good clues or suggestions. And we mustn't forget Vehnemoor as a possibility."

§

Soon after Joe's group arrived at Celle, news circulated through new prisoners from the Front of a recent Allied attack on German lines in the River Somme region. The British called it the Big Push again, launched at 7:30 A.M. on 1 July 1916 across the River Somme. With the French Army battling the Germans at Verdun, the British aimed to break through the northern German defences in hours, offering relief for the French at Verdun.

The Allies prepared 19 mines for the first day of the Somme. They comprised a series of underground explosive charges planted in secret by tunnelling companies of the Royal Engineers digging beneath the German front lines on the Western Front. These companies made two significant contributions to the opening attack of the Battle of the Somme. First, by preparing the mines. Second, by organizing a series of shallow Russian saps[55] from the British front line into no-man's-land. This allows the infantry to attack the German positions at Zero Hour. The 19 mines comprised eight huge and eleven lesser charges deep in the chalky ground. These were "overcharged" to throw up top lips of the earth for screening and to give an advantage to the attackers when they captured the resulting craters [56].

Joe met and talked to prisoners arriving from that battle.

"Hello, soldier," said Joe to one of them. "From where are you arriving?"

"Hello, my friend. My name is Simon, and I've just arrived from the Battle of the Somme," said the new prisoner. "Have you heard of that one?"

"Good to meet you, Simon," said Joe. "Aye, I have heard of it. One of your companions I just talked to told me the British detonated huge mines and bombarded the lines for an entire week. That must have helped?"

---

[55] Sapping is a term used in siege operations to describe the digging of a covered trench (a "sap") to approach a besieged place without danger from the enemy's fire. The purpose of the sap is usually to advance a besieging army's position towards a fortification.

[56] Jones, Simon (2010). Underground Warfare 1914-1918. Barnsley: Pen & Sword Books.

"Aye, they did," said Simon. "The bombardment and mines were horrific, but they did their job. And we expected them to reduce the number of Boche. At 7:28 A.M. on the first day of the battle, two minutes before the attack, we detonated two gigantic mines. One was called Lognagar, and the other 'Y Sap'. They were under a German field fortification known as Schwabenhöhe (Swabian Heights) near the village of La Boisselle," said Simon. "We were right there."

The Lochnagar mine, named after Lochnagar Street, the trench from which they dug the gallery, used 60,000 pounds of explosives. Y Sap contained 40,000 pounds of explosives. The bombs caused massive eruptions, and they considered the sound of them the loudest human-made noise in history. Reports suggest people heard it as far away as London. [57] The blast of Lochnagar left a crater 98 feet deep and 330 feet wide, which British troops captured and held. A Royal Flying Corps pilot reported a column of earth from the explosions reached 4,000 feet into the sky. But, despite every effort by the British to conceal the burrowing, the Germans heard the British tunnelling and moved their machine guns. [58]

"The Germans were still there," said Simon. "There was no sign they were weaker, even though the mines killed many of them. Those that survived just slaughtered us with

---

[57] Waugh, I., "WW1 Trip to the Somme." Old British News. Archived from the original on 19 October 2014.
[58] Norman Ferguson, The First World War – A miscellany, Summersdale Publishers, Chichester, UK, 2014

their bloody machine guns, hundreds of them! It was terrible. Our artillery increased the number of shells, and the German guns opened up on no-man's-land. It was deafening; the fumes were choking me, and we couldn't see well because of the dust and clouds caused by exploding shells. It was hell on earth. I thought they would blow me to pieces. As I was walking, I saw my mates dropping into the mud ahead and on both sides. I didn't know how long I would live. It was a nightmare, and I don't know whether my fellow soldiers are still alive."

"Well, Laddie. I have met a few arriving here," said Joe. "So, keep searching; you may find your mates. Oh, and be careful of what you call the Boche. They get upset over words like Hun."

"Have you been in the trenches, soldier?" asked Simon

"Aye, for a brief time in September '14," said Joe. "We were in the first trenches of the war on the Aisne. But they didn't protect us much. They had dug them quickly before we arrived, and they were so shallow we couldn't hide or protect ourselves very well. I believe your trenches are now much better."

"I suppose so," said Simon. "Hundreds of miles of them are now dug from the North Sea to the Swiss border. And our trenches aren't simple anymore. They are complex rabbit warrens with a front-line trench, a support trench behind that and a reserve trench behind that one, linked by communication trenches. They are at least 8 feet deep to protect men and allow them to walk upright. These trenches are never straight but dug in a zigzagging or stepped pattern, with straight sections kept less than a dozen yards. We had combat trenches broken into fire bays connected by traverses. While these block the view of our soldiers along the trench, it ensures the enemy can't enfilade the line; if a bomb, grenade, or shell lands in the trench, the blast doesn't travel as far. And sometimes we dig a trench into no-man's-land as a listening post."

"We had an enfilade or two on the Aisne and a few accidents where our men fired on our men farther forward," said Joe.

"Grenades and shells exploding in or behind our trenches were an enormous problem. It was chaotic. I didn't think I'd live through it."

"Aye, it can be chaotic for sure," said Simon. "We build our trenches much better now. We dig them deep, revet the sides of our trenches with sandbags, wire mesh or wooden frames, and build shooting steps into firing bays off the trench. We cover the floor of the trench with wooden duckboards. In wetter places, we raise the floor on a wooden frame under which we make drainage channels. We call the banked earth on the lip of our trenches facing the enemy the parapet. And to protect us from shells exploding behind us, we have higher embanked rear lips of the trenches called the parados."

"Ours were nowhere as good as that," said Joe. "We couldn't stand or even sit. We had to crawl everywhere; eating, relieving ourselves and facing the enemy was awkward. We often lay in mud and water and had no protection when shooting our rifles. And we had to sleep in it, too."

"Well, we now have dugouts built from 8 to 16 feet into the rear of the support trench," said Simon.

"The best dugouts are the officers' offices, dining rooms and bedrooms. And we have firing bays where we can shoot when standing."

"Howay, you laddies had it better than we did early in the war, that is for sure," said Joe. "How much time do you face the enemy?" asked Joe.

"Our time in a front-line trench is often short, maybe from as little as one day to two weeks at a time before being relieved," said Simon.

"Then we spend time in the support line, reserve line, or resting well behind the lines. We spend a quarter of our time on other non-fighting activities such as hospital, travelling, home leave, and training courses. It's very organized these days and not too bad as long as they don't send you over the top. Then your chances of living are much reduced."

"How is it on the Western Front, now?" asked Joe. "How dangerous is it?"

"During the day, snipers and artillery observers in balloons made movement dangerous, so the trenches are quiet," said Simon.

"It was during these daytime hours that we amused ourselves in various ways, for example, reading or playing cards. Because of the danger of daytime activities, trenches are busiest at night when darkness allows the movements of troops and supplies. We also maintain and expand the barbed wire and trench complex or do reconnaissance of the enemy's defences at night. Sentries in listening posts out in no-man's-land listen for enemy patrols and working parties, or any clues the enemy is preparing for an attack, such as digging tunnels."

"They moved my battalion from our billets at the town of Albert into the trenches a few days before the attack, close to La Boisselle. There two of the largest explosions, Lognagar and Y Sap, happened," said Simon.

"So, there we were on the day of the attack. One thousand nervous British soldiers packed into every front line, support, reserve and communication trench, waiting for our turn to attack the enemy. First, at 7:20 A.M., we heard an enormous explosion in the distance. I've since heard it was at Hawthorn Ridge, and somebody set it off early. That explosion alerted the Boche that something was afoot, so they were waiting for us. Then, at 7:28, all along the line, the rest of the mines exploded."

"How did they do those explosions?" asked Joe.

"185 Tunnelling Company started the tunnel for the Lochnagar mine on 11 November last year," said Simon.

"179 Tunnelling Company, who took over in March this year, completed it. They sank the shaft for the Lochnagar mine in the communication trench called Lochnagar Street. It was a deep incline shaft, meaning that they didn't drop straight down but sloped it with a decline of between 1:2 and 1:3 to a depth of 95 feet. They started it 300 feet behind the British front line and 900 feet from the German front line. Then, they built the gallery and filled it with 60,000 pounds of explosives.

"They say we bombarded the German lines with one million seven hundred thousand shells for a week before the Battle of the Somme began on 1 July. They meant this bombardment to destroy the German barbed wire defences and trenches."

The Army delivered 5,000 tons of ammunition daily for the British guns during the offensive. However, because of poor manufacturing practices, thirty percent of the rounds didn't explode, so they left the German fortifications intact to a great extent. [59] For transportation from the railheads to where they had concentrated the masses of troops and guns, the British relied on motor vehicles to replenish supplies; this was slow and insufficient. They carried 20,000 long tons (at

[59] Norman Ferguson, *The First World War – A miscellany*, Summersdale Publishers, Chichester, UK, 2014

2,240 pounds per long ton) daily during the attacks along a 12-mile front [60].

"When the whistles blew at 7:30 A.M., thousands of us climbed out of the trenches, clambered over the top and walked insanely toward the German line," said Simon.

"The Germans opened fire with every gun, machine gun and rifle they could find. That's when the slaughter started—7:30 A.M. on 1 July. They told us to go over the parapet's top and walk towards the Hun. Walk! So, when the whistles blew over the top, we went. One after the other, we obeyed our orders and walked into the killing field; the Boche mowed our boys down with machine guns like pigeons. That was the worst day of my life. I don't know how many survived that first day. But I know I lost most of my mates. I was lucky, I guess. A blast knocked me unconscious, and the Hun captured me. So now I'm here, grateful and guilty to be alive because so many died; thousands!"

After the first day, with a gain of only one mile, the British suffered over 57,000 casualties, including some 19,000 fatalities. But despite this carnage, the British High Command under Field Marshal Haig was unwilling to reverse their plan.

"I can't believe what's going on over there," said Mike when Joe informed his companions of the first day of the

---

[60] Henniker, A. M., *Transportation on the Western Front 1914–1918*, (2009) [1937].

Somme Offensive. "We had it bad enough. But nineteen thousand men killed on the first day? The generals have lost their minds."

"Aye, Mike, it was a terrible massacre," said Joe. "The soldier Simon I talked to was in shock. He explained everything in detail, repeating how they went over the top and walked toward the enemy. Walked! He said it was horrific."

"What about those mines?" asked Walt. "They say they were the most massive explosions in history."

"Aye, can you believe it?" said Joe. "They say they heard it in London, 200 miles away!"

They called this first of many battles on the Somme the Battle of Albert. They named it after one of the principal French towns behind the British lines. It lasted from 1 to 13 July. Thirteen British and 11 French divisions fought against 6 German divisions, resulting in 107,000 Allied and 55,000 German casualties.

But the slaughter at the Somme continued for eleven more battles.

"I've met a few South Africans arriving from the Somme," said Joe one evening. "The Germans captured them at the Battle of Delville Wood, the third battle of the Somme Offensive from 15 July to 3 September. They are from the 1st South African Infantry Brigade and are arriving in large numbers. They told me a few painful stories of what they had experienced in that little forest on the Somme."

Empire and War

"What did they tell you, Joe?" asked Walt.

"Well, they said that two weeks after the launch of the Somme Offensive, the Battle of Delville Wood started on 15 July," said Joe.

"It was between the armies of Germany and South Africa at Bois d'Elville. It was a thick stand of trees east of Longueval on the Somme. The Australian troops translated the name of this place into Delville Wood. It started during the second battle on the Somme, the Battle of Bazentin Ridge, on 14 July. General Douglas Haig, Commander of the BEF, planned to seize the German positions between Delville Wood and Bazentin le Petit."

"The 1st South African Infantry Brigade made its Western Front entry into the war as part of the 9th (Scottish) Division under the command of Brigadier-General Henry Lukin. It captured Delville Wood on 15 July. They held the wood until 19 July but at a high cost in casualties. But once occupied by the Brigade, the Germans tried to retake the lost ground more than once. But we defeated them since massive defensive firepower had turned a battlefield into a soggy wetland of mud."

The battle achieved its goal and was a decisive victory for the British, but it was costly in lives. British attacks and German counterattacks on the wood continued for seven weeks. By the end of this fight on 3 September, the number of South Africans dead was 2,500. One hundred twenty-one officers and over 3,000 other ranks formed the Brigade on the morning of 14 July. Only 29 officers and 751 other ranks were present at roll call when they gathered the unit a few weeks later. It ended just before the Battle of Flers–Courcelette (15–17 September), the seventh British general attack in the Battle of the Somme.

That was only one of the hundreds of engagements that raged during the Battle of the Somme.

§

The British Introduce a Formidable New Weapon

News soon arrived in the camp of a historic battle involving a new British weapon.

"I've just heard of another battle on the Somme, which involved a new British weapon they call a tank," announced Joe one day. "They are saying it was historic."

"What the hell is a tank weapon?" asked Mike.

"I'm not sure, but from what they've told me, it's a huge armoured vehicle with a gun and other weapons mounted on it," said Joe.

"They say it can crush the barbed wire defences and cross over trenches."

"How can it do that?" asked Walt.

"A soldier from that battle told me they are long armoured vehicles with a new mechanism of tracks for moving it forward," said Joe. "It can cross over or even crush machine-gun nests,"

"I can't imagine it," said Mike. "It sounds dangerous."

"Aye, that it is for sure," said Joe.

"They say it will change land warfare in the future. My contact told me the Battle of Flers–Courcelette launched on 15 September. It was the seventh assault fought during the Somme Offensive by the French Sixth Army and the British Fourth Army against the German 1st Army. It inflicted so many casualties on the German front divisions, and the capture of the villages of Courcelette, Martinpuich, and Flers was a major victory for the British. Still, the German defensive success on the British right flank made wider use of our secret weapon and the cavalry impossible."

The British used tanks in this battle for the first time in history. The Canadian Corps and the New Zealand Division fought for the first time on the Somme. Their crews gave names to their vehicles, such as Chablis, Champagne, Daredevil 1, and Diehard. The Mark I tank weighed 28 tons and moved forward at a top speed of 3.7 mph. It provided shelter for infantry troops falling in behind them when attacking the enemy. Conditions for the crew inside the vehicle, with an exposed engine and uncertain ventilation, were unfavourable. They categorized tanks with 6-pounder guns as males, while those with only machine guns were females. [61] The tanks took the Imperial Army by surprise. However, the Germans fought back, destroyed many tanks by artillery fire, and damaged others with armour-piercing bullets fired from rifles and machine guns. Of the thirty-two tanks capable of launching the first attack, only nine made it across no-man's-land to the German lines.

After a fierce battle, the British gained 2,500 yards overall and captured High Wood, moving forward 3,500 yards in the centre, beyond Flers and Courcelette. Fourth Army troops crossed Bazentin Ridge, exposing the German rear-slope defences beyond ground observation. They considered the attack successful and a British victory because the Allies won 4,000 yards of the third position and the intermediate line. But that wasn't the end of the Battle of the Somme.

The British began arrangements at once to follow up on the tactical progress of the Battle of Flers–Courcelette by launching another battle. After supply and weather delays, the Battle of Morval started on 25 September, and the Reserve Army continued the next day at the Battle of Thiepval Ridge. September was the most costly month of the Battle of the Somme for the German armies, which suffered about 130,000 casualties. With the German losses at the Somme, Verdun and on the Eastern Front, the Allies brought the German

---

[61] Norman Ferguson, *The First World War: A Miscellany*, Summersdale, Chichester, UK, 2014

Empire closer to military collapse. However, the Allies didn't achieve their strategic aim of a decisive victory.

"A British victory," announced Joe to his companions when the news arrived. "They consider the Battle of Flers–Courcelette a British victory. Our new secret weapon won the day!"

"I'd drink to that," said Mike. "If I had a beer."

"That's a winning bet for me," said Walt.

§

First Sea Lord Winston Churchill sponsored the project to develop the tank, which was financed from the Navy budget. In February 1915, he appointed the Landships Committee, which oversaw the design and production of the first British tanks. The Chairman of this committee was Eustace Tennyson d'Eyncourt, Director of Naval Construction at the Admiralty. Minister of Munitions Churchill continued to support the landship project that could "revolutionize land-based combat." This development was the most revolutionary advance since introducing the cavalry horse 3,000 years earlier! And the British needed it since the cavalry had become helpless with the launch of the machine gun.

They built the first tank vehicle, nicknamed Little Willie, in August and September 1915 at William Foster & Company. Foster's was an agricultural machinery company based in

Lincolnshire. They showed the prototype of the new Mark I Tank to the British Army on 2 February 1916. First called Landships by the Landships Committee, they nicknamed production vehicles "tanks" to preserve secrecy. Factory workers referred to the prototype as the tank because it resembled a steel water tank. The name stuck. The first use of the forty-nine Mark I Tank shipped to the battlefield was at the Battle of Flers-Courcelette on the Somme on 15 September 1916. Many assaults didn't make it, but a third attack crossed the line. The Army rushed the tanks into this battle too soon against the wishes of Winston Churchill and tank developer Major-General Ernest Swinton. However, the fight provided valuable design feedback and clues about their potential to affect the war's course.

§

Second Anniversary as POWs—20th of October 1916

The 20th of October 1916 came and went, leaving Joe and his mates depressed by their unchanging lot. They had been POWs for two years, and there was still no end to the war foreseeable. The Germans had used them in work parties since arriving in the camp, but they earned next to nothing. Cellelager issued coupons to use in the canteen, but these had no other value.

They perceived that the Germans now doubted the Kaiser's promised historic victory. News from their families and friends on the streets was becoming bleaker. Morale was faltering even more than hitherto for everyone within the camp. German civilians suffered from constant negative news from the Fronts, and specific supplies dwindled in the shops. The war was taking its toll on everyone.

Within their small circle of trusted friends, talk of escape was cropping up more often than ever. They longed to return home. Late one night after lights out, Joe, Mike and Walt huddled in their corner of the cabin and spoke in low tones.

"I've had enough of this," said Joe, "I need to get home to my family."

"Aye, I agree," said Mike. "It doesn't look like a camp for a simple escape. Look at the fence, the guard towers and the lights! How can we get past all of that?"

"True," said Walt. "The problem is, we're 160 miles from the border. That's a long way to go without being noticed. But my investigations have found there may be another way out."

"How?" asked Joe.

"By getting transferred to Cellelager VI at Vehnemoor," said Walt. "That camp is thirty miles from the Dutch border in empty moorland. I've heard it might be easier to escape from there."

"How do we get to Vehnemoor?" asked Mike.

"Easy. We need to wangle a work transfer," said Walt. "I'll talk to the guard and tell them we want to get to a smaller camp if possible."

"Is Cellelager VI a smaller camp?" asked Joe.

"Very much so," said Walt.

"Well, then, it's worth a try!"

"Yes, but we need to find a map. The guard told me Vehnemoor is near Bremen and Oldenburg, the Dutch border and the North Sea."

Mike accepted that challenge, and Joe proposed he work with Walt to get the transfer.

"We must be careful," Joe said. "They mustn't think we are trying to wangle anything other than a change of scenery and work."

The rest agreed and set about their tasks. It took a while. The marras enquired about Vehnemoor and hinted they might be available to work there if the Kommandant needed them. True to form, Mike found a prisoner who had been to Vehnemoor a few times and had worked throughout that region. He sketched a simple map for him from memory.

§

Despite the massive losses, Field Marshal Haig persisted with the Somme Offensive until 19 November 1916. When they ended the offensive, the British were still three miles short of Bapaume and Serre, part of their planned first-day objectives! The Battle of the Somme resulted in total losses on the British side of 420,000 men; the French casualties numbered 200,000, and German casualties numbered 450,000 to 680,000 men!

"More than a million troop casualties!" scoffed Mike when they heard of it. "A million soldiers mean nothing to those bloody bastards, nothing!" He was angry!

"How is this possible?" asked Joe. "We know how terrible it can be over there, but that's unhinged. Loopy!"

"We are in another world, Laddies," said Walt. "There has been nothing as insane as this war!"

§

On 18 December 1916, the Battle of Verdun ended. The most protracted single battle of the War had raged between the French and Germans near Verdun in Eastern France for nine months, three weeks and six days. Launched on 2 February 1916, the Battle of Verdun was part of an unsuccessful German campaign to take the offensive on the Western Front. The Battle of Verdun was one of the most violent events of the Great War. It's remembered as the "battlefield with the highest density of dead per square yard." [62] At its conclusion, despite a million casualties and vast quantities of munitions spent, neither side had gained any more territory.

This news travelled fast through the French portions of the camp. Joe heard this news on the following Sunday, Christmas Eve.

"My God," said Walt when he heard it. "Another million casualties. This year has been horrific! Two of the biggest battles were on land, and one was at sea—Verdun, the Somme, and Jutland. Millions of British, Canadians,

---

[62] Horne, A., The Price of Glory: Verdun 1916 (Penguin repr. ed. [1962]). London, 2007

Australians, New Zealanders, Indians, French and Germans dead! We are witnessing the end of the world as we knew it, Laddies."

"Aye, wounded or captured millions more," said Mike.

"How did we get into this shite predicament?" asked Walt.

"Well, I can tell you what I know about how we got here," said Joe.

"I followed it and made notes, and I can tell you about it if you want, but it may take a while."

The men wanted to hear it, and Joe told them how the Great War started and upset so many lives back in 1914.

"Yes, but don't blame us if we cry," said Mike.

§

Memories of Peace in 1914

"I thought England had changed when I returned from Africa and India in 1906, but by early 1914, we were living in a completely different world," said Joe.

"The Royal Family, the British Army and the Royal Navy kept the old Victorian traditions of pomp and ceremony without change. We still had the grand events of the British Empire, such as the military parades, coronations and Durbars. But so much else had changed since Queen Victoria passed.

Empire and War

"Before we left for South Africa in Queen Victoria's time in 1899, we lived in a quiet, simple world. We got around on foot or in horse-drawn or steam trams. The wealthy got around on horseback or in horse-drawn carriages. While we were there, South Africa had no automobiles, just horses, horse-drawn carts, trams, and trains - armoured trains. Rushing electric trams, automobiles, trucks, and motorbikes surrounded us when we returned to Edwardian Britain in 1906 from India. They were becoming more common on the streets. Instead of steam, these modern vehicles use petroleum. By 1914, they had replaced many horse-powered means of transport, and we saw the most amazing change with aeroplanes and airships flying over Tyneside. Even the means of communication were changing."

The most critical Victorian-era technologies were the steam engine and the telegraph. Land transportation during the early Victorian Era used age-old means like horses, mules or oxen. However, steam-driven locomotives, ships, and traction vehicles took over during the Victorian Era, and we still use them in public transport, industry, and agriculture. Steam engines drove many sectors. Steam-driven ships and railways allowed much faster transport of materials and products to and from the four corners of the globe. And look at the telephone. It has changed long-distance communication and allows the Government to control the far reaches of the vast British Empire from London via cables deep in the oceans. So much has changed how we do things.

These inventions typified the Edwardian world of the early 20th century, but technological experimentation and development were speeding up by then, creating a far more mechanized and modernized world. These technological advances significantly impacted the world of work, home life and leisure time.

In 1876, Alexander Graham Bell was the first inventor to be granted a United States patent for a device replicating the human voice over the wires. Many others further developed this instrument. The telephone was the first device in history that enabled people to talk with each other over interminable distances. Although the US led the introduction and use of phones in the latter part of the 19th century, the UK followed suit. And its use sped up during the Edwardian era. They regard the period between 1912 and 1914 as pivotal when they further developed telephone technology and trunks in Britain. As tensions with Germany increased, Britain needed a sophisticated telephone network to enable faster communication. The wealthy merchant classes had private phones installed early to better communicate with their business interests. But from 1912, many aristocrats and gentry installed telephones, too. They were installing more and more phones in private homes. Then, they set up call offices in public places such as railway stations and general stores, introducing the working classes to the technology. It hadn't replaced the telegraph, but the modern telephone added a whole extra dimension to communications.

Many more valuable inventions appeared during this period, too, with a dramatic impact on business and leisure activities. The American Eastman Kodak Company introduced the Brownie camera in 1900. Costing $1[63], it opened photography for the common man. The Edwardians invented the first electric typewriter, the first radio receiver in 1901, and the neon lamp in 1902 and by 1914, they were in widespread use. In 1906, the Victor Talking Machine Company released the Victrola, a famous gramophone model for the next two decades. In 1907, Thomas Edison invented the Universal Electric Motor, which had enormous potential for future uses; by 1914, many trams, trains, and industrial machinery used electric motors. Oscar Gregory developed the Photostat machine, beginning the modern era of document imaging; King George V later used this machine to distribute mass personalized handwritten communications with individual soldiers and subjects. The B. F. Goodrich Company created the hookless fastener, renamed the Zipper, in 1913. A tsunami of inventions and new products was being introduced to markets and taken up by consumers at an astonishing rate.

---

[63] The equivalent of $29.89 in 2018

"The changes we were experiencing were so valuable, don't you think?" asked Joe then. "Sure, many of those changes helped the upper classes more than us. But our lives have also improved, don't you think?

"When King Edward died, his son, King George V, followed him. Most of us didn't know then that King George V of Britain, Kaiser Wilhelm II of Germany and Tsar Nicholas II of Russia were cousins. They were all grandsons of Queen Victoria and all competing to be the Top Dogs of Europe.

"Those of us in the shipyards of 1914 witnessed first-hand what they called the arms race with Germany. We were building so many more warships in the Tyneside shipyards. So much was changing with our laws, and unions and the labour movement had grown strong. I can still remember that night in early 1914 at the Rolling Mill Pub when we discussed our feelings on the changes happening on Tyneside.

"Mike, you said you liked the old days of Queen Victoria and King Edward and the peace we enjoyed among ourselves. It's one thing fighting an enemy, but do we need to fight amongst ourselves, too? Why do we need labour movements and unions and the socialists? I know they mean well to do the right thing for us, but they are causing too much trouble. You couldn't walk to the pub in the evenings without them approaching you and pushing a protest notice, a strike placard, or whatever on you. Arguments on things that never worried us are happening between brothers and friends. Why? I, for one, didn't like it!"

"I said that, and I know what you mean," said Mike. "At least in the old days, we knew where we stood and who our friends and enemies were. Before the war, you never knew. One day, you could have a friendly conversation with a marra. The next day, he shouted at you because you wouldn't join a labour meeting or a picket line! So much was changing. And it happened so fast!"

"That is for sure," said Walt. "But was it not for the better? Automobiles, horseless trucks and motorized bikes make moving around quicker and easier. We can say the same about aeroplanes, although all these machines became dangerous in the wrong hands in this war."

"The arms race between Britain and Germany led to more warships and weapons. Many more! And it has spread to the rest of Europe, hasn't it?" I said.

The region's powers devoted their industrialized resources to manufacturing equipment and weapons for a pan-European conflict. Between 1908 and 1913, the military spending of the European powers increased by fifty percent. The increased investment of the Royal Navy and its allies meant that Tyneside and the other shipbuilding regions of Britain were booming and optimistic in the summer of 1914. There were fourteen shipyards along the Tyne, building vessels from massive luxury liners such as RMS Mauretania to tugboats, ferries, wherries and warships—lots of naval ships! From 1910 to 1913, Joe's employer, Hawthorne Leslie, commissioned over thirty vessels, of which a third were destroyers. They said that at Palmers Yard in Jarrow, "iron ore went in one end, and a battleship came out the other." Swan Hunter of Wallsend, on the opposite bank of the river, was one of the best-known shipbuilding companies in the world. It held the world record for gross shipping tonnage constructed per year. In 1913 alone, the Tyneside shipyards completed 100 ships, many of them warships.

At the heart of this industrial district flowed the River Tyne, swarming with ships and smaller vessels. Massive wooden staithes stood high above the docks, the filling points for 20 million tons of coke for transport to 400 ports worldwide. As Britain's primary fuel, coal production and its use had increased since the mid-nineteenth century. Coal exports were a prime source of income for the British economy.

Behind the staithes, shipyards, and docks were scores of engineering workshops and factories. They varied from ironworks and chemical plants to roperies and potteries, visible for miles by their columns of smoke by day and the flares of their furnaces by night. They produced much of the four million pounds of manufactured goods, leaving Tyneside by the river yearly. Only a tenth as much came the other way. Newcastle-Elswick, with the Armstrong Works and Shipyard and other plants, was the north bank home to Europe's most prominent industrial complex.

The booming shipyards and burgeoning coal pits and factories could offer jobs for every able-working man in the region. It was a time when men laboured with their backs and hands while women stayed at home, cooked and raised families. Families were extensive, and the weekly round of washing, cooking and cleaning dominated women's lives. The works' siren defined men's lives. They lived in cobbled streets lined with new terrace flats. These terraces were uniform two-storey dwellings, with each floor having its entrance and household. They were tiny living quarters, and thanks to the boom, Jarrow was one of England's most congested urban areas.

So, by 1914, life for the working and middle classes in Great Britain and Europe was flourishing and peaceful on the surface. The industrial towns were bustling, and there was full employment. The workers left their terraced homes early in the morning with their lunch boxes and returned to their wives and families in the evenings. Life for them was arduous but stable and predictable. Food was on the table in most homes but the poorest and most unfortunate. Thanks to various reforms, life improved for many, including children and the aged.

Newcastle had upscale department stores and enough cinema and theatre seats to cater for visitors at least once a week. There was plenty of open space and parkland for recreation. Two hundred electric trams carried a million passengers a year in Newcastle alone. And the route to the coast had the country's first electric train outside London, luring day-trippers to the beaches in their thousands on summer bank holidays.

The emerging middle classes emulated the wealthy and focussed on the welfare and education of their children. For them, too, life had become predictable and pleasant. The rich enjoyed a whirlwind existence of fancy balls, soirées, garden parties in summer and the hunt in winter. They sent their sons to Britain's best schools and universities and educated their daughters to become the best wives for privileged men. Their lives mirrored the comfortable and predictable lives of their ancestors.

The English countryside in 1914 was still the long-established patchwork of walled or hedged fields broken occasionally with dark copses or forests and interspersed with ancient villages. Seasonal patterns such as the planting, caring for, and harvesting of crops governed life in agricultural areas and made employment possible for many. Theirs was a peaceful existence steeped in tradition and regional customs, living off the land with abundant food. Horses were still the primary means of transport and beasts of burden. Yet, one heard of internal combustion automobiles in the countryside more and more since the estate owners and gentry bought them. And in the fields, petroleum-powered tractors replaced Victorian horse teams and steam-powered traction engines.

The same was true of the grand houses and country estates with their armies of domestic staff, gardeners and farm workers. Life had been this way for centuries with minimal change. It was a peaceful and fulfilling existence.

§

"Little did I or those around me know how our world would soon change so completely, as for millions of others across Britain and Europe," said Joe.

"With my job in the yards in the summer of 1914, we weren't well off, but we had enough. We had settled into a pleasant family lifestyle in Jarrow. My Jarrow marras and I from the Boer War became active reservists in the 2nd Battalion of the Durham Light Infantry. We attended regular meetings and other events related to that regiment at the Newcastle and South Shields depots. The nickname of this regiment is 'The Faithful Durhams,' and we belonged to that spirit. And every summer, we made one or two big family outings to the beach at South Shields."

Outings to the beach were always a special event for the Rutherfords, as for the other working-class families of Tyneside. They only happened once or twice a year in the spring and summer during pleasant weather, but not always

Empire and War

on the same days. In July 1914, the Rutherfords joined in the escape from industrial Jarrow once again, just as they had before Joe and his marras departed for South Africa. The women prepared picnic lunches while the men gathered the children and any implements such as beach pails, shovels, and other sports items needed for such an occasion. On this Sunday, everyone forgot their worries and dressed up in their best clothes as always. The men wore their best shoes, suits and straw boater hats, and the women dressed up in their Sunday finery, including their fancier straw women's hats. As usual, they told the children to wear beach clothes under their Sunday attire. They had one of their infrequent baths the night before and looked their Sunday best. The last thing on the Rutherfords' minds was the trouble brewing in Europe. Then, they headed off as a family in high spirits to the train station. The men carried the lunches and any bags of extras packed by the women.

Joe, his wife Mary, his young son John, his infant daughter Violet, three brothers, six sisters, and their children gathered for the occasion. But besides the Rutherfords this year, most of the Mary's Burgess family was joining them, as were Mike, Ruth, Jack and Fred. Among the Burgesses were Mary's brothers, John Robert, William Souter, James and Harry. Most of her sisters joined them, too.

At the station, the working men bought return tickets for the family to South Shields. Then they waited for the new electric train that soon appeared, making its way into the station much quieter than the old steam locomotive. It was a lovely sunny day, and everyone was excited for the day ahead.

South Shields is a coastal town on the south side of the mouth of the River Tyne, four miles downstream from Jarrow. In a peninsula setting where the River Tyne meets the North Sea, it has six miles of the North Sea coastline and three miles of riverfrontage. The massive North and South Piers dominate the mouth of the Tyne. The Leas comprise long beaches, dunes and coves, and dramatic limestone cliffs topped by a grassy expanse. They cover three miles of the coastline. It was a favourite Sunday destination of the miners and shipbuilders of the South Tyne urban and industrial sprawl.

From the South Shields railway station to the beach was half a mile, a pleasant walk along Ocean Road on such a lovely day. But this wasn't a quiet outing alone. The train was full of hundreds more labourers and their families. It was deafening to hear the screams and laughter of children and the shouts of parents admonishing their behaviour in public. They packed the station as they poured out of the train for the stroll along Ocean Road to the beach. The beach was so packed that there was no place free to move unless you arrived early. But nobody minded this. Relaxed and not working, they had a lovely time with family and friends, away from the daily routine. Life was enjoyable on Sundays in England in the summer of 1914.

But much had changed since their outing in 1900, just before Joe left for the South African War. For a start, the adults were fourteen years older, and the fashions had changed. Joe was now thirty-three years old, and his eldest brother was forty-four. The women wore the more elegant working-class clothes of the time with long flowing skirts and enormous hats. The men dressed much the same as before but with slight improvements to their suits and hats. But what stood out most was the plethora of motorized vehicles becoming more widespread. Many grand chauffeur-driven tourer cars and limousines from companies such as Wolseley and Rolls Royce drove refined gentlemen and ladies as owners and passengers to their destinations. But there were many less expensive self-driven cars on the roads of 1914 England. These included the AC (Auto Carriers), Vauxhall, Morgan, Calcott, Calthorpe, and the Ford Model T introduced from America in 1911, to mention but a few. There were many motorcycles, bicycles and horse-drawn carriages on the roads, too. Together, they created a din that rose above the usual hubbub of the town on weekends such as this. 1914 was no doubt much noisier on the roads than 1900.

They joined the hoards at the beach, but not before agreeing on a meeting place should anyone get lost in the crowd. The children tore off their outer layer of clothes and raced to the water's edge. The parents shouted reminders not to venture too far into the water and to stay together since none could swim. Then, the adults flung off their shoes and socks. The men rolled up their trousers and the women their skirts. Then they wandered into the frigid water at the beach's edge, watching the children. The younger adult women, such as Ellinor and Elizabeth, twenty-eight and twenty-five, had worn tight-fitting full-torso swimsuits under their dresses. They could throw themselves into the breaking waves further out into the sea.

After an hour of playing on the beach, they retired to the Marine Park to find a quieter spot for lunch. Finding just such a lovely place under a tree, the women spread the picnic blankets and emptied the contents of the lunch baskets into the centre. Then, everyone gathered around to enjoy the goodies the women had prepared for the picnic.

After lunch, the children played on the lawns of the Marine Park within sight of the adults lolling away the afternoon. They had no reason to worry. Prosperity boomed in Tyneside, and they ignored the usual political distractions of these troubled days with ominous clouds building in Europe.

The men distanced themselves from the women and children and addressed the current events and rumours. It was unavoidable.

"We're not gonna have a war," said my eldest brother, William. "It's a European problem!"

"I agree," said George.

"Well, I've learned that Britain has an alliance with Belgium, and if the Germans attack Belgium, we have to help them."

"There's so much talk, I don't know what to believe," said William, irritated by the word of potential troubles.

"Our government can't be that sackless [64]," said George. "Surely they know what their people want, not war."

"Our regiment is ready for whatever happens," I said. "And so am I if needed."

"And here we go again, young man," said William. "Didn't you learn your lesson with that last war? And what will become of your family?"

"I'm hardly a young man, William. I've lived through one war, and I won't have much choice," I said. "As a reservist, I'm on call."

"Da said it right years ago. You should never have joined the army!" said William.

"Now you think you are my Da?"

Since it was a family argument, Mike, Jack and Fred kept out of it even though they were on Joe's side. Joe got the last word on that topic.

---

[64] Geordie for lacking braveness, boldness, assertiveness.

"We must support our King and country no matter what happens. How'd it be if no one protected this country and our families?" I said, somewhat vexed with my older brothers' disdain for the great British Army and the unfolding events. "How would you enjoy living under the Kaiser's rule?"

And that was the end of the discussion. It was a conversation repeated many times across the breadth of the British Empire in 1914. Inexperienced men became excited by the prospect of war and foreign adventure while it filled the cynical elders with foreboding. Many had been there during earlier conflicts. And despite the cautions, hundreds of thousands of young British men prepared to join this war should it start. Something brought out the pull of patriotism in the face of such a loathsome enemy to bear. And the romanticized and imagined escapades of combat were just too irresistible to hold them back for long! Joe had his misgivings. It was too familiar, déjà vu.

"Here we go again," Joe thought. "What can we do about it? The decisions are all made by haughty men at the top."

§

The British press carried reports and debates over what the start of such a conflict might bring. They spoke of the Schlieffen Plan, the German operational plan for a designated attack on France through Belgium and Luxemburg. So they didn't expect any surprises should war begin. But Belgium had her neutrality guaranteed by Britain in 1839. The frequent discussion of this now-public plan fuelled increasing apprehension in Britain, Belgium, Luxembourg, and France.

In contrast with England's busy industrial northeast, the French region of Picardy north of Paris was a quiet agricultural landscape with rolling wooded hillocks and pastoral valleys. The only sounds of guns were from occasional hunters. Picardy comprised the Aisne, Oise and Somme Rivers. The adjacent regions of Artois, Champagne-Marne and French Flanders were very similar: hillier in places and flatter in others, with ancient villages and small, bustling centres of commerce and residential comfort.

A main road in that area is the Chemin des Dames in Picardy, nineteen miles long and running along a slight ridge between the valleys of Aisne and Ailette. It gained its name in the 18th century as the route taken by the two daughters of Louis XV, Princesses Adélaïde and Victoire. The road gained its name from the Ladies of France, Princesses Adélaïde and Victoire. It was only a carriage road then, but it was the most direct route between Paris and the Château de la Bôve. The château was the home of Françoise de Châlus, a former mistress of Louis XV, Countess of Narbonne-Lara and lady of honour to Adélaïde, whom the princesses visited often. To make the passage more comfortable, the count had the road surfaced.

The Chemin des Dames runs through a peaceful pastoral region of rolling grain fields and forests. Grand châteaux or manor houses and separate farm buildings dotted the route, tucked between the green and gold patchwork quilt of the farming fields and thick forests. Deer, wild boar and other wild creatures populated these forests. Skylarks twittered their songs high above the pastures while a symphony of birdsong filled the woods. Tiny villages lay in the river valleys, with well-maintained vegetable gardens and fruit orchards. Meadows nurtured herds of sheep and goats, and the occasional cow formed grass collars around the villages and forests. Walled ancient churches and graveyards hovered on the outskirts of the settlements, with manicured flower gardens and tall evergreen cypresses standing guard. Apart from the occasional farm vehicle or rider, there was no traffic on these quiet roads. Apart from farming and the occasional rifle shots for wild game in autumn, anything other than total peace was unthinkable.

In July 1914, the harvest was in full swing, and the fields were alive with farmers and their extended families scything the grain crops. Women and children sang traditional songs that provided the right rhythm while collecting and beating the grain heads to release the cherished seeds. Older men raked the discarded hay into enormous pyramids of straw at the same pace.

Here and there, ancient towns with their houses, workshops, shops, churches and municipal buildings rose out of the rural greenery. Château Thierry was just such a bustling Champagne town on the River Marne near Picardy, fifty-six miles from Paris, its nearby rolling hills endowed with vineyards. The Champagne harvest began in early September, so the vines were undisturbed, their grapes still ripening.

To the north of Picardy was Belgium. Sharing borders with France, the Netherlands, Luxembourg and Germany, Belgium comprises the western coastal Dutch-Flemish Flanders region, the central and southern French Walloon Region and the French-speaking Brussels Capital Region. West Flanders lies on the North Sea coast, with a flat, low-lying polder landscape enclosed by dykes. It's a region blessed with fertile fields of grain, corn, sugar beets, vegetables and fruit, and its farms are small family businesses by tradition. They also farmed pigs, poultry, dairy cattle, and ornamental plant cultures such as flowers. In Wallonia, the French-speaking part of Belgium, the emphasis was on pasture-based cattle breeding. As in France, the harvests had begun, and the meadows were very busy, the farmers expecting good yields. The harvesters sang their traditional songs according to the rhythm of their work.

Empire and War

There was no hint of the imminent struggles to shatter the peace and everything else in their path. In Flanders, the spring poppy season had long passed, but here and there, a single flower or two shone scarlet against the golden backdrop of the cropped wheat stalks. However, the peace and tranquillity of these farming communities were short-lived. In the palaces and military headquarters of the surrounding countries, tensions were increasing daily, and they were preparing contingency plans for war.

Joe had followed the news coming out of Europe and London. This news dominated towards the second half of 1914 in Britain due to the events in Europe as it slid down the slippery slope into war. As always, he kept his marras and brothers informed about these developments. The most dramatic news events occurred during a large gathering of the British and German fleets at Kiel on the Baltic Sea, northern Germany. Lunch over, Joe continued his story.

"I had read that there was a big navy gathering in Germany at a port city called Kiel," Joe told his POW companions. "A few of our best warships travelled through a canal from the North Sea to that city."

After widening to accommodate Dreadnought class battleships, the Kaiser reopened the sixty-one-mile Kiel Canal or Kaiser-Wilhelm-Kanal in June 1914. This widening meant modern warships could travel from the Baltic Sea to the North Sea without going around Denmark. This canal was of utmost strategic importance to the Germans since it saved 250 nautical miles for their navy to reach Britain should war start. For this commemoration in Kiel, the British had dispatched the dreadnought battleship HMS King George V (1911) and a squadron of British ships. They were under the command of Vice Admiral Sir George John Scott Warrender and attended the Kiel Regatta at the end of June. The goal was to show off the modern British ships and inspect the German fleet.

"I recall our conversation from back then."

§

Memories of Kiel Week in Pre-War Germany

"I heard guys at work talking of our ships going to Kiel," said Mike at the time.

"I saw pictures in the newspapers of the ships lined up, anchored offshore from the port," I said. "There were a few of our warships, including the battleship King George V (1911), the German warships and the Kaiser's grand yacht."

"Why were they there, Joe?" asked Mike.

"There's a big yacht gathering at Kiel annually," I said. "They call it Kiel Week or the Kiel Regatta. Magnificent sailing yachts from Germany and elsewhere go there to take part. It's a big show. They made HMS King George V fast to a buoy in Kiel Port. The King George V-class battleships were a group of four dreadnought battleships built for the Royal Navy in the early 1910s that they sometimes called super-dreadnoughts. South of King George V lay the German Fleet Flagship, the Kaiser Class dreadnought battleship Friedrich der Grosse (Frederick the Great) commissioned in 1911 too. They moored the Kaiser's 390-foot royal yacht SMY Hohenzollern (1878) behind that. The rest of the British ships anchored north of her, and on the east, they moored the Hamburg-Amerika cruise liner Viktoria Luise (1900) between two buoys. During this sailing event, they berthed Viktoria Luise in Kiel every year, and she became the centre of influential society for the occasion. Between the moorings and the harbour were dozens of sailing yachts of various sizes visiting to compete in the regatta.

"The Kaiser inspected HMS King George V, and they held the last state banquet on board the Hohenzollern on 25 June 1914 to entertain officers of the British fleet. They also gave Vice-Admiral Warrender a tour of the German battleship; the Admiral's wife, a guest onboard the Viktoria Luise, was with him.

"There were many parties and sports events the admiral attended. The papers said they arranged sporting competitions between British and German teams. The German officer guiding the admiral claimed the Germans won most of the games, except for football. He also claimed that the English sailors were small compared to the Germans. The German papers said 70 men from HMS George V were under seventeen. The German officer thought there were too many older sailors on board."

"What a bloody cheek," said Mike. "How can we be smaller than the Germans? And don't they have young cadets on their ships? Well, at least we won in football."

§

Memories of how The Great War started

During Kiel Week, the fateful news arrived of the deaths of Archduke Franz Ferdinand of Austria and his wife Sophie, Duchess of Hohenberg. A fanatical Bosnian-Serb student, Gavrilo Princip, shot the heir to the Austro-Hungarian throne and his wife on 28 June 1914 in Sarajevo, Bosnia. This news threw Europe's allies into a state of concern and confusion. Still, Admiral Warrender's last farewell message, in line with the spirit of the visit and the welcome they had received, was "Friends in the past, friends forever."

Joe didn't have to announce the assassination to his friends. They knew it as soon as the news arrived in Great Britain. The headline of the *Daily Mail* on 29 July 1914 was "Murder of the Austrian Heir and his Wife." It spread in a flash through every level and corner of British society.

"So, they killed a pair of haughty people," said Mike. "What's the problem? Why is everybody so concerned?"

"Because there's talk of war," I said. "That's what the papers are saying. Any excuse, any spark for war. And they say our politicians are in a panic."

"Shite," yelled Jack. "We don't need that again, do we?"

"Howay, man, we could use excitement for a change," said Mike.

"Not that kind, Mike," I said. "Well, not for me."

Diplomatic manoeuvring, known as the July Crisis, started at once between Austria-Hungary, Germany, Russia, France and Britain. To end Serbian interference in Bosnia, Austria-Hungary issued the July Ultimatum to Serbia—a series of ten impossible demands which they contrived to start a war with Serbia. Throughout July 1914, the newspapers only talked about the war. In no time, the nation deteriorated into a state of preparing for what they were calling "the inevitable."

"Look at this," Joe announced then while holding a newspaper with several pictures of warships spread across its front page with the headline *Great Britain is ready for War*.

"Can you believe it? Are we heading into war again?"

After the Kiel visit, Vice-Admiral Sir George Warrender commanded the British Grand Fleet. With war considered imminent, they ordered the Grand Fleet to first move to Scapa Flow in the Orkney Islands of Northern Scotland. It was a time of extreme European tension, culminating in the naval race with Imperial Germany. Instead of the annual exercises, there was a Fleet Review, an open demonstration of the might of the Royal Navy. The Admiralty wanted to test the "machinery of mobilization," too.[65] Then, on 18 July 1914, the Royal Navy assembled its ships at Spithead for a Royal Naval Review. Two hundred and thirty-two vessels anchored at Spithead, including 59 battleships, 55 cruisers, 78 destroyers, smaller craft, 17 seaplanes and over 70,000 officers and ratings. Because of the size of the fleet, the review went from 18 to 29 July. King George V inspected part of his fleet daily from the Royal Yacht. On the 29th, the Admiralty sent the order to prepare for war and the warships left for their war stations.

"I showed my marras the many photographs in the day's newspaper," said Joe.

"Hmm, impressive," said Mike then. "We have that many warships?"

"Aye. Very impressive," said Jack.

"It seems we have that many ships and more worldwide," said Joe.

"But if war starts, they'll call us up, Laddies."

Remember that? Must I continue?

§

---

[65] J.R. Hill (ed.), The Oxford Illustrated History of the Royal Navy, Oxford: Oxford University Press, 1995

"When Serbia accepted only eight of the ten demands in the ultimatum," I said. "Austria-Hungary declared war on Serbia on 28 July 1914."

"Then, on 29 July, the British Admiralty sent a warning telegram to the Fleet. At 2:10 P.M. on the same day, the British War Office sent telegrams ordering a precautionary period. The British Expeditionary Force (BEF) had been drilling for weeks and were ready and tuned into any signal to move into battle."

"The German Empire mobilized on 30 July 1914. Still holding a grudge because of the German winning of Alsace and Lorraine over forty years before in the Franco-German War, France ordered French mobilization on 1 August. Germany declared war on Russia on the same day."

"On 30 July, more by luck than planning, most of the Territorial Army troops, including the 2/DLI, were at their annual camp at Whittington Barracks Lichfield, Staffordshire. They were 16 miles north of Birmingham, as part of the 18th Brigade of the 6th Division, where they had been since September 1913. They hurried soldiers to their war stations guarding vulnerable points on the coast and along railway lines and docks [66]."

"On Thursday, 30 July 1914, the headlines read, '500,000 Austrians invade Serbia. Germany has given Russia

---

[66] John Sheen, *The Steel of the DLI (The 2nd Battalion of the Durham Light Infantry in War 1914-1918)*, Pen & Sword Books, 2009.

twenty-four hours to declare her intention to mobilize her army.'

"Then on 1 August, the headlines read, 'Russia Declares War on Germany'."

"We met again at the pub on Saturday, 1 August," said Joe to his fellow prisoners.

"Everybody was talking of war and Empires," said Mike. "I thought we were the only ones to have an Empire."

"Aye. It's because that's the only thing newspapers are reporting on these days. The British Empire, German Empire, Austro-Hungarian Empire, Russian Empire, Turkish Ottoman Empire, French Empire and the so-called alliances and war. They are all talking more and more of war."

In 1914, Empires made up of mother nations, dominions, and colonies contained most of the world's peoples. The British Empire was by far the greatest in size, population and wealth; the might of its navy and the extent and experience of its army were supreme. But by 1914, Britain was no longer the dominant economic power in the world. It still dominated the seas and had the world's largest shipbuilding industry. But Britain was losing its dominance and being outperformed by Germany in coal, iron, chemicals and manufacturing small machinery and equipment.

Next in strength were the German Empire, the French Empire, the Austro-Hungarian Empire and the Russian Empire. Other empires of the time included the Italian Empire, the Ottoman Empire, the Japanese Empire, and the Republic of China, which were not kingdoms but had vast populations. Spain and Portugal once controlled mighty empires. They had divided the world in half between them from the 15th to the 18th centuries but had since vanished.

"What do you mean by alliances, Joe?" asked Jack.

"Alliances are the agreements between countries and empires to get even bigger and more robust in case of war," I said. "They've been doing this for a long time and are then allies of one another, friends to help each other should war break out."

Since the latter part of the 19th century, the British government considered Germany the most significant threat to its empire. The Triple Alliance of 1882, where Germany, Austria-Hungary and Italy agreed to support each other if attacked by France or Russia, only increased this anxiety. France and Britain felt threatened by the Triple Alliance because of the rapid growth of the German Navy and Army. So, both these countries signed a solid understanding known as the Entente Cordiale in 1904. Three years later, Russia, who feared the growth in the German Army, joined Britain and France to form the Triple Entente.

"Why are they talking of war?" asked Jack.

"Because these empires have been racing to grow their navies and armies. Each needed to believe that they're the greatest," I said. "It's crazy. Nobody knows why, but everybody is getting ready for war."

"And what if somebody makes a mistake?" asked Mike. "I suppose then we will go to war. I agree, Joe. It's crazy!"

"And how do we stack up against these new Empires?" asked Jack.

"I don't know. The Royal Navy is still the strongest in the world, but I don't think our army is anymore."

The Royal Navy, the military strength of Britain for centuries, was still a dominant force. With the launch of HMS Dreadnought in 1906, the British Empire had expanded this lead over Germany. By 1914, they had equipped the Royal Navy with 18 modern dreadnought battleships, the latest technology in warships, with six more under construction. It had ten modern battlecruisers, 20 Town-class cruisers, 15 scout cruisers, 200 destroyers, 29 older pre-dreadnought design battleships and 150 cruisers built before 1907. The Royal Navy had a fleet of 73 submarines at its disposal. It was a formidable force!

But Britain had reduced its army by July 1914 to 250,000 regular troops, half the number it had committed to the 2nd Anglo-Boer War. One hundred and twenty thousand of these soldiers were ready for war as the British Expeditionary Force (BEF); the army had stationed the rest throughout the British Empire. British troops were in Britain's overseas possessions except for the dominions of Canada, Australia, and New Zealand, whose armies were loyal to Britain. There was also a small home-based Territorial Force, a volunteer reserve unit of the British Army since the Haldane Reforms of 1908.

"And now we have a service of fighting aeroplanes," I said. "Imagine that, Laddies? We didn't have that during the Boer War, only observation balloons."

Joe was referring to Britain's emerging air force. They had set up the Royal Flying Corps (RFC) in May 1912. By 1914, the RFC had 110 planes and six airships. The aeroplanes of the RFC in 1914 were the biplanes BE-2, Farman MF-7, Avro 504, Vickers FB5, F.E.2 and the Bristol Scout. Britain established the Royal Naval Air Service (RNAS) on 23 June 1914. It became the air arm of the Royal Navy under the Admiralty's Air Department.

"And who are our allies?" asked Mike.

"The rest of the British Empire. France and Belgium. There are others, but I can't remember them all."

The British Imperial allies included the dominions and colonies of Canada, Australia, New Zealand, India, South Africa, and Newfoundland, which were not yet part of Canada. In 1914, the other British alliances included France, Belgium, Russia, Serbia, Japan and Montenegro.

"OK, so France is important," said Jack. "But Belgium is tiny, isn't it?"

Empire and War

"Aye. France is our most important ally, and Belgium is a tiny country," I said, "But their ports are so near ours. So, if the Germans were to take them, they'd be right on our doorstep. The army calls the Belgian alliance strategic."

France was still an agricultural country and one of the world's leading trading nations in the first decades of the twentieth century. However, its industrial production output was lower than that of both Germany and Britain. In January 1914, the French Army comprised 800,000 French and 46,000 colonial troops. The French Armée Coloniale (Colonial Army), or La Coloniale, involved soldiers recruited from French West and Central Africa, Madagascar, New Caledonia and Indochina. They deployed most of their vast armies inside France, the majority along the eastern frontier with Germany as part of Plan 17.

Plan 17 was a scheme of mobilization and concentration adopted by the French General Staff in 1913 in readiness for a war between France and Germany. With the fear of war, they mobilized a further three million men during the summer of 1914.

Expenditure on the French Navy doubled between 1910 and 1914. By the summer of 1914, France had 19 battleships, with another 14 on order, 32 cruisers and 86 destroyers. It had 34 submarines and 115 torpedo boats, too.

France formed the French Army Air Service or Aéronautique Militaire in October 1910. France led the world in pioneering aeroplane design, and by mid-1912, they had five small squadrons, or "escadrilles." This service had grown to 132 machines in 21 escadrilles by 1914.

"And what are we up against, Germany?" asked Mike.

"Germany for sure, Mike," I said, "But their allies too, such as Austria-Hungary, Italy and Turkey."

Germany's empire had grown from 200,000 square miles in 1900 to 1,000,000 by 1914. Germany had claimed a few colonies in Africa. German South West Africa, the Cameroons, Togoland and German East Africa were colonies under its control. Other territories controlled by Germany included Northern New Guinea, Samoa and the Chinese province of Shandong. However, the German Empire was still small compared to the British Empire's 11,400,000 square miles.

However, Germany's industrial and economic power had burgeoned after Bismarck unified the independent states and founded the empire in 1870. Germany's rate of industrial development had been the fastest in the world over several decades. Between 1880 and 1913, coal production increased by 400%. Steel, chemicals, engineering and armaments had risen, too. In thirty years, Germany's international trade had quadrupled. Between 1870 and 1910, the population of Germany increased from 24 million to 65 million. Over 40 percent of this fast-growing workforce was in industrial enterprises. However, 35 percent were still working in agriculture, ensuring that Germany could produce enough food for its people.

By the start of the twentieth century, experts recognized Germany as having the most efficient army in the world. It practised conscription for short-term military service followed by a more extended period in reserve. In 1914, the regular German Army comprised 700,000 men.

Germany was slow to recognize the potential of aeroplanes, but they formed the German Army Air Service (GAAS) in 1912. By 1914, Germany had 246 planes and 11 airships, Europe's most significant air force.

The 'Central Powers' aligned with the German Empire. It comprised the Austro-Hungarian Empire with 8 million troops, and from August 1914, the Turkish Ottoman Empire, which had almost 3 million combatants.

"And is the Kaiser the nasty bloke we need to look out for?" asked Mike.

"Aye, he's the colossal problem," I said. "And he's gearing up for a fight. He is Queen Victoria's grandson, you remember. Think of it; it's too crazy!"

Kaiser Wilhelm II was born in Potsdam in 1859, the son of Frederick III and the Queen Consort of Prussia Victoria Adelaide Mary Louisa, daughter of Queen Victoria. Wilhelm's upbringing was strict and authoritarian. They educated him at the Kassel Gymnasium and the University of Bonn. Wilhelm became emperor of Germany in 1888 following the death of

Frederick III. At the time of Wilhelm's accession to the throne, Otto von Bismarck was German Chancellor. But the elderly Bismarck was unable, or unwilling, to manage the new Kaiser as he had done his predecessor. Wilhelm II relieved him of his office two years later.

From the mid-1890s onwards, Kaiser Wilhelm II, the first grandchild of Queen Victoria and Prince Albert, and his government ruled the German Empire. Wilhelm had a withered left arm six inches shorter than his right as a congenital disability. This handicap left a mark on his psyche, and Wilhelm was aggressive. He believed in strengthening Germany's armed forces. Wilhelm used Germany's robust economic base to pour significant resources into building the Imperial German Navy (Kaiserliche Marine). He was in a rivalry with the British Royal Navy for world naval supremacy. In 1914, the German Navy under Grand Admiral Alfred von Tirpitz was the second largest in the world. It had 14 dreadnoughts, 22 pre-dreadnought battleships, four battlecruisers, seven modern light cruisers and 18 older cruisers. The Imperial German Navy was to become the first to use submarines on a large scale in wartime. It had 30 petroleum-powered subs and ten diesel-powered subs, called U-boats from Unterseeboot ("undersea boat"), with 17 more under construction in 1914.

"I've read that the German Army has 4 million troops," said Joe, "And they claim they can hurry them into battle at the speed of lightning."

"My God," said Mike. "That sounds very dangerous!"

"Aye and Wilhelm supported the Boers against the British during the 2nd Anglo-Boer War of 1899-1902," said Joe. "He hated his uncle King Edward VII too, calling him Satan. And as already mentioned, Wilhelm II, George V and Tsar Nicholas II of Russia, another ally of ours, are first cousins, all descended from Queen Victoria!"

"So, on 1 August, Germany declared war on Russia," said Joe. "Belgium mobilized on 2 August. Then, the Germans sent a demand because the French had crossed the border into Belgium. On 3 August, a Monday bank holiday in Britain, Germany declared war on France. The Imperial German Army crossed the border into Luxembourg and threatened to move into Belgium."

§

Remembering an Outing to South Shields

"I remember how our family took a day off from the worries of the possibility of war to gather at home rather than go to South Shields," said Joe.

"It was a warm summer bank holiday on Tyneside on 3 August 1914," said Joe.

"However, there were no outings from Jarrow to the beaches of South Shields that day. The North-Eastern Railway Company (NER) had cancelled special excursion trains, spoiling many plans for the usual escapes from the urban industrial areas. Since our annual outing to South Shields earlier in the summer, the Rutherford family gathered for lunch at my eldest brother William and Jane Nesham's home. It had been my father Thomas and Susannah's house until he died in 1910. As the head of the family, my mother, Susannah, still lived with William and Jane, and she was in charge of our get-together. The entire family arrived with Mary, who was seven months pregnant with our third child. Mike, Jack, and Fred were there to commiserate with us. At first, we avoided talk of war."

"This trouble in Europe is ruining our sport," said George.

"I agreed. There's not much happening in football."

"It wasn't a great season for the North East this past year," said Mike.

"Nee, Mike. Not good," said Jack.

"Middlesbrough in 3rd position, Sunderland 7th and Newcastle 11th," I reminded them. "Not good."

As always, William opened the discussion on the pending conflict. "Well, with this so-called war, there won't be much football! And he was right when he said. 'But ye lot won't be around, so it won't matter, will it'"?

"So, you now believe there will be a war, William?" I asked.

"Well, if I listen to ye lot, I believe it," he said.

"At that point, the women overheard the conversation and pulled the men back into the womb of the family," said Joe.

"We forgot the war for a while, and as we downed many Broons, the atmosphere became more jovial."

§

On 4 August, German troops poured into neutral Belgium according to the strategy defined by the Schlieffen Plan. This plan resulted from a 1905 German General Staff 'thought experiment,' as they called it. It later became a deployment plan and a set of recommendations for German commanders to carry out in a war with France. It planned for German forces to advance westwards through Belgium and northern France, with the right flank swinging around to encircle France's capital. The plan provided for a giant claw 400 miles wide of seven German Armies marching out to surround Paris. The German High Command intended the war to last no longer than forty days, ending before Christmas! In a speech to his troops, Kaiser Wilhelm told them, "You will be home before the leaves fall from the trees [67]."

---

[67] Norman Ferguson, *The First World War: A Miscellany*, Summersdale, Chichester, UK, 2014

As the German forces rushed towards Belgium, trains packed with troops crossed the famous Hohenzollern Bridge at Köln, or Cologne, once every ten minutes. [68] Early that morning, General von der Marwitz's cavalry corps rode several miles east of Brussels across the Belgian border. Behind them, disembarking on the large platforms of the border stations, were the principal elements of the three armies of the German right flank. These troops belonged to Alexander von Kluck's First Army, Karl von Bulow's Second Army and Max von Hausen's Third Army. They were to invade between the Ardennes to the south and the Maastricht Appendix, a Dutch territory protruding from the north. They marched through Belgium and then turned to France. On their left, the Fourth and Fifth Armies formed around Metz, German Lorraine and Trier, Germany. Farther south, the Sixth and Seventh Armies held the bulk of the rest of the German provinces of Lorraine and Alsace. [69]

As mentioned, the Belgians had an alliance with England. When the German Army crossed their eastern frontier, Britain sent a demand to Berlin to withdraw its forces from neutral Belgium. [70] This demand received no response.

---

[68] Norman Ferguson, *The First World War: A Miscellany*, Summersdale, Chichester, UK, 2014

[69] Richard Holmes, *The Western Front*, 1999

[70] John Sheen, *The Steel of the DLI: The 2nd Battalion of the Durham Light Infantry at war 1914-1918*, Pen & Sword Military, 2009

In Germany, the British ambassador met with the German Chancellor.

The Chancellor said, "For just a scrap of paper, Great Britain would make war on a kindred nation who desired nothing better than to be friends with her."

That 'scrap of paper' was the Treaty of London, signed by Austria, Great Britain, France, Prussia and Russia in 1839, which guaranteed Belgium's neutrality.[71]

British Foreign Secretary Sir Edward Grey gave a speech in the House of Commons that day to rally the nation. This talk was headline news, along with Germany declaring war on France on the same day. That evening, as Sir Edward watched the lamplighters outside his London office, he remarked:

"The lamps are going out all over Europe, and we shall not see them lit again in our lifetime." [72]

§

"So, late on 4 August, Great Britain declared war on the German Empire," said Joe.

"Winston Churchill, First Lord of the Admiralty, described the scene in London when the ultimatum expired, and Britain entered the Great War."

---

[71] Norman Ferguson, *The First World War: A Miscellany*, Summersdale, Chichester, UK, 2014
[72] Ibid

Empire and War

"It was eleven o'clock at night, twelve by German time, when the ultimatum expired," said Winston Churchill. "Someone threw the windows of the Admiralty wide open in the warm night air. Under the roof from which Nelson had received his orders, a small group of admirals, captains, and clerks, pencils in hand, waited. Along the Mall from the direction of the Palace, the sound of an immense concourse singing God save the King floated in. On this deep wave, there broke the chimes of Big Ben, and as the first stroke of the hour boomed out, a rustle of movement swept across the room. They flashed the war telegram reading, 'Commence hostilities against Germany' to the ships and establishments under the White Ensign all over the world. I walked across the Horse Guards Parade to the Cabinet room and reported to the Prime Minister and the Ministers assembled there that the deed was done." [73]

"So, there you have it," said Joe. "The war for Britain and its allies had begun! The British called it the 'Great War,' the Americans called it the 'European War,' and the Germans came to call it 'Der Weltkrieg,' the World War.

"Have you heard the news this morning, Laddies?" I asked my marras on the morning of 5 August. "We're at war with Germany, can you believe it? Let's proceed to the regimental depot immediately."

---

[73] Best, Geoffrey, Churchill: A Study of Greatness (2002)

Empire and War

Since Britain was at war, Canada and the other members of the British Empire were also at war because of their legal status as British Dominions and partners. They left foreign policy decisions in the hands of the British Parliament. How Canada and the other Dominions reacted to the war and what measures they took to support Britain was up to their governments. Thus, the Canadian Parliament met in an emergency session on 18 August, for example, to debate the nature and extent of that support. [74]

§

"I think I'll stop there for today," said Joe. "If you are interested, I'll tell the story of our mobilization, training and departure for the Front another day."

To a man, his companions thanked him for another informative war story. They had lived it and mulled it over in their minds so often. But Joe's descriptions crystallized their experiences and added explanations for many things they had not hitherto understood.

§

---

74 https://www.canada.ca/en/news/archive/2014/08/canada-beginning-first-world-war.html

Memories of 1914 Mobilization

"On 5 August 1914, the assembly for the war started," said Joe.

"The regular 2/DLI Reservists arrived as early as 6 A.M. The depot had arranged tea and rations for the arrivals. Doctors conducted medical examinations throughout the day, and the men received their kits after passing. The paperwork was done, so they welcomed the reservists into the 2/DLI. They then sent the recruits and reservists for hair and moustache cuts to regulation lengths. Command number 1,695 of the King's Regulations read: *The hair of the head will be kept short. The chin and the underlip will be shaved, not the upper lip. Whiskers, if worn, will be of moderate lengths.* [75]

"Regular reservists reported sober and on time. But the men of the Special Reserve battalions, 3/DLI and 4/DLI, were late and often under the influence of alcohol. These long-overdue arrivals were to follow the leading party after it had deployed [76]."

At sea on 5 August, the Royal Navy light cruiser HMS *Amphion* (1911) caught and sank the German Navy minelayer SS *Königin Luise* (1913). The "Kaiserliche Marine" (Imperial German Navy) commandeered the *Königin Luise*, a German

---

[75] Norman Ferguson, *The First World War, A miscellany*, Summersdale Publishers Ltd., Chichester, UK, 2014.

[76] S.G.P Ward, Faithful, *The Story of the Durham Light Infantry*, 1962

steam ferry, at the onset of the war and repurposed it as a minelayer. The Germans were laying a minefield forty miles off the Thames Estuary when Amphion caught and sank her. SS *Königin Luise* was the first naval loss for the Germans in the Great War. But all around the British Isles, the Royal Navy deployed vessels of all sizes to patrol its waters.

§

War Diary: Lichfield, Aug. 6, 4 am

301 Reservists arrived under Maj. Robb.

"Major A. K. Robb of the 2/DLI, the adjutant of the Durham University Officers Training Corps, rounded up the ready reservists and marched them to the depot," said Joe.

"The battalion had wired from Lichfield its need for 685 men to bring it up to its war complement. Three hundred and eighty-four soldiers left for Lichfield on 6 August. Altogether, 1020 reservists turned up, with less than 1% absentees, and it went without a hitch."

"The men gave no trouble, and arrangements worked well," said Major Robb.

§

War Diary: Lichfield, Aug. 6th, 7 am

The Precautionary Period Detachments returned.

"On 6 August, the Prime Minister appointed Lord Kitchener, who we know from South Africa, Secretary of State for War," said Joe.

"Kitchener decided immediately to raise New Armies for the war effort."

"On the seas, the Germans lost a ship on 6 August, and so did we," reported Joe. "They lost the men we rescued from the sinking German ship."

"Serves them right," said Mike.

"So, has the navy war started?" asked Jack.

"Aye," said Joe. "The German navy is going after our ships, and our navy is going after theirs."

"One hundred and thirty-one of our sailors dead on the second day!" said Mike. "Man, this war looks far worse than the South African War already."

In a cruel twist of fate and events on 6 August, HMS Amphion struck mines laid by the SS Königin Luise and sank within fifteen minutes. When Amphion went to the bottom, one officer and 131 seamen lost their lives. An unknown number of German crewmen of the Königin Luise rescued by HMS Amphion perished, too. On the same day, HMS Bristol (1910), based in the West Indies, became the first British warship to engage with the enemy. She pursued the light cruiser SMS Karlsruhe, evading a confrontation.

Right after they declared war, the Royal Navy took its toll on German sea-borne commerce as "prizes captured at sea." They seized many German vessels lying in the harbours of Great Britain. The navy announced on 6 August that since the war began on the night of the 4th, they had captured 20 German merchant vessels. Six were sailing ships, and the rest were steamers, representing about 40,000 tons of shipping. British and French warships seized them in British territorial waters. Among the more notable captures by a British gunboat was the 3765-ton barque Perkeo bound for Hamburg with oil cargo and the 1314-ton steamer Franz Horn. They also detained the crew of the cargo ship Dryade when they seized it at Warrington in the Manchester Ship Canal.

By 25 August 1914, the total number of prize vessels and cargo detained in the British Isles was 112. They captured 82 in England, 25 in Scotland and 5 in Ireland!

§

War Diary: Lichfield, Aug. 7th, 4 am

384 Reservists arrived under Lt. CONANT, who had taken the colours to the depot.

"They assigned my marras and me to D-Company," said Joe.

"That was the start of a month of movements around Britain while they assembled various components of the 6th division and strengthened it with reservists. The 2/DLI was a part of that initiative. They also started training recruits for transfer to the Front. The men were in friendly spirits and keen to get to the battlefields. But they first travelled by train to Lichfield in the Midlands. They billeted the men briefly at Whittington Barracks."

Whittington Barracks on Whittington Heath, Lichfield, was the site of one of the best-attended race meetings in the Midlands during the 18th century. It was once the grandstand of the racecourse, but the army repurposed it as a barrack for the soldiers of the Prince of Wales's North Staffordshire Regiment.

"There they bivouacked us under canvas on the heath next to an impressive building with small towers," said Joe. "We settled in and readied ourselves for whatever awaited us.

"I thought we were going to Belgium," grumbled Mike.

"Well, I guess we need training before we go, Mike," I said.

"We had our training in South Africa," said Mike.

"True, and in the Reserve, but these chaps have not had theirs," I said. "But this is a more modern war, so I guess they want to bring us up to date."

"Are they training us here?" asked Jack.

"Nee. I've heard we are only here for a short while and will move on for our training once the division has reached its full complement," I said.

"Howay, but what a send-off we had from the barracks in Newcastle," repeated Jack, "and I felt so proud marching to the station."

"Aye. Everybody was there to send us off," said Mike. "A great farewell!"

"And we had a splendid time on the train," I said. "Everyone was in such high spirits for going off to war!"

"Aye, except for arriving at 3:30 in the morning and marching the three and a half miles to the barracks," said Mike. "I need to sleep!"

"While at Whittington Barracks, raucous drill sergeants assigned to each company disciplined us," said Joe.

"The sergeants barked orders to the crowd of reservists and recruits, getting them into line and shouting, 'You had better prepare yourselves for the challenges ahead of us. And, you had bloody well better see that your uniforms and kit are tidy and your boots polished to perfection.' The sergeants marched us nonstop from our arrival until we moved on to our next stop."

§

War Diary: Lichfield, Aug. 7th, 8.25 am

Order was received to move, and the Battn paraded at 10 pm. The harness, intended for months, had not arrived, so wagons were manhandled to the station.

"The 2/DLI received orders to move to Dunfermline, Scotland, for training on 7 August," said Joe. "They had requested horse harnesses for the wagons, but these hadn't arrived. So, we dragged the carts full of kit and equipment to the train station by manpower to prepare for our departure the next day."

On 7 August 1914, the famous Field Marshal, now Secretary of State for War 1st Earl Kitchener, appealed for one hundred thousand volunteers. Lord Kitchener had become well-known through his victories in Sudan and South Africa. The King created him, Viscount Kitchener of Khartoum and the Vaal in the Colony of Transvaal and Aspall in the County of Suffolk. The army prepared a poster with a memorable image of the Field Marshal in uniform with his handlebar moustache looming large.

This recruitment drive, run throughout the Empire, received an overwhelming response. Recruits inundated the recruiting offices, with over 10,000 men enlisting in the first five days. [77] The success of this campaign led to the Americans copying this poster when they joined the Great War in 1917, using Uncle Sam as their unique and recognizable recruiter.

When Joe saw this advertisement, he recalled his experiences leading up to the South African War. He asked

---

[77] John Sheen, The Steel of the DLI: The 2nd Battalion of the Durham Light Infantry at war 1914-1918, Pen & Sword Military, 2009

himself, "Why are so many men rushing to join the British Army to take part in another war?" Joe then answered himself based on his experience: "boredom, unemployment, poverty and patriotism; the wish to be part of an effort to protect the British Empire."

For the unemployed, it was a paying job. The appeal targeted employed, bored, or dissatisfied men, promising them world travel and adventure. He thought these were the principal reasons for the Boer War, but in 1914, a strong aversion towards the Germans was an added motivator. Joe realized nothing could halt this phenomenon now, save an unlikely change of direction away from war.

For Kitchener's drive, the army set up local recruitment centres in Territorial Army drill halls or local town halls throughout Great Britain. Volunteers went through a cursory medical examination and, if fit, swore an oath of allegiance and accepted the "King's shilling." [78] They then returned home to await their call. The lowest permissible age was eighteen, but recruitment officers often turned a blind eye to healthy, mature-looking underage youths [79].

Enlisting was straightforward if one had patience. Sizeable crowds of men surrounded the recruitment offices, with the police attempting to keep order. Once inside, they

---

[78] To "take the King's or Queen's shilling" was to agree to serve as a sailor or soldier in the Royal Navy or the British Army. The practice officially stopped in 1879 but the term is still used as a form of slang.

[79] Martin Pegler, *British Tommy 1914-1918*, Osprey, Oxford1996

filled in an attestation form with the help of a recruitment officer. The biggest challenge for many was their age. Many a sergeant looked over the keen and hopeful sixteen-year-olds and dismissed them with a "Hop it, and come back tomorrow when you're eighteen," followed by a conspiratorial wink [80].

The recruitment medical examination was superficial and quick. A doctor checked for visible defects in eyesight, teeth and chest. Tuberculosis was still endemic amongst working-class men, and they rejected sufferers immediately. They told those considered the sound of mind and body to return home and wait for their instructions to arrive. Many denied men took their chances at other recruiting stations where they heard of lower standards[81].

Many men received joining instructions for training battalions within a week; others wondered whether the army wanted them. It was déjà vu for Joe and his marras; they had experienced the same when joining up for the South African war.

§

---

[80] Martin Pegler, *British Tommy 1914-1918*, Osprey, Oxford1996
[81] Ibid

War Diary: Dunfermline, Aug 8th, 2.15 pm

Battn. HeadQrs and A, B Coys arrived: The C.O. looked at positions in the neighbourhood, and the Companies proceeded into Billets, followed shortly afterwards by the remaining companies.

"On 8 August," said Joe, "We began our move to Dunfermline with companies A and B."

Dunfermline is a town and parish, a former Royal Burgh, in Fife, Scotland. It sits on the elevated ground three miles from the northern shore of the Firth of Forth, 17 miles northwest of Edinburgh. Dunfermline was the capital of Scotland until the brutal murder of James I at Perth in 1437. The royal family felt safer in Edinburgh Castle as burghs such as Dunfermline and Stirling could not offer adequate protection to defend the nobles.

On 8 August 1914, Parliament passed the Defence of the Realm Act (DORA) without debate. This legislation empowered the British Government's executive powers to gag published criticism, imprison without trial, and commandeer economic resources required for the war effort.

They organized the British Army in England and Ireland as an expeditionary force comprising six infantry and one cavalry division. The chief ministers, including Lord Kitchener, Secretary of State for War, met on 5 August. Kitchener was in Britain on his annual summer leave between 23 June and 3 August 1914. He boarded a cross-Channel steamer to start his return trip to Cairo, where he had been Consul-General of Egypt. However, they recalled him to London to meet with Prime Minister Asquith. The chief ministers sent four infantry and cavalry divisions to France on 9 August. Against cabinet opinion, Kitchener predicted a protracted war lasting at least three years. He saw it as requiring vast armies to defeat Germany, causing enormous casualties before the end came. Kitchener stated that the conflict "will plumb the depths of human resources to the last million.

At the outbreak of the war in August 1914, the British regular army was a small professional force. It comprised less than 250,000 regular troops organized in regiments of Guards: Grenadier, Coldstream, Scots and Irish. It included another 68 regiments of the line, the Rifle Brigade, thirty-one cavalry regiments, artillery and other support arms. Nearly half of the regular army was overseas in garrisons throughout the British Empire. The Royal Flying Corps was part of the British Army, comprising 84 aeroplanes at the outbreak of the war.

The Territorial Force supported this regular army and the reservists. The regulars and reserves totalled a mobilized force of 700,000 men on paper. However, only 150,000 men were available, and authorities rapidly transformed them into the British Expeditionary Force (BEF) for transfer to the continent. This force comprised six infantry divisions and one cavalry division. By comparison, the French Army mobilized over 1.6 million troops in 62 infantry divisions in 1914. The German Army assembled 1.8 million soldiers in 78 infantry divisions.

§

There were no entries to the 2/DLI War Diary on 9 and 10 of August. The rest of the battalion, including the marras' D-Company, was underway to the assembly at Dunfermline. Joe and his marras once more entered the train station at Newcastle with others for the journey north.

"Here we go again, Laddies," called Mike as we entered the station. "I haven't been on trains so much since I returned from India."

"That's the same with me," I said. "I haven't travelled since returning either."

"Well, go back an extra twenty years for me, Laddies," called Fred. "But I was returning then from South Africa and the 1st Anglo-Boer War."

"Right, Grandpa, you don't have to remind us how old ye are," called Jack.

"I'm just looking for a wee bit more respect, Jack," said Fred.

"Aye, Fred. That you'll get from us," said Joe with sincerity and a laugh.

"How long is this trip to Dunfermline?" asked Mike of the conductor as we mounted the steps into the car.

"Three and a half hours if you're lucky, soldier," said the conductor with a broad grin. "But longer if we hit too many cows."

"Well, better cows than Scots," said Fred with a hearty laugh.

§

Message from the King for the BEF

On 9 August, King George V gave a personal message to the BEF as it prepared to embark for France. In it, he assured his soldiers that their welfare was paramount in his mind. He expressed his confidence in them. The words struck a chord, and they used them on headstone inscriptions, commemorative scrolls and medals.

Buckingham Palace

"You are leaving home to fight for the safety and honour of my Empire.

"Belgium, whose country we are pledged to defend, has been attacked, and France is about to be invaded by the same powerful foe.

"I have implicit confidence in you, my soldiers. Duty is your watchword, and I know your duty will be nobly done.

"I shall follow your every movement with the deepest interest and mark with eager satisfaction your daily progress. Indeed, your welfare will never be absent from my thoughts.

"I pray God to bless you and guard you and bring you back victorious."

George, R.I.

9th August 1914

The BEF was the first British contingent sent to the Western Front at the start of the Great War. Planning for the BEF began with the Haldane reforms of the British Army carried out by the Secretary of State for War Richard Haldane from 1906 to 1912. The Official British Historian Brigadier-General James Edmonds later wrote. "In every respect, the Expeditionary Force of 1914 was incomparably the best trained, best organized and best equipped British Army ever to leave these shores. [82]

"When the BEF entered the war, it was only 100,000 strong," said Joe. "It had a cavalry division and two Corps of

---

[82] Walter Reid, *Architect of Victory: Douglas Haig.* Edinburgh: Birlinn Ltd., 2006

infantry divisions each. Field Marshal Sir John French was in overall command."

Sir John French was a sixty-two-year-old cavalryman who had made his reputation in the Second Anglo-Boer War. Major-General Edmund Allenby commanded the Cavalry Division. Sir Douglas Haig commanded I Corps, comprising the 1st and 2nd divisions. A dour Lowland Scot, Haig had served on French's staff before and during the Boer War. They were strange characters. One officer commented, "French was a man who loved life, laughter and women, while Haig is the dullest dog I ever had the happiness to meet."

On 9 August, the Town-class light cruiser HMS Birmingham (1913) rammed and sank the German submarine U-15 off Fair Isle, northern Scotland, halfway between the Orkney and Shetland Islands. It was the first U-boat claimed by the Royal Navy.

Taking stock of the Durham Light Infantry in August 1914, its status had transformed. It had grown from the original two battalions of one thousand men each at the turn of the century to four by 1914. The 1st Battalion, renowned for contributing to the Relief of Ladysmith during the 2nd Anglo-Boer War, was in Nowshera, India, in August 1914. The 2nd Battalion was at Lichfield, part of the 18th Brigade in the 6th Division. The 3rd (Reserve) Battalion was at Newcastle upon Tyne, a depot training unit. It moved on to mobilization in South Shields, which remained part of the Tyne Garrison. The

4th (Extra Reserve) Battalion was the depot and training unit at Barnard Castle, County Durham. It moved on to mobilization for the Tyne defences.

The Durham Light Infantry raised five battalions in August 1914 to mobilize a Territorial Force, the 5th through the 9th. They were to recruit another six battalions, the 10th through the 15th, as part of the New Army in September 1914. This recruitment drive increased the total complement of the regiment from 2,000 to 15,000 men within such a brief period, thanks to Kitchener's recruitment campaign. The response was phenomenal!

§

Memories of the Arrival at Dunfermline

"At midday on 10 August 1914, we arrived at Dunfermline in a downpour," said Joe. "The army handed out waterproof sheets to shield us from the rain. Huddled under our waterproofing, my marras and I were waiting for accommodation at Dunfermline after a day of train travel from Whittington Barracks Lichfield."

"Aye, what I remember from that arrival," said Mike, "was the rain pissing down in sheets."

"Did you hear of the message for the BEF from the King?" I asked my marras.

"Aye, what an honour for the men of the Expeditionary Force," said Mike. "And for us, once we get there."

"A worried man, I imagine," I said. "His is a colossal job for sure."

"For sure," echoed Mike.

"And we need not worry?" asked Jack

"I don't know, Jack," I said. "We will fight a much bigger army than we did in South Africa—much, much bigger! Our army is much smaller than the German army. So, I guess they should cause us to worry."

"Then why are we going?" asked Jack

"For the same reasons we went to South Africa, Jack," I said. "It's our duty."

"I've heard that before," said Mike. "Isn't that what we said before going to South Africa?"

"Aye, Mike. But that was a far-off war. This war is on our doorstep," I said. "The Germans are marching through Belgium, a small country close to our shores. Where will they go next? France? England? It's 21 miles across the channel from Calais to Dover. They could do that with ease. We must stop them. We are protecting our homes and families here in England. Who else will do that if not us?"

"Aye," said Mike. "I get it!"

"Aye, me too," said Jack.

"And me," said Fred. "We don't want them here. We have to stop them."

"Did you chap hear of that poor soldier who shot himself at Whittington?" asked Mike.

"Aye, he was a 2/DLI bandsman; the Army told him he couldn't join the rest of us for active duty in Europe," I said. "I heard his name was Robert Archer Ferguson, from London. Concerned about his behaviour, a fellow soldier followed him to the bathhouse, which Ferguson had entered and locked the door. Soon after, the soldier heard a shot in the bathhouse and called for help. As they entered the bathhouse, they found him dead with the rifle barrel still in his mouth."

"Shite! Is that any reason for killing yourself," asked Jack?

"It's a bloody shame," I said. "Our officers are saying he is our first casualty of the war."

The army was short of accommodation at Dunfermline for the large numbers of troops, so they quartered the troops in local homes and municipal buildings until 11 August. That's when the battalion was to go into camp at the Transy Estate (shortened from Transylvania). Others ended up in one of the Carnegie libraries. They billeted still more in the town hall.

The drill sergeants said route marching and the breaking in of army boots was a priority. They enlisted men with the colours for seven years. [83] Some soldiers could have left the army as long ago as 1906, like Joe and his Marras, when they completed their tours. However, others may have only been out of the military for months or weeks. The one

---

[83] Meaning recalled to their regular regiments

thing they had in common was the fact they had, as infantrymen, the ability to fire fifteen aimed shots in one minute [84].

"They billeted me in the home of Mr and Mrs Jamie Kennedy, whose three sons had left for training with the Black Watch," recalled Joe.

"So, ye are heading to France too, Laddie," said Jamie, opening a conversation before supper that evening.

"Aye, sir, I am," I said. "We don't know yet whether it will be France or Belgium."

"Well, I'm proud of ye, Joe," said Jamie. "Our sons are going too. They have joined the Black Watch and the Royal Highlanders and are in training at Aldershot. I believe they are in the 1st Battalion, part of the 1st Brigade in the 1st Division."

"Is this their first stint with the Army?" I asked.

"Aye, for two of them. But our eldest Donald was in South Africa," said Jamie.

"I don't believe it. Me too!"

"He was with the 2nd Battalion then as part of the Highland Brigade commanded by Major-General Andrew Gilbert Wauchope. They suffered heavy losses at the Battle of Magersfontein in December 1899. The Boers killed the General, too. Donald got injured and spent the rest of that war

---

[84] John Sheen, The Steel of the DLI: The 2nd Battalion of the Durham Light Infantry at war 1914-1918, Pen & Sword Military, 2009

in hospital recovering," explained Jamie with pride. "But he's fine now."

"That was before my time, sir," I said, "I only arrived in March 1901 after the biggest battles. The Boers wounded me, but it wasn't too serious. I served in the Cape Colony, Orange River Colony and the Transvaal, but we were fighting off the Boer guerrillas or repairing their damage nonstop."

"Good fur ye," said Jamie, "Protecting your King and the Empire. And now you and Donald are off to another war! This one started by the Boche."

"Aye. That I am," I said as we both rose to join Mrs. Kennedy at the supper table.

"We retired after dinner, rising bright and early the next morning," said Joe. "Mrs. Kennedy served an excellent full Scottish breakfast of porridge, eggs, bacon, sausage, black pudding, kippers, baked beans, grilled tomato, toast, tattie scones, marmalade and tea. With a full belly and well-rested, I thanked my hosts and was on my way to join the battalion on the next leg of our journey."

§

War Diary: Dunfermline, August 11th

The Battalion went into camp at TRANSY, ½ mile from DUNFERMLINE RY. STN

Empire and War

"More news of the war arrived on 12 August," said Joe. "On that day, Great Britain formally declared war on Germany's ally, the Austro-Hungarian Empire. With that, the whole of Europe was at war with itself."

"On that day, no sooner had we arrived at the Transy Camp than the army ordered the 2/DLI to join the rest of the 6th Division at Cambridge. So, on 13 August at 11 P.M., we found ourselves on another train heading south."

"Bloody hell," said Mike. "I wish the army could decide what to do with us. First, they sent us south to Whittington Barracks Lichfield. Then they send us north to Dunfermline. And now, after two days in Scotland, we're heading south again to Cambridge. I wish they'd make up their minds."

"Well, at least we're moving by train and not marching. In that way, we can see much more of the United Kingdom. Maybe they couldn't billet enough of us at Dunfermline. So, they're sending us to Cambridge instead?"

"Sure, moving by night," said Jack. "What can we see by night?"

"Aye, well, I guess they move us when the trains are available. Remember our travels by train in Africa and India? We travelled from Cape Town in the South to the far Northern and Eastern Transvaal in South Africa. We travelled in India from Calicut to Wellington, then from Wellington to Secunderabad to Lucknow and Bombay in the North. We have seen the world with the Army."

"Aye, it's been grand. That's why we joined."

"We arrived at Cambridge at 3 P.M. on 14 August and marched to a vast camp under canvas. There, we stayed for three weeks of training in hot weather until the army had formed the 6th Division in full. The military designed training to toughen us up and to test our endurance. Marching drills, bayonet fighting, musketry and trench digging were part of this training, too. [85] But it was so hot that year; I heard at least one recruit died on the drill parade [86]."

§

Before the BEF left England on 14 August, Sir John French received written orders from Lord Kitchener. These focussed on the relationship between Sir John French and the French Army and went straight to the heart of the politics of the Western Front. Kitchener attended school at Montreux, Switzerland, and he served with a French field ambulance unit in the Franco-Prussian War. He was fluent in the French language and understood the French mentality.

Sir John French's confidence in an Allied victory was unbounded as he dined in Paris on 14 August. French noted in his diary that *"the usual silly reports of French reverses"*

[85] Martin Pegler, British Tommy 1914-1918, Osprey, Oxford 1996

[86] John Sheen, The Steel of the DLI: The 2nd Battalion of the Durham Light Infantry at war 1914-1918, Pen & Sword Military, 2009

were *"all untrue."* [87] He visited Joffre the following day. Then, on the 16th, he travelled to Rethel on the Aisne to meet Charles Lanrezac, who commanded the French Fifth Army during the outbreak of the Great War. They preoccupied the latter with reports of German forces moving to his north, and the meeting was unsuccessful. Sir John's knowledge of the French language was lacking. He asked Lanrezac if he thought the Germans proposed to cross the Meuse at Huy. The French general shrugged his shoulders and said: "Tell the marshal that the Germans have gone to the Meuse to fish."

"I've heard Emperor Wilhelm II of Germany thought little the BEF," said Joe.

"They say he issued an order on 19 August 1914 to 'exterminate the treacherous English and walk over General French's contemptible little army.' In later years, the survivors of the regular army thus dubbed themselves The Old Contemptibles."

The Germans, French and Belgians fought several encounters along the eastern border of France and in southern Belgium, each side jockeying for position. Along this front, German armies numbered 1.3 million troops in seven armies. They swept into Luxembourg and Belgium as per the Schlieffen plan. The allies counted 1.25 million French, 117,000 Belgians and 70,000 British troops. The Battle of the

---

[87] Adam Hochschild, To End All Wars: A Story of Loyalty and Rebellion, 1914-1918, 2011

Frontiers along the Western Front comprised the battles of Mulhouse in southern Alsace, 7–10 August; Halen in Belgium, 12 August; Lorraine, eastern France, 14–25 August; the Ardennes, south-east Belgium, 21–23 August; Charleroi, Belgium 21–23 August and Mons, Belgium 23 August.

"Private John Parr, a reconnaissance cyclist, was the first British soldier who died in action on 21 August at Obourg in Belgium on the Western Front," said Joe.

"On 22 August, the BEF reached the coal mining town of Mons, Belgium, known as Bergen by the Flemish-speaking Belgians," said Joe.

"Just after 6:30 A.M., British cavalryman Captain Hornby became the first British soldier to kill a German soldier," said Joe.

"Hornby was fighting on horseback with his sword against a German lance. His squadron became the first unit of the BEF to fight the German army outside Mons on 22 August 1914."

"The Army alerted a troop of 4th Royal Irish Dragoon Guards north of Mons of the approach of German cavalrymen at 6.30 A.M. on Saturday, 22 August," said Joe.

"The Guards mounted their horses and gave chase in the first attack of the BEF in the Great War. Corporal Drummer Edward Thomas fired the first British shot of the war. He fired it in combat near the Belgian village of Casteau, close to

Mons. It was the first British shot in Europe since the Battle of Waterloo in Belgium 99 years before.

This battle saw the soldiers using lances and swords in a war that would see the advent of advanced military technology. A British commander returned with blood on his sword, a tradition that would soon end.

22 August 1914 went down in infamy as the deadliest day of the Great War. On that day, less than three weeks into the conflict, the Germans killed 27,000 French soldiers, many of whom were from the African colonies of Morocco, Senegal and Algeria. One division alone, the 3rd Colonial Infantry Division, lost 228 officers and over 10,000 other ranks, including 3,800 men taken prisoner. They killed two generals, wounded another, and captured yet another. Most of the French commanders perished. Among the divisional artillery, only one officer survived.

"The bloodbath in Europe had begun!" said Joe.

§

War Diary: Cambridge, Aug. 23

The DEAN OF DURHAM came from DURHAM and held a service for the Battalion on Sunday, 23 Aug.

Whilst at Cambridge, Battalion and Brigade training was carried out.

"Back in Cambridge, the 2/DLI was still in training," said Joe. "As a reservist, I didn't go through induction. Before shipping out to South Africa, I had done my basic training and received updates on the latest modern warfare as a reservist. I explained to my company the practice they were to get."

"Training starts with basic training for physical fitness, running drill and marching."

"However, the cocky and impatient drill sergeant took over from me.

"Aye, basic training teaches you discipline, how to follow commands, how to march, basic field skills and how to handle weapons," barked out the drill sergeant. "We'll have you laddies trooping and running nonstop. You'll do severe obstacle courses, shooting and bayonet training from early morning until late night." The sergeant let it sink in, then continued. "It's tough! Exhausting! You may beg us to stop, but believe me, lads, this training is essential and can save your arses when you arrive at the front."

"You will receive basic training in first aid, trench-building, barb-wiring, and other things you need to know to protect yourself on the front. Later, once you have specialized in the infantry as a rifleman, machine gunner, rifle grenadier, signaller or bomber, you'll receive courses in those specialization areas. You'll learn to look after your weapons, get shooting lessons and practice with live ammunition. We'll also teach you how to attack the enemy and drive your bayonet deep into his gut." To which the recruits looked at each other, either grimacing or grinning.

The battalion seconded Joe during recruit training to help the drill sergeant as an example of what the recruits should become and assist in any other way he could.

After this first training session, the marras commented.

"You did well out there," said Mike with a wink.

"Aye, you impressed us, Joe," said Fred with an enormous grin.

"Maybe, but instructing is not for me," I said. "The drill sergeant did much better."

"Well, he is loud and commands respect for sure," said Jack. "So those recruits trembled in their boots."

"We'll need every military skill we can get," I said. "Have you heard what's going on across the Channel?"

"Aye," said Mike. "Word is going around about the German advance. I've heard it's getting rough over there."

"That's for sure," I said. "The Boche are racing through Belgium towards France and us. On 23 to 24 August 1914, the first battle of the war fought by the BEF was at Mons, Belgium. In this struggle, the BEF stopped the Germans. And so began a month-long fight, 'Great Retreat' to the River

Marne in northern France. The British suffered over 1,600 casualties but stopped the German advance at the Marne."

"Aye, we did," said a companion listening to Joe's story at Hamelin Camp. "We stopped them dead in their tracks. I was there."

"That's the way it went for us," called another. "Well told, Joe."

"Aye, thanks, Joe," said yet another.

"That all happened over two years ago," said Walt. "Here we are still in bloody POW camps in Germany."

"Aye, and the war rages on," said Joe. "They are saying 1916 was the worst year so far for casualties."

As 1916 ended, the twelve battles of the Somme resulted in total losses of 420,000 British men, 200,000 French, and 450,000 to 680,000 Germans. The Battle of Verdun resulted in 540,000 French and 430,000 German casualties.

There were other struggles on the Western Front during 1916, the most notable being the Battle of Hulluch. At that battle, the Germans unleashed cloud gas attacks on British troops from 27 to 29 April 1916. That was near the village of Hulluch, one mile north of Loos in northern France. The gas used by the German forces for this battle was a mixture of chlorine and phosgene, which they first used on 19 December 1915 at Wieltje, near Ypres. The Germans concentrated their gas enough to penetrate the British PH gas helmets. These attacks were part of an engagement between the II Bavarian Corps and British I Corps divisions. The British suffered 1,980 casualties, of which 1,260 were gas-related, and 338 died. The Germans had 1,500 gas casualties.

Using poison gas by the principal belligerents throughout the Great War was a war crime. Its use violated the 1899 Hague Declaration Concerning Asphyxiating Gases and the 1907 Hague Convention on Land Warfare, which prohibited using "poison or poisoned weapons" in warfare [88].

With joint casualties of well over two million men, the battles on the River Somme and at Verdun made 1916 the bloodiest year of the Great War.

§

Recalling the Mobilization of the Great War

Christmas and New Year's, or 'Saint Sylvester's Day' or just 'Sylvester' as the Germans call it, came and went. The guards gave Joe's cabin notice they were being transferred to another camp. When asked where they were going, the guards told them they were moving to Cellelager VI for a while. They didn't tell them how long they'd be staying there. Cellelager VI at Vehnemoor was part of the Cellelager group of work camps.

---

[88] Thomas Graham; Damien J. Lavera (2003). Cornerstones of Security: Arms Control Treaties in the Nuclear Era. University of Washington Press.

"Oh, you will love it there," their guard said, chuckling with glee. "It is cold and wet with Raureif (freezing fog or hoar frost) at this time of the year. And lots of Torfmoos (peat moss)."

A collective protest arose from their fellow prisoners.

"Perfect!" whispered Joe to his marras. "The Germans won't have any suspicions. They will think we don't want to go."

§

But on a Sunday before they left for Vehnemoor, Joe recounted the mobilization and start of the war in August 1914.

"As we finished loading the compartments with the war kits, I told the sergeant we were ready just in time. 'War must soon be upon us'."

"Aye, that it will be, Joe," said the sergeant, "I believe we will hear tonight."

"The army refined the mobilization orders for the Durham Light Infantry in the summer of 1914. Every Reserve officer and man at the depot knew what they needed when the time came. At the 2/DLI depot, each reservist had a compartment with his necessary equipment. [89] As an active reservist, I assisted in the preparation. I had the latest army

---

[89] John Sheen, *The Steel of the DLI: The 2nd Battalion of the Durham Light Infantry at war 1914-1918*, Pen & Sword Military, 2009

uniform and was familiar with the newest infantry rifle, but other field items were fresh."

In August 1914, they kitted the British soldier out with the 1902 Pattern Service Dress tunic and trousers. They coloured the thick woollen tunic with dark Indian khaki. There were many pockets where the soldier could store personal items, such as the soldier's AB64 Pay Book, First Field Dressing, cigarettes, photos, etc. The army issued puttees, another Indian invention, to wrap around the ankles and calves for protection and support, and standard boots with hobnail soles [90.]

Besides the uniform, they outfitted the British soldier with the kit required for battle. The British were the first European army to replace leather belts and pouches with webbing, a sturdy material made from woven cotton. The 1908 Pattern Webbing equipment the soldiers received comprised a wide belt, ammunition pouches, bayonet frog and attachment for the entrenching tool handle. There was a collapsible spade in a web cover, a water bottle carrier, a small haversack and a sizeable pack. The pack was for carrying the soldier's greatcoat, a blanket and a mess tin. Inside the haversack were personal items, a knife and, when on Active Service, unused portions of the daily ration. The

---

[90] Chappell, Mike (2000). British Infantry Equipments 1908–2000. Osprey Publishing.

complete set of 1908 webbing could weigh over seventy pounds [91].

"The duty officer hand-recorded the first log entries in the War Diary of the 2nd Battalion of the Durham Light Infantry from Tuesday evening 4 August 1914," said Joe.

"The battalion was at multiple locations between its Precautionary Period stations in South Shields and at the 2/DLI Headquarters at Whittington Barracks, Staffordshire, near Lichfield."

War Diary of the 2nd Battalion D.L.I., 18th Brigade, 6th Division, Lichfield, August 4th, 6.30 pm[92]

Order to mobilize received. 1st Day mobn 5th August 1914

When mobn was ordered, the Precautionary Period Detachments under Maj MANDER were in their allotted places, i.e.

1. Head Quarter Bat. At South Shields under Maj MANDER, 400 men (of whom 137 were

---

[91] Chappell, Mike (2000). British Infantry Equipments 1908–2000. Osprey Publishing.
[92] The National Archives, 6th Division, 18th Infantry Brigade, 2nd Battalion Durham Light Infantry, August 1914 – March 1916, Document 724

provided by the 1ˢᵗ Bⁿ P.W.O. W. West Yorkshire Regt.) and Capt. HARE and Lieut. YATE less the sub-detachments:

   i. Capt. Best, HEPBURN Dock, 21 men

  ii. Lt. Taylor, Oil Depot, S. Shields, 25 men

 iii. Lt. Norton, FRENCHMANS BATTERY, S. Shields, 25 men

  iv. Lt. Grey-Wilson, PALMERS DOCK, JARROW, 20 men

"As recorded in the War Diary that day," said Joe, "Major Morant received the telegram ordering mobilization at 6:30 P.M. on the evening of 4 August. The battalion's years of practice made the procedure routine. Yet the wording of the telegram, '*mobilize stop to acknowledge*,' came as a complete puzzle to everyone involved. One depot commander wired back, 'I have stopped mobilizing.' [93] The telegram might have read 'mobilize stop, acknowledge stop' in telegram speak. It was a minor detail that soon cleared up and didn't delay the 2/DLI mobilization long.

"Major Hubert Morant commanded the Durham Light Infantry Depot, which had moved from Sunderland, County

---

[93] John Sheen, *The Steel of the DLI: The 2nd Battalion of the Durham Light Infantry at war 1914-1918*, Pen & Sword Military, 2009

Durham, to Fenham Barracks in Newcastle upon Tyne, Northumberland. The Durhams shared these premises with the Northumberland Fusiliers in 1884.

"When they received the order to mobilize, most of the 2nd Battalion regulars were in Whittington Barracks Lichfield," said Joe.

"However, a detachment of two hundred and sixty-three men under Major Mander was at its Precautionary Period stations in South Shields, Hepburn Dock. It also had men at the South Shields Oil Depot, Frenchman's Battery, South Shields and Palmers Dock, Jarrow. My marras and I joined this contingent since it was closest to where we lived, but they soon transferred us to Major Mander's station in South Shields." [94]

Later that evening, on 4 August 1914, Joe was preparing himself for departure with Mary without uttering a word. The children were asleep in bed and unaware of the monumental events unfolding around them.

"Thanks, Mary," I said as Mary handed me my belt. "Light compared to my old leather one, isn't it?"

"Aye, Joe," she said with a heavy heart. I had gone through this before, but for Mary, it was her first experience preparing for war, which made her apprehensive. So many thoughts and worries swirled in her head. How would she

---

[94] John Sheen, *The Steel of the DLI: The 2nd Battalion of the Durham Light Infantry at war 1914-1918*, Pen & Sword Military, 2009

cope without Joe? How would the children deal with his absence? Would a soldier's salary be enough to feed their family?

"Come on, Mary," I said while hugging her. "I know it's not easy, and I don't want to go to war again. But thanks to the Germans, we must go through this. The Government doesn't think it will last much more than a month or two. They are saying we'll be back before Christmas. Please understand I can't stay behind and let others fight the battles to protect us. While I still can, I must be part of it. You will receive most of my pay from the army to care for the house and children."

"I understand, Joe," whispered Mary. "I hope it won't last too long. Now, make sure you write as often as you can. And make sure you include words for the children."

"That I will do, my love," I said, "I'll try to write every day if time allows." So, after my kisses for my sleeping children, last goodbyes and a long hug, Mary straightened my uniform with tears in her eyes.

"Stay safe," she said while hugging me again.

"Be strong, my darling," I said before leaving. "We have no choice in this matter. The Germans have made sure of that."

"So, after one last kiss on her forehead, I grabbed my rifle and left home, hurrying to the allotted meeting point. I wasn't eager to go to war again, but my sense of duty forced me. My old marras, Mike and Jack, soon joined me. And Fred soon joined us, too, wearing a broad smile and his threadbare and outdated blue and red uniform from his days in the army. We all greeted him and slapped him on the back."

"Here we go again," called Mike.

"Aye; left, right, left, right," joked Jack.

"Steady, you lot," called out Fred, trailing behind, "Give an old man a break, not so fast!"

"Are we ready?" I yelled with a giggle. "Keep up with us, old man. And trade that uniform in for a fresh one."

"Aye, Joe," they all said, quickening their pace. "We're all with you; just getting warmed up. Eight years after our return to civilian life, we were in active service once more and heading towards war in Europe."

§

Memories of our First Act of War

Seizure of the German Merchant Ship
Albert Clement

War Diary: Lichfield, August 4th continued

On the night of 4 August and into the early hours of the 5th of August, Major D'Arcy Wentworth Mander, aided by Captain Harry

Hare and Lieutenant Victor Yate with 30 men, seized a German merchant ship lying in the Tyne.

When Britain declared war, the Government ordered British forces to impound German ships and properties. On 4 August, a German crew had just moored their vessel called the *Albert Clement* at Tyne Dock. Tyne Dock is in South Shields on the south bank of the River Tyne. It took its name from the North Eastern Railway's large dock on the river built in 1859 to handle Tyneside's coal exports. At its height, the export trade there amounted to seven million tons of coal transported via the four huge staithes built to ease the loading.

"We were in South Shields when Major Mander's detachment, including Captain Harry Hare and Lieutenant Victor Yate, moved to impound the Albert Clement. It was lying at Tyne Dock, and we arrested the crew. We quickly marched to the dock and boarded the German ship cautiously."

The *Albert Clement* was a tiny, nondescript German steamship built by Neptun Werft AG in the North German Hanseatic City of Rostock in 1904. It was a steel single-screw steamer with one deck fitted with electric lights, a recent improvement to shipping. It was 234.2 feet long with a 35.3-foot beam and a gross tonnage of 1,166 tons. At its launch in

1904, the owners named the ship after a distinguished Rostock businessman, *Albert Clement.*

"This must be one of the first actions in this war," I whispered Joe to my marras!

"I'm sure you're right, Joe, whispered Mike in return."

"As we boarded, two German crewmen met us at the gangway," said Joe. "The sailors couldn't speak English, but from their behaviour, the Major surmised they understood what was happening. We could see they were worried, and they stepped aside without resistance, raising their hands on high instead."

"Someone has forewarned them," said the Major to Captain Hare. "They must know that we have declared war."

"Lieutenant Hare chose two soldiers and stayed behind to guard the sailors while the rest of us headed for the bridge with the major," said Joe.

"There, we found the captain waiting. He was a scruffy-looking chap with a long beard and a wide moustache. He was not the best example of a sea captain, but what could one expect of a coal carrier?"

"Good evening," said Major Mander. "The British Crown is impounding your ship, Captain. You and your crew are under arrest, but we will treat you well if you don't resist."

"The captain was calm as he surrendered and understood English," said Joe. "He led the major and his men to the rest of the crew below deck."

"England and Germany are at war," explained the major to the crew, unsure how many understood him. "You are under arrest. Do not resist, and everything will be fine."

"The Captain translated the major's words into German," said Joe. "The major left Lieutenant Hare and a few soldiers behind to guard the ship until the Navy relieved them. We then marched the captain and crew to the South Shields police station, where they jailed them. It went well enough; the major was in complete control and was the perfect gentleman, as always. It may well have been one of the first ships and crews captured by the British in the war."

"I must admit I felt sorry for them. They looked like our pitmen, their faces weathered by the sea and blackened with coal. They may have been from the engine room. This war is not their fault; their Kaiser started it. Oh, and they arrested a Pastor Singer of the German Sailors Home. A party of soldiers escorted him to the police station, too."

§

6. *Christmas 1916*

Soldiers were no longer amenable to a truce by 1916. The war had become very bitter after the devastating human losses suffered during the battles of the Somme and Verdun, and poison gas and flamethrowers and all the rest.

However, American special war correspondent Percival Phillips[95], embedded with the British Armies, published an article titled "Pantomimes, pictures and pierrots" with the *Daily Express* on 24 December 1916. [96]

"The British armies in the field are determined to make this Christmas merry. Despite the unavoidable disadvantages of mud, morose Germans, and alfresco celebrations in front-line trenches, they look forward to a day of genuine cheer tonight. And you will find the true Christmas spirit tomorrow in the dug-outs and billets behind the British front.

"I saw much evidence of this holiday atmosphere in Picardy today as I motored for miles through the area behind the Somme battlefield. Thousands of British soldiers were preparing their temporary homes for tomorrow's feast, and everywhere, there was the same cheerful activity unconnected with the business of war.

"The trucks crawling along the roads carried puddings by the hundredweight. Their drivers beamed at the ovation given these munitions of Christmas in the villages through which they passed.

---

[95] Sir Percival Phillips was born in Brownsville, Pennsylvania, USA, in 1877. He worked for various American daily newspapers and established himself as one of the country's leading war correspondents. In 1901 Phillips moved to England where joined the recently formed *Daily Express*. In August 1914 Phillips was sent to Belgium where he was attached to the Belgian Army. He covered the invasion of Belgium, and in 1915 Phillips became one of the five journalists selected by the government to report the war on the Western Front. After a long and successful career, Percival Phillips died in 1937.

[96] https://www.open.edu/openlearn/history-the-arts/history/christmas-war-1916-festivities-the-front

"Cottages, stables, even farmyards, were being decorated with whatever materials the temporary occupants could rake together from the little shops. The mobilization of gifts from home proceeded under the eyes of experts, who organized the food resources of their respective units with admirable discretion.

"Christmas celebrations will differ according to the situation of the men. I imagine that most front-line battalions will eat their dinner in peace if the prevailing calm of the battle area foretells tomorrow's conditions.

"At one place, a few Saxons hoisted the usual placard (the Saxons would rather write than fight). They urged their British opponents to 'kindly keep quiet Christmas, and we will do the same.' But no Christmas truce has or will occur, whatever the wishes of the homesick Germans, and there will be no fraternizing by opposing armies. One does not expect a significant spurt of activity.

"Doubtless, the gunners will send over their usual quota of shells, for these gentlemen work in all weathers, Sundays and holidays included. They consider an exchange of high explosives an inevitable feature of the routine operations.

"Battalions in rest have organized a variety of entertainments, and some of the Christmas productions are excellent. They are producing pantomimes in several divisional areas. One permanent 'pierrot' troupe, which gladdens the hearts of a Scottish division, appears tomorrow night in a new and ambitious programme worthy of any first-class London hall.

"They have prepared it for this Christmas entertainment, written and produced by professionals, and completed with new scenery and elaborate costumes.

"This Christmas production will occur every night in a barn seating 500 soldiers. The divisional band furnishes the music, and seats are available at various prices, the highest being ten pence.

"Even the poor survivors of the devastating districts will have Christmas dinner. I know of one underground refuge in Arras, where they will assemble and feed many local carefree children.

"There is a pathetic little Christmas tree in one of these cellars of Arras. It's a tiny, stunted handful of green, decorated with three or four candles that they secured with infinite labour to make a few children glad tomorrow.

"Day after day, the German guns send their high explosives into Arras, where some families still live and work. Children play and study in the safe retreats underneath the stricken town. None have less cause to look forward to a merry Christmas than these penniless refugees haunted day and night by the shells of their enemy.

"Yet, if they cannot be merry, they are full of hope and courage. If you knew what the people of France think of

Germany's call for peace, talk with the inhabitants of Arras. None of them will awaken on Christmas morning with a prayer for peace."

§

1917—The year of desperation

7. Transfer to Celle VI Vehnemoor Work Camp

One morning at the start of the New Year 1917, the guards awoke the men even earlier than usual. They gave the prisoners time to gulp weak coffee and eat black bread saved from the previous night. Then, the guards mustered them and did a roll call, noting that a few men were missing. The guards began a search for the missing prisoners, who they soon found hiding in their barracks. They shoved them back to roll call with loud cursing and occasional slaps to the back of their heads.

"We have a train to catch! Thanks to your lost friends here, we must run to the station late."

They were soon running along the road, loaded with their gear: clobber, blankets, washbasin, bare mattresses, and wooden clogs the Stalag had issued them before leaving. "You'll need these," the guard told them. It was still dark when they entrained for Bremen, seventy miles away. So, they settled in for the ride in a third-class passenger wagon with no other passengers at the back of the train. As the train moved into its monotonous rocking ride, the men could see they were heading northwest, bringing them nearer the sea and Holland!

They sat in the Hauptbahnhof at Bremen on the North Sea, the second largest seaport in Germany after Hamburg, for two hours. The sign stated that they built the impressive train station between 1886 and 1891, with architecture and style befitting the era.

"Why aren't we sitting in Newcassel station waiting for someone?" asked Mike.

"Aye, you've got an excellent point there, Mike," said Joe. "They are similar, but this one looks newer. The people rushing around look different, too."

"I'd prefer to be waiting for a train to Hamelin," said Walt with a grin. "I wouldn't mind seeing Traudle again."

"You and your Traudle," said Mike. "Don't you have a nice English hinny waiting for you back home?"

"Why are we not here escaping to Holland, Walt?" asked Joe.

"That would never work," said Walt. "The Germans would send descriptions of us to the police, and they'd catch us out here in the open."

"Aye, or on the train to Holland," said Mike.

"I'm sure you're right there," said Joe, again sinking into silence.

"It's good to know that you are thinking about that," said Walt after a while.

So, after two hours, they continued their journey under guard by another train to Oldenburg, another thirty miles to the west. At four o'clock in the afternoon, they arrived in

Oldenburg, detrained and marched the remaining ten miles southwest to Cellelager VI.

Arriving at a canal, they loaded their packs on an available skiff, then pulled this along by ropes as they walked further. The path followed the channel with peat sheds along its bank and the occasional barge boat loaded with peat. Along the way, they noted how flat and wet the landscape was in this part of Germany. A thick mist carrying a pervasive smell of the sea enveloped them. They could only see a few yards but noticed many diggings with neat piles of peat blocks scattered in the bog. It was then they realized the work they'd be doing in this working camp, where they arrived late that evening in total darkness.

As they entered the encampment, they saw it was small and had fewer prisoners. At most, there were 300 or 400 prisoners at Celle VI instead of the thousands interned at Cellelager.

The camp guards marched them to their barracks at once.

"Bunks stacked three high as usual," noted Mike. "There was also a stove, a table and enough chairs for half of us. I guess they expect us to meet or eat in two shifts."

There were a few small windows in each cabin, but they didn't allow enough light in, so the authorities provided paraffin lanterns. The thin wooden floor was without a covering, and since the wind flowed beneath the cabins, the bare boards were frigid in winter.

"This cabin is bloody cold," said Mike.

"Aye; you're right there," said Joe. "Maybe it will be warmer once we get that peat burning in the stove."

On the first night, they slept on empty mattresses under their Red Cross blanket and two German-issue covers apiece. It was cold and damp, but by then, the peat stove was glowing hot to fend off the chill.

The Germans had built the camp on the flat ground of a slight rise above the peat and waterline. One step from the door landed one in fresh mud and puddles. It soon became plain what the reason for wooden clogs was!

The typical routine of this camp was the same as the others Joe had experienced. Reveille sounded at five or earlier in summer. The prisoners arose, dressed and filled their mugs with tea without milk and sugar. The wise ones saved their bread from the night before and could have it with their tea. Then there was a roll call when they gave the mixed group of prisoners a chance to volunteer for work, not that there were many choices. The POWs answered the roll call in their language, either with the English word "Present," the French word "Présent," the Russian "Bot," pronounced "Vot," or the Flemish "Hier." At noon, there was soup and another roll call. At five o'clock, there was an issue of black bread made from potato flour. According to the Canadian prisoners, there were no books or papers; the canteen sold nothing but matches, notepaper, and something that tasted like buckwheat honey.

It was January, cold and dark. The fog rolled in most nights and often hung around for a few days before clearing for a day or two. There was every ruse for the prisoners not wanting to work in this camp. At every opportunity, the inmates found reasons not to work in the peat bog, such as constant rain and sleet, poor health, coughing or sore chests. However, the biggest reason for not wanting to work was not to help the Germans. Every day, they devise novel ways of avoiding work. "Nicht arbeiten" was the frequent lament. This camp was slack enough, so they often got away with it.

One morning, as the guards were making up a working party, they reported they were short of bodies.

"Everyone attended roll call last night," said the sergeant in charge. "The guards were alert. So, no one could have escaped. Where are they? Find them."

After much commotion, cursing and running around searching, they found the delinquents hiding rolled up in their mattresses. This trick only worked briefly until the guards included a cabin search for their morning mustering.

Joe met a Canadian prisoner who had been there a while.

"A few of the smart prisoners scrubbed the table or swept the cabin floor at inspection time," he told Joe.

"That way, they fooled the guards into believing someone had assigned them to that menial work. The guards then left them alone! Guards gone, they returned to their bunks to while away the frosty morning hours. Clever, eh?"

"Aye," said Joe. "If it works."

"The Kommandant came in one day to inspect the huts before the prisoners left for work," the Canadian said with a grin. "Bed-ridden prisoners were present in large numbers, sitting up and enjoying life as invalids while those preparing for work stood at attention next to their bunks. The Kommandant was in terrible humour and yelled: 'Schweinstall' (pigsty) at the sight of the mattresses and how the men had left their beds and clothes. He shouted, 'This is disgusting; you must fix your beds. They are shocking.' But the soldiers he cursed were the obedient ones preparing for work."

"Did you scum hear the Kommandant?" asked a guard. "Tomorrow, we will come again, and this place must look clean and proper."

"He ignored the more insolent prisoners, who were lounging in their beds laughing at him," said the Canadian. "He didn't say another word, and after those few angry words, he left, mumbling as he went."

This unusual exchange surprised Joe and his marras.

"That was strange," said Mike. "Those guys walked all over the Kommandant. We have never seen that with a Prussian officer up to now."

"Has it always been this way?" asked Joe. "It was much tougher and more disciplined at the other camps where I've been."

"I know," said the Canadian. "I've experienced enough of Germany and German methods to know this camp cannot last. Something will happen; either they will move us, or there will be a new Kommandant and a fresh set of guards."

On another day, Joe was talking to his new Canadian friend.

"Has anyone ever escaped this camp?" asked Joe.

"A few," the Canadian said. "I'm planning to as soon as I can!"

"How did they get out?" asked Joe.

"It was before my time," said the Canadian. "I believe they escaped during the day somehow. I know a little about it and can tell you what I know."

Joe realized escaping from the camp would be a significant challenge. After inspecting Celle VI's security, Joe told his marras, "The campground is 300 feet long and 75 feet wide, with nowhere to hide, even at night. I've done a thorough check. They built a 10-foot high barbed wire fence enclosure by setting long posts deep in the ground and stretching thick wire guys with a wire stretcher. These wires were so taut that one couldn't widen them. A few feet inside this outer fence is an ordinary barbed wire fence with several strands. It makes a no-man's-land, which the guards forbid the prisoners from entering. Outside the camp at the northwest corner is the hut where the guards live when not on duty. They keep an enormous and vicious-looking watchdog in a kennel there. The camp is lit up at night by enormous arc lights 60 feet apart. They position guards outside and around the encampment. Not only that, but bog and water surround the entire camp. I don't think it would be easy to escape from inside this camp!"

§

8.   *Escape Attempt from Celle VI Vehnemoor Camp*

That night, Joe discussed what he had learnt from the Canadian. "We need to escape while working outside the camp," said Joe. "We need a map and a compass."

"What do we need a compass for?" asked Mike. "We know we have to go west, so we'll just go west!"

"What about in fog or at night?" asked Joe. "How are you going to know where the west is then? We cannot escape in broad daylight. We must slip away in a thick fog and travel at night so they cannot see us. Knowing where you are going isn't easy unless you understand the heavens or have a compass. Not even the heavens will help us during those long foggy periods here."

"Hmmm, right," acknowledged Mike. "So, we need a compass. How to hell are we going to find one of those?"

"You'll find one, Mike," said Joe. "I know you will, but we must all try."

And before long, Mike found one.

"I made a trade with a Russian of a few British cigarettes for a simple compass that works," said Mike one day. "I've checked it out by the sun, and it works. So, what's our plan?"

"Well," said Walt. "We get out of here daily to go to the diggings."

"Aye, that's it," cried Joe. "That's it. We must disappear during the day when we are out at the diggings. We need the perfect foggy day for that."

"That shouldn't be too difficult," said Walt. "Every day is foggy here, at least in the morning."

The penny had dropped. For the next few days at the diggings, they became astute observers. They made a note of every detail. How observant the guards were, how they could slip away without the guards noticing. They observed their surrounding countryside on a cloudless day and memorized all noteworthy landmarks, such as single trees and woods—no buildings were visible. And they calculated how far they needed to get into the surrounding countryside during fog before being invisible to the camp, etc.

Each night, they huddled and compared notes in a whisper.

"I have noticed that a few guards are not as sharp as others while working at the diggings during the day," said Walt.

"Maybe we can find a sleepy one that won't see us slip away before they call us to return to camp?"

"Hmmm," said Mike. "Maybe that could work. Let's watch and see if we can find one."

"We need to decide what to take with us," said Joe. "We need to prepare to last several days in this miserable country. We will need enough bread to keep us going for a while. Water should be available for drinking, I'm sure. It's everywhere here."

"So, we need to stash whatever we have in the lining of our greatcoats to carry with us," said Walt.

"Make sure we hide the compass and the knife Mike has magically found. We must keep them ready."

"I think I've found our sleepy guard," said Joe one day. "An old guy often huddles in whatever shelter he can find against the weather while we work. That old guy with messy hair and a beard. If we are careful, we can slip away without him noticing."

"Gunter," said Mike. "We call him Gunter. That's his name."

"Good. Then we must find a way into Gunter's workgroup," said Joe.

They attached themselves to his workgroup as soon as they could. When working, they kept together and became more observant as they worked. And they learned how to separate from the group, disappear into the fog, and sneak around unnoticed. They even worked through the procedure and practised it a few times to make sure everyone knew what they had to do.

One day, the opportunity presented itself. They had been digging for a while, piling up the peat moss at one spot far from the camp that day. A thick fog rolled in and enveloped everything, and they all but disappeared, separated from their group while still digging. Then, well before the guard issued his departure instructions, they ducked behind a pile of peat bricks.

"Now's our chance, Lads," Joe whispered. "Let's make a run for it."

"Aye," said Mike. "Let's go, but with no noise!"

No one appeared to notice them missing, including the guard, so they eased themselves toward the canal path and into the gloom. Tall grasses grew on the outer side of that footway, and they slunk deep behind it and made a crouched getaway.

But the canal and path were heading southeast, not in the direction they needed to go. So, once the marras had run 300 yards, they found a trail heading west and took it, moving as fast as they could without making a noise.

"This way, quick now, lads," said Joe. "They still haven't noticed, or we'd hear an uproar."

They pushed on through the bog even though the going got tough. Despite a thin sheet of ice, the men broke through it, sinking to their knees first and then to their thighs in freezing water and mud.

"Shite, lads," said Mike. "How far do we have to go in this bog?"

"Shut your gob and keep going," said Walt.

"Aye, we daren't give up now," said Joe.

With incredible stamina, the three arrived at the edge of the bog after several minutes of an exhausting slog through the mud. There, they found a small copse of juniper and birch trees under which they collapsed from exhaustion and collected themselves.

"We've made it this far, lads," said Joe.

"Aye, for the time being," said Mike. "Still, we mustn't wait too long in case they come after us."

They rested for an hour, but when they heard the alarm go off back at the camp, it spurred them into action. They were at least a mile away by then, but they could see the arc lamps sweeping the gloom as the fog reduced them to a bright, moving glow. They continued for two more hours while the darkness of night enveloped them.

"I don't think they'll come after us now," said Joe. "They'll be after us soon enough in the morning. Let's get a brief rest and continue as soon as possible."

Exhausted, they dozed off into a restless slumber for an hour. Then, the marras pushed westward into the night, occasionally stopping to check their compass using a match for light. By early the following day, it was still dark, and the fog hadn't dissipated. So, after a quick breakfast of stale bread, the escapees rechecked their bearings and headed even farther west. Their simple map showed a village called Friesoythe should not be far away, and 30 miles beyond that was the border. They needed to skirt the town with caution.

They had worked out by walking three miles per hour. They could reach the borderline by nightfall. The track was much more accessible now, with hard sandy soil and heather interspersed with many small paths. They thought the secondary trails must have been from animals, most likely sheep or goats. Sure enough, they soon saw evidence of this with little piles of dung occasionally. Further on, they sometimes encountered sheep munching on grass and other wild plants.

This terrain continued for the entire day as they walked on through it. Then they heard voices and the sound of farm animals through the rising fog and realized they were approaching a farmhouse or a village.

"Quiet, lads, not a sound," whispered Joe. "Let's give this village a wide miss."

The marras became far more cautious and didn't utter a sound. They could just see the village buildings as they found a way around them. They saw no one and assumed that no one had seen them. So, the village behind them pushed on as fast as possible.

By mid-afternoon, the fog lifted as fast as it had descended. The marras then found themselves exposed on a flat grassland plain and heath interspersed with small stands of conifers. They reckoned they were only a few miles from the Dutch border. Everything was bright white from hoar frost except them, making them very visible from a distance. There were no more voices or animal noises, so they felt assured of their safety. It focused them on their destination, not noticing what was approaching behind them. Then, two hours later, looking over his shoulder, Joe saw an advancing line of soldiers stretched out and moving towards them across the terrain. The soldiers lowered their rifles, ready and gleaming in the waning sunlight. One soldier in their centre had an enormous dog on their scent, leading the soldiers towards their quarry.

"Should we run for it?" asked Mike.

"Don't anybody run or even move," said Walt. "If we do that, they will shoot us!"

That was excellent advice since they were within the comfortable range of German rifles. They stood rigid in agreement and waited, shivering from the cold and fear, until the soldiers caught up with them. They realized their first try to escape had failed. The most they could hope for now was that the punishment was not too severe!

"Will they shoot us?" asked Mike.

"I hope not," said Joe. "I'm not ready for that!"

"That makes three of us," said Walt.

Soon, soldiers surrounded them.

"Sorry, English," called one of the German soldiers with an enormous grin. "Did you think you could get away from us?"

The others laughed and took hold of the three escaping marras.

They weren't far from the town of Friesoythe. So that is where the soldiers led them for transport back to camp. The Kommandant awaited them when they arrived, and the guards led the prisoners to him. He looked livid and bellowed, "Englishe Shweine (English Pigs)! Do you think you can make me look stupid? Did you think you could get away from me? You left a long trail through the bog we could follow, you idiots! I am furious! I must think of a suitable punishment for you tomorrow. Go to your cabin. I never want to see you again!"

And that was that. No more screaming. No more fuss. The escapees never saw the Kommandant again; he stomped into his quarters and didn't re-emerge. The guards remained civil, rationalizing this episode as POWs getting lost in the fog and trying to make a run for it. They couldn't blame them. These escapees were most fortunate; another camp, another Kommandant, and they were alive.

"Maybe the Canadian was right, and this camp is on its way out," said Joe.

"Or maybe it's a sign that ordinary Germans are tiring of this war too and want to see it end."

"You may be right," said Mike. "This war has gone on long enough. For the Germans and us."

The next time he saw the Canadian, he expressed regret that their attempt had failed.

"I'm so sorry you didn't make it, Joe," said the Canadian.

"Thank ye," said Joe. "We were maybe two miles from the Dutch border,"

"Better luck next time, my friend," said the Canadian.

"Thank you, Canuck," said Joe. "If there's a next time. We'll now have a target on our backs. I'm sure it won't be so easy next time."

The following morning, they learned their little group was returning to Cellelager before being transferred to Soltau camp further north. What that meant, they did not know. However, none of their companion prisoners were angry with them or blamed them for their transfer. They admired them for their courage and determination. "Never mind," they said. "You can try again from wherever we are going next. But we've not heard good things about this Soltau camp."

§

9.   Internment at the Soltau POW Camp 3 February 1917—11 November 1918

After a quick 27-mile transfer from Scheuen, Joe's group arrived at Soltau camp on 3 February 1917. It was their third German POW camp, not counting Celle VI, which belonged to Cellelager.

"This place is massive," said Joe to his mates as they entered the encampment.

"Well, let's hope it's better than the others," said Mike.

"Looking at the surroundings as we came here, it's remote," said Walt. "Did you notice the tracks on the way here? It looks as if it's a troop exercise zone. The army surrounds us here! And we're too far from the Dutch border."

"So, no chance of escape," said Joe.

"You may be right," said Walt. "Let's get settled in and get to know the place first. Who knows, maybe we'll get another chance from a working camp?"

The Soltau Camp's size awed Joe and his marras. The Germans purpose-built Soltau Lager, another Imperial German 10th Army Corps POW prison camp, between 1914 and 1915. The camp was the largest POW camp in Germany during the Great War, capable of holding seventy-five thousand inmates at its peak. It comprised eighty barracks accommodating a thousand inmates each in two linked camps. Wide avenues of sand provide plenty of walking space between the barracks. A massive power and heating plant serviced the entire encampment, its chimneys acting as landmarks. There were churches, kitchens, a central canteen, a YMCA gym and several sports fields. One-third of the POWs were Belgians; a further third were Russians; 20 percent were French; 12.5 percent were British, and the rest were a few Italians. They assigned Joe and the newcomers to barracks in a section populated only by British POWs. While they had mixed nationalities throughout the camp in 1914-1915, the German authorities later separated nationalities within the large encampments. Soltau in 1917 was one such camp.

The Soltau Stalag dispatched fit POWs out to fifty outlying branch labour camps. The Germans used prisoners to work in their war effort more than ever since so many millions of German men had gone to the Fronts. They implemented a general plan to make non-disabled prisoners prefer leaving the crowded and dreary prison camps in favour of working in the smaller work camps. Of the total number of inmates at Soltau, they only allowed 10,000 to stay in the main encampment while the others left on work details. They held back the sick, the disabled, those incarcerated for criminal acts, sergeants, adjutants, civilians, POW Association board members, and clerical workers to stay behind in the camp. Many of these men were in hospitals, military prisons, or camp administration buildings[97].

"I have heard they mine salt around here. We may find ourselves back in mining," said Walt.

"No shipbuilding close by?" asked Joe, tongue in cheek.

"Haha, not likely, Joe," said Mike.

They found Soltau a much better run camp than the others they had experienced. They ran it according to Prussian tradition: no-nonsense with far more discipline. There was no possibility of sleeping in or avoiding work parties unless you were certified sick by the camp doctors. They didn't tolerate any relaxing or sightseeing outside the camp either. The Kommandant, a prim and orthodox elderly Prussian colonel, was very strict and ran a "tight ship." He insisted that his guards and the prisoner representatives do the same.

Although there were sports and entertainment facilities, they administered them according to a fixed set of regulations governed by the camp authorities. As a result, they only allowed their friendly football matches under camp rules. The

---

[97] Pursuit of an 'Unparalleled Opportunity': The American YMCA and Prisoner of War Diplomacy among the Central Power Nations during Great War, 1914-1923. by Kenneth Steuer as well as www.1914-18.be

rulebook ran everything. Life as a prisoner of war was becoming more controlled, desperate and ever more tedious as the war progressed.

The camp provided meals for the prisoners out of well-equipped and clean kitchens. Much the same as Celle, they received three meals a day. In Stalag, they get coffee or tea and soup in the morning. For lunch, the kitchens provide meat or fish with vegetables. And in the evening, they gave the prisoners soup and bread. The bread was of such quality the Kommandant said he and his family ate it, too. [98]

But…

"They are giving us less food," said Mike.

"Aye, much less," said Walt.

"Even the soup seems weaker," said Joe.

"So, what is going on," asked Mike. "They haven't fed us enough in these camps. Are they trying to starve us to death?"

"Good point," said Joe. "Thank God we still get the care packages!"

"Is it because they have so many prisoners here?" asked Walt. "This place is much more cramped than Celle. Have you noticed how they've packed us in here? One thousand to a barrack is a lot of sardine prisoners!"

---

[98] A. Euster, Dr C. De Marval, Rapports on visits to POW camps in North Africa and Germany, International Red Cross, Geneva/Paris, May 1915.

"Aye, you can't move unhindered between the barracks with the crush out there," said Joe. "It's an enormous problem!"

"Aye, and that's why I like to go to the working camps," said Mike. "They are not so crowded."

The men complained that their food rations were smaller than the portions they had grown used to, so the care packages became more vital than ever. Agricultural work parties, with the possibility of more generous food rations, became prized work assignments. But Soltau allowed the prisoners to plant vegetables such as potatoes and spinach to supplement their meals.

There was a large canteen where the men could buy food, personal care products and clothing items at fixed low prices. Besides the clothes they wore when they arrived, the camp quartermaster provided shirts, socks, underwear, shoes, coats, and wool blankets subject to strict rules based on deemed need. They issued mattresses, too, filled with wood wool[99].

There was a post office which allowed the prisoners to send home two letters a month and one postcard per week. They permitted exceptions to this rule when family circumstances such as marriages or deaths required it[100].

---

[99] A. Euster, Dr C. De Marval, Rapports on visits to POW camps in North Africa and Germany, International Red Cross, Geneva/Paris, May 1915.
[100] Ibid

And there was another unique aspect of life at Soltau: the prisoners ran the camp themselves through elected representatives. Guards did not interfere with their everyday lives while in the Stalag[101].

§

By 1917, the Great War had moved into a third and final phase in the battlefields and the POW camps. As the war progressed into this last phase, feeding prisoners of war became more difficult for the Central Powers.

Food shortages were the first crisis of this period to hit the German people; more would follow. The ongoing Allied naval blockade stopped the food imports that Germany had become used to in the pre-war years to feed its burgeoning population of 70 million. Shortages included butter, margarine, cooking fat, sugar, potatoes, coffee, tea, fruit and meat from the scarcity of cattle feed. Homegrown foodstuffs first went to Germany's soldiers. They rationed the rest to the civilian population using coupons to buy particular items on designated days. This rationing caused food lines as everyone lined up at nearby shops from dawn to get their ration before the shop ran out. The food situation worsened year by year, becoming critical in early 1917 after the entire German potato crop failed. The food shortage weakened

_____

[101] Ibid

German soldiers fighting on the Western Front compared to their well-fed enemies; these soldiers survived on a fraction of the typical calories. [102]

As the food shortage became acute in Germany, substitute ("ersatz") products became available. These substitute foodstuffs included coffee made from chicory, herbs, berries or other inventive mixtures. There were substitutes for milk, sugar, bread, eggs, marmalade, cocoa and chocolate, none of which tasted like the original item[103].

The many inmates to care for were becoming expensive and difficult to manage. Feeding their citizens was enough of a problem, but feeding POWs was becoming a severe burden for the Central Powers with the increasing food shortages. This burden led the Germans to provide prisoners with exact quantities of ration as they allocated German civilians. However, German troops received more rations than the prisoners. From 1917, in many of the leading German POW camps, the smallest calorie ration set by the German administration was being provided to prisoners. This reduction of food for the POWs was a breach of the Hague Conventions, which stated that prisoners must eat the same food as the captor army's troops. Food parcels sent from the prisoners' home state, their families, their national Red Cross, or other

---

[102] https://www.historyplace.com/worldhistory/firstworldwar/brit-breadline.htm
[103] Ibid

charities limited the impact of food shortages for most prisoners. Likewise, for POWs working in agriculture, food provided by the farmer's employees offset the effect of food shortages. Farmers continued treating POW labourers the same way they handled peacetime hired labourers. [104] But the worse it became in the war for the Central Powers, the worse it became for their citizens, soldiers, and foreign prisoners.

The military authorities estimated that there were 2.4 million soldiers from thirteen nations in Germany's 300 POW camps during the Great War. The largest nationality among these captives was the Russians, followed by the French prisoners.

The German prisoner-of-war camp system developed from an improvised scattering of ad hoc primitive camps in 1914-1915, often at or near existing military barracks and urban centres. But by the end of 1916, they had developed a sophisticated system of primary, industrial-scale encampments. Soltau was one of these.

§

---

[104] Kramer, Prisoners in the First World War, 2010

Significant Developments on the Western Front

Soon after Joe's party arrived at Soltau, news circulated in the camp of significant developments in the French battlefields and a disaster in the English Channel.

"I don't know what this means," said Joe one day. "I've heard the Germans in Eastern France have retreated to their so-called Hindenburg line." [105]

"Does this mean the Germans are giving up?" asked Mike.

"I'm not sure," said Joe. "It sounds like an important development."

Operation Alberich was the code name of this German military operation. During the Battle of the Somme in 1916, two salients formed between Arras and Saint-Quentin and from Saint-Quentin to Noyon. The Germans planned Alberich as a strategic withdrawal of German troops to new positions on the shorter and better-defended Hindenburg Line. The line ran from Arras to Laffaux, near Soissons on the Aisne, closer to Belgium. General Erich Ludendorff was reluctant to order the removal and hesitated until the last moment. However, the retirement took place after months of preparation between 9

---

[105] The Hindenburg Line, Siegfriedstellung in German, or Siegfried Position, was a German defensive position built during the winter of 1916–1917 on the Western Front during the Great War. The line ran from Arras to Laffaux, near Soissons on the Aisne.

February and 20 March 1917. The German retreat shortened the Western front by 25 miles. It freed up 13–14 divisions for the German strategic reserve to defend the Aisne front against the Franco-British Nivelle Offensive.

The Germans began Operation Alberich on 9 February 1917. In the region, they were busy abandoning; they dug up railways and roads, felled trees and polluted water wells. They destroyed towns and villages and planted many mines and other booby traps. [106] The Germans transported 125,000 non-disabled French civilians from the region to work elsewhere in occupied France, while they left behind children, mothers and the elderly with minimal rations. On 4 March, General Louis Franchet d'Espèrey, commander of Groupe d'armées du Nord (GAN, Northern Army Group), advocated an attack while the Germans were preparing to retreat. General Robert Nivelle, Commander-in-Chief of the French armies since December 1916, only approved a limited strike to capture the German front position. The French lost a chance to upset the German withdrawal. [107] It took place from 16 to 20 March, retiring 25 miles and giving up more French territory than that gained by the Allies from September 1914 until this operation. [108]

---

[106] Simkins, P.; Jukes, G.; Hickey, M., *The First World War: The War to End All Wars.* Oxford: Osprey, 2003.

[107] Rickard, J., "Robert Georges Nivelle (1856–1924), French General." History of War, 2001.

[108] Simkins, P.; Jukes, G.; Hickey, M., *The First World War: The War to End All Wars.* Oxford: Osprey, 2003.

During the German withdrawal, the British Third Army and Fifth Army captured Bapaume on 17 March; they also occupied Péronne on 18 March, further extending their position on the Somme.[109]

§

Besides the promising news, the POWs learned of a significant tragedy in the English Channel through arriving South African prisoners. On 21 February 1917, a large cargo steamship, the Darro, collided with the British troop carrier SS Mendi in the English Channel south of the Isle of Wight. The Mendi sank, killing 650 people, most of whom were black South African troops. The sinking was a significant loss of life for the South African military and was one of the early 20th century's worst maritime disasters in British waters. It remains South Africa's worst sea disaster to this day.

SS Mendi had sailed from Cape Town carrying eight hundred and twenty-three men of the 5th Battalion of the South African Native Labour Corps (SANLC) to serve in France. She called at Lagos in Nigeria, where they mounted a naval gun on her stern. She next called at Plymouth and then sailed up the English Channel toward Le Havre in northern France, escorted by the Acorn-class destroyer HMS Brisk.

---

[109] James, E. A. (1990) [1924]. A Record of the Battles and Engagements of the British Armies in France and Flanders 1914–1918 (London Stamp Exchange ed.). Aldershot: Gale & Polden.

Mendi's contingent was a mixture of the characteristics of many British merchant ships. The officers, stewards, cooks, signallers, and gunners were British; stokers and other crew were West Africans, most of whom were from Sierra Leone. The SANLC men aboard her came from various social backgrounds and various South African provinces and adjacent territories. Most had never seen the sea before this voyage, and few could swim. The officers and NCOs were white South Africans.

At 5 A.M. on 21 February 1917, there was a thick fog ten nautical miles south of St. Catherine's Point on the Isle of Wight. The Royal Mail Steam Packet Company cargo ship RMS Darro rammed Mendi's starboard quarter in an accident. The ramming breached Mendi's forward hold. The Darro survived the collision, but Mendi sank, killing six hundred and seven black South African troops and thirty crew.

It was a tragedy that has since faded in most memories.

§

During April, another significant development on the Western Front affected the Germans and prisoners alike.

"Howay, Laddies, I've heard excellent news for a change," said Joe. "The Americans and their materiel are arriving in vast numbers."

"Well, it's about bloody time," said Mike.

"Aye," said Walt. "Now we can defeat the bloody Boche at last."

"Then go home to our families," said Joe. "Let's not give up on our plans to escape. It could still take a while for this war to end."

"We agree with you there," said Mike, seconded by Walt.

The Americans declared war on the Germans on 6 April. That was massive news for the Allies and horrible news for the Central Powers.

The United States had announced a strict neutrality strategy at the war's outset. President Woodrow Wilson wanted to smooth the path to a peace arrangement amongst European adversaries. He sent his top associate, Colonel House, on peace missions to the two sides. Edward Mandell House was a capable American negotiator, a government official and a presidential advisor, known by the courtesy title Colonel House, even though he had no military experience. But despite his best efforts, each side remained sure of triumph, and they disregarded his peace recommendations.

On 7 May 1915, the German submarine U-20 sank the British liner RMS Lusitania, a sister ship to RMS Mauretania, with 1,200 passengers on board losing their lives. Despite losing 128 US citizens, the Americans maintained their neutral policy. However, it was a severe shock, creating a loud diplomatic outcry across the British Empire and the US.

President Wilson said, "America is too proud to fight," demanding an end to German attacks on passenger ships.

Germany complied at first, but in January 1917, they resumed unrestricted submarine warfare on merchant ships.

Then, German Foreign Minister Arthur Zimmermann invited revolution-torn Mexico by telegram to enter the war as an ally of Germany against the US. Germany offered to send Mexico money and help it recover the territories of Texas, New Mexico and Arizona. Mexico had lost seventy years earlier during the Mexican–American War.

British intelligence intercepted the telegram and passed the information on to Washington. That act proved too much, and an enraged Wilson released the Zimmerman note to the public. Americans saw this deed as a basis for war. President Wilson announced the break in official relations with the German Empire before Congress on 3 February 1917. And when German submarines sank seven US merchant ships, he approached Congress, calling for it to declare war on Germany. Congress voted on and agreed to declare war on 6 April 1917. The US declared war on the German Empire on the same day, with an army of just 378,000 men.

Then, the US military moved at lightning speed during April 1917. On 2 May, the first US destroyer flotilla arrived at Queenstown, Ireland. The first use of the convoy system for an Atlantic crossing was on 10 May. On 18 May, the US Government introduced the Compulsory Service Act or "draft" to increase the number of soldiers. The US Army began training recruits at 32 large camps, each housing 25,000 to 55,000 soldiers. Twenty-four million American men registered for the draft, almost a quarter of the US population. [110] The US mobilized over four million military personnel and enormous firepower for the Great War.

On 25 June, the first contingent of US troops landed in France, with General John Joseph "Black Jack" Pershing leading the American Expeditionary Forces. He rejected British and French demands that they should integrate American forces within their armies. Pershing insisted the AEF run as an independent unit under his command, although individual American divisions fought under British control. He allowed it to integrate African-American teams into the French army, too. Because of these developments, the scales of the conflicts tipped in favour of the Allies.

From that point, the men noticed that German attitudes towards them had changed. The Kommandant and guards became more aggressive and antagonistic. Unsure of victory, they made the lives of the prisoners more challenging. They added an extra hour of work to an existing interminable day. They further reduced rations, and the Kommandant ordered

---

[110] Norman Ferguson, The First World War, A miscellany, Summersdale Publishers, Chichester, UK, 2014.

the number of care packages distributed to be fewer. Rumblings began throughout the camp. Friendly banter and barter between prisoners and guards stopped. The men heard rumours that the guards were meting out punishments for the most minor misdemeanours. They learned a favourite sentence was tying soldiers standing against a pole for hours, or even days, irrespective of the weather. It became ugly, and anxiety was rising among the British POWs!

"Aye, the Yankees have entered the war," said Joe one day.

"On our side, I hope," said Mike, tongue in cheek.

"Mike!" called Walt. "Why would they join the Germans?"

"I don't know," said Mike. "You never know with the Yanks. They supported the Boers in the war against the British Empire."

"Nonsense," said Walt. "There were just two or three notorious Yanks that fought with the Boers."

"Aye," said Joe, "there was John Hassell and his band of American Scouts and the Arizona Kid and Dynamite Dick. Oh, and Colonel John Blake and the Irish Brigade. Remember them?"

"Aye, I remember them too. But those Yanks were just a handful of mercenaries hired by the Boers. They were never a serious problem for us, and most fled through Mozambique when the going got too tough for them!"

"The Americans arriving in this war is an excellent move," said Joe. "Up to now, we have been getting nowhere. Nothing has changed for two years except millions of our boys are dead. Maybe now, with four million Yanks on our side, we can finally end this bloody war!"

"I agree, Joe," said Walt.

"Me too," said Mike, hurting still from Walt's comment, "We need to knock the bloody Hun out of this war!"

§

By 1917, a deadlock had gripped the Western Front for two years. Many battles raged from 1914 to 1916, resulting in millions of casualties but no progress for either side. Europe grew weary of the war, and the Allied high command needed a breakthrough. The Allies observed the German army's weakening and reasoned that a significant victory, achieved by breaking through German lines, could end the war sooner. As a result, they planned to assault the German trenches at the town of Arras, 113 miles north of Paris. They hoped the British assault, supported by the Canadians, Australians, Newfoundlanders, New Zealanders and South Africans, could break the impasse on the Western Front and achieve an Allied victory.

The Battle of Arras began on 9 April 1917 with early efforts of Canadian forces under Commander Sir Julian Byng, resulting in the capture of the strategic Vimy Ridge. This victory delivered significant gains for the British troops in the centre of the attack. By late evening on 12 April, the Canadian Corps was in control of the ridge but suffered over ten thousand casualties, including three and a half thousand dead. The victory at Vimy Ridge was more than just a decisive battlefield victory. For the first time, the four Canadian divisions were in a coordinated assault together, with men from every region of Canada involved in the battle. Brigadier-General A.E. Ross, Director of Medical Services for the Canadian Expeditionary Force, declared after the war, "In those few minutes, I witnessed the birth of a nation." Vimy Ridge symbolized the sacrifice and success of the young Dominion of Canada in the Great War.

But by the time the Battle of Arras had ended on 16 May 1917, the British advance had faltered. Even though they considered it a British tactical victory, the fight did not result in the hoped-for breakthrough. They deemed it 'indecisive,' The British suffered 158,000 casualties in the assault, compared to a German loss of 120,000.

§

The next major event was the Battle of Messines. This battle was an attack from June 7 to 14 by the British Second Army under General Sir Herbert Plumer, supported by the

Canadians, Australians and New Zealanders. It was near the village of Messines in West Flanders, Belgium. The British aim was to capture the German defences on the Passchendaele Ridge. The ridge ran from Ploegsteert Wood (Plugstreet) in the south through Messines and Wytschaete to Mount Sorrel. It gave commanding views of the British defences and back areas of Ypres to the north. The British intended to advance to Passchendaele Ridge, depriving the German 4th Army of the high ground, capturing the Belgian coast and moving it to the Dutch frontier.

The battle began with the British detonating 19 mines beneath the German front positions, which devastated them and left 19 enormous craters. They followed this with a creeping barrage 700 yards deep, protecting the British troops as they secured the ridge with support from tanks, cavalry patrols and aircraft. They improved the effects of the British mines, barrages, and bombardments through advances in artillery surveys, flash spotting, and centralized control of artillery from the Second Army headquarters. These attacks moved the front line beyond the former German Sehnenstellung (Oosttaverne line), and they considered them a British success. Both sides of this battle had 25,000 casualties.

§

The Death of Harry Burgess

On 8 July 1917, Mary's 2nd younger brother, Henry (Harry), died a hero of the Western Front near Lille-Armentières. Harry joined the army when he was young and was a sergeant with the 262nd Siege Battery of the Royal Garrison Artillery at the time of his death. The Royal Garrison Artillery deployed the Siege Batteries behind the front line to destroy enemy artillery, supply routes, railways and stores. They equipped the batteries with heavy Howitzer guns, firing large calibre 6, 8 or 9.2-inch shells in a high trajectory. But on this fateful day, the German gunners lobbed a massive projectile onto Harry's battery. Most of the men perished, but Harry survived at first. After later dying of his wounds, they buried him at Trois Arbres Cemetery, Steenwerck, near Armentières, France. He was twenty-five years old.

Harry's death once again threw the Burgess and Rutherford families into mourning. And once more, John Robert Jr. led the way, organizing another Burgess memorial and wake. They now directed their fears towards the remaining Burgess brother, William Souter, on the Western Front and Joe in Germany. Would they lose them as well? They had heard there had been one and a half million British casualties by this point of the war. The war stacked the odds against William Souter and many others, making it home alive!

And once more, the family called upon the tormented old vicar to read a eulogy he now had to give too often to comfort the grieving families of Jarrow.

With that, the vicar repeated the words he had repeated so many times during this war. He bid the Rutherfords and Burgesses goodbye and crept home to weep. It was getting far too much for the old man. The toll of this war was showing even at home. The two families did the same. These were terrible, terrible times!

Joe's following letter from Mary told him the news.

"My dearest Joe,

"Our Harry has died on the front. He was such a sweet man, and we will miss him terribly. Our family is shrinking. We now pray for you and William Souter to make it home alive.

"The children are growing and full of mischief. They don't know their Da, but I hope they will soon.

"I am working hard and making ends meet. It is fine. The women are making sure the home front keeps going.

"Loving you and missing you, Mary."

Joe wrote back to her at once.

"My dear Mary

"I'm grief-stricken once more over our dear Harry's death. He was an excellent soldier. But soldiers know their business is death, which can come when God wills it. Take pride in the fact he died fighting for his King and country. He died a hero. I am sometimes sorry that I can't still be back in the trenches doing my duty. But then I'm grateful to be alive so I can return to you and the children.

"Keep a brave heart, my love. This horrible war will end soon, and we will be together again.

"Kisses and hugs to you and my children. Joe."

§

In another British political development in July 1917, despite protests and strong vocal disproval from the Conservatives, the Prime Minister appointed MP Winston Churchill Minister of Munitions. It was a post outside the cabinet, and his duties there were administrative. However, as a principal tank sponsor, it could be a significant move.

§

The war pounded on through 1917. In August, Joe updated his companions on Western Front events:

"After the disaster of Arras, the French fought the Second Battle of the Aisne from 16 April to 9 May. This battle was part of the so-called Nivelle Offensive, another attempt to be victorious over the German armies in France. But, it was a total disaster for the French Army. It involved over a million troops and 7,000 guns, achieving little territorial gain instead of the 48-hour advance the French had planned. And it ended the career of French Commander-in-Chief Robert Nivelle.

There was a widespread mutiny in the army, too. The French suffered 187,000 casualties, and the Germans had 168,000 losses.

"We followed that with the Third Battle of Ypres or the Battle of Passchendaele. Compared to the battles fought at Ypres in 1914 and 1915, this long-prepared offensive at Passchendaele on 31 July 1917 is the most notorious. Soon, prisoners captured at Passchendaele arrived here, and I've heard horror stories of the terrible bloodbath of that battle."

Joe stitched his bits and pieces of information on Passchendaele into a story for his companions one evening.

"The Battle of Passchendaele was a campaign for control of the ridges south and east of the Belgian city of Ypres in West Flanders," said Joe.

"Passchendaele lies on the last ridge east of Ypres, 5 miles from Roulers junction of the Bruges to Kortrijk railway. The station at Roulers is on the principal supply route of the German 4th Army. They've told me that the generals had wild objectives, unexpectedly bad weather and that Field Marshal Haig made poor decisions that led to horrific losses."

"So what's new?" asked Mike. "It's always the same. The generals decide, and the men die. They call Haig 'The Butcher'!"

"Aye," said Joe. "Haig hoped to break through and liberate Belgium's North Sea coast, from which German U-boats were operating. [111] So, the Allies launched the offensive under General Sir Herbert Plumer from the Ypres salient on 31 July. Before the attack, over 3,000 guns poured four and a half million shells on the German defences. But again, the bombardment didn't silence the German machine guns. Many of those machine guns were in concrete pillboxes. Following that bombardment, our troops, supported by dozens of tanks and a French contingent, attacked the German trenches.

"The explosions of millions of shells and pouring rain had turned the battlefield into a thick mud swamp with scattered water-filled craters deep enough to drown a man. And the hidden graves of soldiers killed in earlier fighting opening up and causing more obstacles made it even worse and shocked our troops."

"Shite," said Mike. "That's bloody awful."

"Aye, but then hundreds of thousands of soldiers on both sides attacked and counterattacked across the mud," said Joe.

"They ran through that mud in a bleak open landscape with no buildings or natural cover. They also ran through the nonstop onslaught of exploding shells, flying shrapnel, and machine-gun fire. My contacts told me that soldiers were falling into the mud and drowning in it! Try to imagine that."

---

[111] "Battles – The Third Battle of Ypres, 1917." First World War.com

"My God, just when we thought it couldn't get any worse," said Walt. "From what I hear daily, this war is becoming hell on Earth!"

"Aye, Walt. That is what I hear, too," said Joe.

"It sounds as if Passchendaele, the Third Battle of Ypres, is ten times worse than our battles at the Aisne and the First Battle of Ypres. And it's not over yet."

"My God," said Walt. "How and when is this battle going to end?"

§

Third Anniversary as POWs—20th of October 1917

The war and bloodshed continued unabated—120,000 casualties in October 1917 alone.

On 20 October 1917, Joe and his remaining band of fellow Ennetières captives once more marked their anniversary as prisoners of war. Their spirits had sunk to new lows. They were much thinner and weaker because of the reductions in. their food portions at Soltau. As they listened to Joe's reports on events, they were asking themselves over and over when this hell on Earth would end. Talk among the British POWs revolved around what impact the Americans entering the war might have and what breakthroughs they could soon achieve. The consensus was that the Yanks would help break the deadlock. Talk amongst the Russians focussed on political developments in Russia, spilling into the rest of the nationalities at Soltau.

"What impact will Russia's revolution have on this war?" asked Mike.

"The rumours say they may back off the war," said Joe.

"The Russians say it is the Tzar who supported the war against Germany, not the general population. With the workers' revolt and imprisonment of the Tzar, they don't want to be part of the war anymore."

"What does that mean?" asked Walt. "How will that affect us?"

Part of the answer came soon enough and spread throughout the camp. On 24 and 25 October 1917, the Bolsheviks in Russia, led by Vladimir Lenin and Leon Trotsky, overthrew the Provisional Russian Government in the October Revolution. They then established the Marxist non-democratic Soviet Government, which prohibited private enterprise and land ownership. Lenin announced Soviet Russia should end its involvement in the war at once, and he renounced all existing treaties with the Allies. The rest of the answer regarding the effect of their withdrawal came soon enough.

"We must wait for what the Germans do next," said Joe.

"The worst that could happen from peace with Russia is that they withdraw their troops from the Eastern Front and send them to the Western Front."

§

The Battle of Passchendaele Revisited

Late in November, Joe gave his companions an update on the end of the Battle of Passchendaele.

"You'll remember I left off after the first terrible Battle of Passchendaele, and it wasn't going so well," said Joe.

"They delayed the next significant effort at Passchendaele until 6 August, which proved a failure too. On 21 August, General Haig told the British government that the end of the German reserves was near, but the struggle might still be severe for a few weeks. By this point, the Germans had killed or wounded 70,000 men from Britain's best assault divisions.

"As the offensive slowed, Haig ordered the 100,000-man Canadian Corps to launch an attack on the Germans occupying the French city of Lens. He hoped this would distract German resources from the primary battle in the Ypres salient. After surveying the German defences, the Canadian commander, Lieutenant-General Arthur Currie, opted to seize the high ground north of Lens at Hill 70 instead. Currie's operation was an unqualified success, and although the Canadian Corps suffered 9,000 casualties, the unit inflicted three times that number on the enemy."

By early September, Haig had come under political pressure from London to halt the offensive, but he pressed forward. That month, they threw Australian and New Zealand divisions into the fight alongside the worn-out British forces. But the result was the same: the Allies bombarded, assaulted, and occupied a section of enemy ground, only to have the counterattacking Germans repulse them.

Joe looked at his notes and continued. "Then, in late September, there was an improvement in the weather and the British situation. Our boys delivered successful strikes on 20 and 26 September and again on 4 October. A creeping artillery barrage won the terrain, and the infantry occupied it. General Plumer had one gun to every 5 yards of Front, and this large concentration of cannon fire crushed the enemy's counterattacks. This positive result and better attack organization helped revive the attacking troops' spirits.

"The Allies launched further attacks on October 12, 22, and 26 and into November, but they made very little progress," said Joe.

"On 6 November, Canadian troops advanced the few hundred yards needed to occupy the site of the destroyed village of Passchendaele.

"Our troops carried out the last assault on 10 November, which won the remaining areas of high ground east of the Ypres salient. With his honour satisfied, Haig finally called a halt to the battle. However, he was no nearer to reaching the Belgian ports that formed his goal than when the Third Battle of Ypres started. His dream of a decisive victory had faded. After the fighting, the British awarded sixty-one Victoria Crosses. The Army granted more Victoria Crosses, 14, for actions on the opening day of the Battle of Passchendaele than on any other single day of the Great War."

British Liberal Prime Minister David Lloyd George, who had tried to prevent the battle without success, used it as an example of senseless waste and poor leadership. The Allies had between 200,000 and 450,000 casualties[112], which makes a mockery of Haig's pledge that he would not commit the country to "heavy losses." Among these casualties were 38,000 Australians, over 15,600 Canadians and 5,300 New Zealanders. The Germans lost between 217,000 and 410,000[113]. These losses occurred for only minor Allied territorial gains over three months and six days, the point of which was unclear.

§

---

[112] Estimates vary, and many are under dispute.
[113] Estimates vary, and many are under dispute.

The First Full-Scale Deployment of the New British Tank

"In the meantime, the most exciting news is that the British launched the first full-scale offensive using our new secret British weapon at Cambrai," said Joe.

"That battle began at 6 A.M. on 20 November 1917. It started with a bombardment by over 1,000 guns on German defences, followed by smoke and a creeping barrage at 300 yards. The bombing and smoke covered the first movements forward of 476 British tanks closing on the German lines in a mass attack. The gains, supported by infantry, were significant. They breached the strong Hindenberg Line to depths of 4 to 5 miles. Each side had 45,000 casualties in this three-week battle, and the British lost 179 tanks. But Cambrai showed how a well-thought-out surprise attack with the mass use of armoured vehicles could break the trench deadlock. When our folk at home got the news, they greeted the first day's success by ringing church bells [114]."

Back at Soltau, the news on Cambrai and the tank's success circulated soon after the battle started, and the British POWs were excited.

---

[114] Miles, W., *Military Operations France and Belgium 1917: The Battle of Cambrai,* 1991

"At last, we've got something powerful the Boche doesn't have," said Joe. "Maybe we can end this war with this new weapon and the American's help!"

"Now, why didn't I come up with that?" asked Mike with a wide grin. "What a grand idea!"

"You're right," said Walt. "Ever since they invented the machine gun, the cavalry use of horses was crazy. The enemy shot them before the horses could reach them. Now, with these tanks, the cavalry and infantry have an alternative way of breaking through enemy lines! From what I've heard about the first tank attack at Flers–Courcelette, they flattened the barbed wire and drove right over the trenches. They blasted with their guns and machine guns as they went. The Germans couldn't believe their eyes and didn't have a chance."

"Aye, but when will the enemy have them, too?" asked Joe.

The Germans were developing their tank, but they spent more time and effort on developing anti-tank weapons at first.

These monumental events of 1917—the Americans joining the fight, multiple Allied victories and the breakthrough and success of mobile tank warfare—lifted spirits at Soltau somewhat. Aeroplanes and airships had become crucial weapons in this war, too.

But talk around camp was also about the Russian Revolution, and nobody in the Soltau British contingent knew what to think of it at first; nobody, except for communist-oriented soldiers, scattered among the British troops. An answer to this question came soon enough, though.

§

The Halifax, Nova Scotia Explosion

Another war-related maritime catastrophe, this time in Halifax, Nova Scotia in Canada, hit the Allies at the end of 1917. On 6 December 1917, two ships collided in the Narrows, a thin passage connecting the upper Halifax Harbour to the Bedford Basin where cross-Atlantic convoys gathered. The French SS *Mont-Blanc*, carrying a cargo of high explosives from New York via Halifax to Bordeaux, France, on behalf of the French government, arrived in Halifax. She was full of explosives, TNT and picric acid, the flammable fuel benzol and nitrocellulose. She was to join a slow convoy gathering in Bedford Basin for a departure to Europe. While slowly entering the harbour at 8:45 A.M., she collided with the unloaded Norwegian ship SS Imo. The Commission for Relief in Belgium had chartered the SS Imo to pick up relief supplies in New York.

Although it was a minor collision, a resulting fire on board the French ship ignited her cargo. It soon caused a massive explosion that devastated the cities of Halifax and Dartmouth. The blast was the most massive human-made explosion to occur before nuclear weapons. It released the equivalent energy of three kilotons of TNT.

It obliterated every building within a 2,500-foot radius of the harbour, including the entire suburb of Richmond. The pressure wave snapped trees, bent iron rails, demolished buildings, destroyed vessels and scattered pieces of Mont-Blanc for kilometres. Not a window in the city survived the blast. Across the harbour, in Dartmouth, there was widespread damage. A tsunami from the explosion destroyed a traditional village of the First Nation Mi'kmaq people who had lived there for generations if not hundreds of years.

The blast killed two thousand people and injured nine thousand others. There was a significant blizzard the day after the explosion, significantly increasing the suffering in the shattered city. Although thousands of miles from the Western Front, the cause of this catastrophe was the Great War.

§

10.   *Christmas 1917*

By the end of 1917, life in the German POW camps was getting desperate. Food was becoming scarcer, affecting German civilians, prison guards and foreign prisoners alike. The POWs still received Red Cross packages, but they noticed the boxes from home were declining. Suspicions circulated in the British camp. The Germans might steal the packages for themselves. It was unthinkable that their families were not sending them! So where were they? The POWs were declining in strength and health and needed those packages to supplement their meagre camp rations. And they required the Great War to end as soon as possible to survive.

1917 had been a pivotal year in the Great War. The US entered the war mid-year. On 16 December, the Russians agreed to an armistice with Germany, Austria-Hungary, Bulgaria and Turkey to end their involvement in the Great War. The "defeat" of Russia meant Germany would no longer be fighting on two fronts. So they could free up their troops on the Eastern Front to join a Spring Offensive in planning for the Western Front.

In between, there had been many battles on the Western Front in 1917, with the Allies making slow progress. However, 1917 still ended with a British loss of 818,000 men.

Christmas 1917 on the Western Front and in the POW camps was a subdued affair. Joe, his marras, and all soldiers on both sides of the conflict struggled to find the traditional "Peace on Earth, Good Will to All Men" accompanying the Christmas season. There was a hint that 1918 was the year of victory and peace. It couldn't come soon enough for most.

§

1918—Endgame and Dénouement

At the start of 1918, the battlefields were quiet as usual during the winter months of January and February. There were far fewer British combat casualties than had been the norm. But the POWs were getting weaker and weaker. With the onset of winter, they hospitalized more and more prisoners as they became ill. Many men developed pneumonia, and deaths in the camp were on the increase. During this war, a quarter of military deaths were from disease.

Joe received another letter from Mary with promising news.

"Dearest Joe,

John Robert told me that Prime Minister Lloyd George and US President Wilson had presented peace plans to their governments. It may still take a while, but that's some positive news.

I know it must be difficult, but please look after yourself for a few more months. Your children and I love you and want you to get home safely and sound.

"All my love and kisses, Mary."

Joe had also picked up on this news through his German contacts.

"I've heard that the US President has proposed a peace plan to Congress," said Joe to his companions one day in late January. "They're calling it his Fourteen Points. Prime Minister Lloyd George made a speech to Parliament outlining British plans for peace, too. Mary mentioned this in her last letter to me, so it must be big news over there. Maybe this year will see the end of this war at last."

"Maybe," said Walt. "Still, we haven't finished the Germans yet. I've heard rumours they might make another big push."

"Well, the war's end can't come soon enough for me," said Mike. "I don't know how much longer I can last."

"You must hang on, Mike," said Joe. "You and I are going home to our families when this war ends. And the first thing we'll do together will be to join the Toon Army for a match in Newcassel."

Both Joe and Walt were right, but no one could imagine the tests the world must endure before they could achieve peace.

On 8 January, Democratic President Woodrow Wilson outlined an elaborate peace plan based on 'Fourteen Points' in a speech to the United States Congress. Wilson called for a League of Nations to guarantee member countries' independence and territorial integrity.[115] Other points included the Germans evacuating occupied territory, creating an

---

[115] Heckscher, August (1991). *Woodrow Wilson*. Easton Press.

independent Poland again, and self-determination for the peoples of Austria-Hungary and the Ottoman Empire. [116]

The speech had a mixed reception in Congress and elsewhere. The talk was well-received by many in the United States and other Allied nations, and even by Bolshevik leader Vladimir Lenin, as a landmark of enlightenment in international relations. However, Republican past president, Teddy Roosevelt gave a warning. "If they build the League of Nations on a document as high-sounding and meaningless as the speech in which Mr. Wilson laid down his fourteen points. It will add one more scrap to the diplomatic wastepaper basket. People would interpret most of these fourteen points to mean anything or nothing. [117]

The Central Powers translated the speech into many languages and disseminated it worldwide as an instrument of Allied propaganda. [118] The Allies also dropped copies of the address behind German lines to encourage the Central Powers to surrender for a just settlement.

"On a sadder note, while commanding No. 3 Canadian General Hospital (McGill) at Boulogne, the doctor and poet Lt Colonel John McCrae died of pneumonia with extensive pneumococcus meningitis on 28 January 1918. He was at the

---

[116] Berg, A. Scott (2013). *Wilson*. Simon & Schuster
[117] Cited in Newer Roosevelt Messages, (ed. Griffith, William, New York: The Current Literature Publishing Company 1919)
[118] Heckscher, August, Woodrow Wilson. Easton Press, 1991.

British General Hospital in Wimereux, France. They buried him the following day in the Commonwealth War Graves Commission section of Wimereux Cemetery, a couple of kilometres up the coast from Boulogne, with full military honours. They transported his flag-draped coffin on a gun carriage and Lieutenant-General Sir Arthur Currie, GOC Canadian Corps. Many of McCrae's friends and staff preceded the mourners, with McCrae's boots reversed in the stirrups of his charger, Bonfire. McCrae's horse was with him and much loved from his departure from Valcartier, Quebec, until his death. Because of the unstable sandy soil, they placed McCrae's gravestone flat, like all the others in the section.

"John McCrae is best known beyond his fellow Canadians for writing probably the most famous war memorial poem ever in May 1915." [119]

According to legend, fellow soldiers retrieved the poem after McCrae, initially dissatisfied with his work, discarded it. *In Flanders Fields* was first published in the London magazine Punch on 8 December 1915. Flanders Fields is a common English name for the World War I battlefields in Belgium and France. It is one of the most quoted poems from the war. Its immediate popularity led to the use of parts of the poem in recruiting efforts and appeals for war bond sales.

---

[119] McCrae, John (1919). In Flanders Fields and Other Poems. New York: G. P. Putnam's Sons

§

11.   The 1918 'Spanish Influenza' Pandemic Begins

In March 1918, over 100 soldiers at Camp Funston in Fort Riley, Kansas, became ill with influenza. Within a week, the number of flu cases increased fivefold. Sporadic flu cases spread throughout the United States, Europe and Asia over the next six months. An April public health report first mentioned this influenza. This report informed officials of 18 severe cases and three deaths in Haskell, Kansas.

The flu spread into Europe. Soldiers in the trenches became ill with what the French locals called "la grippe," with symptoms of sore throats, headaches and a loss of appetite. Although most contagious in the cramped, unfavourable conditions of the trenches, the soldiers recovered within a brief time, so doctors at first called it a "three-day fever." Because of more rumours, they feared it had spread to the POW camps with the recent prisoner arrivals. And in no time, the first cases appeared at Soltau Camp. The Kommandant ordered extra strict measures, isolating new prisoners. Camp doctors worked day and night to combat the outbreak.

§

Early in the New Year, Joe, his closest companions and many other weakened prisoners became ill as they did every year in winter. But as winter moved into spring, it became clear that this year was different, with many POWs becoming sick and some dying. The prison Kommandant ordered a temporary lazaret to house the rising number of ill inmates. He quarantined this hospital for fear of the infection spreading. Word circulated that the same thing was happening in the other POW camps, on the Western Front, and elsewhere. The doctors had heard an unknown flu virus was spreading in the US and Europe, so they didn't want to take any chances.

"I hope I get over this bloody head cold soon," said Joe. "It's gone into my chest."

"Aye, that goes for me, too," said Mike. "I'm feeling bloody shite."

"Well, Laddies, we get this every year," said Walt. "We are very run down after our three years here. We haven't been eating enough, and I don't know about you, but I'm feeling weaker by the day. That can't be any good for fighting off a cold."

That statement got complete agreement from the marras and many others within earshot. Diseases were a constant companion of the soldiers on the Western Front throughout the war. The rats and other vermin in the trenches, coupled with disgusting, unhygienic and often wet and frigid conditions, created the perfect environment for infection. But for the first three years in German POW camps, they had not been too ill except for colds in winter. But at this stage of the war, the death toll in POW camps was increasing through malnutrition and illness.

"We must hang in there, Laddies," said Joe.

"Aye, Joe," said Mike. "I agree with you. But for me, at least, it's been getting harder. I just don't have the energy I used to have. The colds last longer and are getting worse."

"Aye, and now they're talking of flu again," said Walt. "They say it's much worse than a simple cold."

Two huge initiatives dominated the rest of the war on the Western Front during 1918: the Germans started the first, known as the Spring Offensive; the Allies launched the second and final assault on the Germans, which became known as the "Hundred Days Offensive."

§

On 3 March 1918, the new Bolshevik government of Soviet Russia and the Central Powers signed the peace treaty of Brest-Litovsk. This agreement ended Russia's participation in the Great War. Threats of further advances by the German and Austrian armies forced the Bolshevik government into a treaty. The settlement stated that Soviet Russia was to default on Tsar Nicholas II's commitments to the Triple Entente alliance. It ceded the Baltic States to Germany and its province of Kars Oblast in the South Caucasus to the Ottoman Empire and recognized Ukraine as an independent state. Russia agreed to pay six billion German gold marks in reparations. When the Central Powers abandoned the Eastern Front, they freed up their armies to take action elsewhere. Between 1 November 1917 and 21 March 1918, the German divisions on the Western Front increased from 146 to 192, with troops drawn from Russia, Galicia, and Italy. This added another 570,000 men to the German armies in the west.

"Have you noticed the Russians are going home?" asked Joe.

"I guess it frees up lots of space here for more prisoners from other nations on the Western Front."

"Trainloads of them," said Mike. "The Germans are ferrying truckloads of Russians to the train station daily."

"You know what that means?" asked Walt. "Trainloads of the Germans from the Eastern Front will go to the Western Front for that German Spring Offensive. I'll open the betting on that one."

The 1918 Spring Offensive, or Kaiserschlacht (Kaiser's Battle), also known as the Ludendorff Offensive, was a series of German assaults along the Western Front beginning on 21 March 1918. German commanders realized that their only chance of victory lay in defeating the Allies before the massive arrival and deployment of American resources. Their short-lived advantage was the return of the 46 divisions freed up by the Russian surrender.

In the Spring Offensive, the Allies lost almost 255,000 men, 1,300 artillery pieces and 200 tanks. They replaced the hardware through the efforts of the French, British and American factories and workforces. German troop losses were 239,000 men, many of them specialist shock troops (Stoßtruppen) who were irreplaceable. [120] In terms of morale, the early German jubilation at the successful opening of the offensive soon turned to disappointment, as the attack had not achieved decisive results. At that point of the Great War, the Germans still outnumbered the Allies on the Western Front by 300,000 soldiers.

On 26 March, the British and French agreed at a strategic conference in Doullens, France, to appoint an Allied Supreme Commander on the Western Front. The Supreme Commander replaced the separate national commanders they had been using to better coordinate their efforts. General Ferdinand Foch, Maréchal Petain's revered chief of staff, accepted the challenge[121].

§

---

[120] Marix Evans, Martin (2002) *1918: The Year of Victories*, Arcturus Military History Series, London: Arcturus.
[121] Ibid

Even so, the Great War raged on the Western Front. The first tank-versus-tank battle between the Germans and the British occurred on 24 April. In an unexpected engagement, the opposing tanks battled it out at Villers-Bretonneux. This fight happened when three advancing German A7Vs met and engaged three British Mark IV tanks, two of which were "female" tanks armed only with machine guns. They damaged two Mark IV "females" and forced them to withdraw. But the "male" tank, armed with 6-pounder guns, hit and disabled the lead A7V, abandoned then by its crew. The Mark IV continued to fire on the two remaining German A7Vs, which withdrew. A British male tank then advanced with the support of Whippet light tanks until the Germans disabled them with artillery fire. The crews abandoned the light tanks, too. German and British teams recovered their vehicles later in the day.

§

On 9 April, Operation Georgette, or the Battle of the Lys, started with a new German Feuerwalze (Fire Waltz) creeping barrage scheme. It was the 2nd operation of the German Spring Offensive. But this German offensive stalled because of logistical problems and exposed flanks. Counterattacks by British, French, Belgian, Portuguese, Canadian, Newfoundland and Anzac forces slowed and stopped the German advance. Ludendorff ended Georgette on 29 April. As with Michael, the losses were 110,000 men wounded or killed each. [122] Again, the strategic results were disappointing for the Germans. Hazebrouck remained in Allied hands, and the Germans occupied a vulnerable salient under fire from three sides. The British abandoned the worthless territory they had captured at an enormous cost around Ypres the previous year, freeing several divisions to face the German attackers.

§

The Death of William Souter Burgess

On 12 April 1918, the Burgess family suffered another blow. The war had killed the third and second eldest of Mary's brothers, Lance Corporal William Souter Burgess, at Ploegsteert, Belgium. Called Plugstreet by the Tommies, Ploegsteert is just north of Armentières, France. William Souter was with the 18th Battalion of the Durham Light Infantry. He was thirty-two when he died, and with his death, three of the four Burgess brothers had succumbed to this war, the fate of so many families in wartime. All three Burgess brothers had died within a tiny warzone around Ypres, near where the Germans had captured Joe. They died within a

---

[122] Marix Evans, Martin (2002) *1918: The Year of Victories*, Arcturus Military History Series, London: Arcturus.

radius of ten to twelve miles of each other! This entire region was now a vast expanse of mud, rubble, tree stumps and rotting bodies.

Once again, the Burgesses and Rutherfords met in mourning at the ancient St. Paul's Church and monastery in Jarrow for a memorial service. And once more, the tired old vicar stood before them to deliver the eulogy. Tears welled up as he struggled to read his prepared speech. He regained his composure, cleared his throat, and began.

"I can't express my sorrow and regret enough as I must once again officiate over a memorial for yet another Burgess son and brother. We gather to remember and say goodbye to William Souter Burgess for his last journey into God's heaven.

And with that last appeal, he bid the Rutherfords and Burgesses a quiet goodbye and dragged his tired body home to weep further. He could stand it no longer. Over the decades, he had given everything he could, but this war had broken him.

The bishop replaced the vicar with a younger man after this service. They said the old vicar seemed to have lost his mind. People would see him walking the paths of St. Paul's Monastery, muttering and raising his eyes and hands to the sky, asking God to respond to his prayers.

§

Joe received the letter from Mary soon after William's death.

"Dearest Joe,

I must tell you that William Souter died in France, too. You can't imagine the grief we are feeling these days. We have lost three of our four beloved brothers. Please look after yourself. I do not want to lose you. You are our last hope. Please, please, my darling—come home soon!

On a happier note, the children are beautiful and growing by leaps and bounds. John Irwin is now almost seven, Violet is a perky five, and Molly is a mischievous three-and-a-half-year-old. I tell them often their father will be home soon and tell them you are a magnificent man and hero.

"My dearest love, Mary."

This letter filled Joe with hope when thinking of his wife and children. But he felt profound grief at the death of another Burgess brother-in-law. He related its contents to his mates.

"The third of Mary's brothers has fallen near Ypres," he said. "All three of them have fallen near where we became prisoners. Why is that place so cursed for our families?"

"It's not only that place, Joe," said Walt. "I have heard that we have had almost a million British deaths in this war. Men have fallen along the entire Western Front in huge numbers. But yours is tragic news, my dear friend. I am so sorry."

Mike echoed Walt's sentiment, as did his mates gathered around him. Their words helped but couldn't stop him from sinking once more into a deep and lasting depression. He wasn't alone; most of his tens of thousands of fellow POWs at Soltau and millions elsewhere felt the same emotional pain, hunger and helplessness. Life in 1918 was too arduous for everyone concerned. Joe had succumbed to it; he felt weak, listless, and had all but lost hope. His letters to Mary had become shorter, his handwriting shaky. And Mary was desperately worried about whether he would make it home.

§

The Spring Offensive Draws to a Close

The further operations of the Spring Offensive were Blücher–Yorck, or the Third Battle of the Aisne, Operation Gneisenau and Operation Friedensturm. Operation 'Blücher–Yorck' from 27 May to 6 June focused on capturing the Chemin des Dames Ridge before the American Expeditionary Forces arrived in its entirety in France. Ultimately, following many Allied counter-attacks, the German advance halted three days after it began. That battle had 137,000 Allied and 130,000 German casualties. [123]

---

[123] Marix Evans, Martin (2002) *1918: The Year of Victories*, Arcturus Military History Series, London: Arcturus.

By May, hundreds of thousands of US soldiers travelled across the Atlantic monthly to fight in the Great War. With 650,000 American soldiers arriving in France, they're growing by 10,000 per day. The 'Doughboys' sped up by leaving their equipment behind and using British and French munitions in the meantime.

Then Operation Gneisenau ran from 9 to 25 June, with 35,000 Allied and 30,000 German losses. In the last Operation Friedensturm, the German offensive stopped and ended on 18 July. These last clashes included the 3rd Battle of the Aisne, the Battle of Messines and the 2nd Battle of the Marne. The five assaults resulted in German losses of over a million men killed, captured, or wounded; they inflicted similar casualties on the Allies. But with the Spring Offensive, the Germans had spent the last of their resources, while American troops and steel kept pouring in to shore up the Allies. The Germans had lost their last chance to win the Great War [124].

The Spring Offensive ended on 18 July. The Allies had regained their numerical edge over the Germans when the four million-strong American Army finally engaged on the Western Front. The Allies collapsed Germany's military. After six months, the strength of the German army had dropped by one million to just over four million fighting men. [125] In August,

---

[124] Marix Evans, Martin (2002), *Over the Top: Great Battles of the First World War*.
[125] Edmonds, J. E., Military Operations France and Belgium, 1918 May–July: The German Diversion Offensives and the First Allied Counter-Offensive. History of

the Allies used this advantage and improved tactics to launch a counteroffensive.

§

During the last six months of the war, conditions in Germany and its POW camps moved into a relentless decline. Food and fuel were scarce. Fuel shortages constrained the mobility of people and goods. German citizens without the means of producing food faced famine. With these immense problems, the morale of the German troops and citizens alike crashed. From mid-1918, soldiers from both sides succumbed to the deadly strain of influenza. Troop losses from the flu epidemic soon exceeded combat casualties, weakening the hard-pressed German Army.

With the Russian prisoners from Soltau and elsewhere sent home, it freed up many barracks for the thousands of new prisoners arriving daily. The French and British sections of the camp were each extended to accommodate their recent arrivals. But the end of the war was approaching!

§

On the night of 16 to 17 July 1918, Bolshevik revolutionaries under Yakov Yurovsky murdered the Russian

---

the Great War Based on Official Documents by Direction of the Historical Section of the Committee of Imperial Defence. III (Imperial War Museum & Battery Press ed.). London: Macmillan, 1939/1994.

Imperial Romanov family. Bolshevik revolutionaries, under Yakov Yurovsky's command, shot and bayoneted the former Czar Nicholas II, his wife, Alexandra Feodorovna, and their five children in Yekaterinburg. It was on the orders of the Ural Regional Soviet. Also murdered that night were members of the imperial entourage who had accompanied them. They included court physician Eugene Botkin, lady-in-waiting Anna Demidova, footman Alexei Trupp, and head cook Ivan Kharitonov. The revolutionaries transported the bodies to the Koptyaki forest, where they stripped, buried, and mutilated them with grenades to prevent identification.

Tsar Nicholas II was one of the three grandsons of Queen Victoria, leading the great armies of the Great War and the first to die.

§

The Second Wave of Influenza Arrives

The second wave of Spanish Influenza emerged at Camp Devens, a US Army training camp just outside of Boston, and at a naval facility in Boston. Between September and November, the second wave of flu peaked in the United States. This second wave was more dangerous and responsible for most of the deaths attributed to the pandemic. New York City's Board of Health added flu to the list of reportable diseases. They required those with flu to isolate themselves at home or in a city hospital. By the end of September, Camp Devens reported over 14,000 flu cases, equalling one-quarter of the total camp complement, resulting in 757 deaths.

In the autumn of 1918, the US experienced severe shortages of professional nurses. They caused these shortages by deploying large numbers of nurses to military camps in the US and abroad and failing to use trained African-American nurses. The Chicago chapter of the American Red Cross issued an urgent call for volunteers to help nurse the ill.

The pandemic flu viruses hit Philadelphia hard, with over 500 corpses awaiting burial, many for over a week. They used cold storage plants as temporary morgues and a manufacturer of trolley cars donated 200 packing crates for use as coffins. Chicago and many other cities across the US closed theatres, movie houses and night schools and prohibited public gatherings. San Francisco's Board of Health requires anyone serving the public to wear a mask and strongly recommends that residents wear masks in public. New York City reported a 40 percent decline in shipyard productivity because of flu illnesses amid the Great War. The 1918 flu pandemic virus killed 195,000 Americans during October alone.

On 11 September 1918, recent Allied successes delighted British Prime Minister Lloyd George when he arrived in Manchester to receive the keys to the city. Female munitions workers and soldiers home on leave cheered his passage from Piccadilly train station to Albert Square. But later that evening, he developed a sore throat and fever and collapsed. He spent the next ten days confined to a sickbed in Manchester town hall, too ill to move and with a respirator to aid his breathing. Newspapers, including the *Manchester Guardian*, underplayed the severity of his condition for fear of presenting the Germans with a propaganda coup. But, according to his valet, it had been "touch and go."

A robust and healthy person before the war, Joe was nothing more than a wisp of a man. He was a virtual skeleton, weakened, demoralized and often disoriented and incoherent because of his poor condition.

Joe slipped again and again into severe bouts of coughing. And he was not alone. The German crisis had weakened the entire prisoner population, sick and struggling to survive in the last months of the Great War. The remaining prisoners were in dire straits. Excessive work hours and malnutrition were taking their toll. More and more men were dropping in their tracks while out on work details. But the Kommandant realized that the end of the war was in sight. As a result, it worried him that anarchy could break out if he let up on the discipline.

The camp doctors also realized that the POWs were in acute stages of starvation and frailty, but they could do little about that. It had overwhelmed them. For the exhausted doctors, the war's end also needed to come now!

After a few weeks, Joe's condition worsened. He was coughing and had a high temperature; the doctors feared he might have developed pneumonia. His quarantine with others in similar conditions prevented anyone from visiting him. But his marras may have been somewhere else in the mass of beds in the lazaret. The doctors were trying to contain the risks of disease spreading in the camp. They had constructed a second lazaret to accommodate the rising numbers of sick POWs. Rumours ran rampant throughout the encampment. Although there was no proof they were suffering from the unknown influenza virus, panic spread.

Illness laid Joe up for many days with a very high temperature. At first, he had uncontrollable shivers, which the nurses tried to abate using blankets.

Then, Joe became delirious often, falling into a semi-conscious state and drifting from one dream to another. One night, he found himself on a train.

§

Delirium

Joe could hear the rapid chugging sound of the locomotive and smell the smoke wafting in from an open window. He looked out of the coach window at the rolling green fields, dry-stone walls, and hedgerows of North East

England. He was on the last leg of his trip home by train, his tour of South Africa and India behind him. Having served six years as a soldier in the British Empire for Queen Victoria and King Edward VII, Joe had matured and was an enlightened and much wiser man.

He re-experienced the journey on the high seas from Liverpool to Capetown via Tenerife. He relived being shot in a nasty guerrilla war in South Africa. He relived his sea voyage from Durban to Bombay and along the Malabar Coast to Calicut. He remembered his time in southern India on an exotic and eye-opening duty tour under the British Raj.

In his dreams, Joe travelled into the African and the Indian interiors by train, returning to England via the Suez Canal and the Mediterranean Sea. He passed Gibraltar into the North Atlantic and was home to Southampton, England. It had been an incredible experience that expanded every aspect of his being.

However, awake on the train, it was grey and damp outside, with mist lingering on ponds and valleys! Joe recalled the heat and dryness of the two continents he had just visited. There was so much contrast between these environments. He knew deep down he was to miss his exotic and exciting episodes in Africa and on the Indian subcontinent and the constant stimulation these countries offered. Smiling to himself, Joe remembered the lovely women in their colourful costumes and the half-naked men of India. He recalled the drab Boers and the naked black native peoples of Africa. Joe had lived and enjoyed his excursion into the world of the great British Empire beyond these English shores. But now he was returning uneasily to a changed and, for him, alien, Edwardian England. Even though it was home, Joe felt it was unknown territory.

He dreamt of his romantic days and nights with Jenny Ambler, the nurse from Jarrow whom he had met in the Cape Colony. She had followed him to the Transvaal and India. But, tired of forever following her man, she stayed in the south at Wellington when the Army moved him north to Lucknow. Joe missed her and had written her a letter when he left her in Wellington. He had still hoped she could join him in Lucknow and Jarrow to continue their relationship in his home territory once they had discharged him from the army.

But she appeared and said, "I look back fondly at our time together, our more intimate moments in Wellington in particular. You are wonderful, and I am very fond of you, Joe. I followed you across South Africa from Matjesfontein to Standerton in the Transvaal, where we had a perfect time after the war ended. I followed you to Wellington in India, where we had a lovely relationship and explored the Nilgiri Mountains together.

"However, when the Army sent you north to Lucknow, it was too much. As I told you then, I had moved enough and couldn't follow you to Lucknow. It hurt me, and I cried over it for days, Joe. But I got over it. I'm contented here in Wellington and don't want to leave it yet. The patients need me. That is what and where God meant me to be. Nursing is my calling, and I am required here right now. I'm sorry, Joe, but I cannot follow you to Jarrow again. Please understand that I am still fond of you and hope we can meet again someday, but for now, my future is here. With sincere fondness, Jenny."

Her letter should have devastated him. But their mutual friend Alice had forewarned him. He knew she had befriended Jacques de Vos, the handsome freed Boer POW from Trichy, whom Joe had invited to Wellington. Joe had read the letter many times since receiving it in Lucknow. It had broken his heart and filled him with sorrow, but he was coming to terms with it. They had spoken of "love" in India, but now she could only say she was "fond of him"? It was his first major heartbreak. He had left Ruth behind when he joined the army, after which they drifted apart. But Jenny was his first genuine love. They had shared so much for so long and planned a future together. So, her decision had devastated him, even though he understood it. But he realized, too, that building lasting relationships while moving around with the army is precarious. Only now, returning home, could he hope to find a lasting relationship and maybe grow a family?

Joe awoke but was still deep in confused thought when a fellow passenger disturbed him.

"Hello there, soldier. Where are you serving here? Or are you one of our brave lads returning home?"

A stranger's sudden penetrating Geordie voice jolted him out of his daydreaming.

"Aye, sir, that I am," he said.

"Where are ye coming from?" the stranger asked.

"Africa and India," said Joe. "I fought with the Durham Light Infantry in the South African war and served in the south and north of India."

"Well done, Laddie! Protecting our great Empire, eh," said the stranger. "Ye must be proud of that."

"Aye, that I am, sir," said Joe with a coy smile. "That I am. But glad to be coming home."

Joe didn't fancy a lengthy conversation or debate on his homecoming then, so he excused himself and escaped to the water closet. On his return, the man had disappeared. So, he returned to his seat by the window to enjoy his arrival at Newcastle Station.

§

Back in the Soltau lazaret, Joe emerged from his delirium wet with sweat and shivering as if outside in the snow. A passing nurse saw his state and called in another to wash him and give him a change of underclothing, hospital gown, sheets and blankets. Joe opened his eyes, and she heard him say, "Home?" Looking at her, he asked, "Am I home, sister?"

"No, soldier," she said with her German accent. "You're still with us here at Soltau." She gave him another dose of aspirin. Bayer had trademarked it in 1899, and it was already very popular. Aspirin was the standard treatment for many ailments, including the 1918 flu, for which they hadn't yet developed a vaccine. He thanked her and lay semi-conscious again beneath his blanket. The shivering had stopped for a while, and he fell into another troubled sleep.

§

Memories of Joe's Arrival Home in 1906

It was 11 July 1906, and when Joe arrived at the station, there were pressing crowds of people coming from other trains and rushing toward the exits. Joe had never seen so many people there; he wondered what brought so many to the centre of Newcastle on a Wednesday. He soon learned King Edward VII and Queen Alexandra were in Newcastle to open a new railway bridge across the River Tyne in the King's name. The royal couples' train had transported them to Newcastle. Rail travel had grown so much in the 19th and early 20th centuries that the bridges of Newcastle and many other cities weren't coping with the increased traffic. Thus, the North Eastern Railway built the new King Edward VII Bridge with over £500,000 to ease the pressure[126]. Even though it wasn't

---

[126] £61.2 million in 2019

complete, the King visited and inaugurated the bridge on 10 July 1906, a grand event.

But that was yesterday. Today, the King and Queen took part in a royal procession through the city centre. Thousands lined the route from the Central Station to Armstrong College and the Royal Victoria Infirmary, which they were to open in a grand ceremony. The Newcastle Chronicle reported how people had assembled in the city streets from the early hours!

Joe left the station and entered the crushing masses, pushing his way through the crowd and the porte-cochere of the station to a better vantage point. He was in his dress uniform, so the people opened a path for him out of respect. After a brief wait and the appreciative courtesies of fellow viewers for a soldier of the realm, the procession arrived.

First, A-Company of Northumberland Hussars rode past Joe. Mounted on their magnificent black cavalry steeds, the Hussars looked regal in their uniforms of dark blue with intricate white and gold braids. Their busbies, sporting scarlet bags with white over red plumes, topped off their elegant manner. The officers in command wore their spectacular dress uniforms and metal helmets with long white horsehair flowing over the back of their necks. Next followed the Royal Artillery Mounted Band, renowned as "the largest mounted band ever seen." This exceptional military band had enjoyed the privilege of leading the Lord Mayor of London's processions. It was also in the funeral procession of Queen Victoria in 1901, where it preceded the hearse. As the band passed the railway station, they played the British Grenadiers March.

King Edward VII and Queen Alexandra followed the musicians in an open carriage with polished maroon-painted bodywork, the king's crest adorning each door. A team of four splendid black horses pulled the wagon with a mounted postilion in a red uniform guiding each pair. Two more coachmen or "shooters" were guards at the rear.

Behind the carriage, two thousand-man battalions of the Northumberland Fusiliers and the Durham Light Infantry followed in dress uniforms. The Northumberland Fusiliers fought in the 2nd Anglo-Boer War and received two battle honours: Modder River and South Africa, 1899–1902. The 1st Battalion of the Durham Light Infantry earned two battle honours: Relief of Ladysmith and South Africa 1899–1902. They then travelled to India to relieve the 2nd Battalion, who returned to Britain and were in this procession. Joe could pick out several of his fellow Durhams from India and South Africa among the marching troops. He was also wearing his medal from the Boer War, The Queen's South Africa Medal with four clasps: South Africa, 1901, Transvaal, Orange Free State and Cape Colony. Joe was a handsome soldier with a handlebar moustache. He was a fine specimen as a soldier, and men and women in the crowd showed their admiration, to whom Joe smiled and winked.

Uniformed and armed soldiers and sailors posted every few yards lined the entire procession route. Police officers ensured the way was open for the parade and controlled the crushing crowds. It was a magnificent performance, and it assured Joe that the British Empire was still alive and well in England and the colonies.

Joe recalled with pride a march through Capetown following their arrival there. It, too, impressed the local inhabitants. That parade numbered 1,000 cavalry horse riders, two artillery batteries with their guns, 4,000 infantry soldiers, and the army medical corps. Joe and his companions said it was "the grandest march in which they had never taken part." He remembered his company's 3-mile march from Green Point to the Capetown train station in early April 1901. They were behind a military band, an Australian battalion and several hundred other troops heading into the interior. His lost marra[127] Billy was still with them then, as were his other marras, and he remembered their smiles and quips as they marched past the young ladies of Capetown. How naïve they were then, before encountering the realities of war. Joe was missing Billy, and his other marras were still in India. Billy hadn't deserved his untimely end in that train sabotage

---

accident. He recalled the fun and dangers they had while in that country. Joe had found ceremonial military marches so uplifting. And this march through Newcastle he had just experienced as an observer wasn't unlike their movements through Capetown. Soon after his arrival, he felt remorse for his plan to leave the military. But that passed before too long.

§

When Joe awoke, it was daytime. He didn't know how long he had slept but didn't feel rested. A nurse saw he was awake and arrived with a bowl of soup. Joe noted that this soup was much better than the camp served the POWs. He enjoyed the soup and found it provided him with a temporary lift. Joe thought, "Why can't they always give us soup like this?"

But after an hour or two, he felt the sweat returning to his body. And the shivers returned, too. Before long, he once more slipped into a semi-consciousness state.

§

Joe crossed the river to Gateshead, free of the crushing crowds, where he caught a tram towards Heworth. He noted that the double-decker tram, steam-driven when he left for Africa, was now electric, an enormous change and a much quieter and cleaner trip. Before 1901, when he headed to South Africa, most tramcars were horse-drawn or steam-driven.

Traffic clogged city streets during the Edwardian era. Horse-drawn cabs, utilitarian carts and wagons rushed everywhere to deliver their passengers and goods. Trams on rails assumed the right of way because of their size. The rest appeared to follow no rules, just as Joe thought in India. And everywhere, the crowds mingled, jay-walked, and dodged the vehicles on the streets and the sidewalks used as thoroughfares for pedestrians and bicycles. And for the first time, he observed a few sputtering horseless automobile vehicles fighting their way through the traffic. It was chaos, but it bothered nobody.

As he walked the cobbled streets from the tram to his parent's home, he noticed nothing had changed during his six-year absence. He passed the typical terrace houses of Tyneside workers as dreary and dirty as they ever were. The sky was a yellowish grey from the factories and terrace houses pouring smoke from their chimneys. The streets were full of playing and screaming children watched by idle adults from the doorways or front windows. Various carts were plying the roads, vending coal, milk, bread, meat, and vegetables, and the carters were barking out their wares at the emerging housewives. At long last, he felt the familiar old signs that he was home. Now and then, old acquaintances recognized and greeted him.

"Welcome back, Joe. You look good in that uniform, gadgie!"

"I can't believe it. A soldier is ye now, Joe? Good for ye!"

"Where have ye been, Joe? Africa and India? Nee, man."

"Looking good, Laddie. Are you coming or going? Coming, aye. Haven't seen ye for a long while."

Joe harboured strange feelings on this homecoming. On the one hand, he was joyful at the thought of seeing his family and old friends again. But he'd miss the bright blue skies, exotic environments, vegetation and wild animals he had lived with these last few years. Their contrast to the ever-polluted industrial North East England was startling.

He first visited his father, Thomas, and his mother, Susannah. They were still living at 171 Heworth Lane, where they had lived since arriving from Ireland and where Joe and his brothers and sisters were born and raised. He had written to them to announce his return but couldn't give them an exact date. It was a working day, so only his mother, Susannah, was there to greet him until his father, Thomas, got home from work. Ma was a quiet, stoic woman who had agreed under pressure to his departure for South Africa but was now very emotional on his return.

"My God, look at you," she exclaimed repeatedly, sobbing while embracing him. "How you've grown! What a fine young man you've become in your uniform. Da will be so proud and pleased to see you." His father, an Irishman first and a Geordie second, had been dead set against his joining the British Army and sailing off to war in the colonies. But his brothers had supported him, and his parents had agreed.

"I've had a purely belta [128] six years, Ma," said Joe. "I've seen so much and learned so much. You can't imagine. But it's grand to be home with you again!"

With that, his mother burst into a wail, but smiling, sobbing, laughing, she held him ever closer. "You, silly bairn of mine. I couldn't say anything, but I never wanted you to leave. But never mind, you're home. And a grown man at that!"

She then made tea and sandwiches for Joe, and they sat while Joe regaled his mother with tales of his travels and adventures.

Later in the evening, his father arrived home from work. Joe opened the door for him. "Hello, Da," he said.

"My God! Look at you," his Da echoed. "I can't believe it! Joseph Irwin Rutherford, what a fine-looking young man you've become! The army has done ye well."

And then his father did something most uncharacteristic for him. He embraced his son and wept.

---

[128] Excellent, fantastic in Geordie

"With the news from South Africa, I didn't think you'd come home to us," he cried. "Still, here ye are. Look at him, Ma. Just look at him."

The emotion settled, and they sat to a special evening meal prepared by Joe's Ma. Joe filled in the gaps of his past six years, entertaining his parents through the supper. They listened without uttering a word, except for the occasional exclamations or requests to explain places or things new to them. It was an emotional and fulfilling homecoming for Joe.

Joe momentarily emerged smiling from his semi-conscious state, looking around to reorient himself before slipping away.

§

The following Sunday, the family arrived at Joe's parent's home for a reunion. The women cried, and the men beamed as Joe hugged them while expressing his joy at being with them again. Alive and well after being so long and far away, it was such a relief to be home. Joe's elder brothers, William and George, who supported his decision, were there with their wives, Jane Nesham and Sarah Ann Joynes. His older sisters, Mary Ann Esther and her husband, Issac Murdock, Margaret and her husband, James Docherty, and Sarah Jane arrived, too. His younger brother Thomas James, his wife Sarah, and his younger sisters Susannah Ballance,

Ellenor and Elizabeth rounded out the full complement of the family.

A half-dozen children of various ages crowded around him, prodding him for as much information as Joe could offer them on his travels while fondling his uniform and buttons. "Had he seen lions and tigers?" "Did you see elephants and buffalos?" "Tell us about Indians and Africans!" "Did they talk like us?" "No? Could he understand them?" He wasn't sure how they knew of these things, but he responded to their immediate and enthusiastic delight as best he could. To them, he was the family hero, home from the wars and the Empire, the only such person in their family. The gathering spent a long time on the street talking and laughing, joined by familiar neighbours, before the immediate family entered the compact terrace house. Filled with the familiar scents of a Sunday lunch of roast beef with the usual trimmings. A rare treat, such a meal was only served on special occasions.

After lunch, a few Newcastle Brown Ales or Broons, as the Geordies called them, appeared as if by magic. The conversation lasted well into the evening as Joe regaled them with elaborate stories of his South African adventures. Forever the raconteur, Joe embellished the episodes, soliciting "oohs" and "ahs" and occasional expressions of shock or laughter as he skipped from one experience to another.

Neighbourhood friends were finding their way to the Rutherford home to congratulate the returning soldier many had known since his childhood. Among them were the Burgesses, John and Margaret, their sons John Robert, William Souter, James and Harry, and daughters Mary Caston, Sarah Ellen, Margaret and Ellen. Joe immediately recognized Mary even though she was only thirteen the last time he had seen her at his departure. She was now a stunning nineteen-year-old woman, and he was most impressed. "Mary is a handsome woman," he thought.

She was demure and elegant in the typical well-turned-out working-class female dress code of the day. She wore a long black A-line skirt falling to the floor and a frilly white blouse rising to cover her neck, polo-style. Her brown hair, styled in a fashionable Pompadour, flowed in a wave from temple to temple, stopping above her brow. A bun completed the look at the back of her head. He promised himself to meet her again as soon as possible.

Joe regaled his audience on his sea voyage to South Africa and the stop at Tenerife.

"It was an island that was more mountainous than you could ever imagine, with the highest mountains covered with snow, even though it was steaming hot at sea level."

"Nee," called his awe-filled audience.

"Aye. We could see a busy town filled with people, horses, and donkey carts from the ship. The harbour was teeming with goods and workers loading sail and steam-driven ships of various shapes and sizes. Cranes on the wharves heaved large bundles of freight to and from the vessels."

"Just like here," called one child.

"Aye, but different," he said. "The town had many white two-storey buildings with white churches every few blocks. They looked so different from our buildings and churches. There were palm trees everywhere the first time we had seen them. But we saw many more in Africa and India. They told us that these strange-looking trees had sweet fruit that the locals collected. Beyond the town, to the south, were vast fields of bright green grass called sugar cane. We didn't know it was sugar cane until a deckhand told us. It amazed us to hear sugar came from such huge grass plants. Imagine that."

"Nee, sugar comes from grass?" they said. "Whey aye, man!"

Joe described Capetown and the mountain journey to Matjesfontein in the Great Karroo. He fascinated them by saying the Karroo is "a vast desert filled with strange plants and wild animals he had never seen before, along with sheep and goats." And he amazed them by recalling his first action at night and his injury at the hands of the Boers at Matjesfontein.

"Oh, Uncle Joe," the children called! "Thank goodness you're not dead."

He laughed when he described the bicycle outing with his marras. He spoke of his chance meeting with Jenny Ambler, a Jarrow lass, and how they had become close.

"Where is she, Joe?" asked William.

"Still in India, William," said Joe, "She stayed in Wellington."

"When will we meet her?" asked William.

"I don't know, William. She has stayed there for the time being. She broke off our relationship."

"Oh, I'm sorry, Joe," said William.

Joe continued to describe De Aar in the northern Karroo and how he had seen one of the notorious "concentration camps," which he told at length to everyone's disgust. Then he elaborated on his company's chance brush with the infamous General Jan Smuts and his Commando. Joe recalled the journey to the Transvaal and the tragedy of train sabotage at the hands of the Boers, resulting in the death of Billy Wilson. They listened to this with shock and grief since they knew Billy well, returning to when he was a boy. And Joe spoke of the Blockhouse lines and the sweeps between them to catch the Boer fighters. He recounted their rescue of a hapless young Boer at the war's end and how they nursed him back to health.

His family listened with astonishment. They had heard the war news and seen the occasional illustrations of the soldiers and blockhouses. However, they were only aware of it at an introductory level, without many details. They couldn't believe the adventures Joe had experienced. The family was proud of him and grateful he had returned to them after such a horrible war.

And the Burgesses, who were almost family, listened with keen interest too, the brothers in particular.

"What a time you've had, Joe," said 14-year-old Harry. "I want to do that one day."

"That's for me too, Joe," said 17-year-old Jimmie, who was working in Jarrow as a baker's apprentice. "I'll be joining up one of these days. Does the army need bakers?"

"I liked your stories about your travels, Joe. You saw much of the world out there," said William Souter, 21. "I'm not ready yet, but the army sounds good."

"Well, Laddies, I'm not so keen on military life," said John Robert, 23. "I'm content here as a bricklayer in Jarrow, thank you. I'm planning to get married and raise a family here soon enough. So, travelling is out of the question for me."

"Apart from the shooting and exploding shells, the army is an enjoyable life," said Joe. "I enjoyed Africa and India. But I'm happy to be back here in Jarrow again. Six years was long enough for me. I'll now try to regain my old job at Hawthorn Leslie."

He was a glorious hero to Mary Caston Burgess, but then, to her, he always had been.

He held back on his Indian adventures for future gatherings. It had been the most glorious of homecomings, but being late on a night before the work week, everyone retired to their homes. Joe stayed at his parents' house, and before the Burgesses left, he renewed his acquaintance with Mary.

"What an adventure, Joe," said Mary. "I loved the way you explained it."

"Thanks, Mary. It was grand," he said, pushing his chest a tad. "It was dangerous too. I have learned so much! You have to, I reckon. You're a proper young lady now, I can see."

She blushed and turned with a backward glance at her hero.

"Let's get together soon and catch up," said Joe.

"Aye, I'd like that," she said as she rushed off to catch up with her family. "Let's do that soon, Joe!"

Another nurse arrived at his bed, wanting to take his temperature and administer treatment; she awakened Joe from his dreams and spoke perfect English.

"Hello, soldier," she said. "Time for a check-up. How are you feeling?"

"Damn awful, Sister," said Joe. "I have a terrible headache, and I'm still sweating and shivering."

"Well, I see your temperature has dropped slightly," said the nurse. "I'm sure you're on the mend. Here, take more aspirin and a bowl of porridge."

"A bowl of porridge?" asked Joe. "I can't remember when I last had porridge."

Joe took the aspirin and ate the porridge. Then he lay awake until he dozed off again.

§

Joe checked in at the Durham Light Infantry regimental headquarters the next day. Following his honourable discharge from active duty, he signed up as a reservist, attached to the 2nd Battalion, since his old battalion was still in India. With their blessing, Joe set out to find employment. He had no trouble finding a job with his former employer, Hawthorn Leslie. With his military experience and his much-improved reading and writing skills, they gave him employment in the "office." He was to act as the go-between for company management and the labourers, a position he accepted but for which he had reservations. On his first day at Hawthorn Leslie, he met his old friend Fred McRae. They had a brief exchange but agreed to meet Saturday evening at their old haunt, the Rolling Mill Pub.

Hawthorn Leslie was working on a half-dozen cargo and passenger-cargo ships and one Tribal or F-class destroyer, the Ghurka, which they launched the following year. But the talk around the yard was that the company would receive more orders from the Royal Navy for more destroyers, torpedo-boat destroyers and torpedo boats within the next two years. The shipbuilders of Great Britain were helping refit the Royal Navy and the navies of several other aligned countries, strengthening their presence on the high seas.

That Saturday, the two friends met at the pub for the first time since Joe's return.

"Well, Joe, how did it go for you in South Africa?" asked Fred.

Fred had been in South Africa on a tour of service with the British Army during the disastrous 1st Anglo-Boer War from 16 December 1880 to 23 March 1881. Joe had consulted with Fred at length before joining the army, and Fred had described his experiences in that war. Fred advised him to join the Durham Light Infantry reserve volunteer engineers.

"Well, Fred, we only got there after the famous battles under Lord Roberts were over," said Joe.

"So, they involved us in what the army under Lord Kitchener called the Guerrilla War. It was a game of cat and mouse, with us being the cats and the Boers being the wily mice."

Joe then described his experiences from his arrival until the war's end. He told him every detail, including the tragic death of their marra Billy Wilson.

"We didn't hear that much on that here, Joe. I'm blown over by what you have described. Too bad about Billy, though," reacted Fred. "He was a fine man. Now, where are Mike and Jack?"

"They're still in India," said Joe. "They stayed on for a few more months."

"Well, I'm glad you made it through the war safe and sound," concluded Fred once Joe had completed his stories. "Did you like the country?"

"Aye, it was everything you told me and more. But it wasn't all good," said Joe. "We saw nothing but destruction and misery! The Boer farms were burnt and destroyed. Dead farm animals were rotting in the fields or on the sides of the roads. Terrible civilian camps, with hundreds, nee, thousands of Boer women, children and older men dying! Worn-out Boer fighters are hitting us wherever and whenever they could, day and night, right to the bitter end. So, the British Army killed as many Boer fighters as possible, or if we captured them, we sent them overseas. And we locked up their women, children, and older men in these terrible camps where they starved. There was no glory! Instead of the grand parades and puffed-up stories of haughty generals at the start of the war, instead of the army-to-army combat, we fought them one-on-one where we could. There was no honour in that war. I have read that our leaders sacrificed the lives of over 22,000 of Britain's sons; the Boers injured over 22,000 of us in battle, and the

Army sent home another 75,000 ill or wounded. But we daren't ask questions, nee! Who could stand up to these high-born men?"

"My God, Laddie," was Fred's reaction. "I can't believe what you're telling me. I can't believe that our army could do such things."

"Aye, Fred, it's hard to believe," said Joe. "The Boers made it so difficult for us; the generals felt they had to. And do you know why they did it, the war? For the gold, the goldmines in the Transvaal. Aye, they had Kimberley's diamonds, but that wasn't enough. They wanted the gold of the South African Republic too."

"Aye, that's what it's all about, Laddie," said Fred. "It's about riches. It's always about riches. We are ready to do anything for the riches!"

"Aye, but I still believe in the King and the British Empire. I still support him. But I'd like to see an Empire without so much greed and loss of blood! But apart from all that," he said with a wry grin, "I loved South Africa."

Fred laughed at his closing words. He had experienced similar brutality with the British Army in India and South Africa twenty years earlier and understood his younger friend.

"Enough of that talk," blurted out Joe, realizing the mood was too depressed. "Let's toast and drink to our reunion."

It was then that Fred announced his tragic news. "Joe, I must tell you that Mary died a few months ago. I'm alone again, and I miss her so much."

"Oh, Fred, I'm so sorry. She was still young," said Joe. "What happened?"

"Aye, that she was, Joe," said Fred, the tears rising. "The doctor told me her tired heart just stopped."

"How can that happen?" asked Joe. "How can the heart of a young woman just stop?"

"I don't know, Laddie," said Fred. "She hadn't been well for months. Mary just got weaker and weaker. I'm sure the doctor did everything he could, and I did everything I could, but she didn't wake up one morning. You can't know how hard it is to wake up next to your wife, dead and frigid to the touch. Believe me, Joe, I wept for days. I couldn't even go to work until I had buried her."

"I'm so sorry, Fred," repeated Joe to console his friend. "She was such a splendid woman. Life can be so cruel. You must find another suitable woman."

"Nee, Joe," said Fred. "I'm not interested in another woman. Mary was the only woman for me."

And with that sad news, the friends called it a night.

§

Joe slipped in and out of consciousness for two more days but noticed his condition improving. The nurses stopped by from time to time, washed him, changed his underwear, gown and sheets and gave him more aspirin. He wasn't through the illness yet but was gaining strength and occasionally slipping into his dreams.

"It's strange, Sister," he said on her next visit. "I seem to relive my years in Africa and India."

"That is very typical of fever," she said. "It shows that your mind is still very active. And I assume your years in Africa and India positively impacted your mind. Why would your mind want to relive this terrible war?"

"Aye, that's a good point," he said before drifting off again....

§

On one September night in 1906, Joe, Fred and his marras Mike and Jack, who had just returned from India, met again at the pub for a long-overdue reunion. After the usual greetings and jesting, they had an update on their favourite sport—football. Joe had been born in Felling, just east of Gateshead on the opposite side of the river to Newcastle. But he was working and living in Jarrow, farther east on Tyneside. So, this tore Joe between Gateshead NER and Jarrow FC at first. But his loyalties, as with many others on Tyneside, were shifting across the river. They joined the "Toon Army" as Newcastle United fans became known. This team was in the First Division of the Football Association, a more prestigious association than the Northern League. So, Newcastle United had gained in popularity even among the Jarrow boys! That same year, Manchester United FC secured promotion to the Football League First Division on 21 April. They knew the team as Newton Heath until just four years earlier. So, the first part of the talk was about what impact that team might have on Newcastle United. The worst news of that year had been Newcastle United's loss to Everton 0-1 on 21 April in the FA Cup Final at Crystal Palace, London. But that was a few months ago, so the evening discussion revolved around the new season.

Apart from football, the big buzz on Tyneside in September 1906 was the imminent launch of the world's largest ship. The RMS *Mauretania*, on 20 September at Swann, Hunter & Wigham Richardson shipbuilders at Wallsend on the opposite side of the river to Hebburn.

"Howay, man, that we've got to see," said Joe.

"Aye, Joe, we must," echoed his companions at the pub.

The excitement had been building for weeks. Joe and his marras were to witness an event they would not forget for many years. Hawthorn Leslie had rehired Joe's marras, too. The shipyard had laid the keel of the world's largest sea-going vessel on 18 August 1904. For two years, the shipbuilders of Wallsend, Hebburn and Jarrow had watched her rise from the keel into a monster of a ship. She was 790 feet long, 88 feet wide at her beam and ended up eight decks high with a draught of thirty-three feet. She was 263 feet longer and broader than the world's largest battleship, HMS Dreadnought, nearing completion in Portsmouth.

"This will be the largest ship in the world. Never mind; it will just be on Tyneside," said Mike. "She will displace thirty-two thousand Gross Registered Tons when completed. We've never seen a ship as grand as this!"

"Now we will beat the Germans on the seas again," said Jack. He mentioned Britain's disappointment when the German liner SS Kaiser Wilhelm der Grosse became the world's largest and fastest ship in 1897. With a speed of twenty-two knots, she captured the Blue Riband from Cunard Line's Campania and Lucania. Germany dominated the Atlantic briefly, much to Britain's shame. By 1906, the Germans had five four-funnel superliners in service, four owned by North German Lloyd and part of the so-called Kaiser class.

However, the American financier J. P. Morgan's International Mercantile Marine Co. was bidding to monopolize the shipping trade, competing with the Germans to regain US ocean travel dominance. It was approaching the peak of mass migration to North America. With burgeoning trade, travel between Europe and America increased, and the competition became fierce. Britain fought back. By 1902, the British Cunard Line, with the British government's support, agreed to build the superliners *Lusitania* and *Mauretania*, with a guaranteed service speed of twenty-four knots. The government loaned £2,600,000 to make the two ships, with the stipulation that they could convert the vessels into armed merchant cruisers or troop carriers if needed [129]. Cunard Line secured further funding when the Admiralty contracted Cunard as their mail carrier for £150,000 annually.

"I can't wait to see this ship in the water and win the Blue Riband for us," said Mike. "We have the greatest shipbuilders in the world, not the Germans or Americans." He was adding his voice to a growing number calling for Britain's reassurance in the face of Germany's burgeoning competition for the high seas.

"Aye, that is true," said Joe. "Mauretania will win back the ribands for Great Britain, you'll see."

"Wait," called Jack. "Howay, man. There she goes!"

With so many shipbuilders along the Tyne, ship launches were commonplace. But this one was to be monumental, and the anticipation had been building in the weeks before her float. Hawthorn Leslie Hebburn lay opposite Swann Hunter, so Joe and his marras had a front-row stand

---

[129] £311 million in 2018

for this grand event. Towards the appointed time on a Thursday afternoon, they could hear the little whoops of yard sirens along the banks of the Tyne. Men dropped their tools and sought the best viewing positions along its docks and yards. Thousands of workers lined the banks as she prepared to slide down her slipway into the River Tyne. And then a relative quietness fell across the entire district. They could hear only the distant sounds of a band playing rousing tunes for the launch viewing platform filled with many notable guests.

"I see it," called Joe. "She's moving!"

"Aye, me too," yelled Mike. "There she goes."

They couldn't see the christening at the ship's bow from their vantage point. Anne Emily Innes-Ker, Duchess of Roxburghe, née Spencer-Churchill, christened RMS Mauretania. The Duchess was the daughter of the 7th Duke of Marlborough and the sister of Lord Randolph Churchill, Winston Churchill's late father. The Duchess gave a brief speech, blessed the ship, and swung the bottle of Champagne at the high bow of the mighty hull. Alerted by the popping bottle, workers struck the blocks and released the chains. And with that, she began her run into history as she slid along the slipway groaning and screeching, observers' cheers rising above the noise.

"Look at her gaining speed," called Jack. "Will she hit our bank over here? Had we not better move back?"

"Nee. They'll have her well tethered," said Joe. "They'll rein her in before she hits us."

Joe and his marras watched Mauretania as she gained speed and emerged stern-first from the vast scaffolding towering above the dry dock surrounding her. She had most of her superstructure in place but was missing the bridge and the four funnels. They then saw her plunge into the river, creating a massive tidal wave.

"My God, beware, Laddies," called Joe. "She could swamp us here."

On and on, she lunged until she appeared to be almost upon them. The river was only 700 feet wide at that point. But with the angle of the drydock, she was emerging with 1,000 feet in which to manoeuvre. Then she strained against the dozens of hawsers that brought her to a firm but gentle stop as the tugboats approached to guide her to her new birth. The wave continued and crashed into the opposite bank where Joe and his marras stood. At that point, Tyneside erupted into one tremendous roar of cheering, clapping and whooping. Every yard, ship and church along the length of both banks greeted the newest grand lady of the seas with their sirens, whistles and bells. They had launched the world's largest ship. Once completed, she would start a career that would include record-breaking Atlantic crossings, a brief time as a troopship, hospital ship and again as a cruise liner.

"Howay, man! That was pure belta," yelled Mike above the din, jumping up and punching the air above him.

"What a great ship," yelled Joe, excited and proud. "She is huge!"

"That was as good as Toon beating Manchester," called Jack, "Champion!"

Joe and his marras counted this historic launch among their most memorable moments for the rest of their lives. It was not only celebrating one ship, shipyard, and shipping line. It was a salute to the working men and women of this premier shipbuilding region of Britain at the pinnacle of its era. They were proud to have experienced it and be part of Tyneside.

After a year of fitting and sea trials, RMS Mauretania sailed out of the Tyne, accompanied by a fleet of smaller vessels of various sizes. She was on her maiden voyage to her home port of Liverpool. Once again, the people of Tyneside turned out to cheer and salute her. As the running mate to RMS Lusitania, built simultaneously at Clydebank in Scotland, she had the capacity for 2,165 passengers. With a guaranteed speed of twenty-four knots, she was the largest ship in the world and the fastest. RMS Mauretania was to leave Liverpool on her maiden voyage to New York on 16 November 1907 under the command of Captain John Pritchard. On the return journey, she captured the record for the fastest eastbound crossing of the Atlantic. In September 1909, Mauretania seized the Blue Riband for the most rapid westbound passage, an achievement to stand for over two decades.[130] Great Britain had won another race for supremacy on the high seas.

The other big news in shipbuilding that year was the launch of the Royal Navy's largest battleship, the HMS Dreadnought, at His Majesty's Naval Base, Portsmouth. They laid the keel on 2 October 1905, and work on the Dreadnought proceeded at a frenetic pace. King Edward VII launched the vessel on 10 February 1906, after only four months on the shipyard ways. Admiral Sir John "Jacky" Fisher, First Sea Lord of the Board of Admiralty, was the father of the Dreadnought. Fisher heard reports of the Japanese defeat of the Russian fleet in 1905 using 12-inch guns. So, he ordered a battleship with ten 12-inch guns and a speed of twenty-one knots, the most advanced warship of the time. Deemed complete on 3 October 1906, Fisher boasted they had built the gigantic ship in a year and a day. *Dreadnought* was the first British battleship to have a uniform main battery. She was the first capital ship powered by steam turbines, making her the most significant and fastest warship in the world at the time of her completion. [131] HMS Dreadnought was a formidable 527 feet long, 82 feet 1 inch wide, displaced 18,120 long tons and had a heavy load draught of 29 feet 7.5 inches. 18 Babcock &

---

130 John Maxtone-Graham, The Only Way to Cross. New York: Macmillan, 1972.

131 Sturton, Ian, ed. (2008). *Conway's Battleships: The Definitive Visual Reference to the World's All-Big-Gun Ships* (2nd revised and expanded ed.). Annapolis, Maryland: Naval Institute Press.

Wilcox boilers produced steam for the turbines driving the propellers via four shafts. Her entry into service on 2 December 1906 was a fundamental change in maritime technology. And her name became associated with an entire generation of high-technology battleships known as the dreadnoughts. But she sped up the naval race between Britain and Germany.

§

The nursing sister awoke Joe again with a thermometer in her hand.

"You are looking much better, soldier," she said. "Let's sit you up and retake your temperature, shall we?"

"I'll try with your help," said Joe.

The nurse took his temperature and said, "Much better, soldier. You are on the mend for sure. But retake these aspirins, just to make sure." She then swept away to another patient on the floor. After a while, Joe slipped into another dream.

A significant event involving the peoples of Britain and the Empire came in 1910. On 6 May that year, King Edward VII died at 68, and his second son George became king. Edward had only reigned for nine years. George wrote in his diary, "I have lost my best friend and the best of fathers. I am heartbroken and overwhelmed with grief, but God will help me in my responsibilities, and darling Mary will be my comfort as she has always been. May God give me strength and guidance in the heavy task which has fallen on me."

The State held a funeral for Edward VII on 20 May 1910. It was the first public lying in state in Westminster Hall. This sad but pompous event was one of European royalty's last and most significant gatherings during the increasing European tensions.

Joe was still in his job at Hawthorn Leslie. And he had grown in stature, both in his working environment and within his neighbourhood. A great raconteur, Joe spent many nights amusing his friends and family at his favourite pub on Saturday evenings or the Community Centre on Sundays. He was well-liked and respected, and he regaled them with stories from the past and present, real and often embellished. Many still remembered his accounts of the South African War before his departure. Despite being born in England, he had inherited the Irish gift of the Blarney Stone.

His new sweetheart was Mary Caston Burgess, a Geordie girl born in Jarrow-on-Tyne on 5 November 1887. When Joe left for South Africa, she was only thirteen years old, and he had just turned nineteen. On his return from India, he noticed she had blossomed into a handsome young woman of nineteen. She had been waiting for him to return, spurning any other advances. After a while, they had become closer and more affectionate towards one another until courtship began with their parent's blessing.

It had taken a while, but at 29, Joe married 23-year-old Mary on 1 April 1911. Mary was four months pregnant with their first child. Before their marriage, Joe lived at 258 High Street, and Mary lived along the street at 239 High Street, Jarrow. Joe and Mary married and moved into a home of their own at 227 High Street, Jarrow, between their parents' homes. Their first child, John, was born there on 23 July 1911.

"Thank you for making an honest woman of me, Joe," said Mary as they entered their new home laughing.

"No, Mary, you have made an honest man of me," he said. "Now we can fill this new home with a large family."

"Aye, that we will, Joe," she said as she surveyed the two-up, two-down terrace house Joe had found. There was a basic kitchen, for which they bought a table and two chairs, and they purchased one enormous bed for one bedroom upstairs. The house was more extensive than needed at that stage, but they planned to fill it.

"Aye, and we will fill this house with furniture soon enough," said the proud man of the house.

These were contented and fulfilling years for Joe. He was in an excellent job and was earning a better wage. He had a caring wife and a young family. Life for the majority in Jarrow was still arduous, but it improved year by year. Joe met his marras and brothers at the pub every Saturday evening.

This regular meeting was a long-standing tradition that began with his father and brothers before the Boer War and continued when he and his marras returned.

"Life is wonderful," was one of Joe's favourite sayings to his marras. "My walk to the shipyards is short at twenty minutes. I leave home early each morning with the lunch box that Mary prepares for me. Yes, we work ten hours, from 7 A.M. to 5 P.M., six days a week. But I have enough money to pay for my home and care for my little family, which is enough for me."

Labour had been pushing for eight-hour days since Robert Owen campaigned for an eight-hour working day for workers in 1817. Owen was a founder of socialism in Britain. He coined the phrase, "Eight hours labour, eight hours recreation, eight hours rest." Even though a series of Factory Acts passed throughout the 19th century, Parliament had not yet passed the eight-hour-day. They had improved working conditions and reduced work hours for factory workers. At long last, they had introduced eight-hour days for miners by an act of Parliament in 1908. However, it took longer for other industries to adopt the eight-hour day.

"I don't mind rising and going to work early in the morning as long as I can be home with my family by 5:30 in the afternoon," said Joe. "In the evening, I arrive home to a smiling and welcoming wife and my baby son."

"Mary first serves tea, and we catch up on family matters and the latest local gossip. I then relaxed and read the daily newspaper while Mary prepared supper. My life as a married man is a damned pleasant one."

Mike, Jack and Fred had seen a significant change in their friend. He had matured into a family man.

"My home time is important to me. My only night out is my Saturday evening at the pub for a time with my marras," thought Joe. "We have been through lots together and enjoy each other's company. Saturday evenings are the only time I have my Broons and partake in more serious manly discussions on working conditions, labour reforms, football and anything else that arises. But we don't talk of the war anymore. That is far behind us."

This alternative lifestyle was sacrosanct for Joe. Yes, murmurings arose about Germany's expanding military, which caused apprehension among the veteran reserve soldiers. But Germany was far from Tyneside and posed no immediate threats, so they never discussed their concerns outside the regimental depot.

One day, when they were alone, Mike gave Joe the news he had been keeping a secret for a while.

"I have a woman in my life now, Joe," said Mike.

"Good on you, Mike, it's time you did," said Joe. "Who is that now?"

"Ruth Anderson," said Mike.

"Ruth Anderson? My Ruthie?" asked Joe.

"Aye," said Mike, "She's not yours anymore, Joe. As you know, she hasn't been for a long time!"

"True, Mike, and that's great. Are you serious?" asked Joe.

"Aye! That I am. We are getting married," said Mike.

The news initially surprised Joe, but then he rejoiced for his friends, Mike and Ruth. Ruth was a local lass, a Geordie. She had long, inky hair and a petite and shapely figure. Mike had always been a lady's man, but relationships had never lasted long for him. Now he was getting married to Joe's old sweetheart.

In contrast to Mike's robust and scrappy nature, Ruth was shy and not very talkative. "Maybe they will make an exemplary couple," thought Joe. "It should make our relationship easier, being married and raising families."

"I wish you both well, Mike," said Joe. "May our families be forever close!"

§

Joe recovered, as did many of his fellow patients in Soltau Camp. Despite any contrary indications or expectations, they lived with the hope this wasn't the dreaded 1918 flu. But many POWs died, and Joe didn't recover fully from his illness. He coughed for months afterwards. This condition became common in the camp, and the doctors watched out for tuberculosis and the effect that contagious disease could have had if it had taken hold. It was a tense time in Germany and the POW camps.

As Joe, now conscious, lay recovering on a cot in the crowded lazaret, he made a few new acquaintances. He started conversations with them, including a fellow Geordie from Durham who had arrived at the camp in November 1917 from Passchendaele.

"Was that battle as terrible as they say it was?" asked Joe.

"It was worse," he said. "In my three years on the Western Front, I'd never lived through such a terrible battle! It rained nonstop for three months, with mud and craters everywhere, and it was freezing. Lads fell flat on their faces and drowned in the mire. That stinking mud swallowed everything—men, horses, mules and even tanks! I don't know how I lived through it, but I guess I have the Hun to thank for finding me and bringing me here before I croaked."

Joe introduced himself. "My name is Joe. What's yours?"

"Aalreet Joe, charmed to meet ye. My name is Billy," he said.

"I had an excellent friend called Billy, who died when we were in South Africa during the Boer War."

"So, you were there too. How long have ye been in this war?" asked Billy.

"Since September 1914, but a POW since October 1914," said Joe.

"Well, I got here yesterday, as ye know. But I don't intend to stay long," said Billy. "So you weren't in the trenches for a long time then?"

"One month was long enough," said Joe. "Good luck, Billy. I tried to escape once but didn't get very far. I'm hoping this war is over soon. We've had enough of these bloody Boche POW camps! This camp is my third."

"Aye, that's for sure, my marra."

Mary received a letter from Joe at long last telling her of his misfortune. She had worried since she hadn't received word from him, and she knew the 1918 flu was spreading in England and killing many.

"Dearest Mary,

"I'm sorry that I haven't written for a while. I was sick with the flu and in bed for a few days. Nothing too serious. I'm on the mend now, so everything is fine. I hope the same for you and the children. Don't worry; this war will finish soon.

"I will write again soon, but I want to get this off before the post office closes.

"I love you, my dearest, more than ever, Joe."

Regardless of his worsening condition, he refused to give Mary any hint he was suffering more than usual. This secret and his ever-present cheery disposition always shone through despite his near-death experience.

But by then, Mary knew too well what Joe had survived. The flu had been devastating Tyneside. She had the flu during the first wave but had recovered. But she had lost friends to this plague, so she knew its terrible consequences.

Known as the Spanish Flu, this pandemic infected 500 million people on every continent except Antarctica. The disease killed between 50 to 100 million people before it was over at the end of 1920.

§

The Allied Hundred Day Offensive Begins

The so-called Hundred Days Offensive was the final Allied blow to the Germans. They didn't call it that, then. The term Hundred Days Offensive does not refer to any individual battle, or a unified strategy. Instead, it was the rapid series of final Allied victories starting with the Battle of Amiens. No one knew how long it could last, let alone 100 days. It was just business as usual, a counteroffensive to the German Spring Offensive, at least at the outset.

If not his old self, Joe had recovered enough to resume his role of keeping his companions abreast of developments in these last days of the war. Fewer prisoners were arriving at this stage, so he had befriended a few English-speaking guards willing to offer him information. Joe still approached his circle of friends within the camp for anything they had heard through the grapevine. And as before, he noted every development and scrap of news he could uncover on bits of paper, even if from the German Guards. Every evening, he passed on this information to his companions.

"The Allies have launched the killer phase of this war," said Joe one evening early in September. "The latest word is that the war will end in two months."

"Hurrah, hurrah," called one listener.

"About bloody time," called another.

"How do you know, Joe?" asked Mike.

"Because we crushed the Germans by the end of their Spring Offensive a month ago," said Joe. "They have fewer men than we do and fewer supplies. They are on the run, and our boys and the Americans, who they're calling the Doughboys, many freshly arrived, will push the Boche back into Germany where they belong."

"Tell us more," said Walt. "We need more positive news at last."

"Okay, so in the opening stage of the Allied offensive, they launched a series of attacks against the Central Powers," said Joe.

"It started on 8 August with the Battle of Amiens. Most of the British soldiers on the Western Front were still robust enough, with many recent arrivals, to meet the exhausted enemy full force. On 8 August 1918, an infantry team, supported by over 400 tanks, 2,000 guns, and 1,900 aircraft, launched an 'all arms' attack. This powerful force punched through the German lines in spectacular fashion. The offensive soon pushed the Germans out of France, forcing them to retreat beyond the strategically important Hindenburg Line."

"General Sir Henry Rawlinson's British 4th Army used 456 tanks in attacks on German positions east of Amiens," said Joe.

"Our forces advanced over seven miles on the first day, one of the most significant advances of the war. The Fourth Army played a leading role in this progress."

Chief of the German General Staff, General Ludendorff, later described that day as the "Black Day of the German Army."

"Four hundred and fifty-six tanks must have made the difference," said Walt.

"Aye, and this battle affected the morale of the troops on both sides," said Joe. "There were vast numbers of surrendering German forces. Six German divisions fell apart, imagine. And we took 13,000 prisoners during the rapid 7-mile advance. Only when the Germans rushed in nine divisions, their last reserves on the Western Front, did the attack slow. The Battle of Amiens involved significant armoured warfare and marked the end of trench warfare on the Western Front, fighting becoming mobile once more. The Tank Corps would deploy hundreds of the latest British tank type, the Mark V, and a smaller, lighter, faster tank called the Whippet. And our rapid advances were a major boost to the morale of our boys."

"Howay," called Mike. "13,000 German prisoners in one battle is amazing."

"Aye, but they were exhausted and rundown soldiers, many sick with the flu," said Joe.

"On 20 August, the French 10th Army took another 8,000 prisoners at Noyon and captured the Aisne Heights where we fought. Then, on 21 August, the British 3rd Army began an attack along a 10-mile front south of Arras. And the 4th Army beside them resumed its offensive in the Somme as the Germans continued to fall back."

"This sounds fantastic," called a companion. "I am so enjoying this, Joe."

"Thanks, my friend. It sure does our morale a lot of good," said Joe.

They paused then so that Joe could gather more intelligence. He continued his feedback later in September.

"On 12 September, the Americans launched their first stand-alone attack as the US 1st Army," said Joe.

"They attacked the southernmost portion of the Western Front in France at St. Mihiel supported by 1476 Allied planes. Allied air support, comprising 1476 planes, bolstered the offensive. Within 36 hours, the Americans took 15,000 prisoners and captured over 400 artillery pieces as the Germans withdrew."

"Howay," called Mike. "Who can imagine 1,476 Allied aeroplanes? When this war started, seeing one or two flying over amazed us."

"Aye, crazy," said Joe.

"Then, on 26 September, the US 1st Army and French 4th Army began a joint offensive to clear the German-defended corridor between the Meuse River and the Argonne Forest. But there, the Germans didn't fall back, and the battle was soon like action from earlier years in the war. In a steady rain, the troops advanced yard-by-yard over the muddy, crater-filled terrain with 75,000 American casualties suffered over six weeks of fighting."

"Haddaway, that's not so good," said Mike.

"Aye, but on 27 September, the British 1st and 3rd Armies, Australians and the US 2nd Corps broke through a 20-mile section of the Hindenburg Line," said Joe.

"That was between Cambrai and St. Quentin."

"Belgian and British troops pushed back the Germans in the Fourth Battle of Ypres on 28 September. Unlike the earlier drawn-out battles, this lasted just two days as the Belgians took Dixmude and the British took Messines."

The unstoppable strength of the Allies confronted General Ludendorff, and the prospect of an outright military defeat on the Western Front faced him. He suffered a nervous collapse at his headquarters on 28 September, losing all hope for victory. He then informed his superior, Paul von Hindenburg, that they must end the war. Then Ludendorff, accompanied by Hindenburg, met with the Kaiser the next day and urged him to end the war. The Kaiser's army was weakening by the day amid irreversible troop losses, declining discipline and battle readiness because of exhaustion, illness, food shortages, desertions and drunkenness. Kaiser Wilhelm took heed from Hindenburg and Ludendorff and agreed with the need for an armistice.

On 29 September, Bulgaria signed a truce with the Allies, becoming the first of the Central Powers to quit the war.

On 2 October, Ludendorff sent a military representative to Berlin to inform the legislature the Central Powers had lost the war. He told them they should begin armistice discussions at once. It shocked the German politicians when they heard the news since the General Staff and Kaiser had kept them in the dark.

On 4 October, President Woodrow Wilson received a letter from the German government, sent via the Swiss, asking for armistice discussions based on his Fourteen Points. The Germans bypassed the French and British, hoping to negotiate with Wilson, who they perceived as more lenient. However, Wilson disappointed them when he responded with a list of demands as a prelude to discussions. These demands included a German withdrawal from their occupied territories and a total halt of U-boat attacks.

The Allies broke through the last remnants of the Hindenburg Line on 5 October. On 6 October, a provisional government proclaimed the state of Yugoslavia, signalling the start of the breakup of the six-century-old Austro-Hungarian Empire in central Europe. Poland, once part of the Russian Empire, proclaimed itself an independent state on 7 October.

On 8 October, the First and Third British Armies broke through the Hindenburg Line, forcing the German High Command to accept that further fighting in the war was futile. Beyond the Hindenburg Line through October, the German armies retreated through the territory they had gained in 1914. The Allies pressed the Germans back toward the lateral railway line from Metz to Bruges. This line had supplied the Germans at the Front in Northern France and Belgium for much of the war. As the Allied armies reached the tracks, they forced the Germans to abandon vast amounts of heavy equipment and supplies, reducing their morale and capacity to resist. The Allies captured 8,000 Germans while advancing toward Cambrai and LeCateau.

The Germans engaged in a general retreat along a 60-mile section of the Western Front in France. As French and American armies advanced on 13 October, they stretched from St. Quentin southward to the Argonne Forest.

On 14 October, the Germans abandoned positions along the Belgian coast and northernmost France as the British and Belgians were advancing apace. Then, on 17 October, King Albert of Belgium entered the city of Ostend on the Belgian coast.

Battles fought during the final pursuit included Selle (9 October); Courtrai (14 October); Mont-d'Origny (15 October); Selle (17 October); Lys and Escaut (20 October); Serre (20 October); Valenciennes (1 November); and the Sambre including Guise (4 November) and Thiérache (4 November).

In those last days of this epic conflict, men were still dying in large numbers. They succumbed to battlefield defeats and disease in the POW camps. The Allies, by then, outnumbered the Germans on the Western Front by close to 400,000 men.

In Soltau, both prisoners and their guards found themselves in a state of desperation and lethargy. Most prisoners were too weak to work, and the camp authorities were too unmotivated to enforce the work programmes. The men spent their days in their barracks, preserving their dwindling energy or outdoors, seeking food—edible weeds, roots, grass, rats, birds—anything they could find to eat.

§

The Fourth Anniversary as POWs—20 October 1918

Joe and his marras' final observance of their fourth anniversary as prisoners of war, on 20 October 1918, was quiet but uplifting. Although they didn't know it, it was three weeks before the war's end. But everyone sensed the end was near. Rumours abounded of the German surrender. Soltau Lager was in chaos since the British had pushed the Germans back over the Hindenburg Line, and everyone knew the war was almost over.

The Kommandant and his guards were still on duty but had become observers and allies instead of disciplinarians. They had become very concerned about their futures and had changed their attitudes towards the prisoners. They passed on what they heard and read within Germany about events on the Western Front. Many other guards had deserted the camp to look after their families at home. They knew only too well it was over, and they had concerns for the well-being of their next of kin.

Emaciated and not up to the rigours of escape, none of the prisoners attempted to flee. They believed their troops would arrive soon to rescue them. Food rations had been sparse for several months, and the prisoners were starving. Most looked like walking skeletons. In the final few months of the war, the care packages from home and the Red Cross had stopped. The men suspected the Kommandant was stashing or even selling them. They had excellent reasons to rise against their captors but lacked the energy or courage to revolt. Where could they go? They also realized that by then, the Germans were starving too.

Weakened and unable to work, they became listless, lingering in the barracks while awaiting the war's end. Large numbers of them got sick, and many succumbed to their illnesses. The 1918 flu was still rampant. Men who had been healthy and spirited throughout their incarceration became shadows of their former selves, including Joe. The war had taken its toll not only on their bodies but on their minds, too. They had lost close friends and endured terrible conditions and atrocities in the trenches and camps. What they had experienced would live with them for the rest of their lives.

Those still strong enough hunted for rats, rabbits, birds, and insects to supplement their meagre rations. But rejoice they could in this moment of triumph. Oh, what glorious days these were! Everyone awaited the imminent truce, peace and rescue.

§

On another evening, Joe and his fellow POWs again sat around a table after their light meal, reminiscing about their war involvement. They discussed what they knew of the conflict for the hundredth time when the conversation switched to heroism. Although weakened, the pending end of war inspired them enough to focus on this vital topic.

"Were we heroes or cowards?" asked Mike.

"I don't think we were cowards, Mike," said Joe. "We fought the enemy in fierce battles before being captured, but I can't say we were heroes either."

"Aye, and the four years we have spent in these camps?" said Walt. "We may not have been heroes, but it wasn't a doddle either."

"Aye, that's true," said Joe. "It's been a constant struggle just to stay alive. And we still don't know whether we'll make it home!"

"Aren't heroes soldiers who do heroic acts in battle?" challenged Mike. "We've heard of many such blokes— Tommies, French, Doughboys, Canucks and even Boche."

Thousands of heroes were on both sides during this terrible "war to end all wars." They came from various walks of life, nationalities, religions, skin colours and purposes. Many rushed into the fight with a sense of patriotism and honour. Others ended up in the war with no wish to be there. But regardless of motivation, when confronted with the horrors of the conflict, they mustered their strength and courage. They threw themselves into the battles without concern for their well-being. They became the heroes of the Great War.

The British Army awarded 634 Victoria Crosses, and the Americans awarded 121 Medals of Honour during the conflict. Many survived despite their risk, but many didn't. Joe and his marras had heard of the most famous ones, but there were many more.

However, the unsung heroes of the war were the medical services of the thousands of health workers—the doctors, nurses and field medics. They devoted their lives to attending to the injured and sick on the battlefields.

"Aye, what of that Doctor Noel Chavasse?" asked Joe. "He wasn't fighting. He was saving lives. But he was a hero, for sure."

Noel Chavasse, a British medical doctor, Olympic athlete and British Army officer, was the only double VC winner in the Great War. He belonged to the Royal Army Medical Corps attached to the King's Regiment (Liverpool). Chavasse was the only man awarded a Victoria Cross and Bar in the Great War and one of only three men to have achieved this distinction[132].

At the Battle of Guillemont in September 1916, enemy shell fragments hit Chavasse while rescuing men in no-man's-land. They say he got as close as 25 yards from the German line. There, he rescued three men and continued throughout the night under a constant rain of sniper bullets and bombing.

---

[132] Ann Clayton, "Chavasse, Noel Godfrey (1884–1917)," Oxford Dictionary of National Biography, Oxford University Press, 2004

Chavasse led rescue and recovery missions in no-man's-land despite aggressive shell fire. However, he took a fatal shot to the head at the Battle of Passchendaele on 4 August 1917, aged 32. Although operated upon, he was to die of his wounds two days later in 1917. [133] Most Tommies knew of his acts of heroism and praised him often.

"Aye, he was a hero for sure," said Walt. "A hero without a weapon and one who cared for soldiers on both sides, a compassionate human being, Joe's point."

"What of the women heroes?" asked Mike.

"I know of a great heroine, Edith Cavell," said Joe. "What about her? She was a much-loved British nurse living in Belgium. Edith Cavell was a true heroine who helped 200 Allied soldiers escape from German-occupied Belgium. Her most famous saying was, 'Patriotism is not enough. I must have no hatred or bitterness towards anybody.' The Germans arrested and executed her by a firing squad in October 1915."

The death of Edith Cavell helped turn global opinion against Germany.

"Aye, those are all grand stories we have heard," said Mike.

"I love the stories of those native Canadian soldiers who fought in this war, even though they weren't Canadian citizens. Why, I don't know. But they are still heroes."

---

[133] "Chavasse, Noel Godfrey (1884–1917)," Oxford Times, first published Thursday 15 June 2006 A lesson of history.

"Aye, I've heard about a few of those, too," said Joe. "One such Canadian native hero is Henry Louie Norwest. What a bloke; he killed 115 Boche."

Canadian Métis sniper Lance Corporal Henry Louie Norwest was born in Fort Saskatchewan, Alberta, on 1 May 1884. That was the year before the Louis Riel Métis Rebellion, and he may well have grown up on stories of the noble warriors in that last resistance. Nicknamed Ducky, Henry Norwest was Métis of Cree and French origins from the Hobbema reserve in Alberta. He served with the 50th Canadian Infantry Battalion, he fought at Vimy Ridge and the Battle of Amiens, which Canada won. Norwest achieved a documented sniping record of 115 fatal shots. Norwest was not only an outstanding marksman but an exceptional master of stealth tactics and camouflage. Because of these skills, they often sent him on reconnaissance missions into no-man's-land or behind enemy lines. In 1917, Norwest earned the Military Medal during the Battle of Vimy Ridge, and the following year, they awarded him the bar for his Military Medal. Only three months before the war ended, Norwest was on a mission to find a German sniper's lair when the enemy sniper killed him. They buried him in the Warvillers Churchyard Extension Cemetery, Warvillers, Somme, France.

"Aye, what about Canadian native sniper with the funny name of Peggy, our Canadian friend once told us about," said Joe?

"I've heard he has shot more Germans than any other sniper in the Great War."

Joe refers to the Canadian hero Francis Pegahmagabow, nicknamed "Peggy," a First Nations soldier from Parry Sound, Ontario. He became the most decorated soldier for bravery in Canadian military history and the most compelling sniper of the Great War. Three times awarded the Military Medal and wounded, he was an expert marksman and scout, credited with killing 378 Germans and capturing 300 more. On 30 August 1918, during the Hundred Days Offensive, they involved Pegahmagabow in fighting off a German attack at Orix Trench near Upton Wood. His company was low on ammunition and in danger of being surrounded. Pegahmagabow braved heavy machine guns and rifle fire by going into no-man's-land and retrieved enough ammo to enable his post to carry on repulsing heavy enemy counterattacks. He received a second Bar to his Military Medal for these efforts, becoming one of only 39 Canadians to receive this honour. He was first awarded the Military Medal for courage in getting important messages to the rear while fighting at the second battle of Ypres, Festubert and Givenchy. He earned his first bar to the Military Medal at the Battle of Passchendaele.

The Canadian Army initially discouraged the recruitment of native soldiers. They were not even Canadian citizens then. But officers saw that many Indigenous men who lived as hunters were skilled marksmen, unlike young recruits from the cities. When natives joined the Army, they became Canadian citizens and had the right to vote in the 1917 election. 4,000 native Canadians joined the CEF and fought under British command. For many, it was a way to regain the warrior ethic that was still alive in the West.

As their energy faded, the men agreed it didn't matter where you came from, your skin colour, or your station in life; whether you were a fighter or medic or POW or woman, you could still be a hero.

"I reckon that there are hundreds or thousands of such heroes on both sides of this war," proclaimed Mike. "That's what I believe."

"Aye, you're right there, Mike," said Joe. "Look at the heroes we know from our trenches—Major Robb, Jackie Warwick, George Harrington, Major Blake and others now dead. They were heroes. And maybe they will also look at us as heroes one day?"

"How do you remember such things?" asked Walt.

"I don't know, Walt," said Joe. "Things just stick around in my memory for a while. But I want to say that heroes aren't just men who kill the enemy. Some heroes also care for their fellow human beings, helping them at every opportunity. For example, the Medical Services on both sides of this war, as we've seen with our German doctors and nurses in this camp. And I'd venture that most of us have done that, too. So, to my mind, we have all been heroes here too. Look at what we have endured for our homeland. These four years have not been for cowards, and I believe many more of us would have died had it not been for our caring fellow prisoners."

Joe's close friends acknowledged his point of view and felt better because of those good words.

§

Countdown to the End of the Great War

But despite his precariously weakened state, an unstoppable Joe Rutherford continued in his assumed role of informer and motivator for his fading companions. It exhausted him further, but he couldn't stop himself.

"President Wilson told the German government on 23 October that an armistice negotiation could not happen with their military or imperial war leaders still in place," said Joe.

"This made General Ludendorff angry, and he rejected the talks as 'unconditional surrender.'

"The Kaiser responded by forcing Ludendorff to resign. So, now the civilian members of Germany's government are conducting the armistice negotiations."

"This is sounding very promising," said Walt.

"Aye, General Ludendorff lost the war for them," said Mike.

"Nee, the Allies won the war," said another. "We defeated them, don't forget."

"Aye, you've got an excellent point there," said Mike.

"The Allies crossed the Piave River in Italy on 24 October," said Joe.

"Seven Italian armies, including British, French and American divisions, were pushing the Austrians out of Italy. In its last significant battle, the Austro-Hungarian Army paid the heavy price of 30,000 soldiers killed and over 400,000 taken prisoner.

"Turkey signed an armistice with the Allies on 30 October," said Joe. "So, they are the second of the Central Powers after Bulgaria to quit the war. French and Serbian troops liberated Belgrade on 1 November. On the same day, after regrouping and replenishing, the Allied armies restarted their eastward march. The US 1st and 2nd Armies attacked the last German positions along the Meuse River near southern Belgium. Then, the Belgians and British moved toward Ghent and Mons in Belgium. Laddies, our enemy is falling apart."

"It's about time," said Mike. "They are well and truly beaten."

By 1 November, Allied troops on the Western Front outnumbered the Germans by a million men. On 3 November, mutiny struck the German Navy at the ports of Kiel and Wilhelmshaven. German sailors refused orders to put to sea to engage in a final colossal battle with the British Navy.

Revolutionary fervour and Bolshevist-style uprisings erupted in German cities, including Munich, Stuttgart and Berlin. The extent of the unrest stunned German leaders and even the Allies, who feared Germany might now succumb to a violent Bolshevist revolution like Russia. The turmoil added urgency to the armistice negotiations. On the same day, the only remaining ally of Germany, Austria-Hungary, signed an armistice with Italy, leaving Germany alone in the war.

President Wilson informed the Germans on 5 November that peace discussions could start based on his Fourteen Points. He insisted that France's Marshal Foch, the Allied Supreme Commander, must first secure a truce.

On 8 November, six representatives of the German government at Compiègne, France, with Matthias Erzberger as spokesman, heard a brusque presentation with armistice terms by Marshal Ferdinand Foch. The conditions included the German evacuation of occupied territory and the Allied occupation of Germany west of the Rhine River. It also called for the surrender of all weaponry, including their submarines and battleships, and an indefinite continuation of the naval blockade.

On 9 November, the Kaiser's Imperial government collapsed in ruin as German politicians proclaimed a republic, with Friedrich Ebert heading the new provisional government. Kaiser Wilhelm then sought refuge in exile in Holland amid concerns for his safety. His generals warned him they could not protect him well enough from the volatile situation in Germany.

As an ultimate irony, the last battle of the British Empire was at the same place as its first battle—the city of Mons, Belgium, of enormous symbolic importance. In August 1914 and November 1918, the region was the scene of clashes between British troops and German soldiers. Mons, the capital of the province of Hainaut, had endured occupation for over four years. On 11 November 1918, the Canadian Expeditionary Force liberated the city under the command of Lieutenant-General Arthur Currie. The 5th Regiment of Irish Lancers accompanied the Canadian infantry. The Irish Lancers had also been in Mons for the battle of August 1914, another enormous coincidence.

At 10:58 A.M., Canadian soldier Private George Lawrence Price of the 28th North-West Battalion, 6th Canadian Infantry Brigade, 2nd Canadian Division, died at 25 in the village of Ville-sur-Haine. He died just two minutes before the armistice took effect at 11 A.M. Price was the last soldier of the British Empire to be killed during the Great War. [134] The villagers of Ville-sur-Haine pleaded to contribute a coffin and bury their fallen hero Price in the nearby cemetery of St. Symphorien. But as with every Canadian soldier killed in action, they laid him to rest, wrapped in a blanket. As one of

---

[134] http://encyclopedia.1914-1918-online.net/article/mons

those ironies of war, they buried this last casualty alongside British soldiers killed near Mons during the war's first battle[135].

Although the news of the imminent ceasefire had spread among the soldiers on the Front, fighting continued until the appointed hour. At 11 A.M., there was infrequent impromptu mingling between the two sides, but something subdued the reactions. A British corporal noted, "The Germans came from their trenches, bowed to us, and left. That was it. There was nothing we could celebrate with except cookies[136]."

"Howay, the man," called Mike. "This bloody war has ended. What now?"

"Are you sure it's over?" asked Walt.

"As far as we know it is," said Joe. "The Kommandant said it was, and he is giving a speech this afternoon."

"We have heard nothing official," said Mike. "Maybe the Kommandant will tell us."

"Aye, maybe," said Joe. "A guard told me 11 November is the big day."

"What will you do now, Joe?" asked Walt.

"I'm first going home to my family," said Joe. "How? I don't know. Once I get there, I will regain my strength and

---

[135] James McWilliams, *The Last Patrol*, first published in November, 1980, by Readers Digest.
[136] Leonhard, Jörn, *Die Büchse der Pandora - Geschichte des Ersten Weltkriegs*, C.H. Beck, 2014

return to work, maybe at Hawthorn Leslie, if they take me back. I want Mary to stop working and to give all her time to raising our children again, of whom there will be more coming that I can guarantee you."

"What about you, Mike?" asked Walt.

"Much the same as my marra Joe, Walt. Home to my dear wife and son; recover from this bloody war; back to work at Hawthorne Leslie and make more children. I will live again! And what about you?"

"I'm first going to Hamelin," said Walt. "I'll ask Traudle for her hand and take her to England. Then, like you laddies, I will get a job in Jarrow and raise a family."

"What a moment," said Joe. "I had almost lost hope for this conversation! We're alive, Laddies. Weakened but alive. And we have lots of living ahead of us."

Then, a cheer went up from the rest of the Soltau companions.

"Alive. And we have lots of living ahead of us," repeated them one and all.

The next day, those prisoners who were strong enough to make it gathered early in the Soltau parade ground to hear from the Kommandant. Of the 70,000 held there at its peak, fewer than 10,000 were strong enough to join the assembly. Then the Kommandant spoke.

"My dear prisoners," he said. "We have been told the Prussian Army has surrendered to your victorious Allied

Command. They are telling us they signed an Armistice in France yesterday, and the guns on the Western Front fell silent. I must tell you, I did not ask for this war. And neither did you. But for four years, we have been fighting each other. I am sorry for that. My job was to guard prisoners of war until the war ended. I did that to the best of my ability. I know it has not been easy for you; this past year has been difficult for all of us. But you have not been alone in your suffering. The German people are starving, too. We have wanted an end to this war for a long time."

"I wanted to tell you what happens now, but I don't know. I'm sure your armies will soon arrive to free you. They will help you get home. Please do not be angry with us. We only did our duty as soldiers and what our commanders ordered us to do. As soldiers, you must understand this. Now, we must all go home to our families. I wish you well."

With those last words, the much-aged Prussian Kommandant performed a faded salute, then about-turned and vanished into his headquarters.

The prisoners stood in silence for a while as if stunned. They didn't know what the camp authorities expected of them now, so they shuffled back to their barracks to await their fate.

§

Empire and War

The Allied Powers had mobilized forty-three million men by the end of the Great War, of whom the enemy killed, wounded or captured twenty-two and a half million. The Central Powers' total force was over twenty-five million, of whom thirteen and a quarter million combatants were in the German Army. When the Great War ended in November 1918, the Central Powers had lost sixteen and a half million men killed, wounded or missing in action.

At the start of the Great War in August 1914, the DLI had only nine battalions: two Regular, two Reserve (old Militia) and five Territorial (old Volunteers). By 1918, the DLI had grown to 43 battalions, 22 of which fought overseas. Most of the DLI's 22 active service battalions fought on the Western Front in France and Belgium. Some saw action in Egypt, Italy, India, Macedonia and northern Russia, but none took part in the Gallipoli Campaign. The Durham Light Infantry lost 13,000 men killed during the Great War, with thousands more wounded, gassed or taken prisoner.

Over 6,000 men served in Lt-Colonel William Hart-McHarg's 7th Canadian Infantry Battalion during the war, suffering 1440 deaths and 3294 injuries during its 45 months on the Western Front. Members of the Battalion earned over 270 awards for gallantry, including three Victoria Crosses, the highest award for valour in the Empire.

Another seven million civilians lost their lives in this conflict. The total number of military and civilian casualties in the Great War was over thirty-seven million. There were seventeen million deaths and twenty million wounded, making it the deadliest conflict in human history up to that point.

However, it wasn't only humans who experienced pain and suffering during The Great War. Animals, including dogs, horses, and other equines, became casualties as well. Sixteen million animals "served" with the British in the Great War. The RSPCA estimates that British service killed 484,143 horses, mules, camels, and bullocks between 1914 and 1918.

Besides the terrible loss of human life, it didn't end there. Eight million horses and countless mules and donkeys died in the Great War. Veterinary hospitals treated over two and a half million horses, curing two million and clearing them to return to duty. The military used horses for cavalry and transport at the start of this war, as they had for centuries. They were first involved in the war in a British cavalry attack near Mons in August 1914. Britain and Germany had a cavalry force of 100,000 men when the war broke out in Western Europe in August 1914. However, the traditional cavalry became obsolete in this war. By the Spring Offensive of 1918, out of the 150 German warhorses used in one assault, only four made it back. German machine-gun fire was the principal reason most horses did not survive. They found mules to have tremendous transport stamina, serving in the freezing mud over the most challenging terrain on the Western Front. [137] Both sides used them to transport ammunition and supplies to the Front, and the majority died from the horrors of shellfire and appalling weather. Also, the armies used many dogs, pigeons, and other animals that had perished during the war. They estimate one million dogs died on both sides of the Great War[138].

The 'War to End All Wars' saw the demise of the German, Austro-Hungarian and Ottoman empires; the Russian Empire collapsed in the 1917 revolution. Only the British Empire remained and expanded one more time. Under the Treaty of Versailles, the British Empire gained another 1.8 million square miles and 13 million more subjects. The League of Nations mandates dispersed the German and Ottoman colonies among the Allied powers. Britain gained control of Palestine, Transjordan, and Iraq from the Ottoman Empire. It took control of Cameroon, Togoland and Tanganyika from the German Empire in Africa. The British Dominions, too, gained territories. South Africa gained German South West Africa, Australia won New Guinea, and New Zealand got Western Samoa. They made Nauru a joint mandate of Britain and the two Pacific Dominions[139].

---

[137] http://www.animalsinwar.org.uk
[138] Melissa Thompson, Mirror, The 9 million unsung heroes of WW1: Dogs, horses and carrier pigeons made victory possible, 31 July 2014
[139] Lloyd, Trevor Owen, The British Empire 1558–1995. Oxford University Press, 1996

US President Woodrow Wilson insisted Germany lose its Royal Family. On 10 November 1918, they sent Kaiser Wilhelm II by train to the Netherlands, which had remained neutral throughout the war, and he entered exile there. [140] His wife and household were with him. They filled 23 railway wagons of furniture and 27 wagons containing packages of various sorts, plus one bearing a car and another a boat, from the New Palace at Potsdam. [141] In the Treaty of Versailles, Article 227 allowed the Allies to prosecute Wilhelm "for a supreme offence against international morality and the sanctity of treaties." But, despite appeals from the Allies, the Dutch government refused to extradite him. King George V wrote that he regarded his cousin as "the greatest criminal in history" but was against Prime Minister David Lloyd George's motion to hang the Kaiser. President Woodrow Wilson rejected his extradition from the Netherlands, arguing that prosecuting Wilhelm could destabilize the international order and cause peace to be lost. [142]

Kaiser Wilhelm wrote once that the war would never have occurred had Queen Victoria, who died in 1901, still been on the British throne. The "Grandmother of Europe" would not have allowed it to happen.

---

[140] Cecil, Lamar, Wilhelm II: Emperor and Exile, 1900–1941, 1989

[141] Macdonogh, Giles, The Last Kaiser: William the Impetuous, London: Weidenfeld & Nicolson, 2001

[142] Ashton, Nigel J; Hellema, Duco, Hanging the Kaiser: Anglo-Dutch Relations and the Fate of Wilhelm II, 1918–20, Diplomacy & Statecraft, 11 (2): 53–78, 2000

A few years earlier, in 1906, Spanish-born American philosopher George Santayana wrote his 5-volume *The Life of Reason: The Phases of Human Progress*. In that seminal work, he wrote one of his most famous quotes:

"Those who cannot remember the past are condemned to repeat it."

§

12. *Dona Nobis Pacem, Grant Us Peace*

Armistice

As mentioned, the Armistice came into effect on the 11th hour of the 11th day of the 11th month of 1918. The generals signed it that morning at 5 A.M. in a railway carriage of Marshal Foch's private train at Le Francport in the Forest of Compiegne north of Paris. The Great War had ended. They had silenced the guns and freed the men from the horrors of that endless bloody conflict.

The news travelled fast around the world. On Tyneside, it arrived early. At North Shields, the first sign of peace was at 8:10 A.M. when locals saw two boats decked out with bunting. At South Shields, they heard the sirens of boats just after 8:30 A.M. By 9:30 A.M., the news had reached the Royal Navy at Scapa Flow in the Orkney Isles. The sirens of naval vessels alerted the people of the port of Kirkwall on Orkney. The people began rejoicing—many flags and much bunting soon appeared, ships blew whistles, and they rang the cathedral's bells[143].

Later in London, Big Ben, which had been silent throughout the war, should have chimed and struck the eleventh hour once more. But it didn't, returning only at noon to a loud cheer from the thousands assembled along the mall and in front of Buckingham Palace. After that, they chanted, "We want the King!" [144]

King George V, Queen Mary of Teck, Princess Mary and the Duke of Connaught walked out onto the palace balcony. A roar went up as the crowds cheered and called, "God Save the King."

By noon, most towns and cities in Britain were awash with cheering, singing, bells and music. Even though the Government had advised people to avoid large gatherings during the flu pandemic, the crowds were enormous and still growing. [145] Church bells across Great Britain that had been silent throughout the war burst into joyful chimes. Citizens fired off maroon fireworks, bands paraded the streets, followed by cheering crowds of soldiers, and civilians rejoiced. Conversation in the Strand was impossible because of the din of cheers, whistles, hooters and fireworks. Processions of

---

[143] Cuthbertson, Guy, "11 November 1918: The day the world turned upside down," BBC History Magazine, November 2018.

[144] *Daily Mirror*, November 12, 1918

[145] Cuthbertson, Guy, "11 November 1918: The day the world turned upside down," BBC History Magazine, November 2018.

soldiers and munition girls, arm in arm, were everywhere. American soldiers, in jubilation, invaded Downing Street. [146] Later that joyful day, King George V and Queen Mary, along with Princess Mary, attended a Thanksgiving service at St. Paul's Cathedral.

At innumerable church services, the emphasis was on triumph and thanksgiving instead of remembering the dead. Ministers quoted the Bible by saying, "God was on the side of Britain and her allies and gave them victory."

The service at St Margaret's Church, Westminster, the parish church of Parliament, was a joyous affair. There was a brief but crowded parliamentary session where they read out and acclaimed the terms of the Armistice with much cheering. The speaker adjourned the House of Commons at 3.17 P.M. He then led the members to the Church of St Margaret's, Westminster Abbey.

The Lords attended the service, too, and the archbishop of Canterbury presided. Psalm 100 opened the simple service: "Make a joyful noise unto the Lord, all ye lands." From outside came the sound of cheering and music[147].

It was a day when people ignored barriers, broke the rules and turned normalcy on its head. They ignored

---

[146] *Daily Mirror*, November 12, 1918

[147] Cuthbertson, Guy, "11 November 1918: The day the world turned upside down," BBC History Magazine, November 2018.

differences in wealth, class, or gender. "Banker and Beggar Walk Side by Side," *The New York Tribune* noted, and soldiers in New York wore women's hats and coats. Back in England, women wore their hair down and gave out kisses[148].

In France, people swarmed into the Grands Boulevards of Paris and other cities. Around the British Empire and America, people rode atop vehicles or hung from their windows as they weaved through the streets waving the Union Jack or Stars and Stripes. Soldiers and civilians linked arms as they commemorated the historic Armistice document that stated German soldiers must evacuate France and Belgium. It demanded they return POWs to their home countries, too.

They signed the armistice early enough for the news to reach Toronto by the early morning of November 11. The Mail and Empire reported that a man who lived on Parliament Street awoke at 4 A.M. to news of the peace. He at once went into the street to announce it to his neighbours. He wore only his pyjamas. Women appeared in the flimsiest of clothing, some covered only with a wrap or kimono, and forgot the cold in the heat of their enthusiasm.

The Mail and Empire also reported. Flags of the victorious nations flew from every home while cars decorated in flags congested the street. Thoroughfares were a seething

---

[148] Cuthbertson, Guy, "11 November 1918: The day the world turned upside down," BBC History Magazine, November 2018.

mass of humanity, a riot of colour, littered and carpeted with confetti, talcum powder, scraps of paper of every known form of carnival paraphernalia. The news of the armistice was an assurance Toronto would know no work for the next twenty-four hours. Streetcar men refused to work, adding extra traffic to the chaos of confusion. During the height of the celebration, Yonge Street was almost impassable, so thick were the crowds of joy-seekers.

Northern lights illuminated the Montreal sky that Sunday night — a harbinger, the newspapers would later say, of the good news soon to come. Bells and whistles marking the Armistice woke at 6 A.M. Montrealers. The word on the street was that the war was over, something Montrealers were initially hesitant to believe. A similar rumour had circulated a few days earlier and turned out wrong. By 8 A.M. on 11 November, newspapers were rushing out special editions that confirmed that after four years and some 20 million dead, the Great War had really ended. The Montreal French-language newspaper *Le Devoir* reported that day, "Workers arrived at their factories with their hearts light, liberated from a significant burden. In the animated streets, pedestrians were brandishing newspapers with enormous smiles, their eyes brimming with fire.

The last year of the war had been especially tumultuous in Quebec. After its outset, the province's francophones took a disinterested view of the conflict, seeing it as a predominantly British imperial affair. However, when the Canadian government imposed conscription in 1917, opposition in Quebec turned violent. Protesters erupted across the province, and someone bombed the Montreal home of Lord Atholstan, owner of the pro-conscription Montreal Star newspaper. A riot in the city that August had left one person dead.

Joe and his fellow prisoners rejoiced but were so weakened that it dampened their celebrations. Mere shadows of their former selves, they were awaiting their next moves. The Germans of Soltau Camp had not abandoned them as they had feared, for then chaos might have ensued, and they might have perished. The Kommandant and many staff had stayed to look after their charges while awaiting their fate. These long-standing Prussian officers and men stood their ground and performed their duties. Their war had ended, too, but they had lost, so what was to become of them now?

"I can't believe this shite war is over," said Mike. "We won! If I had the strength, I'd get up and dance."

"Aye, over four years later," said Joe. "We're still alive."

"Only just, though, Joe," said Walt.

"I wonder what's going on at home," said Joe.

"Dancing in the streets, I reckon," said Mike.

Back in Tyneside, women, children, shopkeepers, and workers were pouring out of their homes, shops, and factories, cheering, dancing, laughing, and crying in Tyneside cities and towns as elsewhere. Mary Rutherford took the day off because of the pending news. She grabbed her three children and ran out with them to join her sisters and her only remaining brother, John Robert Burgess. They had lost three of their younger brothers in this war. The Burgesses had paid the ultimate price for peace. The Rutherfords rushed towards their eldest brother William's home, where they often assembled as a family to celebrate the war's end together. They rejoiced at the war's end and the imminent return of their brother and Mary's husband, Joe Rutherford. Joe had survived the first battles of the Aisne and Ypres and four years at three POW camps with their work details, meagre food rations and rough living conditions. Their families knew these facts because the newspapers had written about them after the war. But now he could come home at long last!

The Rutherfords and the Burgesses joined the tidal current of humanity flowing towards the centre of Jarrow. They had left their children in the care of grandmothers Susannah Rutherford and Margaret Burgess.

"I can't believe this war is over, and Joe is coming home," called Mary to the others.

"Nor can we, Mary," said William Rutherford. "Nor can we. To be getting Joe back alive is such a relief."

"We took long enough, but we finished the Hun," called John Robert Burgess. "We sure did, didn't we?"

Overhearing John Robert, another nearby called out, "Aye, me marra, we sure did!"

"Curse the Huns!" yelled another.

"The Great War is over," said yet another. "Let bygones be bygones. We now need to move forward."

With that, they joined in the hysteria welling up around them. The joy of victory and the end to the horrific Great War was ubiquitous. Then, as the official news continued circulating, and the crowds merged, their cheers became a roar. Pandemonium broke out in the streets of Jarrow, Hebburn, North and South Shields, Gateshead, Wallsend and Newcastle upon Tyne. Tyneside was among the thousands of regions of Great Britain, Canada, Newfoundland, Australia, New Zealand, France, Belgium and the United States celebrating the victory. Besides the church bells silenced by the war now peeling again, factory and ship sirens howled along the river. The press later wrote that the news spread along the Tyne "like fire among the bracken. By eleven o'clock that morning when the Armistice took effect, the man, woman and child who did not know the glad tidings was rare." [149]

Everyone within earshot threw up their arms and laughed their hearts out. "What a joyful noise," shouted an ecstatic Mary.

---

[149] Jo Bath, Great War Britain: Tyneside, Remembering 1914-18, 2015

Empire and War

The ever-vigilant British Minister of Munitions Winston Churchill sent a telegram to munitions factories for their notice boards on 10 November. He ordered continuous production to continue unabated even if the war ended. But despite Saturday being a working day, they ignored the order, joining the workers of other factories, collieries and shipyards of Tyneside downing tools. Across the River Tyne, "munitionettes," in their fawn and blue overalls, poured from Armstrongs of Elswick towards the centre of Newcastle. [150] One group found a wagon distributing beer bottles for Deuchars' Scottish brewery and, helping themselves, ran off laughing.[151]

"Here's to Deuchars and the victors," they called while skipping off with their loot.

Children gathered improvised instruments such as tin drums and comb-organs, "from which they tried to produce a melody." In Hebburn, pipe bands paraded the streets, and scratch bands, playing weird and soul-disturbing airs, joined in the festivities. [152] Women created street decorations from pictures cut from newspapers, wild ferns and flowers. [153] Men lit bonfires around Tyneside, drawing crowds to them like moths. Many revellers burned effigies of Kaiser Wilhelm II and

---

[150] Local term for the women working in the munitions factories
[151] Jo Bath, *Great War Britain: Tyneside, Remembering 1914-18*, 2015
[152] A scratch band is a hastily thrown together band of musicians who haven't necessarily played together before.
[153] Jo Bath, *Great War Britain: Tyneside, Remembering 1914-18*, 2015

his son, the Crown Prince. Images with placards around their necks hung on makeshift gallows. The Belgian refugees across the river in Elisabethville burnt a straw Kaiser figure and paraded with torches and Chinese lanterns. They played music through the night until 6 A.M. the following day. According to the newspapers, Belgians walked to Newcastle, "where they sang the French Marseillaise national anthem." [154]

Hundreds of citizens, including the Rutherfords and Burgesses, gathered at Jarrow Town Hall in Wylam Street to cheer their mayor and the other assembled dignitaries. They announced the war's end while holding up a piece of paper as a testimony. The mayor thanked the families of Jarrow for their "great and painful sacrifices and hard work over the terrible years of the Great War in Europe." His speech drew the cheers of hundreds of Jarrovians.

"This is such a wonderful moment, Mary, don't you find?" called her sisters.

"Aye, better than wonderful," called Mary. "I hope Joe is having such a moment, too."

"I doubt Joe and his marras will celebrate there as much as we are here," yelled John Robert. "I suspect they are still in harsh conditions over there."

"Aye, I'm sure you're right," said Mary.

---

[154] Jo Bath, *Great War Britain: Tyneside, Remembering 1914-18*, 2015

But soon, the crowds restrained their celebrations because of regrets for the human losses of the past four years. Local papers reported the celebrations were less frenzied than those following the Relief of Mafeking eighteen years earlier, during the Second Anglo-Boer War. Older people, who had suffered the most, left most of the Joy-Day, as they called it, to the younger generations. The veterans, including many invalids, were silent. While others from his workshop went out to rejoice, one of them "went home sad, for I have lost four brothers and a sister in the war." The Burgesses were mourning their three lost brothers. In the hospital wards of the wounded, the *Journal* said, the soldiers were "the last to make merry."

However, one nurse said, "It filled them with holy joy and satisfaction." [155]

The Burgesses and the Rutherfords, while remembering their losses, were celebrating Joe's imminent return on this day, too.

As the celebrations subsided, the crowds became mournful and went to church in droves on Sunday, 12 November. Three thousand citizens packed into Newcastle's St Nicholas Cathedral for a Thanksgiving service. The newspaper called it "one of the most impressive and most attended ever recorded." Most other churches held services

---

[155] Jo Bath, *Great War Britain: Tyneside, Remembering 1914-18*, 2015

that morning, from St Mary's Catholic Cathedral to the Methodist chapels. [156]

The Rutherfords and Burgesses took part in the Sunday service at their historic church, St. Paul's, at the Monastery in Jarrow. That is where the old vicar had christened and married most of them and led the mourning and remembrance of their fallen brothers. The old vicar attended, expressionless and mumbling to himself. But the new and younger vicar officiated the service.

After the service, the Rutherfords and Burgesses gathered with their other friends outside the church. The new vicar raised their spirits. He was a young man full of vigour and excited them over "the fresh life energy emerging on a post-war Tyneside."

"Excellent service," said William Rutherford. "Just what we need now to get back on our feet."

"Aye," agreed John Robert Burgess. "He was right. As hard as it might have been, we must put it behind us. The war was unnecessary. Four years of misery, millions dead or maimed. We lost our three brothers. Your Joe and millions more lost four years out of their lives. Such a tragedy. At least yours will be home soon, William."

"Aye, none too soon, I say," said William. "Mary and their children need him back. We need him back."

[156] Jo Bath, Great War Britain: Tyneside, Remembering 1914-18, 2015

"Aalreet Mary," said Sarah James, one of her closest school friends, "aren't ye happy? I'm delirious! Your Joe and my Harry will soon come home to us!"

And Ruth was there too. "Little Mickey and I will have our Mike back soon, too. Not soon enough."

"Aye, Sarah and Ruth" said Mary, "Not soon enough. I wonder what they are up to right now."

"Packing, I reckon," said Sarah, laughing.

"Packing what?" asked Mary. "I don't think they have much."

It took several days for normalcy to return on Tyneside as elsewhere. On Sunday the 12th, Agnes Hall's Quayside coffee shop did not open because they had nothing to serve customers; they had sold everything the previous day. Tobacconists reported running out of supplies well before midday. Trams were not working apart from a few early morning trams assigned to take people to work, but they were empty. And three trams full of flag-waving conductresses toured the streets. Many people went into town on what should have been the start of the workweek with their female driver. Most workers were to return to work on Monday the 13th, but most didn't. Many took off the entire week. They reported Whitley Bay's promenade to be busier than ever seen in November. Packed cinemas showed pictures of war heroes on the screen instead of adverts, and everywhere, people asked each other, "How did you hear the news?" [157] This Armistice was a moment they'd remember for the rest of their lives. And indeed, we still celebrate it as Remembrance Day.

The authorities presented children with an Armistice celebration basket with pictures of the King, war leaders, and the Lord Mayor. Field Marshal Haig sent children a signed photograph of himself with a message. Prime Minister Lloyd George visited Newcastle on 29 November as part of a nationwide tour. He packed the Tyne Theatre, the Pavilion Theatre, and the streets along his route. The Lord Mayor presented him with the Freedom of Newcastle.

But uppermost on everyone's mind was the return of the surviving men and women from the Western Front and the POW camps.

§

The Journey Home

Alas, that took time. It took many months for the British Army to demobilize the soldiers of the Western Front. They started with priority workers, such as miners and skilled artisans, followed by those who had served the longest. During the Great War, the Germans captured close to seven thousand officers and one hundred and seventy thousand

---

[157] Jo Bath, Great War Britain: Tyneside, Remembering 1914-18, 2015

British and Commonwealth men on the Western Front alone. Of these, the Germans held seventeen thousand captured at the battles of the Marne, Aisne and Ypres for all four years of the war, Joe and Mike among them. From the first day of the Armistice, those living and waiting on the River Tyne watched the return of various ships to Tyneside, but few had soldiers on board.

As the Allies evacuated the troops from the trenches or the POW camps, they first moved them into demobilization camps. There, they showered, and medics checked them for lice, shaving their heads if they found any, and any other signs of ailments or unhealed wounds. Once cleared by the doctors, they waited naked except for a numbered piece of wood around their necks. Orderlies then wheeled in clothes racks full of items for men of all sizes. So, the men rushed around, finding the wardrobes that matched the number on their piece of wood. These were their uniforms and old pre-war clothes, washed, fumigated and disinfected. They were not to bring French or German vermin back home to Britain! For those dressed in their old clothes, it became too clear they had lost much weight during this war.

On their penultimate day on a wintry December day near Boulogne on the coast of France, soldiers queued in thick snow for breakfast. It took a while for the cooks to prepare the meal, which comprised tea, bread, and a large tin of Tyne Brand herrings from North Shields, Tyneside. They huddled in clean, fresh-smelling clothes, including their army-issue greatcoats against a bitter wind.

"What's taking them so bloody long?" asked Mike.

"Aye, we're freezing out here," complained another.

"Well, we've waited four years for this," said Joe. "I can wait a little longer."

Then, a long queue of men streamed past the kitchen table and received tea in their mess tins. They then moved on to a second cook, who handed them two large slices of fresh bread.

"Howay, Laddies," called Mike. "I haven't felt so good in a very long time. And Tyne Brand herrings, a Christmas present from home?"

"Aye, Mike," said Joe. "As hungry and grateful to the Army as I am, I can't face herrings right now."

"Nor can I," said Walt. "Who cares? We will soon cross the channel and head for home."

They left much of it on the ground surrounding the tables since no one could find the appetite to eat tinned herring on such a chilly morning.

"Never mind, chaps," said Joe. "We're on our way home for Christmas on Tyneside."

The following morning, the men hoped for a cooked breakfast of bacon and egg dip. However, the British Army again provided them with tea, bread and a galvanized iron bath full of mashed-up herring with a large wooden spoon.

Most malnourished returning prisoners held their noses and avoided the herrings, but others tucked into them. At 10 A.M., they marched to the docks, where civilians crowded to wave, clap, and blow kisses to show their support to a victorious departing British contingent. They boarded a Royal Navy ship for England, which soon left.

After a seven-hour trip, they arrived and moored at Tilbury on the River Thames. Too late to disembark, the men made themselves as comfortable as possible and slept on board that night. Small boats took them off the ship early the following day.

"Howay, Laddies, what a feeling to be back on English soil," called Joe, to which he got a firm round of approval.

"Not quite home," said Mike. "Still, close enough."

Military Police directed them to a large harbour shed, where they received a food parcel and cocoa before boarding a train at Tilbury Station. At 10 A.M. sharp, they started their journey north to the Ripon Dispersal Camp, West Yorkshire. As early as May 1918, officials prepared the procedures and structures for demobilization, but they completed them in November. The British Isles were sub-divided into twenty "Dispersal Areas," each with one or two associated "Dispersal Units" to which they sent men for demobilization. They routed the soldiers to dispersal units depending on where they intended to live. Ripon was for men returning to Counties Durham, Northumberland and Berwick-on-Tweed [158].

They arrived at Ripon at 1:30 A.M. the next day. The staff fed them a hot meal and announced reveille for 8 A.M. Those who didn't want a suit could draw 52s 6d instead[159].

The following day, after breakfast, they walked to Ripon station, where they embarked on the last stage of their journey. At 1 P.M., the train drew into Newcastle Central Station.

The Army had notified Mary that Joe was in good health and arriving at Newcastle Station on the planned date and time. William had arranged for a friend with a delivery lorry to take them to the station and drive them back to Jarrow. It was an emotional reunion! But it wasn't the only one. As they met Joe, dozens of other Tyneside families, including Joe's long-time friend Mike O'Brien, embraced their returning heroes, laughing and crying. Mike's wife Ruth was there with Mike Junior at her side. Little Mike had been born during the war, so this was Mike's first meeting with his son. It was a joyous occasion with copious laughter and tears, but somewhat overwhelming for returning POWs.

---

[158] https://www.longlongtrail.co.uk/army/other-aspects-of-order-of-battle/dispersal-units-for-demobilisation-purposes-1918-1920/
[159] George Russell Elder, From Geordie Land to No Mans Land, Authorhouse, 2011

After a quiet gathering at Joe's home, their families left him to become re-acquainted with his little family of Mary, John, Violet and Molly. He had not seen Mary or his children for four years and had never met little Molly. She was now four years old. John Irwin was seven, and Violet was five. Joe wasn't a broken man, but, as with most returning veterans, his years in the war had scarred him. Mary approached her exhausted husband slumped in his old armchair at home and, sitting on the arm of the chair, embraced him.

"Welcome home, my dearest man, welcome home," she said, looking into his eyes and smiling. "You made it back to us."

Tears welled up in his eyes as he said, "Thank you, dear wife. For a while, I didn't believe I'd make it."

"Well, make it you did. And now I will nurse you back to health. I want to see you smile and laugh again."

"Aye, smile and laugh again," said Joe with a weak smile. "That will be grand."

Then she turned to her children, who were waiting with anticipation.

"Children, this is your Da," explained Mary. "John, I'm sure you don't remember him, but he remembers you as a wee bairn. Violet, you were too little to remember him. And Molly, you are meeting your Da for the first time. But I wrote to your Da while he was away, telling him all about you. So even though you don't know him yet, he remembers you. Your father is your big Christmas present this year."

Joe's eyes lit up, and his mouth gave a weak smile. "I sure remember John and Violet. And your ma told me so much about you. And I love you so much."

The children were shy and shuffled back and forth and into each other, then they said in unison, "We love you too, Da," and ran forward to embrace him. But only for a moment before retreating again to their mother. Joe broke into muted laughter with tears. He was sore and weak, but oh, so glad to be home with his family after the horrible agony of that war.

Mary sat with the children while they stared at their long-lost father. Joe enjoyed in wonder this scene, which was so strange to him after four years away under the worst of circumstances. He had observed Mary with their sisters on the way home and had noticed a remarkable change in them. Gone were the demurred and subservient girls he had known before the war. Now, they were women, full of confidence, street-wise, with calloused hands and weathered faces. He noted they were in command of their lives and their families. The war had changed them too! Prime Minister David Lloyd George declared how important women had been to the war effort, saying in a speech:

"It would have been impossible for us to have waged a successful war had it not been for the skill and ardour, enthusiasm and industry which the women of this country have thrown into the war." [160]

Women supported the war effort on the home front in many military roles but volunteered and served in various noncombatant functions. By the end of the war, 80,000 had enlisted. The majority served as nurses in various nursing organizations or, from 1917, in the Army with Queen Mary's Army Auxiliary Corps (WAAC). They divided the WAAC into cookery, mechanical, clerical and miscellaneous sections. Most stayed on the Home Front, but 9,000 women served in France [161].

The Great War had ended. Joe and hundreds of thousands of other prisoners were soon home, safe if not sound. Joe's recovery and healing could now begin. He and so many more needed time and understanding, so everyone in his family agreed to help with his healing in any way they could. He thought he needed lots of readjustment to find himself again in the changed world he was returning to.

"Bear with me, Mary," said Joe to his wife. "I'll be strong and useful for you in no time, you'll see. And I promise I'll never go off to war again."

Late that night, Joe and Mike ventured out to enjoy the freedom of peacetime and to take in the sounds and smells of Tyneside once more. They met outside Hawthorn Leslie, and

---

[160] Bob Whitfield, *The Extension of the Franchise, 1832-1931.* Heinemann, 2001
[161] Women's Auxiliary Army Corps, National Archives.

as they stood there looking over the yards and listening to the sounds of labour, tears welled up in their eyes. But these were not the tears of sorrow; they were the tears of immeasurable relief and joy. The two marras had been through two of England's early-twentieth-century wars together. They had lost close friends and brothers along the way, but now they were back with their families, alive!

As they parted ways that night, Joe and Mike threw their arms around each other and hugged for the longest time.

"We have gone through so much together," Joe said as Mike nodded with tears in his eyes.

"We're haem, Joe. Home," said Mike. "A fresh start in life begins for us both now. One we have waited for so long, me marra!"

Then, tears pouring down their cheeks, Joe returned to his sleeping family and Mike to his.

§

On 14 December 1918, David Lloyd George, who had led the country for the previous two years, won a landslide victory in the General Election. He did this on the back of his campaign pledge to make "a country fit for heroes."

The election was notable because, provided they were over 30 and their or their husbands owned property, they could vote in a general election for the first time. Thanks to the

Representation of the People Act, eight and a half million women were finally eligible to vote, not yet enough, but still democratic progress.

Needless to say, Mary, Ruth, and most of their sisters and friends didn't own property. However, they still rejoiced in this promising development after fulfilling the roles of men throughout the war. They could see that their time was coming soon.

§

13.   *Christmas 1918*

After four Christmases in the POW camps of Germany, Joe and Mike and thousands more Allied men were spending Christmas with their families and friends at long last. Sadly, many more were still awaiting their homeward journeys. Soldiers interned in POW camps across Europe faced an uncertain wait to find out when they would return home. Following the war's end, Germany's chaos and civil conflict led to the later labelled German Revolution ('Novemberrevolution'). It wasn't as easy as walking out of the camp a free man and arranging passage across the Channel or North Sea to get home.

Despite the War's end, Christmas 1918 was a muted celebration. The 1918 flu pandemic did most of its damage in the spring and autumn of 1918. But it was still around and only finally ebbed in the spring of 1919, although some historians believe a fourth, much less virulent wave continued into 1920. So, people were still under warnings to remain vigilant and take precautions against infection, even if they had survived the first waves. On Saturday, 21 December 2018, the weekly number of Spanish Flu deaths in the UK had fallen to 1,029. It had reached its deadly peak in November when 8,000 people died in the first week alone. However, there was no scientific explanation for why the number of flu deaths had dropped.

Having avoided Christmases together because of the flu for many years, the UK public had to decide whether it was safe to meet with family and friends this Christmas. But many did so despite the UK's hospitals struggling to keep up. So, newspapers reported a mad rush on present buying around the country, with some shopkeepers even operating a 'one-in-one-out' policy as a social-distancing measure. Of course, everyone was required to wear a face mask.

Despite their physical condition, Joe, Mike, and most other returning veterans wanted to celebrate their long-awaited Christmas with their families and friends. By Monday, 23 December, Joe felt strong enough to venture out to buy Christmas presents for his family. Mary had already done that, but seeing his desire to contribute, she suggested she would accompany him as a companion and helper. So, she asked her mother to look after the children for a couple of hours. Joe was delighted with her offer and dressed his best for their first outing into familiar Jarrow surroundings. He donned his mask and straw Boater hat and, holding on to Mary's waste, launched himself into the streets of Jarrow for the first time since arriving home.

"This is so lovely," said Joe. "Our first outing together. What a joy!"

"It is doubly for me," said Mary. "For a while recently, I didn't think it could happen again."

After a 30-minute walk, they found themselves on Grange Street near Jarrow Town Hall on the corner of Wylam Street. People and dozens of children visiting the shops packed the town centre. They passed a greengrocer selling Christmas trees, being watched by a dozen excited children of various ages. Joe suggested to Mary they maybe buy a small one for their children.

"What a splendid idea," said Mary. "They have been making decorations for school so they could make and bedeck the tree with their own ornaments. They passed a crowd of children of all ages watching a Punch and Judy puppet show outside the Town Hall. They noted they should bring their children the next day, Christmas Eve. They entered a toyshop where Joe bought toys for each of the children from Father Christmas."

Then, not wanting to overdo it on Joe's first excursion, they returned home after buying a small tree. That Christmas

Eve, the Rutherfords, Burgesses and O'Briens attended a Midnight Service at the home of the Venerable Bede St. Paul's Monastery and Church. The grandparents tended to the children.

But Christmas Day was to be the best Joe and his little family had ever had. It began on Christmas morning with the children delightedly opening their presents under their first tiny Christmas Tree, which they so treasured and decorated. Mary prepared a special breakfast of pancakes with butter and sugar that she had miraculously conjured up. They had not only adapted to their long-lost father but wouldn't leave his side. They played for a few hours until Mary's and Joe's families arrived with more presents, vegetables and a turkey.

While the women piled into the tiny kitchen to prepare the Christmas lunch, the men talked about football and anything other than war. The children played their hearts out. Then they heard a loud knock on the door. Mike and Ruth were dropping by to wish Joe and his family a Happy Christmas. Joe fought back the tears as he and Mike stared at each other for a long while without a word. Then, they threw their arms around each other, laughed and cried with Joy as four years of hardships vanished. Then everyone else did the same in solidarity—it was a profoundly emotional moment, releasing four years of tension and agony.

After a few hours, the meal was ready. So, they perched wherever they could find level space in the tiny dining room to enjoy the first Christmas lunch together since the start of the Great War. What joy they all had that Christmas 1918, as did families across the British Empire, Europe and the USA. The war was over, and life could return to normal.

§

Joseph Irwin Rutherford and his fellow prisoners soon received a hand-written letter from King George V.

Buckingham Palace
1918

The Queen joins me in welcoming you on your release from the miseries and hardships you have endured with so much patience & courage.

During these many months of trial, the early rescue of our gallant Officers and men from the cruelties of their captivity has been uppermost in our thoughts. We are thankful that this longed-for day has arrived, & that back in the old Country, you will be able once more to enjoy the happiness of a home & to see wonderful days among those who anxiously look for your return.

George R.I.

Empire and War

For his service in the Great War, they awarded Joseph Rutherford the 1914 Star, the Victory Medal 1914-1918, and the British War Medal 1914-20.

7415 Private Joseph Irwin Rutherford
Durham Light Infantry
24.11.1881 - 27.12.1964

www.ingramcontent.com/pod-product-compliance
Lightning Source LLC
Chambersburg PA
CBHW030534260626
47157CB00006B/2019